ROMAN III
THE WRATH
OF
BOUDICCA

K.M.ASHMAN

CANELO

First published in the United Kingdom in 2013 by Silverback Books Ltd

This edition published in the United Kingdom in 2022 by

Canelo
Unit 9, 5th Floor
Cargo Works, 1–2 Hatfields
London, SE1 9PG
United Kingdom

A CIP catalogue record for this book is available from the British Library.

Print ISBN 978 1 80032 371 1
Ebook ISBN 978 1 78863 931 6

Look for more great books at www.canelo.co

Printed and bound in Great Britain by Clays Ltd, Elcograf S.p.A.

1

Prologue

The Lands of the Trinovantes
Britannia 40 AD

Boudicca was ten years old when she learned of her fate. A trading party from the Kingdom of the Iceni, a great tribe on the east coast of Britannia, had come to the lands of the Trinovantes and spent a week in the compound of her father, himself a king in his own right.

A great feasting took place on the last night. Gifts were exchanged and trading treaties agreed between the two peoples before the real business of the visit was discussed. Eventually agreement was made and the men of both tribes moved their attention to the flasks of wine and skins of ale that lay in abundance around the giant roundhouse which held the Trinovantian council. Soon, considered words of wisdom and guarded calculations of worth were replaced with tales of masculine debauchery and bravery in battle. A trait shared by all Britannic tribesmen.

Boudicca knew that something special was happening that night but had no idea what it could be. Such things were not for the ears of children, even daughters of kings. The sounds of revelry lasted deep into the night and the racket of drinking men meant she lay awake for hours, staring into the darkness of the roundhouse she shared with her mother and two sisters. Finally she left the warmth of her furs and walked over to the dying fire in the centre of the hut, poking the embers to stir the lazy flames from their fiery slumber. A movement behind her made her jump but she smiled when her mother sat alongside her and wrapped her own blanket around them both.

'Noisy lot, aren't they?' said her mother quietly.

Boudicca nodded.

'Are they going in the morning?' asked Boudicca.

'They are,' said her mother.

'What did they want?' asked Boudicca.

Her mother hesitated and looked down before turning to look at her.

'Boudicca,' she said, 'we live in hard times. Messengers ride between tribes telling of a threat from a faraway land.'

'The Romans,' said Boudicca.

'Yes,' said her mother. 'Even as we speak, they gather their forces across the sea and it is said they will assault our shores before next the snow falls.'

'But I have heard father say that Caratacus will lead an army against them and drive them into the sea.'

'And he will I'm sure,' said her mother, 'but there is always the chance he will fail, so we have to make sure our own people's interests are looked after.'

'I don't understand,' said Boudicca.

'Your father is a great king, Boudicca, but we are one tribe amongst many. It is his duty to forge alliances with other tribes.'

'Like the Iceni?' asked Boudicca.

'Exactly,' said her mother. 'Have you seen the tall man who leads them?'

'Yes.'

'Well he is called Prasatagus and he is their king. He has come here to seek our swords in an alliance against the Romans, should the need ever come.'

'Then that is good,' said Boudicca.

'It is, but there is a price to be paid and it is only fair that you know the cost.'

Boudicca waited silently, dreading the words that she guessed would be coming.

'Boudicca…'

'It's me isn't it?' said Boudicca before her mother could continue.

She looked down as if in shame. 'I'm sorry, my darling,' she said, 'but we need a blood bond and he has asked that you become his bride.'

'When?' asked Boudicca.

'Not yet,' she said, tucking a lock of Boudicca's long red hair back behind her daughter's ear, 'but there has been agreement you will not be promised to another. When you have reached fifteen years, you will be taken to the lands of the Iceni to become his queen.'

Boudicca stared into the flames, absorbing the news. She did not know much about the ways of adults but knew it was an important path that lay before her.

'Are you alright, Boudicca?' asked her mother gently.

Boudicca nodded in silence.

'There is no need to be frightened,' said her mother.

'I'm not afraid, Mother,' said Boudicca, 'only worried that I make you and father proud.'

'Oh, Boudicca,' sighed her mother, pulling her closer into her embrace, 'you already do, every minute of every day and who knows, one day the whole of Britannia will be proud of you too.'

Boudicca snuggled in closer and both mother and daughter stared into the comforting flames, not realising that within a generation, Boudicca's name would unite a kingdom and send fear into the very souls of an empire half a world away.

Chapter One

The Lands of the Silures
60 AD

Prydain walked into the village, leading his horse by the reins. A group of ten men followed, each leading his own horse as well as a pack mule. Though his accompanying men wore warm animal furs against the last of the winter snows, Prydain insisted on wearing an oiled leather cloak lined with sheepskin, a leftover habit from when he had served in the legions seventeen years earlier. His long black hair was tied back, as was the way of the Silures and one side of his face was tattooed with Celtic imagery. A short sword hung from his belt and a broadsword was strapped across his back, a testament to the dangerous times they lived in.

The line of men walked through the village toward the stables and as the news of their arrival spread, people came out of their warm roundhouses in excitement. Children walked alongside the warriors, asking questions about the expedition, while women looked with interest at the packs carried by the mules. As they reached the stables an old man wrapped in a heavy horsehair blanket ducked out of a hut, helped by an elderly woman. Prydain allowed his horse to be led away and walked over to greet him.

'Prydain, you have returned,' said the old man.

'We have, Kegan,' said Prydain, 'and are happy to be back.'

'Did you have any trouble?'

'If you mean with the Romans, then nothing worth worrying about. Their patrols stumble through the forests like wounded bears and we know of their presence long before they are near enough to cause us any problems.'

'It has always been so,' said Kegan, 'and is a trait that aides us. However, my manners escape me, come into the warm and you can share the tale in comfort.'

'I will check the horses are cared for,' said Prydain, 'and then the single men. After that, I would be honoured to share your hearth.'

'As it should be,' said Kegan with a nod. 'I will see that the wine is warm.'

Kegan returned into the hut while Prydain followed his men to the stables. The village was situated on the banks of a small stream, deep in the southern mountains of the Khymru. It was protected on all sides by thick forests and could only be reached by those who knew their way through the tangled maze of forest trails. Many villages were hidden in a similar manner and though the Roman patrols were rare in the area, the Silures took no risks. The Romans had already subdued all the border tribes as well as the great Deceangli in the north of the Khymru.

However they had not had much success with the Silures mainly due to two things. One was the forbidding nature of the country with steep mountains and heavily wooded valleys, while the other was the evasive nature of the Silures tactics. Unlike the other Britannic tribes, the Silures refused to meet the invaders in face to face battle but instead relied on hit and run tactics, striking any unprotected patrols with devastating speed before melting back into the protective embrace of the country they knew so well.

Since the defeat of Caratacus at Caer Caradog five years earlier, the Romans had made many attempts at subduing the Silures but always came up short. Occasionally they would find a village but usually it would be empty and even though they burned those they found, the effect on the troublesome tribe was minimal.

At the stables, the slaves unloaded the pack mules overseen by some of Prydain's warriors. Piles of furs lay along the walls as did sacks of grain and dried meat. Though many of the border tribes had bent their knee to the Romans, they still nurtured hatred and secretly supported those men who continued to be a thorn in the invaders' side. Subsequently, these supply trains were commonplace throughout the south of the Khymru, especially in winter when hunting was poor and access to trade markets was denied by Roman patrols.

'Get the fresh skins to the women for cleaning,' said Prydain, 'and take the food to the elder council. They will ensure it is distributed fairly.'

When he was sure the supplies had been sorted and the horses rubbed down and fed, his attention turned to the men.

'Cullen,' he said, addressing a tall warrior. 'There are bed spaces in the long house for you and your men. Take the deer you killed this morning and a skin of wine to celebrate our success, you have earned it.'

Cullen nodded in gratitude.

'Thank you, Prydain. As usual it was an honour to ride with you. I am only sorry that our blades never tasted Roman flesh.'

'I fear that day will come soon enough, Cullen. In the meantime enjoy the venison and the warmth of the fires. I will have some of the slave women sent over.'

Cullen hoisted the deer onto his back and led six of the patrol toward the single men's longhouse on the other side of the stream.

'What about us, Prydain,' asked a giant of a man nearby, 'do we not also deserve a deer to celebrate?'

'I fear we would need a herd of deer to feed your appetite, Gildas,' laughed Prydain, 'but you are right. The married men should take something as well. Each of you take a wolf fur for your wives, perhaps it will make them more accommodating when you lay alongside them tonight.'

'It will take more than a wolf skin to thaw his wife,' laughed a voice, 'she is colder than steel in winter.'

The rest of the men laughed while Gildas scowled. He was bigger than anyone in the tribe and had killed many men in battle but there was one person who could put him in his place; his woman.

'She may be cold to you,' said Gildas, 'but when she thaws, she is hotter than a blacksmith's furnace. Besides, I did a little trading of my own back there and I have this little trinket.' He reached into his tunic and withdrew a necklace of coloured river stones. 'When she claps eyes on this, she will rip my clothes off faster than you can drink a mug of ale.'

The men laughed as they finished their work and after selecting the wolf furs from the packs, made their way to their family's huts. Prydain selected a particularly beautiful pelt, predominantly white with patches of grey, before making his own way over to the hut of Kegan.

Kegan was the clan chieftain and after the battle of Caer Caradog five years earlier, it was Kegan who had given Prydain a place amongst his people. Since then Prydain had earned the respect and trust of the whole clan and had grown particularly close to the chieftain.

'Prydain, come in,' said Kegan, 'be seated.'

Prydain sat on a pile of furs situated near the fire. He was often invited to the hut of the chieftain and felt comfortable in his presence. The old woman who had helped Kegan walk outside brought over a bowl of Cawl, the staple diet of their people during winter.

'Thank you,' said Prydain, taking the bowl gratefully. It had been days since his last hot meal.

Kegan didn't eat, but watched the young man as he finished the broth. Finally Prydain sat back and smiled toward the woman.

'Thank you, Cara,' he said. 'Excellent as usual.'

'We had to kill a cow,' said Kegan, 'but our people were starving. These supplies have come just in time.'

'They will last but a few weeks,' said Prydain. 'As soon as my men are rested, we will set out again.'

'Take a few days,' said Kegan. 'The snows are melting, as is the ice. Soon we will be able to cast our nets and travel further afield for the hunt.'

'Still, one more trip will ease the transition,' said Prydain.

Kegan nodded.

'It is a shame it has come to this,' said Kegan. 'I remember the time when our beams groaned from the weight of dried meat. Hunts were always fruitful, even in winter but the constant crashing of Roman boots frightens the deer deeper into the forest. Perhaps next winter we will stock up earlier.'

'We cannot go through this again,' said Prydain. 'Our men get restless and demand blood. We hide in the forests like scared rabbits while the Romans torch our villages. This is not our way, Kegan. Since when have the Silures avoided our enemies?'

'I feel your frustration, Prydain but you know we cannot beat these people on a battlefield. Even you have said this around many council fires.'

'I know,' said Prydain, 'and I stand by my words, but we cannot just stand by and let them absorb our lands.'

'But they have no fortress in the Khymru,' said Kegan. 'Their patrols are a nuisance but when the snows melt, we will be able to hunt and when we are strong again, we will take the fight back to them. That is our way, Prydain, to hit hard and disappear like the mist before they have time to draw their weapons.'

'And it is a good tactic,' said Prydain, 'but only against small forces. The day they decide to set up a fortress in our lands, our attacks will be like flies to a bull and make no mistake, Kegan, that day will come.'

'Perhaps so,' said the old man, 'but it is hard enough surviving today, the tomorrows will have to wait.'

The rest of the evening was taken up with drinking wine while Prydain told Kegan about his trip. They had laden the pack mules with iron ore from the local mines and sent the trading party north to the lands of the Ordovices. Their lands were more open and their harvests had been good, enabling them to be in a strong position for trading. In addition, as they had a direct trading route with the Deceangli further north, and access to Roman goods, it was a way for the Silures to access necessities during these hard times.

Cara retired to her bed space behind a wicker screen and Kegan produced some chewing root. Both he and Prydain chewed on the fibrous material before placing it between gum and lower lip to allow the mild narcotic to take effect.

'These are hard times, Prydain,' said Kegan.

'They are,' agreed Prydain, 'but when the snows are gone, we will be able to assemble the tribe and agree a strategy to slow the Roman advance.'

'You think this is possible?'

'I think they can be slowed,' said Prydain, 'but I fear their patience. To them, time is an ally and they are in no rush. Whether it is in our lifetime or that of our children, unless the tribes unite then I fear their presence is inevitable.'

'Then perhaps it is better to do as the Cornovii and bend our knee.'

'Every minute of freedom is precious,' said Prydain, 'and is worth fighting for. I have seen how Rome treats its slaves and I would not wish it on anyone.'

'Yet we too have slaves,' said Kegan.

'Our lowest slaves are treated as kings compared to those of the Romans,' said Prydain.

'Do you miss your former life as a Roman?' asked Kegan.

'I never was a Roman,' answered Prydain, 'I just grew up there. Once I learned my true heritage, then I knew where I belonged.'

'But you spent your childhood there, surely there is something you miss?'

'I miss the warmth of the sun,' said Prydain, 'and sometimes as a child, I swam in the sea near my master's farm. I can tell you, Kegan, there is no comparison between the seas of Rome and the seas of Britannia.'

'I do not see the attraction of swimming in any water,' said Kegan. 'That is for the fishes.'

'All Roman soldiers can swim,' said Prydain, 'it is part of their training.'

'I hear you killed your father,' said Kegan quietly.

Prydain glanced over.

'He was no father to me,' he answered quietly before leaning over to throw some extra wood on the fire. 'He was simply the man who raped my mother. As far as I am concerned, my father was a man called Karim, a gladiator who saved me from death in the arena when I was a baby. He was more of a father than my true father could ever be.'

'Is Karim still alive?' asked Kegan.

'I don't know,' said Prydain. 'I haven't seen him for almost twenty years. If he is, he is an old man by now.'

They fell quiet for a few moments as Kegan allowed Prydain his memories.

'Tell me, Prydain,' said Kegan eventually. 'Why is it you haven't taken a wife in all these years?'

'I don't know,' said Prydain. 'There have been several women through the years but none that I wanted to build a home with.'

'A man needs a woman to keep him warm as he gets old,' said Kegan.

'Perhaps,' said Prydain, 'and there is still time for me but until then, there are women a plenty to fulfil my needs in the bed furs.'

'Whores and slaves are fine for fire,' said Kegan, 'but short on warmth, I have found.'

Prydain laughed.

'Kegan, since when have you worried about my marital comfort?'

'It has been on my mind often these past few months,' said Kegan. 'I am getting old and fear this will be my last winter. If the gods see fit to take me to their fireside, then I see no better man to lead this clan than you.'

Prydain paused and stared at Kegan for several moments.

'I am honoured,' he said eventually, 'but you will outlive us all.'

'Perhaps,' smiled Kegan, 'but these things must be talked about. If you are agreeable, I will decree you as my successor and seek the approval of the elders. I do not think there will be objection though it would smooth the way if you had a woman at your side.'

'Ah, hence the talk,' laughed Prydain. 'So why can't a warrior clan be led by a single man?'

'We are indeed a warrior clan,' agreed Kegan, 'but value the family. It would be better to be led by a man with similar values.'

'Well,' said Prydain, standing up. 'I am honoured to be considered but can't promise to find a woman just to achieve the position.'

'And I do not expect you to,' said Kegan, himself standing up. 'All I am saying is don't be so quick to push them from your furs in the mornings. Perhaps one of them may be worth keeping.'

Prydain smiled.

'I will take on board your thoughts, Kegan but until then, I will continue to share the single men's longhouse.

Now I will go to my bed before you start talking about children.'

'One step at a time, Prydain,' laughed Kegan, 'but that is a conversation my wife is waiting to have with you.'

Both men laughed and grabbed each other's forearms in friendship.

'Until the morrow, Kegan,' said Prydain. 'Perhaps we can hunt fox together.'

'I fear my hunting days are done, Prydain, but you are always welcome here. Sleep well.'

Prydain left the hut and walked through the dark village thinking about the conversation with Kegan. Although he had been with the Silures for almost sixteen years and was a blood relation of their leader Hawkwing, his Roman upbringing was always in the background and meant he was never fully accepted. Perhaps this would be a way of finally getting that acceptance. As he neared the single men's hut, the sounds of drunken revelry got louder and he sighed as he realised it was going to be a long night.

Chapter Two

The Lands of the Iceni
Britannia — 60AD

Rianna couldn't remember her mother, for she had died from the cough when Rianna was very young. Her father too was nothing more to her than a story told by others, as he had been killed in a conflict between clans before she had been born. Such orphaned children were usually looked after by any surviving family but in Rianna's case there had been none, so the six-year-old child's fate had been unclear. However, the gods had been kind, for in her few years as a carefree child, she had befriended another little girl and every day they played the games of children in the dust of the Trinovantian village. Even at six years old, it was obvious they would be lifelong friends and the village soon became used to seeing them side by side, Rianna's jet black hair a sharp contrast to the fiery red locks of her little friend, Boudicca.

When Rianna was orphaned, Boudicca beseeched her mother to help and they took Rianna into the king's household, essentially as a servant but within weeks she had become part of the family.

Subsequently they had grown up together as sisters, even attending the warrior training that every Trinovantian undertook, male or female, and despite their different heritage, this was where Rianna excelled.

Even at fifteen, Rianna could match many men with a sword and was a better rider than most. Her temper was fiery and despite many young warrior's attempts to woo her, she remained staunchly independent, deciding that her fate lay in her own hands and would never be decided by any man.

Both girls had become inseparable, so on Boudicca's fifteenth birthday when the whole of the Trinovantes lined the dirt road to say goodbye to their warrior princess, Rianna rode beside her as servant, confidante and lifelong friend. That had been fifteen years earlier and now they were just as close as ever.

—

'Do you remember the day we arrived here?' asked Rianna as the two women sat on the riverbank, dangling their feet into the cool, clear water.

'Like it was yesterday,' said Boudicca. 'Who'd have believed it was fifteen summers ago?'

'I bet Prasatagus remembers it,' laughed Rianna. 'The entire village lined up at the gates with flags and banners to welcome his gentle bride and we galloped in from the other direction covered in dust and sweating like oarsmen.'

Boudicca laughed at the memory.

'I can see his face now,' she said, 'he was furious.'

'Well, you have to let them know where they stand,' laughed Rianna.

'We fought like cat and dog for the first few weeks,' said Boudicca.

'I know,' said Rianna. 'I used to cry myself to sleep at the sound of your weeping and often the guards had to hold me back from running in with my blade.'

'It wasn't so bad,' smiled Boudicca, 'and anyway, the making up was always the best bit.'

'I heard that as well,' said Rianna with a smile, 'in fact half the village did.'

'Rianna,' shouted Boudicca, punching her friend on her shoulder, 'you never said so.'

'Well, we couldn't help it,' laughed Rianna, 'you are a bit, shall we say, vocal?'

'Oh no,' gasped Boudicca in mock shame, 'how can I ever face the village again?'

'Don't worry,' laughed Rianna, 'we're used to it now.'

'Rianna, stop it,' laughed Boudicca, 'you make me sound like the whores at the slave markets.'

'Well, it has been said,' replied Rianna.

Boudicca squealed and pounced on her friend, laughing hysterically as they wrestled in the spring grass. Finally they both lay on their backs, looking up at the passing clouds.

'He's a good man you know,' said Boudicca.

'Who?' asked Rianna.

'Prasatagus.'

'I know,' answered Rianna.

Boudicca turned to face her, propping herself up on her elbow.

'You don't like the way he deals with the Romans, do you?'

'He is my king, Boudicca, as you are my queen. It is not for the likes of me to question the decisions of such people.'

'Oh stop the king and queen nonsense,' said Boudicca, 'and talk to me as a friend. These past few months I have seen you fret more than I ever have.'

Rianna sat up and turned to face her friend.

'Boudicca,' she said, 'it is obvious to all that Prasatagus is not well.'

Boudicca's face dropped slightly.

'It is but a passing illness,' she said, 'and he will get better soon.'

'And I hope he does,' said Rianna, 'I really do, but what if he doesn't? What if he is summoned to meet his gods and leaves you and the girls to deal with the Romans on your own?'

Boudicca's features softened at the mention of her children. She had borne Prasatagus two daughters soon after the ceremony and they had quickly become adored by all in the Iceni. Proud and stubborn like their mother, yet intelligent and fair of face like their father.

'Rianna, you know we have an arrangement with Rome,' she said.

'A Roman's words mean nothing,' said Rianna.

'Catus Decianus is the Procurator,' said Boudicca, 'and his word is true. Since we rallied against Scapula thirteen summers ago, Rome has feared the strength of the Iceni and has paid us a fortune in gold to buy our peace. In return we provide them with supplies and guarantee them safe passage through our lands. Why would they change this agreement now?'

Rianna grabbed Boudicca's hand in hers.

'Because if Prasatagus dies,' she said, 'then they could take the chance to change it in their favour.'

'Rianna,' answered Boudicca, 'I appreciate your concern but in the event of his death, the king has made arrangements to appease the Romans. He has paid one of their scribes to write a testament leaving half of our kingdom to Rome whilst leaving the remainder to me and his daughters. The Romans place great store in such things and they will be grateful for our continued alliance.'

'Boudicca,' said Rianna, 'all I am saying is to be careful. The Romans do not recognise women as leaders, only men.'

'I have met Decianus on several occasions,' said Boudicca, 'and he recognises our sovereignty. Fret not, Rianna. Our people are fed, our weapons show rust from little use and our children laugh in freedom each day. We may not like the fact the Romans are here, but we lost the chance to drive them out when Caratacus faced him alone at Caer Caradog and no other tribes rallied to his call. All we can do now is live life the best we can and look after our own people.'

A voice echoed on the breeze and both women turned to see who called.

'It's Lannosea,' said Boudicca referring to her youngest daughter. She stood up and walked up the slopes of the riverbank to see the twelve-year-old running across the pasture toward her.

'Mother,' called Lannosea, 'come quickly, it's Father.'

'What's wrong?' shouted Boudicca, breaking into a run.

'He has collapsed,' shouted Lannosea through her tears, 'and calls your name in pain.'

Boudicca looked over toward Rianna, a look of devastation on her face.

'Go,' shouted Rianna, 'I'll look after Lannosea. We'll catch up with you.'

Boudicca ran to her horse and within seconds she was galloping across the plain, her long red hair blowing behind her like the flames of a fire. Rianna ran up to Lannosea and put her arms around the sobbing girl.

'Don't worry, child,' she said, 'Prasatagus is a fighter and he has suffered worse before.'

'I don't think so, Rianna,' sobbed the girl, 'I have never seen him look so ill. I think he is dying.'

Rianna tightened her grip and held the young girl until she stopped crying. Finally she eased Lannosea away from her.

'Where's Heanua?' asked Rianna gently, referring to Lannosea's fourteen-year-old sister.

'She's out riding,' said Lannosea. 'I know not where but father's servants have sent riders looking.'

'Right,' said Rianna. 'Let's get those tears dried and get back to the village. Your mother will need you at her side.'

Lannosea nodded and wiped the tears away with the heel of her hand.

'There's only one horse,' she said her voice still shaking.

'And he is as strong as an ox,' said Rianna. 'Come on, let's get going.'

Within moments both women were astride Rianna's horse and following in Boudicca's wake, both unaware that their lives had just changed forever.

—

Boudicca sat on the rocky escarpment, looking out over the lands of the Iceni. On a nearby hill was the fort they would use in times of conflict should they ever come under attack and in the valley below lay the village where she and Prasatagus had brought up their children in safety.

Beyond that lay the rolling hills of the Iceni, the bountiful land that fed their tribe and provided safety for her people. Though born into the Trinovantes, she had been embraced by these people and now considered herself Iceni through and through. Behind her, the grass on the top of the hill was a little greener than that on its slopes, benefitting from the regrowth after the inferno of her husband's funeral pyre six weeks earlier.

The ashes had been blown away by the wind and any remnants of firewood or human flesh had been collected up and cast into the holy waters of the river, as was their way, leaving no memory of the great king who had once ruled these lands.

The past few weeks had been a blur for Boudicca. Her grief was profound but her people looked to her for leadership and she knew she had to be strong. Since Prasatagus' heart had given out, her days had been filled receiving tribute from the hundreds of smaller clans who made up the great Iceni. Riders from miles around poured into the valley for the funerary rites and even her ailing father had made the tiring journey from the Trinovantes to pay his respects.

The funeral was like nothing seen by any of those in attendance. The pyre was constructed on the hill and three female servants hurled themselves into the flames to join their master in the afterlife; if it wasn't for her daughters, Boudicca would gladly have joined them. The flames could be seen for miles around and everyone who saw its light knew that a great king passed that day.

It had been a hard few days but eventually the visitors had left, leaving the valley in peace once more. Life had returned to a semblance of normality and every day she rode up to the escarpment to sit and watch the sun set over the Iceni.

On these trips, Rianna insisted on riding with her but always stayed back with the horses as Boudicca wrestled with her grief. It was on one such evening that she heard Boudicca gently call out her name.

'Rianna, attend me.'

Rianna walked over and stood alongside her friend.

'It's beautiful isn't it?' said Boudicca, looking to the setting sun.

'It is,' said Rianna.

Boudicca tapped the ground beside her.

'Sit,' she said. 'Share this moment with me.'

'Are you alright?' asked Rianna as she sat.

'I am,' said Boudicca. 'My thoughts are clearing and I wanted you to see this.'

Rianna looked toward the horizon and saw the distant forested hills ablaze with the red fire of the setting sun. Above them the sky faded from purple to black as the sun fought its daily battle to remain in control of the heavens, but eventually disappeared, leaving only fiery reflections on the few clouds above.

'I have never seen it so beautiful,' said Rianna.

'Nor have I,' said Boudicca, 'and that is why I will not seek out this view ever again. I think this is a sign, Rianna, a sign from Prasatagus to move on and lead our people forward. He sent this sunset to say goodbye and I think it will never be bettered.'

Rianna sought out her friend's hand.

'I think you are right,' she said. 'It has the beauty of your man's heart and it is a fitting memory to his name.'

They waited in silence as the sky darkened and only when

22

the stars started appearing in their droves, did Boudicca stand to leave.

'It is done,' she said. 'It is time to move on.' She turned to Rianna. 'Thank you for being here, Rianna. I couldn't have got through this without you.'

'I will always be at your side, Boudicca, until death itself.'

The two women hugged before making their way to the horses. As they rode back to the village, they talked of the business of the following day.

'Our scouts tell us that the delegation from Decianus is but a day's ride away,' said Rianna.

'I am aware of their proximity,' said Boudicca, 'and we will greet them not as subjects but as fellow rulers.'

'The way it should be,' said Rianna before adding, 'how is your spirit, Boudicca?'

'What do you mean?' asked Boudicca.

'Does grief dampen your fire or do you still harbour the need to beat me?'

'Is this a wager?' asked Boudicca, recognising the playful challenge in her friend's voice.

'Well,' answered Rianna, 'you are Queen of the Iceni now. Perhaps it is time to ride in a cart?'

'Not as long as I can breathe,' laughed Boudicca.

'Prove it,' said Rianna.

Boudicca didn't answer but pulled up her horse to stand beside Rianna.

'Like the old days?' asked Boudicca eventually.

'Like the old days,' agreed Rianna.

'Then on my mark,' said Boudicca. 'One, two...'

Before she could say three Rianna had dug her heels into the haunches of her horse and gained a few strides advantage over her friend as the race began.

'Oh, Rianna,' laughed Boudicca as she spurred her own horse, 'I should have known.'

–

Two days later, the nobles of Boudicca's tribe gathered in the centre of the village, waiting for the arrival of the Roman deputation. They knew a large force had camped nearby and many were nervous why Suetonius had sent so many men at arms. This was supposed to be a meeting to determine on-going trading terms and no conflict was anticipated. Despite this, they had amassed several hundred warriors of their own, who formed a large circle in the village clearing, an impressive sight in itself.

To one end of the clearing stood a high back chair carved from a single piece of oak embedded with hundreds of precious stones. Celtic designs of intricate artistry wove their way around the chair and the seat was padded with the finest purple silk, a rarity indeed in the lands of Britannia. This was the throne of the Iceni and it was designed to display the wealth and power of the tribe.

Several paces in front of the throne was another ornate chair and though this was also decorated with intricate carvings, it held no precious metal and was lower than the other, designed for visitors of lesser importance than the Iceni ruler.

A runner raced across the clearing and stopped before the roundhouse of Boudicca. Rianna ducked out of the low doorway and faced him.

'Well?' she snapped.

'They are here,' gasped the man. 'They are riding toward the village as we speak and will be here in a few moments.'

Rianna returned inside.

'It's time to go, Boudicca,' she said.

Boudicca nodded and turned to her daughters.

'You two stay here,' she said, 'and watch from the doorway.'

'But we can't see anything from here,' whined Heanua, 'the people will be in the way.'

'Stay here,' repeated her mother. 'When we know it is safe, perhaps I will send for you.'

The girl huffed in defiance but knew better than to argue with her mother. Boudicca kissed them both and donned her multi-coloured cloak before fastening it with a large golden brooch. She pulled her long hair from beneath the cloak and let it hang down her back.

'Ready?' asked Rianna.

'Ready,' confirmed Boudicca and followed her friend out to the clearing. Her people parted to let her through and she took her place on the bejewelled throne.

'Let them in,' she called and the gates of the stockade were pulled open by a group of slaves.

All heads turned to see the visitors, fully expecting a parade of brightly coloured legionaries to march in to the sound of drums and trumpets. Instead, a dozen riders galloped in and reined to a halt just short of the throne, followed by a cohort of running men, each fully armoured and covered in the dust of travel. Immediately they circled the clearing, each holding their Pilae outward toward the surrounding onlookers.

The leader of the horsemen dismounted and handed the reins to a comrade before removing his riding gauntlets and banging the dust from his tunic. He removed his horsehair crested helmet and hung it from the pommel on his saddle before looking around the arena, seemingly ignoring Boudicca. Finally his gaze fell on the queen and a smirk played around his mouth. He walked toward the lesser chair and paused before looking over to the queen.

'Is this for me?' he asked.

Boudicca nodded silently, hardly able to contain the anger she felt at his obvious indifference to her station. The officer sat down unceremoniously.

'Get me a drink,' he ordered.

Despite her ire, Boudicca nodded to a servant who brought over an ornately carved silver goblet, filled with wine.

The man examined the intricate designs on the goblet before drinking deeply. Finally he cast the half empty tankard from him in disgust.

'I've tasted better horse piss,' he said and Boudicca made to rise from her seat before being forced back down by the hand of Rianna.

'So,' shouted the man, looking around, 'who is in command here?'

'I am,' said Boudicca, her voice shaking with pent up rage, 'and I demand to know the name of the man who abuses the hospitality of an ally.'

'Really?' asked the officer, looking her up and down in feigned disinterest. 'What a novel idea.'

Before Boudicca could react, the man continued.

'So be it,' he said. 'In the absence of a real ruler I will address you. I am Tribune Quintus Virrius and am here in the name of Seneca the Younger, advisor to the Emperor of Rome.' He held out a hand and another officer ran over to place a scroll in his grasp. Virrius unrolled the document and stood up to read the proclamation.

'Let it be known,' he read, 'it has come to our attention that the great Prasatagus, King of the Icenic clans and ally to Rome has passed on to the next life, leaving his lands without heir or kingship. Rome offers her condolences to those he leaves behind but knows that Prasatagus would expect fair outcome to those he owed debt. To this end, Seneca hereby claims the repayment of all loans paid to the Iceni over many years with immediate effect complete with all interest due.'

'What lies are these?' shouted Boudicca. 'We owe Rome no debt.'

Virrius lowered the scroll and stared at Boudicca.

'Really?' he asked in feigned amusement. 'If I'm not mistaken, the cushion upon which you sit is of eastern silk. The beads around your neck are jade, are they not? And even the cloak around your shoulders has been woven by Numidian weavers. Are you telling me that your trade routes extend so far from your shores?'

'They are gifts from Suetonius,' snarled Boudicca, 'as well you know.'

'And the wines, the luxuries, the many baskets of coin over the years? Are you saying these too were also gifts?'

'They were tribute to my husband,' said Boudicca.

'Tribute?' laughed Virrius. 'For one who claims majesty enough to lead a tribe as great as the Iceni, you display a breath-taking ignorance. Rome pays tribute to nobody, Boudicca; the world pays tribute to Rome. You and your husband lived in luxury at the expense of Nero's purse on agreement that it would one day be repaid. Today I am here to collect that debt.'

All around the clearing the crowd started to get restless and voices called angrily above the walls of spears, causing the soldiers to brace in case of any sudden rush from the onlookers. Boudicca raised her hand to calm her people.

'You know well this is fabrication,' she said, 'yet I feel Prasatagus saw this day coming and made suitable preparation. We too have our scrolls, Virrius, and the king left instruction written in the language of your people. In it he bequeaths a treasure a hundred times greater than any debt you allege so cut short the politics and we will reach agreement.'

'Spoken like a man,' said Virrius, 'so be it. Where will I find this great treasure you speak of? I would feast my eyes on this mountain of gold.'

'There are indeed mountains,' said Boudicca, 'but golden they are not, except to those born into their shadows. These past two days you have seen the treasure for you have ridden through the midst of it. Prasatagus has decreed that on his death, half of the Iceni Kingdom would be bequeathed to Rome in return for favoured trading terms and continued friendship. Everything south of the hills you passed yesterday back to the great river will become the property of Rome. The sweetest grazing and fallowed land as far as the eye can see. Deer-filled forests and streams sweeter than the purest wine. A place fit for an emperor. This is our gift, a treasure that cannot be measured against silk or coin but in beauty and land. Managed well, it will repay your so-called debt within two seasons.'

'Half a kingdom,' mused Virrius, 'and what about the other half?'

'It will remain with the Iceni,' said Boudicca. 'Ruled by myself as Queen and handed down to my daughters when I die.'

'Ah,' said Virrius. 'Now that could be a problem.'

'A problem?' asked Boudicca, 'I don't understand.'

'Let me put it this way,' said Virrius. 'When our gold laden carts turned up at your doors over the years, did you take a look and think, ah, there is a cart full of gold but I will take only half?'

'I don't see the similarity,' said Boudicca.

'Oh come on, Boudicca,' said Virrius, 'the comparison is obvious. I see an un-ruled land in debt to Rome and you offer half. Explain why I would accept such a feeble proposition.'

Boudicca's eyes narrowed at the implications.

'The other half is not on offer,' she said quietly.

'On whose decree?' asked Virrius. 'Yours? I think not, Boudicca. Prasatagus was a clever man but we tolerated his games knowing his time would end. You people see only to the next harvest but Rome is patient and plans many generations into the future. These scrolls have gathered dust they have been written so long. Your kingdom is no more, Boudicca. I claim it in the name of Nero and in full payment of the debt of Prasatagus.'

'No,' shouted Boudicca standing up. 'You cannot do this; these are our lands and have been since time dawned. If there is a debt then we will pay but in gold and corn, not with the resting places of our ancestors.'

'Too late, Boudicca,' said Virrius. 'The gold we will have, the corn we will have. But we will also have your cattle, your people and your lands. You can stay here and play at being Queen but it will be under our rule and at our whim. Submit gracefully and you will hardly see a difference. You will continue to live in your lands but will send tribute to Camulodunum. A schedule of taxes has been drawn up already. Cattle, gold, iron and slaves. All will be due in monthly payments starting immediately.

Meet the tally and you will enjoy our patronage. Defy Rome and feel our wrath. What is it to be?'

To one side a commotion broke out in the crowd and both Virrius and Boudicca looked over to see the cause.

'What goes on there?' shouted Virrius.

'Mother,' came a shout, 'they won't let us through.'

Virrius turned to Boudicca.

'Your children?' he asked.

'My daughters,' she confirmed.

'Let them through,' called Virrius and watched as the two girls ran to their mother's side.

'Pretty girls,' he said. 'It would be a shame if something was to happen to them.'

'You wouldn't dare,' snarled Boudicca.

'Wouldn't I?' asked Virrius. 'My work here is done, Boudicca. Tonight we will camp outside your walls. Tomorrow you will sign a treaty handing over all your lands to Rome.'

'And if I don't?'

Virrius laughed.

'You will,' he said and turned to go. As he walked back toward his horse, a rock flew through the air and smashed against his unprotected head, causing him to fall to his knees, his forehead pouring with blood. For a few seconds everyone stared in disbelief, unsure what had happened. Virrius got slowly to his feet and turned to face Boudicca as one of his men ran forward.

'My lord, are you alright?' he shouted.

'I am fine,' growled Virrius, still staring at Boudicca with loathing. To one side four soldiers dragged a struggling man from the crowd and threw him to the ground. Virrius glanced down toward the man in the dust.

'Is this the man?' he asked.

'Yes, my lord,' said a soldier. 'Do you want him killed?'

'Killed, yes,' he growled, 'but he is just one flea on an infested rat. Crucify him along with a hundred more and for each man crucified, add a woman and a child. This rat needs teaching a lesson.'

'No,' shouted Boudicca and ran forward toward him.

'Seize her,' shouted Virrius above the rising clamour of the crowd, 'and silence the rest of them – use blades if necessary.'

Two soldiers grabbed Boudicca and wrestled her to the floor. The arena broke into pandemonium as the Iceni surged forward in anger, keen to support their queen. The soldiers reacted with swords and the air echoed with the sounds of screams as blood flew in all directions. A Cornicine echoed in the morning air and within moments, hundreds more auxiliary infantry ran through the gates with swords drawn to help subdue the angry tribe.

In amongst the confusion, Rianna grabbed the two girls, realising the danger. There wasn't much she could do to help Boudicca but she could help the children.

'Come with me,' she said.

'But what about Mother?' cried Heanua.

'She will be fine,' said Rianna, 'come quickly.'

'But…'

'Heanua,' snapped Rianna, 'you have to be strong. Your mother would expect it. You are a future queen and have to be kept safe.' They made their way through the crowd toward the huts.

'Where are we going?' asked Lannosea.

'To the horses,' said Rianna, 'we have to get out of the village.'

'But there are more Romans out there.'

31

'We'll go out of the side gate,' said Rianna, 'hopefully we can get a head start and if we can get to the forest, they will never find us. We will have to ride hard though; do you think you can do that?'

Both girls nodded.

'Then come quickly,' said Rianna. 'We have to go.'

Back in the square the extra soldiers had brought the crowd under control and everyone fell to their knees at sword point. Dozens of bodies lay around and the dust was blackened by their spilled blood. Boudicca was held down by two legionaries as Virrius addressed the crowd.

'Listen to me,' he roared, 'you are no longer allies, you are servants of Rome. The woman who squirms in the dust at my feet is supposed to be a queen. Witness what we think of this claim.'

Two soldiers dragged Boudicca to her feet and stretched her arms out between them. Another officer drew his Pugio and cut away the brooch that held her cape. Within seconds her tunic was also cut from her body and she stood naked from the waist up. Despite her humiliation, she stood upright with head raised. Another soldier approached and gave Virrius a thin branch of hazel.

Virrius stripped the thinner twigs from the makeshift whip and swished it through the air, enjoying the way it flexed in flight.

'That's a very pretty chair you have there, Boudicca,' he sneered, 'let's see if we can put it to good use.'

The two soldiers dragged her to the throne and bent her over the rear of the frame. Virrius walked over and ran the makeshift whip gently down her naked back. The crowd fell silent as they realised what was happening.

'You people should know when you are beaten,' he said, 'but just in case, let me give you a reminder.' Without any more warning he drew back the whip and lashed it full force across her back, cutting deep into her flesh.

Despite her resolve Boudicca screamed in pain and it echoed around the village.

Over and over again Virrius whipped the queen until her back was a mess of ripped flesh, and her blood splashed against him. By the ninth stroke, Boudicca was unconscious but he gave her three more lashes before stepping back. The two men holding her over the chair let her fall to the dust. Virrius turned to the people and walked over to face them.

'This is what we think of your queen,' he shouted, 'a mere servant to be beaten as we see fit. As she bleeds, so will you.' He gestured for his horse and mounted before turning to face the nearest Centurion.

'Centurion Rammas,' he called, 'I will return to the marching camp. Identify the nobles of this so-called tribe and send them in chains to Rome.'

'And the rest of the village?' asked the grizzled Centurion.

'Your men have worked hard these past few months,' he said, 'it is yours to do with as you will.'

All around the soldiers started cheering and Virrius rode out of the village with the rest of the officers. When they had gone, Centurion Rammas turned to face the terrified villagers before looking at the grinning faces of his command.

'Well,' he shouted, drawing his Gladius, 'you heard the man, what are you waiting for?'

A few hundred yards away, Virrius heard the screaming start in the village behind him and knew there would be few survivors that night. He did not fret at the thought for it was how things were done and the village was just one more spoil of war. Soon he was back in his command tent within the marching camp, writing a letter to Seneca. An hour later, an orderly asked permission to be admitted.

'Enter,' said Virrius.

'My lord, you are requested outside,' said the orderly.

'What for?' asked Virrius.

'I think you should see for yourself,' said the orderly.

Virrius followed him outside and saw a mounted Batavian scout patrol waiting on their horses. One of the riders held the reins of another horse with two young girls tied together on its back while another carried the body of a woman.

Virrius's eyes narrowed.

'These are the daughters of Boudicca, are they not?'

'We believe so, my lord,' said the lead rider. 'We found them trying to escape in the forest.'

'Un-chaperoned?'

'This woman was with them. She put up a fight but fell at my sword.'

'Is she dead?'

'No, my lord.'

Virrius walked up to the girls and stared up at the older one.

'Your eyes show hate,' he said.

'Where is my mother?' asked the girl.

'Probably dead by now,' said Virrius without compassion.

34

The younger of the two gasped and burst into tears but Heanua just stared at the Roman.

'Then you had better kill me too,' she said, 'for one day I will cut your throat.'

Virrius smiled.

'You have your mother's spirit,' he said.

Heanua spat and the Tribune closed his eyes as the spittle ran down his face.

'Such a shame,' he sighed as he wiped away the spit. 'You could have made such pretty slaves.'

'I would rather die,' she answered.

'Really?' he said. 'So be it.' He turned to the Batavian cavalryman. 'Decurion, they are yours.'

'What would you have me do with them?' asked the soldier.

'When was the last time your men enjoyed the company of women?'

'Six weeks, my lord, in the whore houses of Londinium.'

'Then this is your lucky day,' said Virrius, 'these will cost you nothing. Give them to your men.'

For a second, nobody moved as the implications sunk in.

'Well?' said Virrius. 'What are you waiting for?'

'No,' moaned the woman on the horse, and both men turned to see her struggling to sit upright in her saddle. One arm was wrapped around her waist, clutching at her tunic to stem the blood from her wound, while the other gripped the saddle horn to stop herself from falling. Her long hair fell untidily around her shoulders and her face grimaced in pain.

'No,' she said again, 'please not this. They are still children.'

'Really?' sneered Virrius. 'Girls are married at such an age in Rome, but I suppose we are more civilised than you.'

'Look at them,' cried Rianna, 'they are girls still in body and mind, the gods will curse you for your violation.'

'Let me worry about the gods,' snarled Virrius. 'Decurion, take them away.'

'Nooo!' screamed Rianna. 'Take me instead, I beg you, let me take their place.'

'You?' shouted the Decurion, struggling to rein in his nervous horse. 'I think not, Witch. I prefer my meat fresh.' He spurred his horse forward and grabbed at the reins of the girls' horse.

'What's happening?' cried Lannosea. 'Rianna, where is he taking us?'

As they passed the wounded Rianna, she spurred her horse, ripping the reins out of the soldier's hands. Before anyone could stop her, she was alongside the children and leaned across to wrap them in her arms.

'Rianna, what's happening?' cried Lannosea. 'What are they going to do to us?'

'Listen,' sobbed Rianna through her own tears. 'You must be brave. What they are about to do, just submit. Do not fight them, do you hear me? No matter what fire you feel in your heart or pain in your body, do not fight them or you will be killed. Submit and survive, that is all that is important. You must survive.'

Before they could answer, her head was yanked backwards as one of the riders dragged her by her hair, throwing her to the floor. Both girls screamed in fright but within seconds, the Decurion was galloping away toward the gates of the fort, leading the girls' horse behind him.

Rianna struggled to get to her knees and looked toward the disappearing girls.

'Be brave,' she whispered but before she could say anything more, an armoured fist smashed into her face, sending her deep into unconsciousness. The last thing she heard was the sound of Lannosea screaming her name as they rode from the camp.

–

Virrius and the remaining guards watched them go.

'What do you want me to do with her?' asked one of the guards, looking down at the woman's body.

'Use her as you will then throw her in the cess pit,' said Virrius, 'I am done here.' Without another word he returned to his tent, leaving the lustful guards staring at the unconscious yet undeniably attractive woman.

'Like he said,' said one. 'Looks like this is our lucky day.'

Both men laughed and dragged Rianna between them toward the lines of legionary tents.

Chapter Three

The Lands of the Deceangli – 60 AD

Suetonius walked around the battlements of the Deceangli fort high above the coastal village of Treforum. From his position he could see the island of Mona across the Menai straits and knew that he had to make a decision in the very near future. Over the last few months his legion, The XIV Gemina Martia Victrix had campaigned amongst the Deceangli clans, putting down any resistance with ruthless efficiency. Finally they had reached the Cerrig overlooking the strait and laid siege to the stone fortress of Idwal, true blood King of the Deceangli. Initially the fort had seemed impregnable, based as it was on the top of a rocky escarpment and Suetonius had resigned himself to a long siege before carrying out a final assault but fate had stepped in and dealt him an unexpected result. Idwal had fallen ill and died, the victim of an ague that struck down half the defenders and when their king and his closest followers were dead, those who were left had no stomach for the fight. Within days they sent out messengers suing for peace and though Suetonius would normally have extracted a severe price from a defeated enemy, he immediately accepted their surrender and moved the legion into the fort while he made his plans.

Over the years the Deceangli had proved a thorn in his side and were amongst the most warlike of the Khymric tribes, but the war had taken its toll and they had become tired of fighting. This was surely the intervention of the gods for though the subjugation of the Deceangli was a fantastic achievement, Suetonius had eyes on a greater prize; the conquest of the Druids.

Across the Straits lay the island of Mona, a large island to the north of the Khymru and spiritual home of the mystical holy men who controlled almost all the tribes in Britannia. Ever since the first days of the invasion, successive governors had vowed to subdue the influential and troublesome Druids, but the defending Deceangli had always proved a difficult hurdle to be overcome before any such assault could take place.

With the defeat of Idwal's people, the way now lay open to fulfil this important tactical mission, but it had come quicker than expected and he had a decision to make. Should he send for support from the other legions, or risk an immediate assault, building on the success and subsequent high morale of the recent victory?

'She is finally within our grasp,' said a voice and Suetonius turned to see Tribune Attellus standing beside him with two wooden tankards of warmed wine.

'She is,' said Suetonius taking the offered wine. 'Yet strangely, despite its natural beauty I do not see the island as a female but a calculating male opponent needing to be destroyed.'

'Well, thanks to your continued inroads against the enemy, we are on the brink of taking the head from the snake,' said Attellus.

'Are we, Attellus?' asked Suetonius. 'We prepared for a siege, not a full-on assault on a well-defended island. The task would be difficult for two legions, let alone one. I find myself torn between two evils. Do I assault with the four thousand men we have, risking defeat against a stronger enemy or do I send a message to the Ninth Hispana and wait for their support, allowing the enemy to prepare their defences with the possible outcome of even more casualties? Either way, the responsibility weighs heavy on my shoulders.'

'Why not consolidate our position here and wait for the time to be right?'

'It will never be right,' said Suetonius. 'The Druids are the beating heart of these people and the longer we wait the more warriors will flock to their cause. A perceived threat to them may be the catalyst for the unification of the tribes, and that is a situation we cannot allow to happen.'

'So what avenue will you explore?' asked Attellus.

'I will allow myself this night for deliberation,' said Suetonius, 'and with the gods' will, the answer will appear with the dawn.'

The two men stared out across the hills toward Mona on the far side of the strait, both wondering what dangers the countless pinpricks of firelights held for them, knowing that whatever they were, sooner or later they would have to be met head on.

\-

A hundred and fifty miles away, Prydain sat alone at the table in the single men's hut. He had been back with the clan for only a few days, yet already he felt the need to ride out. He took another drink of his ale and glanced down at the young woman in his bed space. She was nice enough but such encounters always left him emotionally empty, a reminder that despite being back amongst his mother's people, after seventeen years in Britannia he still didn't feel at home. Perhaps Kegan had been right and it was time to settle down. The young woman was sleeping soundly and it seemed a shame to throw her out into the cold; she was just as much an outcast as he, for since she had been taken as a prisoner from the neighbouring Dobunii, she had no choice but to make her living as a whore.

Prydain drained his mug and stood up. With a sigh he grabbed his cloak and walked out into the night. Within minutes he was in the stable, whispering quietly to his horse.

'Hello, Blade,' he said, rubbing the sturdy horse's neck. 'Do you have room for me here? I need the company of someone who understands me.' The horse looked on with little interest as Prydain lay on a nearby pile of hay and pulled his cloak about him.

'You're a horse of few words, Blade,' he said, 'but that works fine for me.'

Within moments the sound of gentle snoring filled the stable as Prydain spent another night in the lands of his mother.

—

'Prydain, wake up,' said a voice.

For a few seconds Prydain struggled to wake.

'Prydain, you must come to the home of Kegan immediately. There has been a development.'

Prydain sat up and forced the sleep from his mind. He had slept surprisingly well and he could see daylight streaming through the stable door. Above him he could see Taran, one of the single warriors.

'What developments?' asked Prydain standing up. 'Is the clan in danger?'

'No nothing like that,' said Taran, 'but the patrols have brought in a prisoner who seeks you by name.'

'Where is he?' asked Prydain, brushing hay from his body.

'With Kegan,' said Taran, 'but it is not a he, it is a woman.'

'Really? A woman riding alone in the forests does not make sense,' said Prydain. 'Is she Silures?'

'No, all she will say is she is from the north. Other than that she refuses to speak.'

'A strange situation indeed,' said Prydain. 'Let's go and see what she wants.'

Prydain walked across the bridge and into the village. All around the people were preparing for the day. Women were carrying the wooden buckets of waste to the cess pits outside of the village, while children ran amongst the huts playing with their siblings. Some of the older men were setting out to collect firewood, whilst others were taking the sheep out of the pens for the first time in days to find fresh grazing. Prydain looked at the children staring at him as he passed. Life was always hard in the villages but he could see their faces were drawn more than usual, a sign of the difficult winter that was thankfully falling away around him. Dogs sniffed at his feet, hopeful for a treat and older people stared at the two warriors striding purposely toward the chieftain's hut.

As he approached, Prydain could see four more warriors talking quietly amongst themselves, obviously still ride weary from their journey.

'Owen, it has been a long time,' he said.

One of the riders looked up and walked forward to grasp Prydain's arm.

'Prydain, my friend. You are looking well.'

'And you too, though the bags beneath your eyes are larger than those alongside your saddle. I thought you patrolled the northern borders?'

'We did, but this woman approached and asked to be brought to you. We have ridden hard these past two days,' said Owen, 'with little rest and even less food.'

'What task drives such urgency?' asked Prydain.

'A strange tale and a claim of common friendship,' said Owen, 'She says you know her and begged audience.'

'Why?'

'She has news of a potential tragedy and claimed you would want to hear it first-hand. At first, we did not believe her but when she retold her tale, I recalled something you shared with us around a fire long ago and I realised there may be some truth to her story.'

'Which is?'

'I think you should hear it from her own lips,' said Owen. 'It is either a farcical tale or a matter that affects Britannia itself. I will leave that decision to you.'

'Owen, either way you have my gratitude for honouring my name,' said Prydain. 'Take your men to the hut alongside the stables and get them fed. There will also be beds there. Try to get some rest before you return.'

'Thank you, Prydain,' said Owen. 'We could certainly do with some rest.' He nodded toward Kegan's hut. 'Whether she tells the truth or has the tongue of a snake there is one thing that is certain.'

'And that is?'

'She has a beauty unrivalled,' said Owen.

Chapter Four

The Lands of the Iceni

Rianna wasn't sure what dragged her from unconsciousness, the pain from the wound in her side or the overpowering smell of human filth that pooled around her. Whichever it was, she wished that she was dead for both were overwhelming. For several minutes she lay in the cess pit, motionless, tolerating the swarms of flies that crawled over her stinking face as her mind adjusted to her hellish predicament. Next to her lay another body, though this one long dead and eyeless from the attention of the crows, its grey flesh showing beneath torn skin where the rats had already fed. Realising she was not about to die, she lifted her hand from the filth and using the dead warrior as a platform, eased her body across the pit toward the sloping edges.

The soldiers' shit clung to her clothes, making her retch uncontrollably and though she would have welcomed death, she would rather die at a sword point or even as prey to wolves for nobody should die like this. Slowly but surely, she dragged herself out of the pit, fully expecting to be discovered at any moment and thrown back to the sound of her tormentors' laughter, but apart from the sounds of birds, the forest remained eerily silent.

Finally she crawled clear and lay on the forest floor exhausted, wanting only to die but as the air in her lungs cleared and her memories started to return, her resolve hardened.

Her body had been subjected to the worst sexual abuses the soldiers could devise but despite the pain and the blood, she knew instinctively that there was no life-threatening damage. The sword wound had congealed and though one side of her face was grossly swollen, she knew she had to survive. Not for herself, but for the girls.

Gradually she pushed herself up to a kneeling position and after catching her breath, forced herself to her feet. The breeze caressed her face and she realised it was heavy with the smell of smoke, the tell-tale sign that the Romans had left, burning the temporary camp behind them.

Clutching at her side she started to limp toward the source of the smoke, hoping desperately that they had left the girls behind and not taken them into slavery, or worse. Within minutes she reached the burning remains of the marching camp, and staggered hopelessly between the fires, searching for the bodies of the children.

'Heanua,' she called as loud as her strength would allow, 'Lannosea, where are you?' Over and over she called out until finally she collapsed in the middle of the clearing, crying quietly at the futility of the task.

'Rianna?' said a quiet voice and the wounded woman looked up slowly to see Lannosea standing a few yards away.

'Lannosea,' she gasped but her forced smile soon dropped when she saw the remains of the girl's woollen dress hanging from her shoulders, the lower half caked in blood from her own nightmarish experience.

'We did it, Rianna,' said the girl quietly. 'We did what you said.'

'What did you do?' asked Rianna quietly, her voice close to breaking.

'We submitted,' said Lannosea, 'we wanted to fight but remembered what you said and this is what they did to us.' She indicated her torn dress and the bloody stains.

'It's alright, Lannosea,' whispered Rianna, 'I know you are hurt, but you are alive.'

'Alive?' said the girl, her voice rising. 'Do you know what they did to us, Rianna? Do you know what those bastards did to me?'

'I know, sweetheart, I know,' said Rianna, reaching out her hand as her own tears starting to flow, 'but the pain will pass. You are alive, that's the main thing.'

'No, you don't know,' shouted the girl, 'those men hurt me, Rianna, those pigs were inside me.'

'Oh, Lannosea,' cried Rianna, walking toward her, 'you must trust me, this will get better.'

'Get away from me,' screamed the girl and stepped backward.

Rianna stopped in her tracks, shocked at the rejection from the girl she had treated as her own. Lannosea wiped the tears from her eyes with the heels of her hands.

'We trusted you, Rianna,' she sobbed, 'you said you would protect us and we went like lambs to the slaughter, not knowing what lay in store. There were six of them, Rianna and each one took their turn while we begged them to stop.'

Rianna's hand flew to her own mouth to stifle the sobs aching to break free.

'Why, Rianna?' asked Lannosea. 'Why did you tell us to submit? I would rather have fought.'

'If you had fought, they would have killed you,' said Rianna, 'and I couldn't allow that to happen.'

'Why not?' screamed Lannosea. 'Don't you think I would rather be dead than feeling the way I do now? What could hell possibly hold that is worse than this?'

'I thought it was the right thing to do,' whispered Rianna.

'Well, you thought wrong,' cried Lannosea, her voice weakening through emotion.

Rianna took the opportunity to run forward the few paces and grab Lannosea in her arms, holding her tightly as the girl fought against her, her twelve-year-old fists venting her anger and shame against the woman who had helped bring her up.

'I'm sorry,' whispered Rianna over and over again until finally Lannosea's arms stopped hitting and reached around to cling on as if she would never let her go, her heart breaking as the floods of tears came.

Eventually Rianna eased Lannosea's arms loose and dropped to her knees to face the girl at her level. She pushed the girl's hair back from her eyes and wiped away the tears as gently as she could.

'Lannosea,' she said, 'we can make this right, I promise, but first we have to find your sister. Do you know where she is?'

'She's dead,' whispered Lannosea, 'they killed her.'

'No,' gasped Rianna, 'she can't be. Where is she?'

Lannosea pointed over to the smouldering remains of a pile of hessian sacks.

'Stay right here,' said Rianna. 'I'll go and check. Don't go anywhere, Lannosea, we will get out of here soon enough but first I must see to Heanua.' She stumbled over and found the older girl's body in amongst some empty grain sacks, flat on her back with her dress still raised above her waist, evidence of the atrocities she had suffered.

'Oh you poor, poor girl,' cried Rianna quietly, dropping to her knees. 'I am so sorry.' She gently replaced the girl's dress below her knees before brushing the hair gently from her eyes.

'You did this,' said Lannosea, who had followed Rianna across the clearing.

'I didn't mean this to happen,' said Rianna. 'I hoped they would let you live. If you had fought, then they would definitely have killed you.'

'Well, we didn't fight and they killed her anyway. So much for your advice.'

'Lannosea, you have to understand...' started Rianna.

Before she could say any more, a groan escaped from the lips of Heanua and Rianna stared down at her in shock.

'By the gods, she is still alive,' she gasped.

'But I thought...' started Lannosea.

'It doesn't matter,' said Rianna, 'she is alive. Quickly, get me some water.'

'From where?' asked the girl.

'I don't know,' shouted Rianna, 'check around the camp, go to the stream in the woods, I don't care, just get some water quickly.'

Lannosea backed away before turning to run.

Rianna cradled the unconscious girl's head in her lap, talking quietly in encouraging tones.

'Hang on, sweetheart,' she said. 'We'll make you better, I promise.'

-

Back in the camp of the Iceni, Boudicca was waking from her own nightmare. A shaman was chanting her incantations over her beaten body and Boudicca realised she was back in her hut. For a few seconds she couldn't recall what had happened but when she tried to move and the fire returned to her flesh, the recollection came flooding back and she relived every cutting slash of the soldier's whip. Suddenly she remembered her daughters and looked up at the shaman.

'My girls,' she said. 'Where are they? Are they alright?'

'I know not, my Queen,' said the Shaman, 'all I know is that they escaped the camp with Rianna.'

Boudicca eased back onto the furs, her mind calmed by the fact they were with Rianna.

'What of the others?' asked Boudicca.

'Many are dead,' said the Shaman, 'killed by the Roman swords. They routed the village killing most of the men. They tried to fight but were unprepared. When that was done, they turned their attentions on the women and children, deflowering the maidens in a drunken stupor. We are tending to those who are wounded but the village is devastated. All your wealth has gone and the elders taken into slavery. There is nothing left, my Queen, they have destroyed it all.'

Boudicca shook her head.

'No, Shaman, you are wrong,' she said. 'They have left the one thing that they should have taken first; they left my life, and as long as I have that I swear I will repay this day. For every man they have wounded we will have retribution. For every woman they have abused we will match their pain tenfold and for every life taken we will slaughter a thousand. Be swift with your ointments, Shaman, for there is work to do.'

'You will need to rest,' said the Shaman.

'I need to do nothing except revenge my people,' answered Boudicca. 'These wounds are flesh deep only; it is my very soul that is scarred. Make me well or I will find one who will.'

Back at the Roman camp site, Heanua, Lannosea and Rianna helped each other into the forest. Heanua was weak from her ordeal but between them, they managed to reach the stream and followed it until they found a reasonably-sized pool.

'This will have to do,' said Rianna.

'For what?' asked Lannosea.

'We have to get clean before infection sets in,' said Rianna. 'It may be too late for me but we must try.'

'It looks cold,' said Heanua.

'It will be,' said Rianna, 'but we must be strong. Filth is the home of infection and you should clean your injuries.'

Without undressing, the girls stepped gingerly into the water and walked toward the middle, gasping as it reached up past their waists. Rianna followed them in and together they crouched until the water covered their shoulders.

'Take off your dresses,' she said, 'and scrub them against the rocks. Beat them until they are clean and then use the clean material to wash your bodies.'

'I don't think any amount of washing will make me clean ever again,' said Heanua.

'This is not just for your body but your spirit,' said Rianna. 'Allow the clean waters of the Iceni to wash away the stain of the Romans. Embrace the biting cold for it will rip away the hurt and the shame. Allow it to help you, Heanua, for these waters are borne of our lands and have nurtured us since we were born. The water gods will help heal your body and mind.'

The girls nodded and set about washing themselves, gently at first but with growing anger. Finally they left the stream and put on their wet clothes.

'Come on,' said Rianna, 'we have to get back to the village.'

Though the distance was only a mile, it seemed to take hours to reach the village. The further they went, the more concerned Rianna became as there was no sign of any of their people. At this time of day there should be all sorts out on the tracks. Traders, hunters, herders or even just children playing but there were none of these and the trails were strangely silent.

Finally they reached the village and entered through the gated wall to a scene of devastation. Most houses were burned down and those that were left had their doors ripped off their leather hinges. All around people were shuffling aimlessly, each nursing their own wounds, struggling to understand what had happened. Bodies lay in their hundreds and women searched amongst them to find their loved ones. Smoke filled the air and in one corner, Rianna could see several makeshift crosses, the crucified bodies riddled with arrows having been used as target practise by the Roman archers.

As they walked through the village in silence, empty eyes stared toward them, seeking explanation for the atrocities – but they had no answers. Eventually they reached the centre and Heanua ran forward to her mother's roundhouse, unable to wait any longer.

'Mother,' she shouted and burst into the darkened room.

'Heanua, you are alive,' said Boudicca. 'Thank the gods.'

The girl ran forward to the bed, her brow furrowing as she saw the injured state of the queen.

'Mother, you are hurt,' she said, and went to embrace her, only to be restrained by the hand of the Shaman.

'Careful, child, her wounds are raw.'

'What have they done to you?' gasped Heanua.

'Nothing that won't heal,' said Boudicca, with a weak smile. 'Where is your sister? Is she with you?'

'She follows,' said Heanua, 'but aides Rianna.'

'Why, what ails Rianna?'

'She fell to a Roman sword,' said Heanua, 'but lives still. I fear she is weakening though for the wound has started bleeding again.'

Boudicca turned her head to the Shaman.

'Send your people to aid them, quickly.'

The Shaman bowed and left the roundhouse. Boudicca turned to face her daughter once more.

'And what of you, child?' she asked. 'How have you fared?'

Heanua's face dropped but despite the gloom, Boudicca could sense the change.

'Heanua, what's wrong? Tell me what hurts you so?'

'Nothing,' said the girl. 'I am well.'

Boudicca's eyes narrowed as she examined her daughter's face.

'Heanua, you are hiding something from me. I am your mother and demand you tell me.'

'Nothing,' shouted Heanua, taking Boudicca by surprise. 'We are well. Both of us are.'

Boudicca forced herself up onto one elbow and reached out one arm.

'It's alright, child,' she said, 'come here. I am sorry, I shouldn't have spoken as I did.'

Heanua paused before walking forward to sit on the side of the bed and lowered her head to rest it on her mother's shoulder.

'I am scared, mother,' said Heanua, 'what is to become of us?'

'There is no need to be scared, child,' said Boudicca. 'The worst is over and from now on, it is they who will fear.' Before she could continue, the door flew open and the Shaman burst in.

'Boudicca,' she cried, 'Rianna has collapsed and is in dire need.'

'What ails her?' asked Boudicca.

'My acolytes attend her as we speak,' said the Shaman, 'but her body burns with the fierceness of a forest fire. I fear she will die.'

'No,' gasped Boudicca, 'I will not let this happen. Help me up.'

'You must not move, Queen,' said the Shaman, 'your own wounds are too severe.'

'Get me up,' said Boudicca again. 'I will attend my friend or die trying.'

Heanua and the Shaman helped the queen out of the roundhouse and across the clearing to where a small crowd had gathered.

'Let us through,' shouted the shaman and the people parted before them.

Boudicca knelt down beside Rianna and felt the shivering woman's skin.

'What causes this fever?' she asked.

'She has a sword wound to her side,' said one of the acolytes. 'The blade has hit no organs but has closed over the cut. I fear there is infection within that needs cleaning.'

'And if we leave it?'

'She will die,' said the acolyte.

Boudicca turned to the Shaman.

'Is there a way to clean the infection?' she asked.

'Possibly,' said the Shaman, 'but she is weak and may not survive the trauma.'

'Tell me.'

'If the cavity is unbroken and only the flesh is cut, we can reopen the wound and scrape out the filth. The wound will be packed with the boiled mulch of the willow and will ease the pain but only the gods will have the final say.'

Boudicca turned to face Rianna whose eyes were half closed in pain.

'Did you hear that, Rianna? We may be able to save your life but there will be much pain.'

'Do it,' gasped Rianna.

Boudicca nodded and turned to the Shaman.

'You heard her,' she said. 'Take her to my hut and give her my bed. You will do everything in your power to save this woman. Her life is your life. Do you understand?'

'I do, great Queen.'

Boudicca turned to face Rianna once more.

'Be strong, my friend,' she whispered, brushing her hair to one side. 'There are things still to do Rianna, retribution to be paid and feats that bards will sing of, but I need you at my side. Do you hear me? Use that strength to fight the poison inside and when you are well, I will be waiting.'

Rianna smiled weakly.

54

'Boudicca,' she whispered, 'the girls.'

'What about them?'

'They have been through a lot and need you.'

'I am always here for them,' said Boudicca.

'No, you don't understand,' said Rianna. 'They need their mother, not their queen.'

Boudicca paused but nodded in silence.

'I understand,' she said quietly.

Behind them the Shaman returned.

'We are ready,' she said.

Boudicca kissed Rianna on the cheek before struggling up to her feet, allowing them access to the wounded woman. Several pairs of hands carried Rianna away and the crowd dispersed, leaving only Boudicca, Lannosea and Heanua in a loose circle, looking at each other in silence. Finally Boudicca gave a tight-lipped smile and held out her arms and after a moment's hesitation, Heanua walked forward into her embrace.

'Lannosea, join us,' said her mother.

Lannosea walked forward but instead of joining her family, she walked straight past and headed for the huts.

Chapter Five

The Lands of the Silures

It took a few seconds for Prydain's eyes to adjust to the dim interior of Kegan's hut. Inside, Kegan and Cara sat at the rough-hewn table opposite a woman who was eating a warm maize porridge. Prydain could only see the back of her from the doorway.

'Prydain,' said Kegan. 'You are here at last. Please meet our guest, her name is Heulwen.'

The woman with the long brown hair stood and turned to greet him.

For a second Prydain was taken aback, for although he hadn't seen her for almost ten years, her face had hardly changed. In fact her maturity had been generous and if anything, her beauty had been enhanced.

'Heulwen,' he said. 'It has been a long time.'

'Too long,' said Heulwen and stepped forward to give him a hug.

'You two obviously know each other,' said Kegan.

'We do,' said Heulwen, 'Prydain fished me out of the river at Caer Caradog. If it wasn't for him, I would have been killed by the Roman cavalry.'

'A compliment ill deserved,' said Prydain, 'As I recall it turned out you were more than able to survive in the wilderness.'

'The wilderness I can handle,' said Heulwen, 'rivers are a different thing.'

Prydain smiled.

'I understand you have ridden long and hard to be here. It's not often we see lone female riders so your quest must be important.'

'Prydain, your manners escape you,' said Kegan. 'Our guest has not finished her meal. Please join us and break your fast.'

'Of course,' said Prydain, 'please accept my apologies.' He sat alongside Heulwen while Cara brought over a bowl of porridge as well as a loaf of freshly baked bread.

'Please, fill yourselves up,' said Cara. 'I would otherwise be offended.'

Both Prydain and Heulwen smiled and broke chunks of bread from the loaf. When they had finished, Cara brought over a steaming jug of weakened honey wine and poured it into four wooden tankards before joining the group at the table.

'A meal fit for a king, Cara,' said Heulwen. 'You have my gratitude.'

'Nonsense,' said Cara. 'All travellers are treated so. It is our way.'

'Nevertheless, your hospitality is welcome. I have not eaten for two days.'

'So where have you come from?' asked Kegan. 'Are you Deceangli?'

'My people have no tribe,' said Heulwen, 'we are the Asbri.'

'The Asbri?' said Kegan, his eyes widening in surprise. 'A people of the shadows, I hear.'

'It is true we avoid others wherever possible,' said Heulwen, 'but our skills are often sought in the way of

57

healing. Caratacus himself was an acolyte and we served alongside him at Caer Caradog.'

'It is also said your people are witches,' said Cara.

'If you mean that we have direct links to the afterlife and cast curses on our enemies, then I am sorry to disappoint,' said Heulwen, 'but if you mean we harness the forces of everything around us to make our lives better, then you are correct and I am proud to be labelled so.'

'Perhaps it is a term we will only use between these walls,' said Kegan. 'Our people are fearful of such things and may not be so accommodating.'

'I will not be here long enough to cause inconvenience,' said Heulwen, 'I come only to seek the aid of Prydain.'

'In what matter?' asked Prydain.

'In the matter of Taliesin,' she answered. 'He is missing and I believe he is in danger.'

—

Prydain's face fell at the information but before he could answer, Kegan spoke up.

'Who is this Taliesin you speak of?' he asked.

Prydain glanced at Heulwen before turning to face Kegan.

'Taliesin is the son of Gwydion of the Blaidd,' said Prydain, 'a warrior of the Deceangli who was killed at Caer Caradog. As he died, I swore to protect his son but as he grew up, I put him in the care of the Asbri.'

'Why?' asked Cara. 'If you swore to look after him, then why give him away?'

'Because he would be safer that way,' said Prydain. 'Taliesin's mother was Gwenno, daughter of Erwyn, chieftain of the Blaidd and as such could one day claim the leadership of that great clan. However, the usurper Robbus seduced Erwyn's wife and snatched the leadership in a day of treachery. Taliesin will one day return to the Blaidd and take back what was rightfully his. It was important that he was brought up in the way of chieftains.'

'And was he?' asked Kegan.

'On the contrary, he was brought up in a humble life,' said Heulwen. 'He has turned out to be a wonderful young man and will one day make an excellent king.'

'Chieftain,' corrected Prydain.

Heulwen looked at Prydain.

'I chose my words carefully,' she said, 'and stand by what I said. Things have changed, Prydain. The Romans have spent these last few years laying waste to clans across the Deceangli territories and many have died in their defence. There is no true blood Deceangli left to lead the tribe.'

'But what about Idwal?' asked Prydain.

'Idwal died ten days ago,' said Heulwen, 'struck down by an ague in the Cerrig at Treforum. His army surrendered without a blow dealt and his sons were carted off as slaves to Rome. Without a leader the Deceangli are on their knees and clans fight amongst themselves for position. The Deceangli need a leader, Prydain, and Taliesin is the last true blood in the line of the princes. He needs to pick up the banner and lead if this country is ever going to resist the Roman occupation. That is why I am here. Taliesin is a grounded boy with maturity beyond his years but his passion for this country often outstrips his sensibility. When he heard that the Romans were intent on laying siege to the Cerrig, he left our village without warning, intent on lending his sword arm to Idwal. Obviously, we pursued him, for his safety is more important than just one more blade against the enemy, but the Cerrig fell before we caught up with him.'

'Was he captured?' asked Prydain.

'We don't know,' said Heulwen. 'Many were taken prisoner and lie in chains within the Cerrig. We can only hope he is still alive.'

'So what do you want from me?' asked Prydain.

'Prydain, I know it is a great ask but we need your knowledge to try and help us free him.'

'What can I do that your own warriors cannot achieve?'

'We have no warriors,' said Heulwen, 'we are a peaceful people and our men are poets or studiers of the stars. If Taliesin is indeed a prisoner, we will need to find a way to free him. Do you remember the few days we spent together fleeing the aftermath of Caer Caradog all those years ago?'

'I do.'

'Well you told me then that you were once imprisoned in the Cerrig. You know the layout of the fortress and can help us find him.'

'Heulwen, I was there for hours only. I'm not even sure if I recall the layout.'

'No man forgets his prison,' said Heulwen, 'no matter how short the sentence.'

'Even if I do recall the layout, how do you intend to overcome a garrison of Romans? Surely not by force of arms?'

'With this,' said Heulwen throwing a bag of coins onto the table. 'The Romans have a taste for gold so we have melted down the Torcs of our people to form the discs they crave. Every man has his price and if we can bribe a few guards perhaps we can free him.'

'But why do you need me?' asked Prydain.

'Because you know the ways of the Romans,' said Heulwen, 'and the bargain may need translation.'

'I can't,' said Prydain. 'I am needed here, with my own people. The winter has been harsh and despite the thaw, it will be difficult until the sun once again warms our skin. Besides, my days fighting Romans are done. If they threaten the lands of my mother then I will fight but until then, I will concentrate on feeding our children.'

An awkward silence fell at the table before Heulwen spoke again.

'Prydain, I didn't want to do this but I must remind you of the pledge you made.'

'I fulfilled my oath,' said Prydain, 'by placing him in your hands. My part is done.'

'Prydain, I take no pleasure in pursuing this but the future of the Silures also relies on the survival of Taliesin.'

'In what way?'

'If we can't return him to his people, then I fear the Deceangli will tear themselves apart, leaving the route open for the Romans to campaign south and if that happens, it is only a matter of time before the Ordovices fall to their swords. After that the Silures are the only ones stopping the Khymru from falling. There is more to this than just the survival of one boy; our nation could well be at risk.'

Prydain turned to Kegan.

'What say you?' he asked.

'Heulwen makes sense,' said Kegan, 'but the decision is yours. Your contribution to this clan has been great and without you our life would be much harder, but the responsibilities are not yours alone. If your heart reaches out to this quest then go with our blessing. If not, then there is a place here for you and when I die, you will become chieftain. Either way there is no shame, only honour. Take some time for it is a dangerous feat you contemplate.'

Prydain looked between them all before speaking again.

'Many years ago my mother needed help and there was nobody there to come to her aide. Subsequently she led her life as a slave in Rome and died at the hands of a monster. If somebody had heeded her call, she may have lived today. My home is here and I have pledged my life to the Silures yet I cannot ignore the plight of this boy. His father and I faced many trials together and when he died in my arms at Caer Caradog, I pledged I would see his son safe to manhood.' He turned to face Heulwen. 'I will honour that pledge, Heulwen. My sword is yours.'

Heulwen's hand crept forward and covered Prydain's own on the table.

'Thank you, Prydain. I will be forever grateful.'

'Then so be it,' said Kegan, standing up. 'The decision is made. Heulwen, you will get some rest while the preparations are made. You will leave in the morning.'

'No, we must leave immediately,' said Heulwen. 'There is no time to lose.'

'The loss of one day will not hinder you unduly,' said Kegan, 'just ensure you are better prepared. Prydain will make suitable arrangements and you will leave at first light. In the meantime, Cara will make up a bed so you can get some sleep. From what I can gather, rest is going to be in short supply in the forthcoming days.'

Heulwen looked toward Prydain for support.

'Kegan is right,' he said. 'This quest is not to be taken lightly and I need time to prepare.'

Heulwen nodded silently in acceptance.

'Come with me, Heulwen,' said Cara. 'The rest is the business of men.'

Kegan and Prydain left the hut and wandered across the village.

'You do realise that the chances of success are limited,' said Kegan. 'The Roman influence has spread like a plague and they have spies everywhere. It will be difficult to even get to the Cerrig and even then, the chances of him being there are slim.'

'I know,' said Prydain, 'but I must try.'

'Then take some men,' said Kegan. 'The spring is almost upon us and times will get easier for our hunters.'

'No, Kegan. They will be needed here.'

'Nonsense,' said Kegan, 'besides, they have warrior's appetites. You will be doing us a favour. Without your men, our food will probably last until next summer.'

Both men laughed.

'I see what you are doing, Kegan but this task is mine alone. I will not lead our men toward a fate I do not control. Their swords may be needed here.'

Kegan stopped and faced Prydain.

'These past few years you have become like a son to me, Prydain. I accept your need to meet your pledge but know this. The gods will be deafened by my prayers until the day you return.'

'I am honoured, Kegan and if the gods are willing, I will return before winter to share that store of good wine you have hidden beneath your bed space.'

'You know about that?' asked Kegan with surprise.

'Everyone knows about that,' laughed Prydain.

'Then on the day you return, we will show it the light of day and there will be revelry the likes of which this clan has never seen before.'

'Then there is no doubt I will return,' laughed Prydain, 'for even the gods will wish to see that day.'

'I will let you get on,' said Kegan, 'but will say my goodbyes now.'

'Why not tomorrow?'

'It is never good for a clan to see the tears of a chief,' said Kegan and held out his arm.

Prydain paused before grabbing Kegan's arm and pulling him in to a manly embrace.

'I care not for comments of fools,' he said. 'I will miss you as a father and if the gods will it, I will return to make you proud of me.'

Kegan's eyes filled up and he nodded silently before breaking the embrace and making his way slowly across the village.

—

The following morning saw Prydain up early to see to his horse. He rode through the village and stopped before the hut of Kegan. Cara led Heulwen out but as expected, there was no sign of Kegan.

'He's gone hunting,' said Cara.

Prydain nodded with understanding.

'Are you ready, Heulwen?' he asked.

'Yes,' said Heulwen, 'though after the food Cara has made me eat, I feel I may need a plough horse to carry me.'

'Nonsense,' said Cara. 'Porridge and Cawl is just what you need to set you up for a long ride.'

'Thank you, Cara,' said Heulwen, kissing the old woman on her cheek. 'Your hospitality has been wonderful.'

'You just stay safe, my girl,' said Cara, 'and be gone before you start this old woman crying.'

Heulwen kissed Cara again before mounting the horse.

'Goodbye, Cara,' said Prydain, 'and remind that old man of yours that I will hold him to his promise.'

'What promise?'

'Ask Kegan,' said Prydain and kicked at his horse's flanks to lead the way.

—

They hadn't travelled more than a mile when Prydain pulled up and looked behind him.

'What's the matter?' asked Heulwen, reining in her horse beside him.

'We are being followed,' said Prydain.

'Are you sure?'

'Positive.'

'Who do you think it is?' asked Heulwen.

'I have a good idea,' said Prydain, 'but we will see soon enough.' A moment later, three men came riding over the hill and galloped toward him.

'And where do you think you are going?' asked one.

'To the Cerrig of the Deceangli,' said Prydain.

'Without us?' asked the second man. 'How forgetful of you.'

Prydain looked around the faces of the three as Heulwen looked on in bemusement.

'Do you know these men?' she asked.

'I do,' said Prydain, 'they are my fellow warriors and closest friends. I did not forget you, Cullen. I thought hard about asking for your aid but there is a chance I will not be returning this time. The dangers are great and the task is mine alone.'

'We live every day with danger,' said the second man, 'since when has that stayed our hand?'

'I know, Taran, but the burden is mine. I made a pledge and honour demands it is paid. You do not owe me anything.'

'It matters not,' said Taran. 'We are coming with you and nothing you say will change our minds. We have our weapons and supplies so all we need from you is the nature of the task.'

'A task that may be the end of us all,' said Prydain.

'And that is why we are here,' said Taran. 'With us your chances are slim but alone they are non-existent. We are coming with or without your agreement. Four swords are better than one.'

'Listen to him, Prydain,' said the third rider, 'for our minds are set. We understand that the Khymru is at risk and is this country no less ours?'

'Of course it is,' said Prydain.

'Then it is agreed,' said the big man. 'This party now has four swords.'

'Five,' said Heulwen, pulling aside her cloak to reveal a side dagger.

'A pretty toy, lady,' said Taran.

'Yet one that can cut a Roman throat as efficiently as any sword,' answered Heulwen.

'Enough,' interrupted Prydain. 'If we are to succeed, we need to work as a fist, not an open palm. Heulwen, this is Taran, the best swordsman I have ever seen and the handsome one there is Cullen. Whilst he is also an excellent swordsman, his main weapon is his silver tongue. Watch him for many a lady has fallen for his honeyed words.'

'A pleasure to meet you, Miss,' said Cullen, taking her hand to kiss it gently. 'Owen was right, you are indeed fairer than the most beautiful flower.'

'Back off, Cullen,' said Prydain. 'You have only just made acquaintance and already you cast your bait.'

'Good to make your acquaintance, Cullen and Taran,' said Heulwen before turning to face the biggest man. 'And you are?'

'I am Gildas, Lady,' he said, 'and fear not for I will keep these two brigands in check.'

'And do you have a silver tongue?'

'Me? Oh no, Lady. My heart is taken by one back in camp.'

'So why are you so keen to leave her?' asked Heulwen.

'Let's just say that though the homecomings are sweet, the goodbyes are sweeter still,' said Gildas. 'But enough banter, do we ride or do we talk like washer women at the wicker?'

'You are right,' said Prydain. 'There is a long way to go.'

'I hear the Romans run riot in the north,' said Gildas. 'Perhaps there will be chance to blood our blades.'

'Our aim is to return a boy to his tribe,' said Prydain, 'nothing more. Once we have him, we will return at full speed to our own lands.'

'Fair enough,' said Gildas. 'So what are we waiting for?'

'Nothing,' said Prydain. 'Lead the way, Gildas.'

Gildas spurred his horse to a trot and the other four riders followed him, each unsure what the next few days would bring but equally quiet in their determination to succeed.

Chapter Six

The Lands of the Iceni

Boudicca stared into the dancing flames of the camp-fire. Her dress was lowered to her waist and Heanua was gently rubbing ointment from the Shamen into the many wounds across her back. Beside her, Lannosea was busy cutting a sheet of linen into strips for fresh bandages. All around, the many campfires stretched away into the darkness, providing circles of welcoming warmth throughout the forest like a swarm of fireflies. Yet all those who sought their comforting heat knew they were safe from prying eyes as the nearest enemy patrols were at least a day's ride away and could not see into the blanket of protecting Iceni darkness. Heanua helped wrap Boudicca with bandages before snuggling into her side, just happy to enjoy the closeness of her mother, a pleasure rarely enjoyed. A figure approached and spoke quietly.

'Boudicca,' said the guard, 'the Shaman seeks audience.'

'Let her through,' said Boudicca.

The mystical woman entered, her body stooped through age.

'Shaman,' said Boudicca, 'I trust you have good news.'

'I do, great Queen,' said the Shaman, 'the fever has broken and Rianna is lost in the sleep of the exhausted.'

'Good news indeed,' said Boudicca.

'We have laid her in one of the carts,' said the Shaman. 'She will need to rest but the gods smile on her.'

'At first light we will sacrifice a bull to their glory,' said Boudicca. 'Pass the word to the people. Our messengers have returned from the clans with promise of support and today I have received a pledge from the Trinovantes. They have long suffered Rome's will and are straining to throw off the shackles. Tonight you and your acolytes will partake of the devil's cap and reveal your dreams. If they are true, then tomorrow we will step out from the shadows.'

The Shaman bowed and left the tent.

-

The following morning saw Boudicca walking out of the forest accompanied by her closest advisors. Behind her, hundreds of her own clan followed, spread across the forest edge like a wave upon a shore. For a second the sunlight caught her eyes, and her hand flew up to shade the early morning glare, but within seconds it fell away again, a shocked response to the sight that lay before her. In the valley below, thousands of warriors stood silently in the sunshine, waiting for the appearance of the woman whose plight had united them as one. Along the high ground hundreds of carts lined up, each carrying supplies and the families of those who had answered her call. Throughout the mass she could see the banners of all the Iceni clans and in the distance, she could see seas of red tunics, the preferred colours of the Trinovantes.

Immediately below her, clan leaders looked up at her, each holding the banner of his own clan. Iceni, Trinovantes and Cornovii were prevalent but there were also clans from the Durotriges, Catuvellauni and Dobunii, each leader testament to their own tribe's weariness of Roman rule.

As she appeared, a great roar rose from the throats of ten thousand men, all cheering the warrior queen. For what seemed an age the cheering continued and Boudicca was shocked to see all the clan leaders bend their knee before her. Heanua tapped her on the shoulder and pointed toward a cart on one side. Boudicca looked over and saw Rianna sitting on the tail gate.

Rianna raised her fist, first placing it over her heart before raising it in salute to her friend. Boudicca copied the gesture before turning to face the impressive army before her. She held her hand high until eventually silence fell.

'Those who can hear my words, carry them to the back so everyone shares this day,' she called. 'Today the people of Britannia lift themselves from the mud. Today we send message to Nero that this land is ours and they have sullied our soil long enough. Never before has such an army been seen in Britannia and let those warriors who have died in our country's defence look down upon us with pride. Leaders of the Trinovantes, Catuvellauni and Iceni, fellow warriors of the Durotriges, Dobunii and Coritani, in the name of our revered forebears, cast away your differences. In the name of Cunobelinus and Caratacus who faced the Romans when all others slept in their beds, unite as one for today we are not the tribes of Britannia, we *are* Britannia.'

Again the crowd roared and this time Boudicca did little to quieten them. She turned to one of her warlords.

'Pass the word for the clans to ready their steeds and sharpen their swords,' she said. 'Before the sun is at its highest, we will take the first steps toward regaining our lands. Gather the clan leaders for council at the far crags. I will attend shortly.'

The warrior nodded and ran from her. Boudicca summoned the nearby Shaman.

'Attend me,' she said and walked over to the wagon where Rianna still sat. 'Rianna, my heart is glad to see you well.'

'I am as weak as a puppy but the witches have done their work well,' said Rianna.

'It was to their advantage that you lived,' sneered Boudicca.

'You have never paid them much respect,' said Rianna, 'yet allow them personal attendance. I have often wondered about this.'

'They are often scaremongers who bode ill for their own purpose,' said Boudicca, 'and I have little time for such talk.'

'Then why humour them?' asked Rianna.

'My views are not shared by the majority,' said Boudicca, 'and my people fall upon the Shamen's words like geese on the corn. Better that I direct their ramblings than banish them, for that would only feed subversion.' Both women looked toward the old crone as she arrived.

'You summoned me, great Queen.'

'I did. Have you partaken of the dream root?'

'We have, Boudicca.'

'And was this day revealed to you?'

'It was, my Queen, but such things are for the enlightened. My pictures can be shared but they are yours to read.'

'Then show me your dreams, Shaman, for the people of Britannia grow impatient.'

'My Queen,' said the Shaman, 'I saw a sacred pond that fed a stream. Many children drank from the stream but it dried up and the children went thirsty. Together they looked to the pond and saw it was blocked by mud. A minnow tried to unblock the mud but a great pike scared it off and chased it around the pond. Finally the minnow grew tired and turned against the pike in a great fight, swallowing up the pike and allowing the stream to flow again, easing the thirst of the children.'

'I knew it,' gasped Boudicca, 'the vision is clear.'

'Is it?' asked Rianna.

'Don't you see?' asked Boudicca. 'The children in the dream are our children of the future and the mighty pike represents the Romans. The fact that it was defeated by a minnow shows that our cause is just.' She turned to the Shaman. 'Take your dream to the people and let them know the meaning. They will stand taller with such magic and look into the enemy's eyes as equals, not vanquished.' As the Shaman disappeared to her task Boudicca turned once more to Rianna. 'My friend,' she said, 'there are great days before us and I am honoured that you will be at my side.'

'And I am proud to stand alongside you, Boudicca. Many lives will be lost before we return to our lands but their sacrifice will strengthen every step of those who follow until not one Roman foot remains on Britannic soil.'

'Then let us make it so, sister or die well in the trying.' The two women embraced before Boudicca left to address the council, cheered on by thousands of warriors as she passed. The die was cast; the war had begun.

Chapter Seven

The Lands of the Deceangli

Three hundred miles away, Suetonius finalised his plans. The engineers had overseen the construction of a fleet of basic assault boats while every vessel for miles around had been seized to add to the makeshift fleet. Onagers and Ballistae, the siege artillery, were unloaded from the carts and assembled along the foreshore in anticipation of the assault.

The command post was still located in the Cerrig and Suetonius held a briefing for his officers in the great hall which once held the warriors of Idwal. When all those summoned had arrived, Suetonius called them to silence.

'Gentlemen,' he said. 'Thank you for leaving your preparations at such short notice. I have summoned you here to relay disturbing news. Our spies tell us that one of the tribes in the east is busy raising an army to provide resistance against us. At this moment there is little information but our spies report their numbers are many and they pose a threat to our settlements in the area.'

'Which tribe?' asked a Tribune.

'Iceni,' said Suetonius, 'though there are reports of others joining them.'

'I thought the Iceni were subservient,' said a voice.

'They were,' said Suetonius, 'but the old king died and his widow is known to be a firebrand.'

'A woman,' said Tribune Attellus, 'why is this of concern to us? Pass the information to the Evocati stationed at Camulodunum and be done with it. They may be reserves but every one of them is a veteran, they will scratch this itch without catching breath.'

'You would think so,' said Suetonius, 'but apparently this itch has already burned dozens of client villages and is reported to be heading toward Camulodunum.'

'Why go there?' asked Attellus. 'Surely they don't think they can have any effect. Villages are one thing but a walled city is another altogether. It is too well defended.'

'This is why I summoned you,' said Suetonius. 'I have reports that this woman is becoming a serious threat and her army could breach the walls of Camulodunum. In normal circumstances I would despatch two legions to swat this insect but the Victrix is spread thinly across the south of Britannia while the Augusta is tied down in the Khymru, keeping the cursed Silures and Cornovii quiet. That leaves us and the Ninth Hispana to deal with the threat. Camulodunum is at least fifteen days march from here and we would arrive too late to reinforce the defences. The Hispana, however, are only a few days away from the settlement and are perfectly placed to defend their walls or better still, address the problem before it arises. To this end, I have sent a team of messengers on fresh horses to instruct Legatus Petillius to lead his legion against the Iceni without delay. I have no doubt whatsoever that the threat, if there ever was one, will be extinct within ten days.'

Heads nodded around the hall. Quintus Petillius Cerialis, Legatus of the Ninth Hispana legion was a veteran of many conflicts and a respected leader of men.

'However,' continued Suetonius, 'as the Ninth will be otherwise engaged it means we are alone in our task against the Druids. We could wait until Petillius has dealt with this annoyance and joins us here but I grow frustrated by the continued delay. Mona has long been a thorn in our side and while the Deceangli lick their wounds, I feel we will never have a better opportunity to silence these so-called priests. Across that stretch of water lays the head of the snake. Remove that, and the rest of the Britannic tribes will writhe in religious agony. My Tribunes tell me we have enough boats to carry half the legion across the strait and if we go when the tide is lowest, we can land on the far slopes within minutes. Make no mistake, for though the enemy do not have a trained army, this is a task equal to that faced by Plautius at Medway. I believe our men have the mettle but let it never be said that my ego outshone the expertise of my commanders. I seek your guidance on this matter. Do we wait for the Ninth Hispana, or do we do what Romans do best and take the battle to the enemy in the face of overwhelming odds?'

As one the hall erupted in shouts from every man present.

'Take the head,' shouted some, 'kill the snake,' shouted others, 'death to the Druids.' Fists pounded on tables while men invoked their own gods in support of the action. As the commotion continued, Suetonius walked slowly through the throng of seasoned soldiers. He would fight alongside any one of them in a heartbeat, but there was one man whose opinion he sought above all others. The gathered officers and Centurions opened before him until he stood before the only man not on his feet. The soldier's helmet lay on the ground and though he was entitled to wear the transverse scarlet crest of a Centurion, he rarely displayed such insignia, preferring to concentrate on the thing that mattered most; soldiering.

With any other man, the lack of response to the governor's rallying call could have been seen as insubordination but with this man it was different. He was the senior Centurion of the legion and as such the leader of the double strength first cohort and though he was a man of few words, he had earned the respect of every man there. All eyes turned toward the two men and silence fell once more, broken only by the sound of a whetstone being dragged slowly along the edge of the Centurion's Gladius.

Suetonius watched him with interest. This man had been there at the beginning and served under Plautius during the invasion seventeen years earlier. His skill with any weapon was legendary amongst the legion and he was the complete soldier, totally committed to the service of Rome. It was an ill kept secret that he had also served in the Exploratores, the specialised unit that operated behind enemy lines and had played a major part in the downfall of Caratacus at the battle of Caer Caradog ten years earlier. Since then he had worked his way up through the ranks to where he was now. His name was Cassus Maecilius and he was the Primus Pilus, senior Centurion and fourth in line of command to the Fourteenth Gemina.

'What say you, Cassus?' asked Suetonius. 'What thoughts swirl around that mind of yours?'

The soldier stopped sharpening his sword and got to his feet. Slowly his gaze swept across the room, meeting the eyes of all those who dared to look directly toward him.

'Suetonius,' he said eventually. 'As you know I will follow you unto hell if that is your command. I hold no fear of these so-called Druids and I will gladly lead my men across the strait to bathe my Gladius in religious blood. But there is doubt in my sword arm. Unlike others present, this woman you speak of worries me. I have had dealings with the Iceni in the past and know them to be one of the more stubborn tribes. If word is spreading that they raise an army, then that is no small news and just the fact that they dare stand against us screams a warning to me. We all know that if this island had the sense to unite, we would need five times as many legions compared to the four now deployed. If this woman is as rabid as they proclaim, she may just be the catalyst to spur such unification. As word spreads about her gall, men will flock to her banner. Warriors from tribes who yet resist will join farmers crippled by taxes in a fight for liberty and there is no army that fights as well as one of liberation. You ask me my thoughts and they are these. The Druids see themselves as invincible and protected by their gods. They are going nowhere and will still be there later in the campaign season for us to pick off at whim. Destroying them will be a political victory only, while in the east a real threat raises its head. Leave the priests for a later time and double march to Camulodunum. Send fresh riders and have the Ninth wait for our arrival before they face the Iceni. With two legions, I agree the battle will be one sided but alone I fear Petillius may come up against a viper not a grass snake.'

For a few moments the room remained silent as those present digested his words.

'Utter horseshit,' snapped Tribune Attellus and the men opened up again, leaving the young Tribune facing the Primus Pilus.

'The idea that a thrown together army of ill prepared barbarians could present a threat to a legion of the Ninth's stature is not even worth a second thought. With respect, Cassus, I believe Petillius will swat this Boudicca aside as he would a fly and then, if he is half the leader, I know he is, continue to wipe the Iceni from the face of the earth for their impudence.'

Cassus didn't rise to the insult. The young Tribune was known as a hot head and didn't mince his words, a trait that the more experienced soldier found quite refreshing.

'You may be right, Attellus,' he said, 'but my opinion was sought and I gave it. I do not doubt our ability to overcome the Druids. I do however believe that Boudicca poses a greater threat.'

Attellus turned to the governor.

'My lord,' he said, 'our men have campaigned long for a chance of glory. Stories abound that the island is full of treasures and our men have fought with the promise of gold as their reward. Gladii sit in scabbards and sword arms grow lazy with the wait. Many before you have proclaimed the Druids the ultimate prize but all fell by the wayside, seduced by the politics of governorship yet you have them at your feet.'

Attellus turned to address the rest of the men.

'Do not doubt the worth of Petillius,' he continued, 'his name resounds around the senate, such is his fame. Let him deal with the woman while we behead the snake. Like every man here I revere the word of the Primus Pilus but with respect, in this matter he is wrong. Take their holy island and Britannia will fold beneath them like a new-born calf's legs. Surely this is an opportunity too great to miss?'

Many voices raised in support until finally the Legatus raised his hand for silence.

'Praefectus Castrorum, report on the task before us,' he said.

The third in command of the legion stepped forward.

'My lord, the strait separating Mona from the mainland ranges from a mile wide to less than a few hundred paces. It is open to the sea and as such is tidal. At low tide, the distance in places reduces to less than a hundred paces though locals report that the mud exposed can be lethal and will trap men in its grip as if in irons. Obviously, this is a situation we cannot contemplate.' He approached the map.

'Our options are these,' he continued. 'If we are to assault Mona, we can do it at only two possible times, high or low tide. The race of the water between those times is too great and our men and boats would be washed away. At high tide, we can launch assault boats here, here and here.' He pointed a dagger at the map. 'Other launch points are available but the far bank is not suitable for quick exits from the boats and they would become killing zones. In addition, our Ballistae and Onagers would be out of range as they would have to be brought back from the water's edge. We would probably prevail but would lose many boats from the defenders' arrows before we made landfall.'

'However,' he continued, 'if we were to attack at low tide, we have observed the waters uncover accessible rocks further into the strait. This means our artillery becomes viable. In addition, the water flow is at a minimum and though the distance is still fifty paces across deep water, it is well within the capabilities of our men and indeed the cavalry.'

'What about the exposed mud?' asked a voice.

'Again, at these points we have observed rocky outcrops at low tide,' said the officer. 'All we would have to do is get across ten paces of mud to access solid footing. After that, it is down to the skills of our infantry.'

'And how is that mud to be bettered?'

'With reed mats,' said the Praefectus Castrorum. 'The locals use them to harvest shellfish at low tide. We have taken this knowledge and are having hundreds of such mats made as we speak. The first wave of boats will contain local fishermen who have been brought up on the straits and know the dangers. They will lay the mats needed to span the distance from boat to rocks, ready for the second wave containing our men.'

'Why would the fishermen help us?' asked another officer. 'Surely as soon as they make the crossing they will defect to the enemy.'

'Undoubtedly,' said the Praefectus, 'but trust me, we have arrangements in place to ensure that won't happen.'

'And the cavalry,' asked another officer, 'is there a role for us?'

'There is, Quintus,' answered the officer, 'though in the second wave. We cannot risk the horses in the mud so once the landing has been secured, your cavalry will enter the water here and here. It is a longer swim but at least there is no mud and the far bank is a gentle sloping beach, ideal for easy exit. By then the far bank will be ours and you will ride to secure the forward edge of the assault while the rest of the legion crosses behind you.'

'Enemy strength?' asked Attellus.

'Unknown at the moment but we have observed movement in the trees on the far bank. Locals have informed us that the Druids have no formal army though there is a clan of Druid warriors that guard the holy men. We understand they are fanatics who will fight to the death to protect their island though only a few hundred strong. Nevertheless, the population of the island is many thousands and they will also protect their priests to the death. We should assume at least equal numbers to our own.'

The governor stood forward once again.

'Architecti, report on preparations,' he ordered.

The officer in charge of the legion's engineers pushed to the front of the gathered officers.

'My lord, we have a hundred barges already constructed, each capable of carrying a Contubernium across the channel in a few minutes. On top of that we have commandeered another twenty fishing vessels as well as a cargo ship capable of carrying a century of archers on her decks. We also have a thousand rush mats completed with a thousand more due imminently. All Scorpios are serviced and are capable of reaching the far shore to provide covering fire. The Onagers have already been tensioned and although most of the far bank is beyond their range there is a spur that sticks out where they can get closer, bringing a stretch of the bank within their reach.'

'Ballistae arrows?'

'Over five thousand in carts to the rear.'

'Fire pots?'

'A thousand, as well as five thousand boulders for Onagers.'

'Tribune Attellus, you were tasked with tactics. Unveil your plan.'

'Gentlemen,' said Attellus, relishing the opportunity to demonstrate his tactical ability. 'The arrangements already discussed should indicate our thinking. However, for clarity, the plan is this. In two days' time, low tide is just before dawn. Before the sun rises, our engineers will drag the Ballistae onto the rocks and the Onagers onto the spur indicated by the Architecti. The lead boats with the fishermen will make the crossing under the cover of darkness and lay the mats across the mud. Hopefully they will be undetected but as soon as the subterfuge is revealed, our artillery will begin the bombardment with fire pots and Ballistae arrows. In the confusion, our cohorts will follow up in boats here,' he indicated the location on the map, 'while the Batavian auxiliaries will swim the wider channels here and here. All first assault troops will be tasked with securing the shore for one hundred paces inland, enabling our cavalry to cross without fear of archers. The rest, gentlemen is standard operating procedure.'

'It sounds straightforward,' said one of the Centurions.

'It is,' said Attellus, 'as are all great plans.'

Suetonius stepped forward once more and all heads turned to face the general.

'A legion is not one sword but many acting as one,' he said, 'and though such decisions fall on my shoulders, the same is often said about a good commander. I have listened to your council and though your concerns are heeded, I have made a decision. As suggested by the Primus Pilus, message will be sent to the Ninth to hold back from engagement with Boudicca unless pressed into self-defence. In the meantime, in two days' time the Fourteenth Gemina will assault Mona with all possible haste to wipe out the Druid's influence once and for all. Gentlemen, you have forty-eight hours to prepare your men for battle. The decision is made.'

Raucous cheering once again broke out and continued as the officers left the hall to return to their units. Finally only a few were left including the governor and the Primus Pilus.

'I hope you are not offended, Cassus,' said Suetonius.

'Why would I be offended?' asked Cassus. 'You asked my opinion and I gave it. The decision is yours to make. It now falls to me to make it happen and I will do that with every fibre of my being.'

'I know you will,' said Suetonius, 'and your direction is welcome but you will not lead the vanguard of our attack, Cassus, that honour will fall to the Gallic auxiliaries.'

For the first time Cassus' eyes showed a flicker of anger.

'That role should be filled by the first cohort,' he said.

'Ordinarily yes,' said Suetonius, 'but I fear that though the crossing is short, the first to attempt it will be going into a killing zone. I have no doubt that we will succeed but I am not going to risk my most experienced men and Primus Pilus before they have chance to draw Gladii.'

'My men will be shamed,' said Cassus.

'An unfortunate situation yet a necessary one,' said Suetonius.

'So are we to be involved at all?' asked Cassus.

'When the far bank is secured, you and your men will be unleashed inland,' said Suetonius.

'Against civilians and children?' asked Cassus. 'A task for lesser men I feel.'

'Yet the most profitable for spoils you would agree?'

Cassus stared at the commander for several moments before answering.

'My lord, can I speak freely?'

'As always,' said Suetonius.

'My lord, my men are the best there are and have handed you many victories. To pull them back from the van will have an effect on their morale as ill as any defeat. I request the decision is revisited.'

'Request denied,' said Suetonius. 'I know you are angry but some decisions are for the greater good. Tell your men there will be other opportunities for glory.'

Cassus took a deep breath before replacing his helmet.

'I will relay your message, my lord, but feel it will be like seed upon barren ground.' Before the general could answer, Cassus saluted and left the hall.

Attellus approached and stood beside Suetonius.

'Sometimes I wonder why you put up with such insubordination,' he said.

'Have you ever seen him fight, Attellus?'

'No, but I have heard he is good.'

'Good isn't the word I would use,' said the general. 'In fact there is not a word I can think of to describe him. You have to see it to understand.'

'He is but one man, General.'

Suetonius turned to stare at the Tribune.

'No, Attellus,' he said finally. 'Sometimes I don't think he is.'

Chapter Eight

The City of Camulodunum

Hundreds of traders stood outside the walls of the city waiting for the giant gates to open, a daily ritual for those locals who frequented the Roman markets. Despite the underlying hatred for the Romans, there was no denying their coins were as good as any and the markets within often held goods that the outlying villages could only dream of.

Camulodunum had once been the Capital of Britannia before the invasion seventeen years earlier but after its surrender to the legions of Plautius, the city had gradually become more Romanised and was now completely under the control of the Empire. In the intervening years, those soldiers who had reached the end of their twenty-six years' service and had retired from the legions, often chose to stay in Britannia and settled in Camulodunum. These were the Evocati, ex-soldiers who were available for reserve duties as required.

Such was the Roman influence, it even had a temple to Claudius, the emperor who had visited Britannia briefly to accept the surrender of the capital on behalf of Rome. Stories were still told in the city of the enormous beasts he brought with him and though children looked up in awe at the storytellers, those who had not witnessed the war elephants with their own eyes doubted the truth of those who had.

As the gates creaked open, the traders mounted their carts and stirred their mules into action, keen to get the best pitches in the market square. Farmers, shepherds and tailors walked alongside each other, each hoping that their goods would be snapped up by the ever consuming Romans, and though the procession was similar to other days, if the Evocati guards had taken more notice and not been so self-assured in their dominance of the populace, they might have noticed some differences.

Where carts had previously had one driver, most now had two. The piles of sacks in the backs of the carts seemed to be a little higher than normal and surely the number of herders had increased. In addition, the number of ordinary people joining the traders seemed larger than normal but despite this, the Evocati stood aside in boredom, resigned to the daily procession that was as necessary to the success of Camulodunum as it was to the villagers.

'By the gods they stink,' said one of the armoured soldiers as the procession of animals and people passed through the gates.

'What do you expect?' said the other. 'Once a barbarian, always a barbarian.'

A passing man threw him a withering look.

'Yes, that's right,' repeated the guard, 'I'm talking about you, stinking barbarian filth. Do you have a problem with that?'

'Actually I do,' snarled the man, and before either soldier could act, he ran across the space between them and plunged a knife into the guard's heart. Another man yelled a warning but sack cloths were thrown back on the carts and dozens of armed men jumped down to attack the remaining men around the gate.

'Alarm!' shouted a guard up on the parapet, but within seconds a flurry of arrows flew upward to cut down any remaining defenders. All around people started panicking and another group of guards ran out from a nearby hut to see what the commotion was about.

Dozens of the men previously dressed as traders threw away their disguises and even women under the protection of hooded cloaks turned out to be disguised warriors, heavy with their weapons of choice. With a frenzy born of frustration they attacked the defenders, each screaming their battle cries as they cut them down.

'We're under attack,' shouted a guard, 'sound the alarm.'

A Cornicine blasted a signal over the sounds of peoples' screams and all across the city the alarm was repeated, alerting the populace to the danger.

One of the attackers ran back outside and waved his sword back and fore above his head giving the agreed signal to hidden eyes back in the treeline. Within moments, hundreds of previously unseen riders broke free from their hiding place to gallop toward the captured gate while behind them the forest shook with the battle cries of ten thousand men.

Dozens of soldiers ran from the nearby barracks to confront those who had taken the gate and despite the fact they had retired from active service, the skills learned over twenty-five years in the legions never waned and the drills kicked in immediately.

'Present shields,' shouted an officer, and immediately the front rank locked their shields together in an impenetrable wall.

'Second rank, ready Pila, on my command.'

The second rank stepped back and prepared to launch the spears designed to bend after impact, rendering them unusable by the enemy.

The attacking warriors closed in, screaming their war cries to intimidate the defenders.

'Steady,' roared the officer, 'release!'

Twenty Pilae sailed above the front rank, taking out over half of the warriors.

'Extended line,' screamed the officer.

The second row spread out on either side of the men in front presenting a solid wall of shields fifty paces wide.

'Close quarter,' shouted the officer, 'advaaance!'

With shields locked together, the whole line marched forward as one, secure behind the solid wall of wood and brass. The remaining few attackers threw themselves on the shield wall in a vain attempt to kill the soldiers behind, only to find Gladii waiting for them. Within moments the last of the warriors fell and the Roman officer realised there was no more threat between them and the open gate.

'Break ranks,' he shouted. 'Get to the gates. We have to get them closed in case of a second attack.' The Evocati ran toward the gate. Those who had maintained an element of fitness outstripped those who had enjoyed the finer diet of retirement but within seconds the soldiers in front stuttered to a halt.

'You men,' shouted the officer, 'what's the problem? Get to the gate, that's an order.'

One of the Evocati turned to face him, fear written all over his face.

'It's too late,' he shouted, 'they are here.' Before he could say any more, two arrows thudded into his back and he dropped to his knees. The officer looked up in shock and mentally said a prayer to his gods as the warrior horsemen thundered into the city, cutting down the Romans as they went. His vast experience told him that resistance was futile and he lowered his Gladii to welcome death, mentally picturing his wife and children as he did, an image cut brutally short by a warrior club smashing into his face and bursting his skull.

From her vantage point, Boudicca could see her army pouring into the city through the main gate. She stood upon a chariot drawn by four black stallions, a gift from her ailing father back in the lands of the Trinovantes. The horses had been given with a simple message.

'A conqueror looks like a conqueror, no less the liber-ator.'

Beside her sat Rianna and though she yearned to ride alongside her queen, her injuries were still raw and she could stand for minutes only at a time.

'It looks like the day starts well, Boudicca,' said Rianna.

'The first steps are taken,' said Boudicca, 'but the race is not yet done. Many men who soldiered for Rome sleep within those walls and swords do not forget how to be swords.'

'The main gate is ours,' said Rianna, 'and look, our warriors spread along the ramparts.'

All along the walls, thousands of warriors waited their turn to climb the assault ladders being thrown up as far as she could see. The defenders hurried to the defence of their city but they had been caught cold and the lack of cohesion meant there were hundreds of smaller battles rather than a concerted defence. Smoke started to spread as the first buildings were set alight and all along the walls, she could see her warriors engaging the defenders with rabid savagery. Bodies were hurled from the parapets and those still alive were torn limb from limb by willing hands. The sounds of battle carried toward her on the breeze and below her position, thousands more waited their turn to vent their rage in the city. A rider galloped up the hill and reined in his horse before her in a cloud of dust.

'My Queen,' he said, struggling to control his panting horse, 'the outer limits are taken and the defenders fall back in disarray. Our warriors run amok in the outskirts while the Roman nobility flee to the sanctuary of their temple.'

'And the people?'

'They beg for mercy at our feet,' said the rider, 'Roman and slave alike.'

Boudicca stared out toward the city again.

'My children begged for mercy,' she said quietly, 'and their cries fell on deaf ears. What difference are their cries to those who now plea?'

'None,' said Rianna.

'Then treat them as they did us,' said Boudicca. 'Spare the slave that joins our cause but let everyone else feel my wrath.'

'What about the women and children?' asked the rider and slowly Boudicca turned her head to stare into his face.

'Has the sounds of battle dimmed your understanding,' she asked. 'I said kill them. Kill them all.'

'My Queen,' shouted the man in acknowledgement and spun his horse to gallop away down the hill.

Boudicca turned to see Rianna staring up at her with cold eyes.

'Is that hate I see in your eyes, Rianna?'

'Hate?' said Rianna. 'I thought you knew me well, Boudicca. No, it's not hate but admiration. Admiration for a woman doing what many men before her said they would do but failed to deliver.' She gestured toward a couple of slaves who hurried over to help her from the chariot.

'Where are you going?' asked Boudicca.

'I am still too weak to ride beside you, friend, but I will not hinder your glory. Ride, Boudicca, taste the triumph that is yours to savour.' She looked toward Camulodunum once more and then down on the thousands of families who had poured from the forest to watch their men assault the city. 'They have waited a long time for this Boudicca, let them taste victory, no matter how fleeting.'

Boudicca followed Rianna's gaze and saw thousands of eyes turned toward her, waiting for the command they knew would come. Older men mingled with boys and women of all ages but each shared three things; anticipation in their eyes, anger in their hearts and knives in their hands.

'You are right, Rianna,' she said, 'so it begins.'

Without another word she rode the chariot forward a few paces and drew a spear from the rack on the side.

'People of Britannia,' she roared. 'Behold the Roman threat running like children before us. Show them why they are right to fear us and take back the infested city of Camulodunum – it is yours.'

As one the throng cheered their support and ran forward across the plain toward the city, a people's army ten thousand strong, every one hell bent on revenge.

For the next few days Boudicca's army rampaged through Camulodunum in a frenzy of retribution. The pent-up rage of the people burned like a firebrand, having seen their capital wrested from their control to be turned into an outpost of Rome. Led by the Trinovantians, they worked their way through the city killing anything that moved. Women were raped and children dragged behind horses as the drunken warriors repaid a debt of seventeen years' worth of subordination. Despite the overwhelming numbers, the Evocati tried their best to defend their families, a futile gesture and they were swatted away like flies. As they were ordered to their deaths in the face of the Britannic hoard, the elders of the city holed themselves up in the last secure place in the city, the temple of Claudius. Built from solid stone and having enormous doors made from the stoutest oak, it was a citadel capable of withstanding the fiercest assault. Inside, dozens of nobles and their families huddled together, still dressed in their finery having run from their villas in fear.

'Father, what is to happen to us?' asked a little girl, looking toward the barricaded door as the attackers beat uselessly against it.

'Fret not, child,' said her father, 'help is on its way. Be brave, this place is blessed by the gods in Claudius' name – it cannot be breached.'

'But how long must we stay here?' asked one of the others. 'There is food enough for a week but after that we will surely starve.'

'A week is more than enough,' said the man, 'we heard whisper of an assault ten days ago and sent word to Procurator Catus Decianus asking for help. We have asked for a thousand men at arms to help us and I have no doubt they are only hours away. Soon these filth will taste Roman steel.'

'A thousand men?' asked the voice. 'There is surely ten times that number attacking us as we speak. They will be outnumbered.'

'A thousand Romans are worth ten thousand barbarians on any given day,' said the councillor. 'But fear not, we have also sent riders to seek out the Ninth Hispana. They are close by and recently laid siege to the Iceni. They too are only days away. Once Quintus Petillius Cerialis hears of our plight he will press an entire legion against the attackers and feed our fields with their blood.'

Murmurs of approval echoed around the main chamber and though the useless attempts at entry continued against the door, the prisoners continued to eat and drink calmly, accustomed as they were to the better things in life.

—

Outside, Boudicca stood before the temple, watching the futile attempts at battering down the doors. Rianna had joined her from her cart and limped to her side.

'Boudicca,' she said.

Boudicca turned to her friend and for a moment her face lit up.

'Rianna, you look much better.'

'Another few days and I will carry your spears on your chariot,' said Rianna. 'Boudicca, I have news.'

'Speak,' said Boudicca.

'Our cavalry have ambushed a column not far from here,' she said. 'They were on their way to relieve the city but found Trinovantian archers instead. Most are now dead.'

'How many?' asked Boudicca.

'Two hundred,' said Rianna.

'Who were they?'

'Reinforcements sent by Procurator Decianus,' said Rianna. 'It seems he thought two hundred cavalry would be ample to deal with our threat.'

'An ill-conceived judgement,' said Boudicca, 'but how do you know this?'

'We took prisoners,' said Rianna, 'and though some went to their deaths with honour others were not so brave and the fires loosened their tongues. In return for their lives they talked like washer women.'

'What news did they have?'

'Not good,' said Rianna. 'Although Decianus underestimates our strength it seems there are others that may not share his stupidity. We were told that riders have been sent to summon the Ninth Hispana and they could be here in as little as a few days.'

'The Hispana,' spat Boudicca. 'The soldiers who devastated our village and violated my girls bore that standard.'

'They did,' said Rianna, 'and they are on their way here. I fear we should leave now and seek the safety of the forests.'

'Why?' asked Boudicca. 'The very pigs that started us on this trail of liberation are within our reach. I hoped it would one day be so but to have them walk into our reach so early in our campaign is a gift from the goddess Andraste herself.'

'Boudicca, we are yet undisciplined and cannot take on a legion.'

95

'Not in open battle, I agree,' said Boudicca, 'but there are many ways to kill a bear. Gather the clan leaders to meet outside the city gates. I will be along shortly to address them.'

'What are you going to do?' asked Rianna.

'I have a temple to demolish,' said Boudicca.

Rianna nodded and limped back to her cart.

Behind her, Boudicca summoned the leader of the warriors trying to break down the door.

'Maccus, attend me,' she said.

The man walked over and removed his helmet, releasing rivulets of sweat to run down his face.

'It seems the doors fight back,' she said.

'They are surely made of iron,' said Maccus.

'Nothing but oak, I feel,' said Boudicca, 'but as hard as iron I agree.'

'Fear not, Boudicca, they will starve before my men leave this place.'

'I have greater plans for your men, Maccus, so time is not generous. Our people tear down this city as we speak but it will be a hollow victory if the temple remains.'

'I will bring woodsmen with fresh axes,' said Maccus. 'We will have the doors open in days.'

'Days we do not have,' said Boudicca, 'though woodsmen are a good choice of strength.'

'I do not understand,' said Maccus. 'The door width will only allow six men to swing their axes at a time which will take days and the steps prevent the construction of rams.'

'Divert your axe men to the forests,' said Boudicca, 'along with a thousand warriors. Drag wood to build a fire against the doors and burn them down.'

'Boudicca, as you know oak burns slowly and it is embedded with bars of iron. It will still take days.'

'Oak burns, iron melts,' said Boudicca, 'and the bigger the furnace, the hotter the flame. Cut down the trees and build me a fire, Maccus. A fire bigger than any we have seen before. Make it bigger than the temple if necessary, cut down the whole forest if needed but I want a pyre such as has never been seen. Do this and I feel the doors will fall to ash before your eyes and when it does, spare nobody inside the blade. Man, woman or child, send them all to hell. You have two days, Maccus, do not fail me – there is a fresh task that needs our attention.'

'What task is this?' asked Maccus.

'A hunt,' said Boudicca. 'We have a bear to kill.'

Chapter Nine

The Straits of Menai

Suetonius looked over the straits between the mainland and the island of Mona. The darkness was falling away and slowly he could make out the preparations that had been made in the previous two hours. Ballistae had been manhandled out across the rocks as far as possible and all along the foreshore, hundreds of men sat wrapped in their waterproof capes against the morning drizzle, each waiting their turn in the assault barges. At the far side of the channel he could see several boats bobbing gently in the gloom, though these were empty, having already served their purpose. Beyond them he could just about make out the shapes of the local fishermen, feverishly laying out the reed mats designed to spread the weight of any men running across them.

Suetonius turned and looked up at the nearby cliff edge, and though it wasn't very high, he knew it was enough for its intended purpose. As the sky lightened, he could make out over a hundred women and children lined up along the cliff edge, each shivering in the dawn chill, some from the temperature, others with fear as their fate unfolded before them. Behind each captive a soldier held an unsheathed Gladius, waiting for the order to force their prisoners over the edge on to the rocks below.

'Watch well, Barbarians,' called the Optio in charge of the prisoners, 'and pray to your gods that your men are successful in their service to Rome. For every man that falls short in their task, two of you will learn how to fly, albeit for only a few seconds.' He laughed at his own joke, oblivious of the sobs of the children.

Out on the far mud banks the local fishermen worked furiously laying the mats, spreading them out and building up layer after layer to increase their weight carrying properties, knowing full well that the encroaching light would soon reveal them to any sentry's eyes on the far shore. Despite their frantic activity, many more stood behind them waiting their turn to unload their cargo. Further upstream hundreds of cavalry stood beside their mounts, comforting them with quiet words as they waited for the battle to start.

Suetonius turned to his Tribune.

'The day is here, Attellus,' he said. 'Give the signal.'

Attellus drew his Gladius and held it aloft for a few seconds before dropping it sharply. Usually there would be accompanying fanfares of massed Cornicines, along with the beating of war drums to herald any advance but in this instance, it was important to harvest every minute of silence. Below them the laden barges pushed off from the bank and over five hundred light infantry, crouched beneath their round shields in anticipation of defending arrows. For a minute or so the quiet was maintained and Attellus thought they would actually get the first wave across undetected but suddenly the silence was shattered by a blood-curdling scream as the enemy spotted the threat.

'This is it,' said Suetonius, 'let battle commence.'

Fifty miles away, Prydain and his comrades sat against a bluff, taking shelter from the driving rain. They had been riding hard for three days, only stopping to sleep for an hour or so at a time and taking it in turns to stand guard against the constant Roman patrols.

One of the riders stood out in the rain, paying close attention to one of the horses.

'There is no way she is going to last until we get to the lands of the Deceangli,' said Cullen, wiping the water from his horse's neck. 'Her best years are behind her.'

'We need to find somewhere to get some proper rest,' said Prydain, 'this rain has taken it out of all of us. If we don't look after the horses, what chance have we got?'

'The Roman influence is everywhere,' said Gildas, 'and the nearest friendly village is miles to the west. It will take us a day to get there.'

'It matters not,' said Prydain, 'without proper rest, we will not get much further.'

'There is a farm nearby where we can get help,' said Heulwen. 'I have shared their hospitality in the past.'

'How far?' asked Prydain.

'Half a day,' said Heulwen. 'If the family still lives there, I think they will help us.'

'Then lead the way,' said Prydain, climbing into the saddle. 'With a bit of luck we may also be able to share some hot food.'

All the riders mounted their horses and followed Heulwen off the hill into the valley below.

'The river passes the farm,' explained Heulwen.

'Are you sure we will be welcomed?' asked Prydain. 'These are hard times and strangers are viewed with suspicion.'

'We will be fine,' said Heulwen. 'My people have provided attendance to many in these parts for many years. This family I know personally.'

For the next few hours the party rode in relative silence, stopping only to rest the horses. Finally they crested a rise and looked down to the farmstead below.

'This is it,' said Heulwen. 'Keep your hands from your weapons and try to look friendly.'

They rode down into the farm while several people emerged from the roundhouses to watch, alerted by the barking of the dogs. A white-haired old man approached them, relying heavily on a staff to help him walk.

'Hwyl, strangers,' he said. 'If you come in peace then there is a welcome here for you. If it is plunder you seek then you will not find resistance for we have little of value.'

'Madoc, it is good to see you again,' said Heulwen. 'I trust you remember me.'

The old man paused before answering.

'My eyes fail me with age,' said the man, 'but if I'm not mistaken that voice can only be Heulwen of the Asbri.'

'Your ears are true, Madoc, and these are my friends. We seek a day's rest and some hot food if you are able.'

'Heulwen,' answered the man, 'you are always welcome here and any friends of yours are friends of ours. Come, dismount and share my home.' He turned to a young boy sitting on a nearby wall.

'Allyn, show our friends to the stable and make sure the horses are tended.'

'Why me?' asked Allyn. 'Why can't they do it themselves?'

'Curb your tongue, boy,' snapped Madoc, 'or it'll be the birch for you.'

The boy mumbled his retort under his breath but jumped off the wall to do as he was told.

'Take no notice,' said Madoc. 'He is a good boy but is very opinionated. His father was killed at Caer Caradog. I try my best but he needs a younger man's influence.'

'It seems he races to be a man while still a boy,' said Heulwen.

'He does,' said Madoc. 'He and his friends play at killing Romans every chance they get. It brings fear to my heart for he grows up too quick. But enough talk, come, join me in our home. You are in luck for we have a sheep's head in the pot and there is enough for all.'

'Thank you, Madoc. As usual your hospitality is generous.'

Ten minutes later they all sat around the inner walls of the smoky roundhouse, each wrapped in sheepskin as their sodden cloaks dried in the heat. A woman stirred the giant pot on the central fire and Prydain's mouth watered at the enticing smell. Finally she fished out the sheep's head and placed it on a wooden platter before hitting it with a large knife to reach the brain within. Wooden platters were passed around and each of the guests was summoned forward for their share of the meal.

Prydain gestured toward Madoc to lead the way.

'No,' said Madoc, 'there is meat enough for all. Your bellies must be small from hunger. Eat your fill.'

Needing no second invitation, Prydain and the other three men held out their bowls for a portion of brain and some of the meaty broth. Heulwen joined them and soon everyone in the hut was dipping chunks of rough bread into stew and eating the feast noisily. Gildas finished before anyone else and looked longingly at the pot.

'Old mother,' he said eventually, 'your meal is fit for the gods and manners forbid I ask for more but once all are fed, I have a silver coin that I would gladly pay for a second bowl.'

'You will keep your coin, Sir,' said the woman, 'for you are our guests, but though the meat is scarce, the flavours of the broth remain and there are roots aplenty within the pot. Fill your bowl as oft as you wish for my heart glows to see such an appetite.'

Gildas smiled widely and approached the pot to refill his bowl, quickly followed by the others who had been too polite to ask. Soon the meal was over, though Gildas pored over the sheep skull, seeking any scrap of meat that may be left on the bone.

'Your hospitality does you proud, Sir,' said Prydain to Madoc, as they watched the big man, 'and we are indebted to you.'

'If a man cannot share his soup with one who hungers, then I feel we are not long for this world,' sighed Madoc. 'So, are you able to share your tale or is it one of secrecy?'

'It is for the ears of the loyal only,' said Prydain, 'and though you have shown your friendship, I would ask that you keep it to yourself.'

'We see few strangers here,' said Madoc, 'and my heart yearns for the old days. I would garner no benefit from a loose tongue.'

Prydain retold the tale of Taliesin and their quest to return him to the Asbri. Madoc listened intently and poured Prydain a tankard of ale as he talked. Finally Prydain was done.

'So,' he said, 'that is our goal. Whether it will be successful or not only the gods know.'

'It matters not,' said Madoc. 'Either you will find him, or you won't. If you survive then it will be a noble task and will give hope to a nation, and if you die then it will be a noble death and the aftermath will be none of your business.'

'A very astute outlook on life,' laughed Prydain.

'Perhaps so,' said Madoc, 'but one that has kept me relatively happy throughout my years. Whatever the gods have in store for us will come to pass and nothing we can do will change it.'

'You may be right, Madoc, but unless we try, we will never know.'

Madoc stared at Prydain for a few moments before speaking again.

'Prydain, you have trusted me with the truth which is an honour. Perhaps I may be able to repay that trust for there is something you should know that may help you in your task.'

'I am intrigued,' said Prydain.

'Come with me,' said Madoc and led Prydain from the hut and across the courtyard to the wood store.

Prydain looked on as Madoc banged on the wooden building.

'Morfan, un-brace the door,' called Madoc, 'the riders are friendly and there is no danger.'

For a few moments there was silence, but finally the door swung inward enough for a man's face to appear.

'Who are you?' asked the man.

'This is Prydain of the Silures,' said Madoc. 'He is a friend.'

'What do you want of me?'

'The riders are on their way toward the Cerrig,' said Madoc, 'and I thought you might have information that may be of help.' He turned to face Prydain. 'Morfan was one of Idwal's soldiers at the Cerrig,' he said. 'When the king died, many bent their knee to the Romans within days but Morfan and others refused to yield. They fought their way out of Treforum and rallied resistance in the forests, but they were quickly hunted down.'

'What has this to do with me?' asked Prydain.

'Morfan, tell Prydain of the boy who fought alongside you.'

The man shrugged his shoulders.

'Not much to tell,' said Morfan. 'Like many others he had the calling to fight alongside the king, but had been with us for a few days only. He was young and obviously inexperienced in warfare.'

'What was his name?' asked Prydain.

'I know not,' said the man. 'We called him Witch-boy for he said he was brought up by the Asbri, a false story, no doubt, but amusing enough.'

'It was true,' said Prydain, 'the boy's name is Taliesin and he is the one we seek. Tell me, does he still live?'

'The Roman cavalry were everywhere,' said Morfan, 'and many fell. Those of us who had resisted scattered before them. Some came south to join with those clans who still resist while others rode east to the Iceni. The boy rode with them.'

'Why eastward?' asked Prydain. 'Surely that way is into the arms of the beast.'

'It is,' said Morfan, 'but there are reports emerging of a great army being raised by Boudicca to oppose the Romans.'

'And who is she?' asked Prydain.

'The widow of Prasatagus, King of the Iceni,' said Morfan. 'It is said she and her daughters were ravished by the Romans after his death and she seeks vengeance, calling on all the tribes to lend their swords to her cause.'

'And is there any truth in this tale?'

'As true as you stand before me. I have heard tell that the Trinovantes have already heeded the call as well as many smaller tribes. Their numbers are in the thousands and growing every day.'

'To what end?'

'The end that we all would see,' said Morfan, 'the death of all Romans.'

Ten minutes later Prydain ducked back into the hut of Madoc and shared the news with his comrades.

'Then this is indeed good news,' said Heulwen. 'At least we know he is alive.'

'We do,' said Prydain, 'yet it brings a whole new set of problems.'

'Such as?'

'First of all we will have to pass through the lands of the Catuvellauni,' said Prydain, 'and we know little of the landscape or indeed who has sold out to the Romans. We will be alone and will have to live off the land as much as possible. On top of that, the very fact that the Iceni are in revolt will put every Roman in Britannia on a war footing and watches will be doubled. We will have to live like Brigands until we find this Boudicca and by then he could already have met a Roman blade. War is not pretty, Heulwen, and if this Boudicca thinks she can lead an army against Rome in open battle, then she is gravely mistaken.'

'I understand that,' said Heulwen, 'but at least this way there is a route through the dangers and our fate is in our own hands. The task has not changed, Prydain, just the location.'

'Fret not,' sighed Prydain, 'I will keep my word. I just wanted to let you know the risks involved.'

'And you have my gratitude,' said Heulwen, 'but I am well aware of the risks and if the gods intend I die on this quest then it is an outcome I welcome. The fate of the Khymru is greater than us all.'

'And what about you?' asked Prydain, turning to his friends. 'Is your path still with ours or does it lay elsewhere? There is no shame in going home for the task has changed.'

'I ride with you,' said Cullen.

'As do I,' said Gildas.

'Taran?' asked Prydain.

'Do you really need to ask?' asked the young man. 'Of course I ride with you and am insulted at the question.'

'Then it is agreed,' said Prydain. 'Tonight we rest but tomorrow we turn east.' He turned to face the old man.

'Madoc, we are in need of fresh horses. I know we ask a lot but do you have any you could spare?'

'I don't,' said Madoc, 'but there will be steeds in the local village for sale. Do you have any coin?'

'No,' said Prydain, 'at least not enough for horses.'

'Wait,' said Heulwen. 'We no longer need the gold coins to bribe the Cerrig guards. We can use some of those.'

'Gold coins will arouse suspicion amongst the Roman spies,' said Madoc.

'It matters not,' said Prydain. 'By the time any word gets to the Romans we will be far to the east.'

'So be it,' said Gildas, standing up. 'We need a dry place to lay our heads and will be gone by dawn. Madoc, do you have such a place?'

'The stable is dry,' said Madoc, 'and there is plenty of straw for your beds. I will have the boy bring over some sheep-skins. Heulwen can share Sioned's hut.'

'Is Sioned still here?' asked Heulwen with surprise. 'I thought she would have left to raise her own family by now.'

'And she would have,' said Madoc, 'but her man fell at Caer Caradog. When he failed to return, Sioned found she was already with child and stayed with us to bring him up.'

'It will be good to see her again,' said Heulwen. 'Does she still use the same hut?'

'She does but shares it with her son, Allyn. I am sure you will be welcomed.'

'The boy with attitude,' laughed Prydain.

'The same,' said Madoc. 'But enough chatter, we all need our rest.'

'You are right,' said Prydain, 'and have been the perfect host. We need to be up before birdsong tomorrow.'

'My aching bones keep me under the bed-furs these days,' said Madoc, 'so I will not be here to see you go. Travel well, friends, and stay safe.'

'Thank you, Madoc,' said Prydain, 'your help today could well aid a nation.'

'Helping friends is more important,' said Madoc. 'Sleep well, friend.'

-

Before noon the following day all five riders were miles away from the farm, each on a fresh horse. In addition

Gildas led a mule loaded with supplies including food, water and an oiled tent for shelter against the spring rains. The gold coins had raised a high level of interest in the village but they wasted no time haggling over the prices and were long gone before any serious questions were asked. Before leaving, Prydain made a point of talking to one of the traders and mentioning they were going south to trade with the Silures. The deliberate lie would spread like wildfire and hopefully hide their trail. Soon they were miles away, and headed out of the Khymru toward the lands of the Catuvellauni.

Chapter Ten

The Straits of Menai

Suetonius stared across the straits with concern. Despite the cover of the Onagers, the civilian fishermen had suffered heavy casualties from the spear throwers on the far shore and the main wave of assault troops had hesitated in the face of the enemy. On the other side of the strait, as far as the eye could see, the Druids and the common people of Mona poured from the treeline and formed screaming lines of defenders, roaring their defiance at the attackers before them. There was no structure or order within their lines just a melee of manic people hurling their insults and challenges across the water. Warriors were interspersed with children and old alike, every one of them as rabid as the next. Naked women, their bodies painted with wode and hair stuck up with animal fats rushed amongst the throng carrying burning torches and brushing the flames against the men's bare torsos encouraging them to feats of bravery. Screams and taunts were joined by war horns and drums, all adding to the growing cacophony from across the water.

'The men have stalled,' said Tribune Attellus, 'what's the matter with them?'

'I know not,' said Suetonius, 'it seems they are entranced by the barbaric display. Get me my horse quickly before we lose the impetus.'

Attellus signalled a nearby groom and within minutes, Suetonius was galloping down the slope toward his confused legion. Though the noise from across the water was indeed loud above the din he could hear the Centurions berating their men for their show of fear.

'Silence,' roared Suetonius and gradually the noise from the Roman ranks stopped. 'Who are you?' he shouted at the men milling at the boats and lined up on the bank. 'For I do not recognise you. Where are the men who bear the name fourteenth Gemina, the legion of glorious heritage from across the empire?'

As he addressed them, Suetonius walked his horse before the gathered ranks, addressing them directly and many lowered their gaze in shame.

'Where are the warriors who defeated Caratacus and Togodumnus?' he continued. 'Show me the legion who defeated Cornovii and Deceangli without breaking sweat for I see them not. They are not here for I do not recognise them. Where is the respect for those who died for the name? Is there none? Are the glorious dead to look down, only to avert their gaze from this shame? Look before you, Romans, and ask yourself what is there to fear? They are old men daubed in mud. Naked and feeble old women shouting nonsense and children calling you names. Is it this that holds you back? Are you, who took Caer Caradog, now afraid of babes?'

'No,' shouted many of the men, rousing from their stupor.

'Can it be that the glorious Gemina now turn away from unclothed heathens and I should ride back to Nero proclaiming tales of cowardice and shame?'

'No,' shouted the men again, though this time with added voices.

'And can it be that this glorious legion that has turned its back on no foe, this family of brothers that crossed a thousand miles to give Claudius a nation, now balks from facing mere barbarians not fit to clear our filth?'

'*No*,' screamed the soldiers, '*never*,' shouted others.

'Then put aside this shame and deliver what it is that we do best,' shouted Suetonius. 'Pick up your arms and stare into the eyes of the enemy. Reach inside for the courage I know you have in abundance and show these heathens that we scorn their displays of pathetic symbolism. Look to your fronts, Romans; before you is the head of the snake, the tribe of the Druids. Beyond them are their sacred groves of gold and precious stones. Swipe away this irritation and the island is yours for the taking. Caskets of gold and silver are there for the picking, maidens untouched await your attentions and treasures enough to make your retirements as luxurious as senators are begging to be claimed. All that stands between you is this strip of water and the farcical display before you. But such things are secondary to that we all hold dearest. The spoils are yours by right, the battle is yours by duty, but your honour is yours by birth.'

'So what is it to be,' he shouted, 'infamy or immortality?'

'Immortality!' shouted the legion.

'Choose your destiny, legionaries,' roared Suetonius, 'shame or glory?'

'*Glory*,' thundered the legion over and over again.

Suetonius looked around his men, knowing there would now be no holding them back.

'Then discard this lethargy and show me the hearts that I know you have. Bring back the soldiers who fought alongside Scapula and send these heathens to hell.' He drew his Gladius and held it in the air. 'Men of the Four-teenth Gemina, for our glorious dead and the glory of Rome, *advaaance!*'

All the carefully laid plans of Attellus were discarded as the legion ploughed forward into the strait. Every boat was filled with the heavy infantry and while those at the front held up their shields as defence against the arrows, the others paddled furiously to cross the small channel. Light infantry swam alongside the boats or clung on to the saddles of the cavalry who had also joined in the all-out assault.

Above them the air sang with the sound of arrows and fire pots, as every ballista and Onager team worked furiously to maintain a hail of missiles upon the enemy on the far shore. Scorpio operators ran as far forward as they could, to place their pole mounted crossbows amongst the rocks and picked off the enemy warriors with deadly accuracy.

Suetonius looked on with a racing heart. It wasn't the tactic they had planned but he had roused his men to such a state he knew their fury needed to be directed rather than harnessed. Before him there were some casualties as men lost their grip on the barges and some boats capsized in the melee but it was obvious the vast majority would land on the far shore within minutes.

'I hope this works,' said Attellus, 'the strategies are discarded.'

'Strategies are sometimes secondary to aggression,' said Suetonius. 'I trust this is such a time.'

Throughout the legion, the Roman's own battle cries joined those of the enemies and the battle drums of the Fourteenth joined with the Cornicines, drowning out the wails of the opponents. Fury registered in the eyes of every man and Suetonius knew he had done his job. This was the legion he was proud to lead. On the far side the first to land were wading through the mud toward the grassy slope leading up to the enemy, but no sooner had they advanced than they were cut down by the spears of the Celts. Blood mingled with mud and fallen men tried to crawl forward only to be entombed by the cloying filth. Behind them the assault continued and fresh attackers braved the onslaught to run over the bodies of the fallen, each time gaining a few more metres before they too were cut down by the defenders' spears.

Seeing the danger, the artillery lowered their aim and fire pots fell amongst the front ranks of the enemy, the flammable oils spraying amongst them and causing panic within their lines. The few moments respite was all the lead legionaries needed, and they rushed forward from their boats to create a double height wall of shields to protect those coming behind. The manoeuvre was self-sustaining and within moments the wall spread outward forming the standard Roman line of assault.

Once the line started to form, Suetonius breathed a sigh of relief. Gaining a foothold on the far shore was always going to be the most dangerous part of the assault, but now they had a century of men across, he knew it was only a matter of time. Every minute that passed saw hundreds more safely across and despite the constant hail of arrows from the enemy, the growing wall of laminated wood and hides meant that few men now fell. New waves of boats were launched containing the next cohorts and as they reached the far shore, those already in position marched forward as one, forcing the enemy back and making room for their comrades behind. The Druid army retreated slowly, keeping their distance from the wall of red and gold shields, unsure how to deal with the monster that crept forward from the water's edge.

Finally, Suetonius judged he had enough across and turned to the flag bearer at his side.

'Give the signal,' he said and immediately a row of flag bearers raised their banners to wave them back and fore. It was the signal that every officer and Centurion on the far side of the river had been waiting for and after a fanfare of Cornicines, the legion fell deathly silent. The enemy also quietened down, looking on in confusion as the ranks of Romans stopped moving and stared over their shields. A single drumbeat rang out across the slopes and ten men marched forward in pace with the drums. A second later, the ten men either side of them did the same, closely followed by the men on their flanks. Within moments, a human wedge had formed, the dreaded Cuneus formation, or the pig's head as it was called by the soldiers, the favoured attack formation against enemy defensive lines.

For the last time the legion halted and a senior Centurion stepped out of the front of the wedge. He drew his Gladius as did a thousand other soldiers and looked around the formation.

'Fourteenth Gemina,' he screamed, 'to glory!' He lifted his sword high before lowering it toward the enemy. '*Advaaance!*'

Every battle drum beat out a marching chorus and the lead cohort advanced to conflict, closely followed by the remaining cohorts. Many warriors broke from their own lines and ran forward to attack the Romans but most fell before they got anywhere near, speared by the Pila thrown from the advancing ranks. Other defenders started to get nervous and despite their rantings and weapon waving, retreated to the protection of the forests.

A white-haired Druid stepped forward, brandishing a staff in one hand and a severed human head in the other. He urged his people to battle and without wielding a weapon of any sort, walked toward the Romans reciting his spells and charms. Within moments a Pilum speared him through the chest and he fell backward into the dirt. As if it was the sign everyone had been waiting for, an ethereal cry arose from the Celts. Immediately they went on the offensive and their warriors ran down to the fight. Behind them their people followed, and the slopes were covered with screaming defenders, men, women and children, all desperate to tear the enemy limb from limb. Thousands poured down the hill and the legion reacted in kind, responding to the sound of the charge signalled by the Cornicines.

–

The result was slaughter. The wedge of the attackers drove through the enemy like a spear, pausing for nothing except to slay any before them. Within minutes they had divided the enemy and turned outward to attack the two flanks. Behind them the supporting cohorts drove into the face of the Celts while on the outward edges, the cavalry bore down on them like a terrible wind, wiping them out with lance and sword. Seeing the risk, more Celts ran forward from the forest to add their weight to the battle and though the Romans were outnumbered, slowly but surely, they edged their way up the slopes toward the treeline. The nature of the ground meant it was hard to keep disciplined lines and the Roman formation fractured, allowing the Celts to get amongst them and what they lacked in discipline, they more than made up for in fanaticism.

The battle ebbed and flowed like a bloody tide, but slowly the greater discipline of the legion told and units fought together rather than as individuals. The lower ground was taken and the fight moved into the trees. The Roman advance halted and consolidated their positions in line abreast. The foreshore was secure and though many had fallen, the legion now had a secure beachhead. Behind them, the feared first cohort was landing in the boats led by the Primus Pilus and he walked up to the Centurion responsible for the successful assault.

'Fabius, your men have fought well,' he said.

Fabius looked back toward the shoreline over the ground littered with the bodies of his men.

'But at what price?' he said.

'The cost is indeed high,' said Cassus, 'but worth paying. Their sacrifice has ensured our forces have a free run inland.'

'What about the survivors?' asked Fabius. 'Many fled inland and will provide resistance.'

'They will be of little consequence,' said Cassus. 'When we have passed through your lines stand your cohort down and see to your dead. Tell your wounded they will collectively take ten percent share of all plunder taken from this shore. I will personally oversee it.'

'Thank you, Cassus,' said Fabius. 'It will be appreciated.'

Cassus looked up and down the shoreline. The entire first cohort was now in formation behind the shields of the front line. Supporting them were a further two cohorts of auxiliary light infantry and an alae of cavalry on either side, a total of almost two thousand-foot soldiers and a thousand cavalry.

'On my signal,' said Cassus, 'open your ranks for us to pass through.'

Fabius saluted his superior and walked away to brief his men. Cassus turned to his grizzled Optio, the experienced second in command of the cohort.

'Ready the men,' said Cassus, 'we waste no more time. We will advance until we either reach the far side of the island or there are no more enemy left to kill. Pass the word, no prisoners, no mercy. I fear the Ninth have need of our services in the east and every day we spend here means a day extra for the Iceni queen to build her army.'

'Understood,' said the Optio.

Cassus turned to the cornicen at his side.

'As soon as Fabius indicates readiness,' he said, 'sound the advance.' He fastened the straps beneath his crested helmet and stared into the treeline. 'Let's get this done.'

Chapter Eleven

The Lands of the Trinovantes

Legate Petillius Cerialis ducked out of his tent and walked toward the east gate of the temporary marching camp. His aides had reported that Virrius had returned and though he knew Virrius would report to him shortly, he was impatient to hear the news.

Every soldier he passed in the camp snapped to attention, suitable acknowledgement to a man of his rank. The camp was large, much bigger than those needed by the smaller vexillations that usually patrolled between tribes, as for the first time in over a year, Petillius had an almost full-strength legion to hand. Word had flown in from all around about the threat posed by the barbarian army and though he was no fool, he held no fear of such rumours, confident in the ability of his men.

Almost five thousand legionaries and auxiliaries lay at his disposal, most of whom were camped inside the temporary walls. They were protected from assault by a surrounding ditch and embankment made from the spoil topped by a wooden spiked palisade. There had been talks about forming a permanent legionary fortress in this location but the decision had been postponed while the governor campaigned against the Druids at Mona.

As he walked, he could hear the commotion of Virrius's men as they sorted out their horses after the two-day mission. Amongst them Virrius's voice rang out above all others, organising and berating his men to greater effort before they could be stood down. Petillius smiled inwardly. Virrius was still a young man but was an excellent officer. He led by example and wasn't afraid to discipline those who fell short of his own high standards.

'Virrius, your return is opportune,' said Petillius.

Virrius turned sharply and saluted the Legate.

'Hail Petillius,' said Virrius, 'it is good to be back. The palisades are as welcoming as the walls of Rome itself. This country is as cold and welcoming as a young bride's mother.'

'Such are the ways of a defeated land,' said Petillius. 'What news of this so-called uprising?'

'We saw no sign,' said Virrius. 'Every village claimed no knowledge and even those we placed under the whip cried ignorance.'

'Were the villages fully populated?'

'As far as we could tell,' said Virrius. 'If this Boudicca has the army the rumours speak of, then it is not from around here.'

'This is a worry,' said Petillius, 'in my experience such smoke is usually accompanied by fire of some kind. Perhaps they are exaggerations.'

'Perhaps so,' said Virrius.

'Who are the prisoners?' asked Petillius, spying a group of four men with their hands tied behind their backs.

'Nobody of note,' said Virrius. 'Our scouts rode them down in the forest. They resisted and two of their number fell before they saw the error of their ways.'

'I see your scouts introduced themselves well,' said Petillius, walking over to inspect the captives.

Virrius glanced toward the blackened eyes and swollen faces of the beaten men.

'Nothing that won't heal,' said Virrius. 'They will bring a good price.'

Petillius drew his Gladius and placed the point of his blade under one of the captive's chins and forced his head up to face him.

'This one looks like he wants to eat my heart,' said Petillius.

'And given the chance he probably would,' said Virrius. 'For one so young he has a temper of a wildcat.'

The boy spat toward the Legate and only the fact that his mouth was dry from dust stopped his bile from reaching the officer.

Virrius immediately smashed his fist into the boy's jaw, sending him sprawling into the dust.

'My apologies, my lord,' said Virrius, 'I will have him crucified immediately.'

'Don't bother,' said Petillius, 'keep the crucifixions for when there are others to witness the futility of resistance. When we are done here, send him south to the tin mines. A lifetime of hard labour draped in chains will help him see the error of his ways.'

Before Virrius could answer, a commotion at the wall made them turn and a horseman galloped through the gate, causing panic amongst the guards.

'Hold that man,' screamed Virrius and soldiers ran forward to grab at the horse's reins. The animal was lathered with sweat from hard riding and the rider slumped in the saddle, obviously exhausted. Eager hands lowered the man from the horse and sat him against a cartwheel while he drank eagerly from an offered water bottle.

'Make way,' shouted Virrius and the group opened up before him.

'Who are you?' asked Virrius. 'And where have you come from?'

The man struggled to his feet before answering.

'My lord, my name is Tubero from a vexillation attached to the command of Catus Decianus.'

'I know of him,' said Petillius, 'what causes this state?'

'My lord, we received a request from Camulodunum to send support to resist a barbarian attack. Decianus sent a full two hundred cavalry to aid the defence but we were ambushed by archers and spearmen. My entire unit fell but I was allowed to ride free with a message.'

'What message?'

'My lord, I am to tell the governor that our time in Britannia is over. Leave these islands now or suffer her wrath.'

'Whose wrath?'

'Boudicca, my lord, Queen of the Iceni.'

'Boudicca,' growled Virrius, 'I knew I should have had her killed.'

'You know of this woman?' asked Petillius.

'I do, she is the woman who claims the throne of the Iceni. I thought we had made her see sense but obviously I was wrong. Leave this to me, my lord. I will take the first cohort and ride to Camulodunum immediately.'

'You waste your time,' said Tubero. 'Camulodunum has already fallen and lies in ashes.'

'What?' gasped Petillius. 'You must be mistaken. Even if the stories of a barbarian army are true, they have no siege engines. How could they breach the walls of a city?'

'By subterfuge and weight of numbers, my lord. I am told they were as ants upon the ground.'

'How do you know this to be true?' snapped Virrius.

'I was taken to see the ruins of Camulodunum myself,' said Tubero, 'and the rest I heard from other prisoners. They destroyed the entire city and showed no mercy to any linked with Rome. Everyone is dead.'

'And the temple?'

'Destroyed.'

'Wait,' said Virrius. 'Why did they let you go untouched?'

'I never said I was untouched,' said the man, and slowly removed his sword arm from beneath his cloak. The end was wrapped in a stinking bloody bandage of linen, evidence of a horrific injury beneath.

'They took the fingers of my sword arm,' said Tubero, 'so I could not return to fight against them. There is no benefit in me lying to you.'

'I believe you, Tubero,' said Petillius. 'Get yourself to the Medicus, perhaps there is something they can do to dress the wounds.'

'The wounds have been sealed in the flames of Boudicca's fire,' said Tubero. 'They wanted to protect against infection so I lived long enough to deliver the message.'

'See what they can do,' said Petillius and turned to Virrius. 'Attend me in my tent immediately and summon the other officers.'

'My lord, there is one more thing,' said Tubero. 'After the sacking of Camulodunum there was a great revelry amongst their people and they openly boasted of their next target.'

'And you heard them?'

'I did. They intend to march on Londinium within the next few days.'

'You are sure about this?'

'Yes, my lord. They made no attempt to hide their intentions for having taken the Colonia, they fear no legion.'

'Thank you,' said Petillius, 'you will be rewarded for your information. Now get that hand seen to.' The Legate turned and marched back to his quarters while Virrius finished dealing with his men.

'Secure the prisoners and stable the horses,' shouted Virrius. 'Stand down and get some hot food and sleep. Something tells me we may be riding back out sooner than we think.'

The men carried on with their duties while Virrius followed Petillius across the camp. One soldier reached down and dragged the beaten boy to his feet and placed a Pugio blade against his throat.

'Enough of your shit, boy,' he said, 'you'll get no such mercy from us. Now, either you come with me peacefully or you won't live long enough to even see those tin mines the Legate speaks of.'

The prisoner scowled but another of the captives spoke up.

'Boy, leave it. We are within the viper's nest and now is not the time to fight. Conserve your strength for a more opportune time.'

Slowly the young boy backed off, realising his comrade was right. This wasn't the time or the place. But one thing he was sure of, there was no way he was going to be a slave of any man and within the next few days he would escape or die trying.

'That's better,' said the guard, 'now start moving.'

The line of prisoners shuffled toward a smaller wooden stockade within the camp. In amongst them, nursing the fresh wound across his face was Taliesin, the last true blood king of the Deceangli.

–

As was normal for a war briefing, all the Tribunes and senior Centurions gathered within the large command tent of the legion commander. Petillius was pacing back and forth, his mind racing with this new information. When everyone had gathered, he briefed them on the news of Camulodunum. The officers were stunned. Most had spent time in Camulodunum on their periods of leave, enjoying the surroundings that the colony had made similar to those back in Rome. Many had friends or family living there and though it was officially forbidden, they knew that many of the soldiers had wives and girlfriends within those walls.

The mood was ugly and voices were raised in anger.

'My lord, we have to leave right away,' shouted one of the Tribunes. 'Perhaps it is not too late to provide aid.'

'The city is burned and the crows pick over our dead,' said Petillius.

'Even in the midst of carnage there are survivors,' said another. 'Our men have families within the city and they may need our aid. They could be hiding amongst the rubble, waiting for help to arrive.'

Petillius held up his hand.

'Gentlemen, I agree the wisdom in providing aid but there is something else to consider. If the stories are true then this Boudicca has a formidable army under her control and whilst I doubt not our ability to deal with her threat, if we split the legion in half then we provide easy targets for her army. This I cannot contemplate so there are three options open to me. Stay here and send news to Suetonius asking for support, ride to Camulodunum in the hope of finding survivors, leaving the route to Londinium open, or seek out this woman and deal with the threat head on. I realise many will have lost loved ones in Camulodunum but to ride there now is a fool's quest. We have been told that this woman's army vented its rage on every living thing and the city is devoid of life. It is tragic but let the pain add strength to our soldiers' arms. I will not lead our legion on a funerary mission when there are thousands more Roman citizens still alive in other towns. If our intelligence is true, they have set their sights on Londinium and with good weather can get there within ten days. Though it is not a walled city as was Camulodunum, its importance is just as great if not more. The banks of the River Tamesas are alive with our trading ships.'

The tent fell silent as the implications sank in.

'I feel the loss of our countrymen,' continued Petillius, 'yet it is the living we should concentrate on, not the dead. I will send word to Suetonius to keep him informed but in the meantime, we march the legion out as soon as possible, not as grave diggers but as soldiers of Rome. We will seek out this Boudicca and face her head on. Let's see how brave her barbarians are in the face of a seasoned legion, not a retired settlement. Tell the men that tomorrow we prepare, for dawn the next day we march to battle.'

The men cheered their support and Petillius turned to Virrius.

'Send out the scouts,' he said, 'and tell them the first to report on the location of this so-called army will have first choice of plunder when barbarians' rotting bodies litter the landscape. Find her for me, Virrius, give me this woman.'

'Leave it to me, my lord,' said Virrius and saluted before leaving the tent.

Chapter Twelve

The Forests of the Trinovantes

Boudicca sat beside a waterfall in one of the forest streams, reciting prayers to her gods in gratitude for her victory. When she was finished, she cast a golden Torc into the water and watched it sink under the surface before turning away to walk back to her camp.

'Rianna, you startled me,' she said, seeing her friend standing close by.

'Me, frighten a great warrior queen such as you? Surely not,' said Rianna.

'Warrior queen? I think not,' said Boudicca. 'Camulodunum may have fallen but I was there in name only; my blade is yet un-bloodied.'

'There will be time enough,' said Rianna. 'When your strength has returned then you can lead us in conflict.'

'Is there time?' asked Boudicca. 'Yes our victory was great, but how long can we keep the alliance together before the tribes revert to the conflict of our ancestors?'

'This is not yet a worry to bear,' said Rianna. 'At the moment, every warrior is drunk on victory and would follow you into hell itself. Just enjoy it for what it is.'

'There is no joy in the victory, Rianna. There is satisfaction and there is comfort in the revenge but I find no joy in ending another's life. It is a task that needs doing and one we will see through to the end, but joyous it is not. Anyway, what brings you out here?'

'I came to find you,' said Rianna, 'we have word from our spies. The Hispana legion has broken camp and is heading our way.'

Boudicca's head turned sharply.

'Where are they?' she asked. 'And at what strength?'

'They are at White-water valley,' said Rianna, 'and march at full strength.'

'If they have left their fort it means they are set on a mission,' said Boudicca. 'This isn't a mercy mission to Camulodunum but a campaign against a foe.'

'Us?' asked Rianna.

'It has to be,' said Boudicca, 'there is no other threat to them in this area.'

'Do you want me to order the army dispersed?'

'Dispersed? Oh no, Rianna, quite the opposite. The bear has smelled the honey and leaves his lair. Summon the clan leaders to meet here at dawn. This is an opportunity too good to miss.'

–

Petillius rode at the head of his legion. Behind him marched almost five thousand men at arms, ranging from the heavily armoured legionary cohorts, to the light infantry and the more specialised units, the archers, spear throwers and slingers. Cavalry units flanked both sides and behind them came the ox-drawn wagons carrying the legion's supplies, itself guarded by a further two cohorts of auxiliary cavalry.

It was an impressive sight, and he knew it would take more than these barbarians could muster to defeat a legion. Since the fleet had landed the four legions seventeen years earlier, there had been minor setbacks but never had an entire legion been threatened, and though it had happened elsewhere in the empire, it was unheard of in Britannia.

They had been on the march for three days, laying waste to every village they could find in an effort to get information about the army of Boudicca, but so far they had heard nothing.

Virrius was riding at his side discussing tactics, when they saw a group of riders galloping toward them. Petillius held up his hand and the buglers sounded the halt. Behind them, the message passed back and the soldiers took the unexpected yet welcome opportunity to rest.

'Who are they?' asked Petillius.

'Batavian scouts,' said Virrius. 'It looks like they have news.'

'See what they want,' said Petillius, and Virrius along with another Tribune rode out to meet the patrol. As they approached, the scout unit reined in their horses and saluted the officer.

'My lord, we have a lead,' said the Decurion in charge.

'Explain,' demanded Virrius.

The cavalryman signalled to one of his comrades to come forward. Virrius saw a woman draped across the saddle in front of the rider. Without ceremony the scout tipped the woman off his horse to land in the mud, before dismounting and dragging her to her feet.

'This woman knows where Boudicca is,' said the rider.

The woman looked up in terror.

'Is this true?' asked Virrius in the Britannic language. 'Do you know where the warrior queen hides?'

'No, Sir,' she said, her eyes full of fear. 'I know nothing of whom you speak.'

Virrius looked at the Decurion with scorn.

'What is this?' he asked. 'We have little time to play games; what makes you think she knows anything?'

The Decurion nodded to the soldier standing beside the woman, who immediately turned and ripped apart the top of her dress. Both officers stared down at the bare-chested woman in silence. Around her neck was an exquisite necklace made from jade and gold, and bearing the likeness of the Roman goddess, Vesta.

Virrius jumped off his horse and examined the necklace closely. It was definitely Roman and could only have been taken from one of the women in Camulodunum.

'Where did you get this?' he demanded.

'I found it,' stuttered the woman. 'I found it in the dirt.'

Virrius slapped her across the head with the back of his hand, knocking her to the ground. He turned to the scout leader.

'Where did you find her?' he asked.

'Outside a village an hour's ride away,' said the Decurion.

'Did they see you?'

'No, my lord.'

'Pick her up,' ordered Virrius.

The soldier dragged the woman to her feet and held her before the officer.

'Now listen to me,' said Virrius quietly. 'I am going to make this really simple so even your pathetic barbarian mind can understand. My men here know your village and no doubt within that village there are families with children. You may even have some yourself.'

The woman's eyes flickered for a second.

'Oh you do?' said Virrius. 'This makes it even easier. Either you know where the warrior queen hides or you don't. If you do, you will tell us where to find her. If you tell the truth, you will be released and no harm will befall you or your village. However, if you don't know where she is, or say you do and then it turns out to be a lie, I will send my cavalry over to your village and before the sun sets this day, they will kill every living adult before the eyes of your children. When they are done, every child irrespective of age or sex will be raped by my men before being crucified. You, lady, will watch all this with your own eyes before having them gouged out by my own hands. The sight of them suffering will be the last thing you see and you will wander blind until you starve to death, knowing it was you who were responsible for the fate of those children. Now, do you understand what is at risk here?'

The woman nodded as tears rolled down her face.

'Good. Then I will ask you again. Where is the army of the warrior queen?'

For a few seconds the woman didn't move but slowly she raised her arm and pointed off to the flank.

'There,' she said, 'two day's ride from here.'

'Are you sure?' asked Virrius. 'For I wouldn't want to have to ride all the way back here to find your children.'

'They are there,' shouted the woman through her tears, 'I swear before my gods I am telling the truth.'

Virrius stared into the eyes of the woman.

'Do you know what?' he said. 'I think you are. Thank you.' Without warning he plunged his Gladius up through the woman's stomach and into her heart. For a few seconds her eyes widened in shock, before she collapsed to the floor.

Virrius climbed back up onto his horse and turned to his comrade.

'It looks like we have found our army,' he said.

'Was there any need for that?' asked the second Tribune.

'Every need,' said Virrius, 'it's the only language they understand.' He turned to the Decurion in charge of the scout unit. 'Decurion, take a hundred cavalry and burn that village to the ground. We are heading east, make sure you join us by dark.'

'Yes, my lord,' said the Decurion, and he and his men rode away to carry out their orders.

Virrius rode back to the legion and joined Petillius.

'My lord, we have the location of the barbarian army.'

'Is it near?'

'Two days ride in that direction,' said Virrius. 'By nightfall tomorrow this woman will be begging for mercy, and this time I'll personally make sure she will never pose a problem to us ever again.'

'Excellent news,' said Petillius. 'Pass word to the legion. We head east with immediate effect. Split into three columns and deploy all cavalry to the flanks. Order the engineers to ride forward and select a suitable place for tonight's marching camp, no more than ten miles from here. We will go firm tonight and assess the situation tomorrow.'

'Yes, my lord,' said Virrius and galloped down the lines to pass on the orders. Within ten minutes the legion wheeled eastward and split into three, each marching half a mile apart for maximum defence. Petillius watched the manoeuvre with pride, impressed at the parade ground precision of his well-drilled command, but unbeknownst to him, hidden within the treeline, others also watched the manoeuvres; people with a vested interest in learning everything they could about the legion. The scouts of Boudicca.

–

The following night, Taliesin sat back to back with another of the prisoners, their hands bound securely. Every minute since being captured a few days earlier he had watched for an opportunity to escape. During the march the prisoners were tied together by the neck with their hands tied behind their backs, and now the legion had encamped for the night, they were lashed together against a stake that had been driven into the ground.

Despite the lateness of the hour the camp was alive with activity, and the air buzzed with the sound of men talking while they sharpened their weapons. Word had come in from the scouts that they had spotted the barbarian army a few hours' march away, and the command had come to prepare to move before dawn. The smell of cooking wafted around the camp as many men took the opportunity to get a hot meal before they went into battle, sitting before their tents in groups and exchanging last messages with their comrades, to be passed to their families should they fall. Others took the opportunity to sleep, anxious to rebuild their strength after the arduous march.

The prisoners watched the preparations, knowing that something was about to happen but unsure of what.

'Do you think they have found Boudicca?' asked Taliesin.

'They must have,' answered Finian, one of the older warriors. 'The whole legion seems to be preparing and they would only do that for a formidable opponent. There are no tribes capable of offering a threat to a legion so it must be Boudicca's army.'

'Then she must be close,' said Taliesin. 'If we can just break these bonds, we could find her and join her cause.'

'Be quiet, boy,' sighed Finian. 'You waste your breath. Even if we could get through our ties, how do you propose escaping from a legionary encampment? It's impossible.'

'We have to try,' said Taliesin. 'If nothing else at least we will die knowing we tried to free our country.'

'Don't be so eager to die,' said Finian. 'Fate will try to kill you often enough in the years ahead – don't try to seek her embrace so quickly.'

'I don't want to die,' said Taliesin, 'but would rather embed myself on the end of a sword than perish beneath the weight of chains.'

'Trust the gods, Taliesin,' said Finian, 'if it is meant you are to kill Romans, then they will clear the path before you.'

As the night continued, the prisoners witnessed the preparations of the legion until eventually the cavalry rode out to secure the routes. Half an hour later, the infantry columns followed them through the gate as quietly as possible. Unlike on the daily march, they had removed the leather covers from their shields and left behind their Furcas, the cross shaped pole that carried their packs containing their personal equipment. Supply carts were left in the camp and the only waggons taken were those containing the Onagers, Ballistae and the mountain of ammunition needed for both. It was an army stripped down for battle and one that meant business. Once they had gone, Taliesin started to struggle against his bonds once more.

'Do you never give up, boy?' asked Finian.

'Never,' said Taliesin. 'There are only a few dozen guards and the civilians left behind. If this is not an opportune time then nothing will be. We have to try.'

An hour later, Finian slept with his head resting on his chest when an urgent whisper dragged him from his much-needed rest.

'Finian,' whispered the voice again with more urgency.

'What now?' he growled.

'I've done it,' said Taliesin. 'My bonds are loose!'

–

Just before dawn Petillius stood alongside his horse in the protection of a treeline. The ground opened up below him and out on the plain he could see the glowing embers of hundreds of campfires, the evidence of an encamped army. Shadows moved amongst the flames as the warrior camp guards patrolled amongst them and Petillius smiled inwardly. There could not have been a better place for a battle, even if he had chosen it himself. Though Boudicca's army was undoubtedly large, the openness of the plains were perfect for his cavalry to deploy behind the enemy and offered ample room for the manoeuvres of his cohorts. Behind him, his legion had advanced almost silently through the forest and was currently forming up within the treeline. Petillius made a mental note to sacrifice a bull to Mars for aiding him in such perfect preparations.

Someone sidled up beside him.

'My lord, the cavalry are in position on the far side,' said Virrius. 'Once the legion advances their spears are waiting should the barbarians run.'

'I don't think they will run, Virrius, I think they are stubborn enough to think they can take us on face to face.'

'Then they think wrong,' said Virrius.

'Are the flanking cohorts ready?' asked Petillius.

'Awaiting your orders,' said Virrius.

'Then we are ready to go,' said Petillius. 'Return to your cohort and await the signal. When it is sent, we will march the legion out onto the plain and assume Cuneus formation. If my suspicions are correct, they will waste no time in facing us across the field and if so, the day will be all but won before a Pilum is thrown.'

'Then I will see you amongst the blood,' said Virrius, and disappeared into the darkness.

–

Petillius gazed down upon the plain as the first fingers of light crept above the horizon. Down below he saw the first reflections from the armour of the legionaries as they manoeuvred quietly into position. Though such a body of men weren't silent, they were far enough away from the Celtic army to go unheard, and they were in position long before any of the enemy were aware of their presence.

The first cohort formed the vanguard of the wedge-shaped formation, while the second to fourth cohorts flanked the formation to the rear. Another two cohorts of auxiliary infantry formed a deep flat line behind the wedge, while another two lay in reserve. The cavalry had been deployed to the far end of the plain using some low-lying hills as cover and all the artillery were in the forest edge behind him, ready to scatter the enemy should they attack.

Everything was in place, and as the sun crept higher, the Legate turned to a man standing nervously at his side.

'Let's wake them up, soldier,' he said, 'give the signal.'

The archer dipped the end of the arrow into a clay pot containing fire embers, waiting until the flames had caught well, before firing it high into the purple dawning sky.

As one, every Cornicine in the legion ripped the morning silence apart as they sounded the advance, and every man paced forward in time to the war drums. The whole legion marched in time toward the enemy camp and from his position on the hill, Petillius could see the barbarian encampment burst into panicky life.

Men rose from their sleep around the fires or from within their animal skin tents to stare toward the noise. Immediately they recognised the threat and within minutes, hordes of armed warriors ran from the camp toward the oncoming legion, donning their helmets as they ran and grabbing spears from the piles at the edges of the camp. The morning air echoed with the shouting of thousands of men as they lined up in loose formation to wave their weapons in defiance at the oncoming Romans.

A few yards away from Petillius, Virrius held up his hand and the drums stopped. Down on the plain the legion's vanguard came to a halt, and the flanking cohorts drew up alongside them to form a strong line abreast. The reserve cohorts set up a deep support and every man stared across the plain toward the vocal enemy.

'We are ready, my lord,' said Virrius.

'Then make it happen, Tribune,' said Petillius. 'The longer we wait, the sturdier their resolve will become. Strike while their senses are still dulled by last night's ale.'

A second flaming arrow split the dawn sky and again the war drums beat out their rhythm. This time every man in the legion below drew his Gladius, knowing full well that this time there would be no signal to halt. Their advance to battle had started.

–

Boudicca lay amongst the damp bracken, shivering from the attentions of the pre-dawn mist. In the distance she could hear the drums of the Romans and her heart raced as she realised they had taken the bait. All around her, thousands of her comrades shivered along with her, the bracken above them offering little protection against the morning dampness. Several times over the past few hours her hidden army had heard the hooves of passing cavalry, as they searched the area for hidden risks but the riders had stuck to the well-used paths and avoided the rougher ground to either side, a decision that had played right into Boudicca's hands.

Chilled fingers flexed around their weapons to get the blood flowing yet resisted the urge to leap out on the passing patrols. There was a greater prize to be had.

Down in the valley the wall of shields advanced toward the barbarian encampment. Above their heads flew volleys of arrows released by the legions archers as well as balls of fire from the Onagers. The defenders charged forward to take on the Romans just as Petillius had hoped and within seconds, hundreds of half-naked barbarians crashed against the wall of shields in a manic attempt to reach the soldiers behind. At first the lines faltered under the weight of numbers, but this was what the Romans did best; head-on conflict with lesser trained opponents, and though the odd attacker managed to get through, they were quickly dealt with by the second ranks. As soon as the initial surge had faltered, the legion went on the offensive and slowly paced forward, each time thrusting their swords between the shields, invariably encountering barbarian flesh. It was a slaughter, but despite their losses, the barbarian army continued the futile assault until finally they broke off and retreated a hundred paces.

'Sound the pursuit,' shouted Virrius, and the signal rang out across the fields to chase the enemy down. The front cohorts broke ranks and ran forward to finish the enemy off. A retreating army was doomed in the face of any Roman assault, for they would pursue them mercilessly until the lack of light meant they could go on no more.

'Signal the cavalry to close in,' shouted Virrius and a soldier with a heliograph sent the signal miles across the plain to close the gap. Down below the battle had broken up into chaos, and individual fights littered the battlefield as far as the eye could see.

The heavily armoured legionaries not only had the better training and weapons but also outnumbered the enemy by at least two to one. It was only a matter of time before Boudicca's army was wiped out.

'There's the cavalry,' said Virrius, pointing to the approaching riders spread across the plain. 'This is going to be easy.'

'Too easy,' said Petillius.

Virrius turned to stare at Petillius, surprised at the concern on the Legate's face.

'Something is wrong,' said Petillius. 'Those men had no chance of breaching our lines yet they attacked them as if we were nothing.'

'That is their mentality,' said Virrius. 'They don't know when they are beaten.'

'If this Boudicca is half as good as they say she is, why would she assault a legion head on?'

'Ignorance,' sneered Virrius. 'After all, she is but a woman. What would they know about tactics?'

'No,' said Petillius, 'this is too easy; besides, that army was only a couple of thousand strong. Where are the ten thousand she is reputed to lead?'

Virrius turned to watch the scattered battle below.

'She knew she would have no chance against formed ranks,' continued Petillius, 'but in an open fight, the odds would be more equal, especially with more warriors.'

'By the gods,' said Virrius, looking again at the spread-out nature of his men. 'You think she deliberately sacrificed those men to get us to break ranks.'

'I do,' said Petillius, 'she has led us into a trap and one which I fear is about to be sprung.'

Virrius turned to the signaller at his side.

'Sound the retreat,' he shouted, 'get them out of there.'

As the man raised his Cornicine to his mouth, an arrow pierced his throat and he looked up in confusion before falling to his knees, clutching wildly at his wound.

Virrius drew his Gladius and spun around to identify the threat.

'Where did that come from?' he roared, and all around him the officers milled about, unable to answer. Suddenly a volley of arrows flew from the forest and men fell all around the Legatus. Within seconds, every signaller lay dead or dying across the hillside, carefully targeted by the hidden archers.

'The trees,' shouted a soldier, 'they are in the trees.' Before Virrius could give any orders, hundreds of men ran from the thick undergrowth of the forest edge. Others dropped from branches while still more seemed to rise from the very ground itself, discarding the mud and leaves that had hidden them from enemy eyes.

'Where are the rear guards?' shouted an officer.

'They must have been taken by surprise,' shouted Petillius, 'form a line and deal with this threat. Guards get a rider down to the reserves; I want at least a cohort up here immediately. Virrius, get a message to the Primus Pilus, he is to retreat from contact and reform the legion. This bitch has lured us into a trap.'

'Yes, my lord,' shouted Virrius and ran over to the horses. Within seconds he was galloping down the slope toward the battle.

–

Boudicca watched as her people were slaughtered below and although every one of them had volunteered to become the bait, it hurt to see so many of them fall. It was obvious they couldn't last much longer yet still she waited. It was important the Roman cavalry were fully deployed before she showed her strength.

'They come,' whispered a voice beside her, and she peered between the bracken to see the cavalry racing to join the battle.

'Wait,' said Boudicca, sensing the frustration in her comrade's voice. 'Just a little longer.' The cavalry spread out into line abreast as they neared the encampment and lances were withdrawn from their leather holders to be levelled toward the enemy. The pace increased and within seconds they were galloping full pelt into the battle, a tidal wave of irresistible force ready to annihilate any who stood before them.

The panicking barbarians faltered in their retreat, not knowing which way to turn to avoid the relentless

Roman advance. People ran everywhere and the cavalry's headlong charge became caught up in the confusion as hundreds of warriors ran amongst them, using their skinning knives against the tendons of the animals. The flow of combatants had stopped in all directions and man stood against man, in a battle to the death with no quarter given. The overall skill and better armament of the Romans meant the barbarians were no match for them, but despite their losses, every moment had been carefully choreographed for this exact scenario. Most of the Roman infantry and all of the cavalry were engaged in unstructured battle and though it looked as if they would be victorious, this was the moment Boudicca had been waiting for.

Casting away the bracken she stood tall on the side of the hill and held her broadsword high.

'Sacred Andraste,' she screamed, 'in the name of our forefathers, lead us this day to victory.' All around, warrior after warrior followed her lead and stood up from their cold hiding places to race down the slopes toward the battle. Thousands of men and women each armed to the teeth with sword, knife or club, emerged from the enveloping bracken as if by magic, and within seconds the slopes were alive with over ten thousand warriors; racing to aid their fellow Britons.

Virrius galloped toward the Primus Pilus deep in the heart of the battle. It was essential the chief Centurion understood the gravity of the situation, for if his bloodlust blinded him to the danger, then the men would assume it was known and keep fighting alongside him.

Virrius glanced up and gasped in despair as he saw the hordes of barbarians racing down to close the trap. He reined his horse in, realising he was too late to reach the furthest ranks.

'You men,' he roared, spinning his horse around, 'fall back and form a line.' Confused legionaries, used to being on the front foot, looked at each other in bewilderment as the officer rode frantically amongst them, barking his orders to all within earshot.

'It is a trap,' he shouted, 'fall back and reform.'

Realisation sunk in and the junior officers amongst them echoed his orders to organise their men, but despite their newfound urgency, it was too late. The main brunt of Boudicca's army was amongst them.

The battle turned instantly as the barbarians ran amok, their war cries adding to the mayhem. Bodies were hewn apart as the Britons took out their rage on the Romans. The sea of half-naked, painted warriors seemed never-ending, and Virrius realised the day was lost.

'Retreat,' he screamed from his horse, 'back to the forest lines,' but though the remaining men tried to make headway toward the sheltering forest, they were hounded at every step and legionaries fell in their droves.

Up on the hill, Petillius stared in horror as his legion was torn apart at the hands of Boudicca.

'My lord, our men are routed,' shouted an officer. 'We need to help them.'

'No,' snapped Petillius, 'it is too late. The witch has drawn us in like a lamb to the slaughter. If we commit what men are left, it will just feed their swords with more Roman blood. My honour demands I die amongst my men but comes second to a greater need, the retention of the Aquila.' He looked up at the golden Eagle standard high on its pole. The Eagle had been cast in bronze and coated with gold, but the value was not in the precious metal but the iconography it represented. The legions of Rome.

'Fetch the horses,' commanded Petillius, 'and order those in reserve to retreat with all haste. Gather back at the fort and prepare the defences. It is too late to help those below but at least we can secure the Aquila.' As the young officer ran to relay the orders, Petillius looked once more down into the valley. Most of the legion had been slaughtered, and those few that remained had formed a square in the centre of the battlefield, outnumbered a hundred to one by enemy attacking from all sides. In amongst them Petillius could make out the figure of Virrius fighting manically amongst his men. As he watched, the last surviving group of legionaries were overrun and Petillius turned away with a heavy heart. The Ninth Hispana had been wiped out.

An hour later, Boudicca walked amongst the carnage. Dead and dying men lay in their thousands all around her, each a contributor to the sea of blood so eagerly absorbed by the thirsty soil beneath. Some cried out in pain, but most just lay quietly waiting for death to arrive. The families of the Britons who had fought searched amongst them, looking for kin who had fallen, to take them away for the death ceremonies.

Young boys from the tribes walked amongst the Roman wounded with their skinning knives, taking great delight in despatching any they found to the afterlife, while the women searched their bodies for jewellery or coins.

Boudicca was quiet. She thought she would have been ecstatic after the battle, but she felt only anger. Anger that it had to be like this in her own country. Anger, that though they had defeated a legion, many of their own people had to fall to achieve the victory.

'Boudicca,' said a voice.

The queen turned to see Rianna walking up behind her.

'Rianna,' she said quietly. 'We did it! We killed the bear.'

'You did it, Boudicca. You were the one with the vision and the audacity to take on the best of the Romans.'

The warrior queen looked slowly around the valley. Everywhere she looked and as far as the eye could see, the ground was covered with bodies.

'But at what price?' she asked.

'A worthwhile price,' said Rianna. 'Yes, many have died, but their sacrifice has shown the way. The Romans are beatable, Boudicca. With courage and leadership, we can now stare them in the eye as equals. No more will we lay awake at night and fear the sound of horses' hooves.'

'Do you think so?' asked Boudicca. 'Do you think this is all it takes to send them scurrying back to their boats, because I don't. I think it will just awaken them to our strength and next time they will be better prepared. This isn't the end, Rianna, but the beginning. There will be other legions that will follow in their footprints. More battles, more pain and more death. Many more will die before we can call ourselves victors.'

'So we will fight,' said Rianna, 'and many may die, but in the end we will prevail. Today you have shown us the way.'

Boudicca looked up once more.

'Tell me, Rianna,' she said, 'what do you see before you?'

'I see a glorious battlefield that will send shockwaves unto Rome itself,' said Rianna. 'Why, what do you see?'

'Me? I see a fork in the path,' said Boudicca. 'A choice to be made, though both options involving a life of conflict. We can either choose the path of resistance, fighting from the trees and picking our battles or we grasp this gift with both hands.'

'What do you mean?'

'Total war,' said Boudicca. 'Ride this wave of victory right into the heart of them, pulling the people with us. We will never again have an opportunity like this, Rianna, and as painful as it is to see our men bleed, is not eternal servitude no less painful? If it were just our lives, I would plunge headlong down the path to war but what of them?' She swept her arm in an arc, pointing at the ten thousand or so Britons now celebrating wildly. 'In their moment of ecstasy most will not contemplate the consequences. What right do I have to ask them to die?'

'The right of a queen,' snapped Rianna. 'You have led us here and you will lead us onward. One word from you and they will follow you to the gates of Rome itself. I understand the burden of queenship is heavy, but that is the price to be paid. You have often proclaimed your hatred of the Roman occupation, yet now you have the chance to end it, you falter. Do not succumb to these demons, Boudicca, stand tall and lead us onward.'

Boudicca stared at her friend for an age before smiling.

'You are right,' she said, 'summon my chariot for if I am to fight this war I will do so as a warrior of our people.'

Rianna smiled and signalled to a group of horse riders a few hundred paces away. Within moments Boudicca was once more aboard her chariot.

'Join me,' she said and Rianna climbed up beside her. 'If we ride out now, Rianna, there is no turning back.'

'Nor should there be, Boudicca. Ride out, for your people await.'

Boudicca urged her horses slowly forward and as the people saw her, they ran to line her route into the heart of the battlefield, dragging the bodies out of her path as she passed. Within minutes they were surrounded by cheering warriors, both men and women, everyone exulting her triumph. Finally she reached the centre where a large body of men stood in a circle, led by Maccus, the clan leader who had breached the temple at Camulodunum. Boudicca dismounted and walked through the throng to see what was happening. Before her a group of legionary prisoners knelt in the dust, their hands tied behind their backs.

'Maccus,' said Boudicca. 'You have been busy, I see.'

'My blade has absorbed so much Roman blood, I swear it is twice as heavy,' said Maccus.

'And what of these?'

'I ordered them spared in case you want to question them,' said Maccus.

'We will carry no prisoners,' said Boudicca.

'Then question them first and kill them later,' said Maccus.

'They have nothing I want to hear,' said Boudicca. 'Cut off their sword hands and send them back to their countrymen. Let them see that though our strength is mighty, we are a just people.' As she turned to walk away, a voice rang out from the prisoners and Boudicca stopped dead in her tracks, her heart racing in her chest.

'Boudicca,' shouted the voice. 'Enjoy your petty victory while it lasts, for as we speak your demise has already been agreed amongst the Roman gods.'

Boudicca turned slowly and stared at the man who was responsible for all this carnage.

'Virrius,' she snarled under her breath.

'Oh, you remember me?' said the Tribune.

'Oh, I remember you, Virrius,' she answered, walking slowly toward him. 'I remember you, and the way you abused our hospitality. I remember the way you raped our women and killed our unarmed men. I remember how you watched as our children's heads were smashed against each other and how you laughed as I begged for your mercy.'

'How about the whip's lash, Boudicca,' he taunted, 'do you remember how it cut deep into your naked flesh?'

'Every last strike,' whispered Boudicca and started to draw her sword.

'So this is it, Boudicca,' said Virrius with venom in his voice. 'When it comes down to it, the great warrior queen of the Iceni resorts to killing a tethered captive. How typical of a barbarian.'

'You call us barbarians,' snarled Boudicca. 'If defending your home against murderers of the old and rapists of children make me a barbarian then I am proud to bear that name. This is not your home, Roman, it is the land of our fathers and we are entitled to defend it with every beat of our hearts. You have come here, killed our men and raped our women. You have taxed us more than we can sustain and as we watched our old die of hunger, you have taken our young to be slaves, leaving us a bleak future. We fight for freedom yet you fight for the greed of one man. Which is the more barbaric, Roman? Ask your false gods that question when you stand in judgement before them.'

Boudicca altered her grip on her sword but before she could move, a commotion to one side made her stop and she watched in confusion as her oldest daughter walked slowly across the clearing, toward the restrained Tribune.

'Heanua,' said Boudicca, but as she stepped forward, she felt a restraining hand on her arm.

'Boudicca, wait,' said Rianna's voice. 'Let it unfold.'

The noise of the crowd dropped to silence as the girl approached the Roman. Virrius' brow lowered, not understanding what was happening, but within seconds he spotted the knife the young girl held at her side.

'Oh, this gets better,' said Virrius, 'you now send a child to do a man's work. Do your worst, barbarian spawn, I die knowing that you and your kind will soon be stamped into the mud by the legions of Rome.' Despite his bravado, a bead of sweat ran down his face and the tone of his voice changed as death approached.

As the girl drew near, Virrius struggled against his captors but they forced his arms out wide and pulled his head back to expose his throat.

His eyes were wide like a scared dog, and he stared at the girl with hatred as she stopped before him.

'Do it,' he snarled through gritted teeth. 'What are you waiting for?'

For a few seconds nobody moved but finally Heanua placed the point of her blade against the Roman's chest, carefully avoiding the area where she knew his heart to be.

'You are wrong, Roman,' she said quietly. 'Your legions may kill us today but there is always a tomorrow. Children not yet born will spill Roman blood as I now

150

spill yours.' As she spoke, she eased the blade slowly between his ribcage and into one of his lungs. Virrius gasped in pain, but Heanua just kept talking as easily as if she was skinning a rabbit.

'You see, Virrius,' she said, 'you represent Rome and I represent Britannia. You are bigger and stronger than I by far, yet it is I who will live the longer. I may not have pierced your beating heart but these smaller wounds will ensure you die slowly and in great pain as you gasp for breath, choking on your own blood.' She withdrew the blade and placed it over the other lung. Again she pushed the sharp knife slowly through the cartilage, unflinching as the mortally wounded man coughed frothy blood over her face.

'Be proud, Roman,' she said, 'for as you die, you are a prophesy of the future that lies before Rome.'

She stepped back and the captors released Virrius to fall in the mud, coughing and thrashing around as he tried desperately to find breath. Heanua threw the knife to one side and turned to walk away, passing her mother without even a glance of recognition.

'Let her go,' said another female warrior, 'she needs some time alone.'

'No,' said Boudicca, 'she doesn't. She needs her mother,' and turned to follow Heanua across the battle-field.

'What about the prisoners?' shouted Rianna. 'What fate awaits them?'

Boudicca paused but did not turn around.

'Burn them,' she said, 'every last one of them.'

Without another word she followed her daughter back to their camp, picking her way between the thousands of corpses littering the valley.

Back in the hills, Petillius rode frantically through the forest, galloping as hard as he could away from the battle. All around mayhem reigned, as the warriors of Boudicca swarmed like bees amongst the trees, slashing wildly at the passing horses. The reserve cohorts were fragmented as each man fought for his life against overwhelming odds, until finally it was a headlong retreat with every man fighting for survival. Those on foot stood no chance, while those on horseback fared much better as they put distance between themselves and the manic enemy.

'Keep going,' screamed Petillius as one of his men swerved to help a comrade. 'We have to get the Aquila to safety. This is not Teutoberg and I will not lose an Eagle.'

Those few who were left forged on, and gradually left the battlefield behind them as they sought familiar territory. Finally, after several hours, they came across a river and a cavalryman reigned an exhausted horse alongside the Legate.

'My lord,' he said, 'I know this river. If we follow it downstream it will take us toward our last encampment.'

'Are you sure?' asked Petillius.

'Yes, my lord. I have ridden this way before.'

'Then lead us back to safety,' said Petillius, 'or I fear this day will never end.'

Once more they forged ahead until, many hours later, the weary horses walked slowly through the gate of the sparsely guarded camp they had left a few days earlier.

A guard ran forward and helped Petillius from his horse.

'My lord, what's happened?' asked the Decurion in charge.

'I will brief you later,' said the Legate. 'In the meantime stand to the guard, every man to the palisades, including the wounded. Break out every weapon we have in the wagons and stockpile them around the perimeter. Each man will eat and sleep at his post, until I personally give the order to stand down. Is that clear?'

'Yes, my lord,' said the Decurion.

'Good. Tell your men to keep an eye out for any stragglers that may find their way back. You can send a patrol out to aid any they find but you are not to engage the enemy. We need every man capable of wielding a sword behind this barrier. Now, arrange food and water to be brought to the palisades for my men. We don't know how much time we have.'

'Yes, my lord,' said the Decurion and saluted before turning away to pass on the orders. Petillius turned to the Tribunus Laticlavius, the young officer learning his trade besides the Legate.

'Dellus, see to the horses,' he said. 'Ensure they are fed, watered and rubbed down. What strength they have left may still be required before this day is done.'

'My lord,' said the young officer, 'there are no grooms available and only a few slaves within the camp. The rest of the men are heading to the stockade as you ordered.'

'Then do it yourself, man,' shouted Petillius. 'Are you yet so soft that you shy from hard work? Thank the gods that the only blood you shed this day will be from blistered hands and not opened chest.'

Only when the men were busy redeploying did Petillius turn to the standard bearer at his side.

'Aquilifer,' he said, using the Eagle bearer's formal title. 'You have ridden hard and carried our standard well. You above all deserve rest but there is a task I would have you attend. I would entrust it to no other.'

'Whatever you command, my lord,' said the Aquilifer.

'Go to one of the empty officer's tents,' said Petillius, 'and seal yourself inside. While there, scrape away the soil and bury the Eagle as deep as your forearm. Once done, arrange the contents as if there was no disturbance.'

'Bury the Eagle, my lord?' asked the officer incredulously.

'You heard me,' said the Legate. 'I hope it is temporary but I fear we may not survive this day, and I will not see her glory in the hands of the Barbarians. Now go, and inform me when the task is done.'

The officer saluted and turned away to his task. Petillius took a moment to adjust his armour and take a drink before heading over to join his men at the palisades. It was not a task normally required of a Legate, but these were desperate times and after all, he was a legionary.

Chapter Thirteen

The Lands of the Trinovantes

Prydain and his comrades had ridden for several days through the midlands of Britannia, heading toward the lands of the Iceni. The spring rains made the going tough for though there were well trodden paths along the route, those they could risk were boggy with mud and the going was slow. Along the way they encountered many local tribesmen but kept themselves to themselves to avoid rousing suspicion and every night they camped deep within the woods in order to light a fire without fear of being seen. One such night, the men were seated around the meagre flames while Heulwen was already wrapped in her cloak beneath the cover of the tent.

'May as well use it up,' said Gildas leaning forward and retrieving the remains of a boar's leg from the fire.

'You'll not find much meat on there,' replied Cullen.

'It's not the flesh I seek but a treat much greater.' Gildas cracked the leg bone with his knife. Carefully he levered away the bone fragments until he reach the end of the marrow with his teeth and pulled out a length of the delicacy, making a great show of how delicious he found the taste.

'What food do we have left?' asked Prydain.

'Some dried mutton,' replied Taran, 'and some grain. We will have to hunt tomorrow or we will go hungry in the coming days.'

'I fear these lands are sparse of deer,' said Prydain. 'The villages are many in these parts and we may have to wander a great distance to find spoor.'

'Then we will have to risk a village,' said Taran. 'We still have coin and without supplies we will fall short of our goal before getting anywhere near.'

'The coin will arouse suspicion,' said Prydain.

'There is no alternative,' answered Taran. 'We have to take that risk.'

'I never thought I would see the day when I regretted having gold coins,' said Cullen.

Prydain laughed.

'I sympathise,' he said. 'We have enough coin to spend a lifetime getting fat yet they may be the death of us.' Silence fell for a few moments as all four men stared into the dancing flames.

'So what do you know of this Taliesin,' asked Cullen eventually.

'Not much if truth be told,' said Prydain. 'I was once captured by his father and offered into slavery but fate intervened and we became the closest of friends. He died in my arms at Caer Caradog and I swore to protect his son. It turns out he is the last true blood prince of the Deceangli and his bloodline is needed to protect the north of the Khymru.'

'He sounds too eager to die if you ask me,' said Cullen.

'Show me a young Khymric warrior who is not as headstrong,' said Prydain. 'The difference is his life is not his to give.'

'So what do we do if we find him?'

'Explain the situation and ask him to return with us,' said Prydain.

'As simple as that?'

'I could knock him out and tie him to a mule,' said Gildas.

'It's an option,' said Prydain, 'but not a favourable one, I fear.'

'Why not?'

'This boy has to be nurtured into a man,' said Prydain. 'It will be hard enough to curb his bloodlust, especially when there is an offensive against the Romans underway. It is important he sees the merit in our mission and travels back of his own free will. If we force him, he will lose honour amongst comrades and will never embrace the role laid before him.'

'We must find him first,' said Cullen, 'and that will be a task in itself.'

'I agree,' said Prydain, 'but I feel if we find this warrior queen, then Taliesin won't be far away.'

'Unless he has already been killed,' said Taran.

Everyone stayed quiet, realising that the possibility of the boy being already dead was very, very high.

'Well, we will find out soon enough,' said Prydain. 'Anyway, let's get back to the problem of getting supplies from the village. Who fancies going in?'

—

A hundred miles away, smoke lay across the island of Mona, swirling between the trees of the oaken forests like a heavy morning mist. However, this was no refreshing cloud of dew droplets but the acrid evidence of the bloody events of the previous two days. Men walked slowly through the smoke in silence, tired and battle-scarred silhouettes, leaning down to check fallen opponents for loot, the right of the victor in these hard times.

Cassus looked on with cold disinterest. His days of looting the dead were long gone and he had enough saved with the legion's treasurer to ensure a comfortable retirement when the time came. His wages were substantial and he had been awarded significant monetary gifts by various commanders during his career, ensuring his days of looting were over.

Suetonius appeared through the smoke.

'Cassus, your victory is total,' he said. 'It seems the whole island is ablaze.'

'Only their sacred groves, my lord,' said Cassus. 'I felt it was important to show them the contempt in which we hold their gods.'

'And their priests?'

'Fuel for the same fires,' said Cassus. 'Their threat was great in volume though insignificant in substance. Thousands have felt our wrath and it was wolves amongst sheep. Those who ran are being chased down as we speak but for sport more than anything. A good exercise for the young men I feel.'

'Let them exercise their sword arms a while longer,' said the Legate, 'but rein them in before dark. Mona is now no more than a graveyard and there are pressing needs elsewhere.'

'A sentiment I share,' said Cassus, 'and I feel this task could have been done by auxiliaries rather than Rome's finest.'

'Your frustration is noted, Cassus, but it was a task that needed doing. I will be returning to the Cerrig shortly to make the arrangements for the march. Join me this evening to share a meal with my officers and together we will plan the next step in subduing this godforsaken country.'

Before Cassus could answer Suetonius walked away, flanked by his bodyguard. Cassus watched him go before summoning his second in command.

'Optio,' he said, 'pass the word; every unit to be back at the camp by dark. I want to be across the strait at the next tide. Let the men celebrate tonight but limit the wine. I feel we will be on the march by noon and any unable to keep up will feel the bite of my Vitis.'

'Yes, my lord,' said the Optio and walked away to share the command. Cassus made his way to the shore to ensure there were enough boats to take the legion back to the mainland. The campaign against Mona had been easier than he had hoped and had been a one-sided slaughter. Ordinarily, the warrior in him would be rejoicing and he would revel in the bloodshed but deep inside, something ate at him. He wasn't sure what it was, but his mind kept returning to the threat of this unknown woman in the east. Boudicca.

–

Taliesin shook his fellow comrade awake. The sky had long turned from black to grey and the low hanging sun fought with the morning rain clouds for the right to dominate the sky. Both men had travelled north to find Boudicca, following the trail left by the marching legion yet careful to stay just off the track in case any Romans had to return to the camp and found them gone. Now they had made their escape, there was no way they wanted to risk being caught again. Each night they laid low in amongst whatever undergrowth they could find, sharing an old horse blanket for warmth. Though they were used to hunger, the complete lack of food meant they were weak and both men knew they couldn't go on much longer.

'Finian, wake up,' hissed Taliesin, shaking the man beneath the blanket.

'What's the matter?' mumbled Finian. 'Do you have food? For if not an empty stomach is easier to bear when sleeping.'

'Finian, something's happening,' said Taliesin. 'There are men in the woods, many men.'

Finian sat up urgently, instantly awake.

'What do you mean?' he asked. 'Romans?'

'I don't know,' said Taliesin. 'If they are, they don't march in formation. They seem to be all around us.'

'I don't hear them,' said Finian.

'Exactly,' said Taliesin. 'They try to keep quiet but since the sun rose, I have heard many pass us by.' As he spoke someone coughed in the distance and both fugitives ducked lower into the bramble thicket.

'Do you think they are searching for us?' asked Taliesin.

'No,' said the older man. 'We are too far from the fort and there were only a few guards left. They wouldn't waste resources on a couple of runaway slaves, at least not during a time of conflict.'

'So what do you think is happening?'

'I'm not sure,' said Finian, turning his head sharply to the right as a voice drifted to him through the woods. 'But we daren't move; we could be stepping straight back into the slave's yoke.'

'I will die first,' snarled Taliesin.

Suddenly Finian threw his arm around Taliesin's head and clamped his hand over his comrade's mouth.

The boy's first instinct was to struggle but when he followed Finian's wide eyed stare, he instantly froze, afraid to move a muscle. Less than ten paces away, a Roman infantry man had emerged from the gloom and sat against a tree to rest. He drank deeply from his water bottle and carefully removed his helmet before placing it beside him on the forest floor. Finally he explored the side of his head with his hands before pouring some water on the mass of bloody hair, matted closely to his skull. He gasped in pain for a second before taking his knife and cutting a large square of cloth from the undershirt beneath his armour. Folding it in a pad he used some more water to dampen the cloth before dabbing it gingerly against the head wound.

Finian eased his hand from Taliesin's mouth and put his finger up to his own lips, indicating his friend to be quiet. Slowly he crawled back through the thicket closely followed by Taliesin until they were out of earshot of the wounded soldier.

'What's going on?' hissed Taliesin. 'That man looks exhausted. Did you see the wound on his head?'

'I did,' said Finian, 'and it's obviously a battle wound. I reckon he has been hit by something, probably a mace and if it wasn't for that helmet, his brains would now be spread across a field somewhere. As it is the wound looks serious enough to be fatal.'

'What do you think happened?' asked Taliesin.

'For him to receive a wound from a mace suggests he has been in very close quarter fighting,' said Finian, 'and that means a tightly fought battle. Romans do most of their killing from afar if they can help it and usually finish off the remainder with their Gladii. This man has been face to face with an opponent and it looks like he came off second best.'

'You think he has fought with Boudicca's army?' asked Taliesin with barely concealed excitement.

'I don't know,' said Finian, 'but it is a possibility.'

'Shhh, what's that?' hissed Taliesin and once again both men ducked as someone approached their position. This time it was a cavalryman riding an exhausted horse. The man's head was hanging low on his chest and one arm, caked in blood, hung loosely at his side, the result of a blow from an axe.

'Look there's more,' hissed Taliesin and as the gloom lightened, they could see the remnants of the shattered legion making their way through the forest away from Boudicca.

'By the gods, Taliesin,' said Finian, 'they are a beaten army. It looks like they met their match with Boudicca.'

'I knew it,' said Taliesin, 'she is the one to drive this filth from our lands. Come on, she can't be far.'

Finian grabbed his arm.

'Where do you think you are going?' he asked.

'To find her of course,' said Taliesin.

'In broad daylight through a retreating army?' asked Finian. 'How far do you think you will get?'

'Look at them,' said Taliesin as another soldier limped past. 'They are a threat no longer; Boudicca has stripped that title from them.'

'Do not fool yourself, boy,' said Finian, 'even a wounded Roman is more than a match for us two. Look at us. We are weak from hunger and haven't a weapon between us.'

'If we stay here much longer, we will be too weak to move anyway,' said Taliesin. 'Who knows how many follow these?'

Finian thought furiously.

'You are right,' he said, 'we have to do something.' He looked around the ground and scrabbled through the detritus until he found what he was looking for, a broken branch the size of an arrow shaft. He snapped one end and picked at the fibres until it had a semblance of a point. He pressed it against his palm and grunted in satisfaction when it produced a spot of blood.

'What do you want that for?' asked Taliesin.

'We may not be a match for most of them,' said Finian, 'but between us I think we can manage one who already has a smashed-in skull.'

Taliesin stared back the way they had come, realising what Finian intended.

'To what purpose?' he asked.

'All legionaries carry food,' said Finian. 'With a bit of luck he may have some left but even if he doesn't, he will have weapons and with those, our task will become much easier.'

Taliesin stared at his friend before nodding in agreement.

'Then we had better strike quickly before he decides to leave,' he said. 'What do you want me to do?'

'Circle around the thicket back to his position but stay low and keep an eye out for any of his comrades. One will be hard enough, more than one and we are dead men. I will circle the opposite way. When you see me, step out into the open and attract his attention. Hopefully he will be distracted long enough for me to get across the clearing.'

'What do you expect to do with that?' asked Taliesin, pointing at the makeshift weapon. 'He still wears his armour.'

'His throat is unprotected,' said Finian. 'We will have one opportunity but if the surprise is made, I can pierce his throat before he can cry out. After that it will be a matter of minutes before he dies. I just hope the gods keep his comrades away long enough.'

Taliesin nodded slowly.

'Then let's get it done,' he said and turned to follow the left edge of the thicket. Finian followed the right side back toward the resting Roman knowing that their chance of success was slim at best, but it was the only one they had.

–

Gerrilius was a Decurion in the third century of the second cohort and though he was an experienced legionary, his heart raced from being so near death. Never had he been in such an unorganised battle, and for the first time since he had joined the legions, he had thought his life was coming to an end. Where they had all come from, he still didn't know. One minute his unit were pursuing retreating barbarians across the plain and the next they were fighting frantically for their lives against overwhelming enemy numbers. The disciplined ranks that were so familiar quickly disintegrated under the onslaught and within moments it had been every man for himself.

He recalled how men he had known for years fell all around him and despite his manic defence, he knew it was only a matter of time before they were overwhelmed. He had heard the orders to retreat and had fought his way back toward the Aquila, but the odds were overwhelming and it soon became obvious he wouldn't make it. Comrade after comrade fell to the barbarian hoard and though he lost count of how many men he killed, he soon came up against a giant of a man wielding a large, metal headed hammer. There was no stand off or calculated conflict and it was all over in a matter of seconds. The warrior came at him, screaming in his heathen language while swinging the giant mace and though Gerrilius managed to duck just in time, it still struck him a glancing blow on the side of his head, denting his helmet and cracking his skull.

Though the blow wasn't fatal, it had knocked him out cold, though not before he had run his Gladius up through the man's stomach and into his heart. Both men fell to the floor, one knocked unconscious and one dead as the battle raged around them. The giant warrior lay across the Roman's seemingly lifeless body and their blood mingled as it ran over Gerrilius' face and dripped to the battlefield floor. Though he didn't know it at the time, it was this carnage that saved the Roman's life as after the battle was over, he was overlooked by the warrior boys despatching the Roman wounded with their skinning knives. By the time he came around, night had fallen and he had managed to crawl away into the relative safety of the nearby woods and staggered back toward the legionary fort many miles away.

That had been the previous night and somehow, he had managed to keep going throughout the hours of darkness, putting a lot of distance between him and the battlefield. Finally he could go no further and knew he had to rest. The pain in his head was overpowering and his fingers probed gingerly at the depression in the side of his skull. He winced as the shattered bone pushed easily inward but hoped the wound was not fatal. He had seen similar battle injuries in other men and some had experienced no aftereffects after the skull had healed. Others however, despite living had turned into gibbering idiots and had become objects of mirth back home in Rome. He believed he would be one of the lucky ones.

Despite the pressing need to continue, Gerrilius knew he had to rest. Although he wasn't out of danger, the effects of the battle, the injury and the travelling through the night meant his body was on the verge of shutting down. He needed sleep and though it wasn't ideal, this thicker part of the forest was going to be as safe a place as he could hope for. His eyes closed of their own accord and he descended quickly into sleep as his body started the long process of healing, not aware that less than fifty paces away, two starving barbarians were intent on killing him.

Back in the Cerrig, Governor Suetonius was delighted and knew he would have tribute paid to him upon his eventual return to Rome. He had lost less than a hundred men in the battle and the island of Mona, so long a thorn in the Rome's side, had at last fallen to their might. Though the battle had been one sided the outcome was almost incalculable in its consequences. Almost every tribe in Britannia was influenced by the Druids, and now their sacred island had been laid to waste, their power would be minimal. It had been a very successful campaign.

Cassus strode along the ranks of the formed-up legion, casting a critical eye over the presentation of his men. The previous night had been one of celebration and many of the soldiers looked worse for wear, but though his tongue was sharp, he withheld the threat of his Vitis, and the symbol of his authority lay idle in his hand. Despite his threat, he was fully aware that these men had just been through a battle and had lost comrades in the fight. They deserved the hangovers they now felt and he would not admonish them in their hour of victory. Besides, the march would soon blow away the cobwebs.

The men mumbled amongst themselves in the early morning chill and spent the time adjusting their packs as they awaited the command to march out. Suetonius was talking amongst his officers awaiting confirmation from his scouts that the way was relatively clear. The few locals who had been allowed to stay in the Cerrig during the Romans' brief occupation watched nervously from the doorways, eager to see the back of the arrogant soldiers. Their presence had been brutal albeit short and many of the locals bore the scars of the soldiers' tempers.

The low murmur of voices was suddenly interrupted by the shout of a lookout and the guards pulled open the gates to allow through a group of riders. Cassus looked over and recognised one of the scout patrols, but amongst them was a rider obviously worse for wear from a hard ride.

The cavalryman almost fell from his horse and was escorted through the massed ranks to stand before Suetonius. Although Cassus couldn't hear the conversation, the look on Suetonius' face told him the rider was the bearer of bad news. Within minutes the rider was dismissed and Suetonius engaged his officers in animated conversation. Finally they all dispersed each running to carry out whatever orders they had been issued by their general. Cassus took the opportunity to approach him.

'My lord, I note the urgency of your manner. Is there a concern I should be aware of?'

Suetonius stared at him for a moment before answering.

'Yes there is,' said Suetonius, 'and on this occasion I am man enough to admit that you were right and I was wrong. Camulodunum has fallen, Cassus. That bitch queen has flattened the city and killed everyone within its walls. It seems there are no survivors.'

Cassus remained tight lipped. He felt no pleasure in being right, just frustration that they were so far away and couldn't offer their countrymen their support.

'What of the Ninth?' he asked.

'No news,' said Suetonius. 'We can only assume they weren't able to get there in time. If they had, Petillius would have crushed this bitch.'

'Perhaps they were already there,' said Cassus, voicing the obvious thought both men harboured.

'No,' said Suetonius eventually. 'That is impossible. The Hispana are good against ten times their number.'

'Until we get confirmation, I suggest we assume the worst,' said Cassus, 'and march the men at double time to offer relief.'

'The arrangements have already been made,' said Suetonius. 'The auxiliaries are riding out as we speak and we will be rid of this Cerrig within the hour. What is the mettle of your men, Cassus? Can they do a fifteen-day march in ten?'

'We will do it in seven,' said Cassus.

'From any other man I would see that as an empty boast but from you, I see it as a fact. Lead us out, Primus Pilus. I feel our legion needs your example now more than ever.'

Cassus saluted and marched away, his demeanour completely changed.

'Centurions to me,' he roared and from all around the Cerrig, the experienced soldiers ran to hear his orders.

'Listen carefully,' he shouted when they were gathered around him. 'The Ninth may be in trouble and we are the nearest available relief. Tell the men to tighten their straps and prepare for double pace. We will march harder than we ever have before and cover twice as much distance. Any stragglers will be left at the wayside until the following carts can pick them up but we will not leave any guards. I want each man to carry two extra water bottles in their pack and an extra ration of Buccellatum. Erase the memory of yesterday's battle for it is done. Our comrades need us now and I will not let them down. Now get back to your men, we march within the hour and will not stop until we share the Ninth's campfires. Now move.'

The Centurions ran back to their commands and within seconds, their raised voices combined to echo around the stone fortress. The mood changed drastically and the legion's hangovers were replaced with what it knew best – military efficiency.

–

Gerrilius opened his eyes slowly. Despite the injury to his head and his desperate need to sleep, he hadn't lasted this long in Rome's army without developing a sixth sense, often the only difference between life and death. Today was no different. A movement to one side caught his eye and he threw himself sideways just as Finian lunged toward him with the sharpened branch.

Gerrilius' training kicked in and as he rolled away he reached for his Gladius, but though his assault had missed, Finian's desperation meant he was just as quick and he pounced on the wounded Roman in a manic fit of rage.

For a few moments Finian dominated the surprised Roman and they grappled in eerie silence, each desperate for an opening to better the other but within a minute the Roman's greater strength and better training told and he punched the Celt hard in the face, making him fall dazed to one side.

Gerrilius staggered to his feet and drew his blood-stained Gladius before limping over to the still dazed Finian.

'Is that all you have?' he spat, 'I am insulted.'

Finian was on his back on the floor, looking up at the giant Roman, knowing full well that he had blown his one chance and there was no chance of mercy.

'Despite my death, you are still defeated, Roman,' he said. 'It is just a matter of time.'

Gerrilius stepped forward to plunge his Gladius into the Celt's gut but as he did, his sixth sense once more screamed a warning, though this time it was a second too late.

With a primeval roar, Taliesin launched himself onto the Roman's back and before the soldier could respond, smashed a fist-sized boulder against the existing injury on the side of the man's head.

The resulting scream of pain matched the intensity of Taliesin's and the Roman dropped to his knees, blinded by the lightning bolts of agony bouncing around his head. Taliesin fell away and looked on in horror as the man held his head in his hands, screaming in pain as his shattered skull cut into his damaged brain.

'Taliesin,' shouted Finian, 'get his sword.'

Taliesin looked over in a daze, as if his friend was talking a foreign language.

'What?'

'His sword!' screamed Finian. 'Quickly before it's too late.'

Taliesin saw the sword lying amongst the leaf litter and bent to pick it up.

'Kill him,' shouted Finian. 'Stick the bastard before he comes to his senses.'

Taliesin walked forward and stood before the kneeling Roman who was still groaning in pain.

'Do it,' screamed Finian. 'What are you waiting for?'

Gerrilius slowly lifted his head and stared at the young man before him yet still Taliesin hesitated. Finally the mortally wounded Roman broke the silence between them and spoke in the Britannic language.

'Do it boy,' he said, 'I am done.'

Without a pause Taliesin drove the Gladius through the Roman's eye socket and deep into his brain. The soldier gasped in pain before falling to the floor, writhing in his final death throes.

Taliesin watched him die as Finian limped up beside him.

'Thank the gods,' he said. 'For a second there, I thought you weren't going to do it. It was almost as if you haven't killed a man before.'

Taliesin looked up at his comrade but said nothing.

'I don't believe it,' said Finian, 'with all your brave talk, I thought you had killed hundreds.'

'One or a hundred,' said Taliesin, 'what does it matter?'

'Nothing I suppose,' said Finian, 'now come on, let's see if he has any food. With all that racket this place could be swarming with Romans within minutes. We have to get out of here.'

Chapter Fourteen

The Lands of the Iceni

Rianna was sitting in the back of a covered cart having her wound dressed by one of the Shaman. Boudicca sat alongside the temporary bed containing the sleeping form of Lannosea, gently smoothing her daughter's hair.

'How is she?' asked Rianna.

'The mind demons plague her,' said Boudicca with sadness. 'The Shaman have invoked the gods' blessings and drenched her with the dream smoke but she still suffers.'

'Has she spoken since the battle?' asked Rianna.

'No,' said Boudicca. 'The last few days she has spent little time outside the cart and stares into the distance. Who knows what horrors beset her?'

'What about Heanua?'

'Her demons are conquered,' said Boudicca. 'She throws herself into swordplay with our warriors alongside the best of them. She craves the opportunity to blood her blade again and I fear her anger may prove her downfall.'

'It is her way of dealing with it,' said Rianna. 'I would let the girl embrace her anger and do what she has to do.'

Boudicca nodded in silence.

'I just wish Lannosea could find her way through,' she sighed, looking down at her youngest daughter. When it was obvious the young girl was finally asleep, Boudicca crossed the rocking wagon and sat opposite her friend before looking out at the wagon train behind them stretching back as far as the eye could see.

'The army grows bigger every day,' said Boudicca. 'We have to be careful it does not grow so big it can't be sustained.'

'The villages give what they can,' said Rianna, 'but many are still going hungry.'

'It is a worry,' said Boudicca. 'We have almost thirty thousand warriors under our banner and the same number pledged from the other tribes. We cannot afford to wait too long or our warriors will drift off to the comfort of their clans.'

'So what is your plan, Boudicca? Do you intend to assault one of their fortresses?'

'To what end?' asked Boudicca. 'Their permanent forts are well defended and we are no experts in siege warfare. Behind palisades I feel they will provide a resistance too great. No, what we need to do is lure them out into the open where our numbers can be brought to bear.'

'And how do you intend to do that?'

'By denying them the comforts to which they have become accustomed. Hit them where it hurts and deny them the goods they rely on so much.'

'Their supply lines?' asked Rianna.

'No,' said Boudicca. 'The supply lines are but veins in the Roman body; we need to cut out the heart.'

'What do you mean?'

'What is the biggest trading town in Britannia?' asked Boudicca.

'Londinium,' said Rianna.

'Londinium,' agreed Boudicca. 'Almost all of their supplies are shipped up the river Tamesas and the town has become an essential hub in their strategy. Deny them access to this and their whole campaign will falter.'

'You mean to attack the ports?'

'Oh no, Rianna, the ports are just the doorways. If we are to do this, we need to wipe out the entire city. By doing so, we will force them to tighten their belts while filling our own food wagons. There is food enough in Londinium to sustain our campaign for many months. It is the obvious choice.'

'But the population,' said Rianna, 'surely there as many Britons as Romans.'

'Perhaps so, but most suck the breast of the Roman Empire and grow fat on the labour of our brothers. Those that bent their knee have made their choice and will pay the price of servitude.'

'Have you shared this with the clan leaders?'

'Some but not all. I have sent word to those tribes who have yet to join us. This is a chance to strike at the Roman heart and we cannot risk defeat. Take Londinium and the Romans will shake in fear behind their palisades.'

'What about defences?' asked Rianna.

'Minimal,' said Boudicca. 'I have questioned many who have been there. Londinium was a mere village just ten years ago but the deep Tamesas has enabled it to grow at a pace that quickly outgrew any defences it may have once had. It is an open city populated by traders, traitors and the Roman gentry who rake in the coin for distributing the supplies. I hear tell of Roman women being carried on litters as if they were in Rome itself while their husbands drink and whore as if they owned the country.'

'When do you plan the attack?' asked Rianna.

'As soon as we have the commitment of the other tribes,' said Boudicca. 'A few days rest and then we will move south. By my reckoning we can be at the outskirts of the city within ten days.'

Rianna nodded.

'Then I have a favour to ask,' she said. 'My wound is healing and I ask your agreement to join in the assault.'

'Can you wield your sword?' asked Boudicca.

'I can,' said Rianna, 'and though there is still an ache, ten days practise will strengthen my arm. Against fat traders it will be more than enough to prevail.'

Boudicca nodded.

'You above all have shared this journey with me, Rianna. The city is rich with plunder and while it is right our people will share the wealth, it is only fair that you too, share in the spoils.'

'The only wealth I seek is that afforded by retribution,' said Rianna. 'My sword arm grows stronger by the day but my spirit aches at the humiliation I suffered at Roman hands. It too needs to heal.'

'Then heal it will,' said Boudicca. 'You will join me in the assault and heal your spirit with the blood of Romans.'

The wagon train ground to a halt and a warrior appeared around the back of the covered cart.

'My Queen,' he said. 'The lead carts have reached the river junction.'

'Good,' said Boudicca. 'Tell our people to make camp, we will rest here for a few days. Deploy scouts on the hills all around us. I want to know about anyone approaching hours before they arrive, no matter who they are. Any sign of enemy troops, sound the alarm immediately.'

The warrior saluted and ran off to give the orders.

'Come,' said Boudicca to Rianna. 'There are other arrangements to be made. I will arrange to deploy the carts throughout the forest and send out hunting parties. You send riders to the local villages and ask them to furnish whatever food they can spare, including cattle. We have an army to feed.'

'Boudicca,' said Rianna as the queen jumped from the cart.

Boudicca turned to look at her friend of many years.

'Tell me what is in your heart,' said Rianna. 'Do you really believe we can do this?'

Boudicca paused before answering.

'I believe this is our greatest chance,' she said. 'Our army grows by the day and we have already defeated an entire legion, a feat unheard of even in the days of the great Caratacus. Only the gods know the outcome but I fear nothing they can send against us. There are but three legions left in Britannia and even if Suetonius fielded all three, I feel our numbers are too great. This is our time, Rianna, the fight back has begun.'

–

Petillius opened his eyes, struggling to realise where he was. As a Legate he was used to waking beneath covers of clean furs, in a tent warmed by a fire pot but today was different. Today he shivered as he woke and blinked the cold rain from his face. The dawn was just breaking and he soon remembered he was still on the palisade along-side his men. His scarlet cloak now lay sodden around his shoulders, clinging to the bronze ceremonial armour he had donned before the battle in anticipation of total victory. Usually it was a stunning burnished emblem of

Rome's authority but now it was just a cold weight against his chest, a humbling reminder of the humiliation he had suffered at the hands of the warrior queen.

More survivors of the battle had trickled into the camp through the night and while their needs were tended by the one surviving Medicus, those who had been there for almost two days stared at the threatening forest edge in anticipation. There was agreement that Boudicca would surely follow the retreating Romans and administer the final annihilation on the remaining hundred or so survivors who had made it back to the fort, so every available man had stayed at their posts for twenty-four hours, taking it in turns to sleep and eat. Despite his station, Petillius had taken his share of the load and had stood alongside the lower ranks as a comrade rather than Legatus, a sign of the close camaraderie of his legion.

'My lord,' said a voice and Petillius looked up at the young officer he had berated the previous day. Tribune Dellus was holding a heavy waxed coat with a fur lined hood in one hand and a tankard of something hot in the other.

'Dellus,' he said. 'You look as bad as I feel. Have you slept?'

'A little,' said the officer. 'While you were sleeping, I rounded up some of the walking wounded and made a broth. There isn't much but it is hearty and will warm you up.'

'Have all the men been fed?'

'Most of them,' said Dellus. 'The last will make their way down as soon as they are relieved. There is enough for all.'

Petillius turned to sit with his back against the palisade wall before accepting the tankard of broth. Carefully he sipped at the meaty liquid, enjoying the heat as it made its way to the pit of his stomach. Dellus produced a hunk of bread from beneath his cloak and waited patiently as his commanding officer ate hungrily, the first hot meal he had eaten for three days.

'It's good,' said the Legate eventually, 'and welcomed by the men no doubt.'

Dellus didn't answer and the Legate saw his eyes were sunk deep within his face.

'How much sleep have you had?' he asked. 'And be honest.'

'There was much to be done, my lord. There will be time to sleep when I am dead.'

Petillius stared for a moment while chewing the last of his bread. The young man had a lot to learn but he seemed made of the right stuff. Finally the Legate stood up and unclipped the sodden red cloak before throwing it to the camp floor below.

'Help me with this,' he said and Dellus unclipped the heavy bronze breast plate, watching in surprise as this too was discarded to the mud below.

'My lord, you may need that before the day is out.'

'A shiny plaything in times of dominance,' said Petillius. 'If I am required to fight for my life, I would prefer the freedom of chain mail.' He took the waxed cloak from the officer and threw it around his shoulders, already welcoming the instant warmth its weight brought. 'First I will talk to the men at the palisade. They have shown great fortitude these past three days and they need their Legate amongst them.'

'I understand, my lord,' said the young officer and turned to leave.

'Dellus,' said Petillius, 'once the last of the men have been fed you will get some rest. At times like these, men show their real mettle and yours will not go unrewarded. You are dismissed.'

'But my lord,' started Dellus.

'But nothing,' said Petillius. 'Our numbers are few and the men need strong leadership. Before this is settled I will no doubt have need of your counsel and your support. You are a Roman officer and as such your leadership will be required in the next few days. You are no good to me exhausted. Now finish your task and get some rest. That is an order.'

'Thank you, my lord,' said Dellus and continued to his task.

Petillius fastened the cloak and spent the next hour walking the earthen ramparts of the palisade. As he went, he talked quietly with the men on duty, thanking them for their fortitude and giving calm assurance that the situation was manageable. The look on many of their faces reflected the shock they felt at the extent of their defeat. Losing a battle was never a good thing but the extent of the rout had affected them to the core. The legion had been routed and the hundred or so in the camp were all that were left from a strength of over five thousand. It had been slaughter. Finally Petillius descended to the fort floor and made his way to his command tent. Though he was tired, he knew there was much to do. They couldn't just stay here and wait to be overrun; they had to take the initiative. Quite what that was, he had no idea, but he knew he had to make a plan, and make it soon.

Chapter Fifteen

The Lands of the Catuvellauni

Prydain rode his horse slowly through the village, leading the now un-laden pack horse. Alongside him rode Heulwen. The group had decided it would be better if the two of them rode in together, as a couple wouldn't be seen as a threat. Back in their own lands, strangers would be made welcome but it was no secret that many Catuvellauni villages had become heavily Romanised over the years and they couldn't take the risk of close inspection. Their features and accents were typically Khymric and would raise too many questions if noticed by any Roman spies.

The main street was fairly quiet and those people who were out paid them little notice. Both riders dismounted at the village centre and tied the three horses at a hitching rail. A boy with a deformed arm ran over to greet them.

'A coin to water your horses, stranger,' he said.

Prydain nodded.

'How much to find some hay to go with the water?' he asked.

'Another two?' said the boy, more in hope than expectancy.

Prydain pulled three coins from within his coat and handed them over.

'Is there a market?' he asked.

'The market gathers later,' said the boy. 'What is it that you seek?'

'Just food,' said Prydain. 'Dried meat, biscuit, that sort of thing.'

'My cousin slaughters the sheep for the herders,' said the boy, 'and always has mutton hanging in his hut. He will be glad to help; his name is Calder.'

'Where is he to be found?'

The boy pointed along a side street where a muddy path wound its way between many small huts.

'At the end,' he said. 'It is easy to find. He keeps pigs in a pen outside.'

'Thank you,' said Prydain. 'We will be back in a short while. Feed the horses well and rub them down. If their coats shine on my return there will be one more coin.'

The boy's eyes lit up at the thought. Four coins would feed his family for days.

'Thank you, Sir,' he said and ran toward the nearby stables to make a deal.

Prydain and Heulwen made their way down the well-trodden path until the smell of the pigs told them they were near.

'This must be it,' said Heulwen, pinching her nose against the stench.

Prydain called out across the pen of black pig filth.

'Hello there, we seek the man known as Calder.'

For a moment there was no response but eventually the small door in the mud wall opened and the oldest man Prydain had ever seen ducked through the opening. His face was a mass of wrinkles and there wasn't a tooth in his bald head. In his hand he held a bloodied knife and a leather apron covered his dirty tunic and leggings. He squinted toward the two friends.

'Who wants him?' asked the man.

'My name is Prydain,' came the answer, 'and this is Heulwen. We are looking to buy food for our journey and understand you are the man to see.'

'It depends,' said Calder.

'On what?'

'On whether you have coin.'

'We can pay,' said Prydain.

'Then there is business to be done,' said Calder, 'come in.'

Prydain and Heulwen waded through the mud, pushing through the curious pigs that sniffed around their feet.

'Go on in,' said Calder, standing to one side. As they ducked through the door Calder looked warily up and down the path. It was always prudent to know who was watching you in these troubled times.

Inside the hut the smell was no better despite a smoky atmosphere. A half-skinned sheep's carcass hung from the ceiling; its hind legs secured in looped ropes suspended from the roof timbers. A pile of un-cleaned furs lay heaped in the corner and several recently butchered joints of meat hung from curved hooks on an A-frame that ran the length of the hut. Despite the smell, Prydain looked around with interest. Life was never easy in the clans and this was more meat than he had ever seen at one time. Heulwen held her hand over her mouth, trying her best not to inhale the stench.

'State your business,' said Calder as he followed them in. 'And be quick, I am a busy man.'

'I can see that,' said Prydain. 'Is all this yours?'

'Of course not,' said Calder. 'Some of the villagers pay the shepherds to look after a communal flock. I do the butchering for them. In return I get the offal and a roof over my head.'

'You live on the offal,' said Heulwen.

Calder leaned forward and picked up the skinning knife from a stone table. Prydain half held his breath, not sure what the old man intended to do. Calder stared into Prydain's eyes for a moment before leaning forward and plunging his knife into another leather bucket and Heulwen gagged as he withdrew a bloody kidney from amongst the entrails.

'The choicest parts,' said Calder and laughed as Heulwen turned to run out of the hut, the vomit already pouring through her fingers.

Prydain watched her go, quite jealous of the fact she was getting out of the overpowering slaughterhouse.

'Typical woman,' snarled Calder. 'Give them a nice joint and they are happy enough, but once they see a bit of blood it's a different matter.'

Prydain didn't answer. It was all he could do to stop himself from being sick.

'So what do you want?' asked Calder.

'Do you have any smoked meat?' asked Prydain. 'Something that will last a journey of several days.'

'You are in luck,' said Calder. 'I haven't got anything smoked but I've got a salted gammon ready to go. One of my masters had a deal with the brewer's son but he fell from his horse and broke his neck. Took him three days to die, it did. My master wasn't happy as they had a deal but his bad luck is your good fortune.' He walked to the back of the hut and lifted a heavy hessian sack before dragging it over and hoisting it up onto the stone table. He peeled the edges back to reveal the yellowed skin of an enormous pig's leg, complete with trotter. 'Nothing wrong with it,' said Calder, swatting away the flies. 'Cut a few slices off and hang them over a fire. Either that or throw some in a pot with a bundle of roots and you've got yourself a soup. Last for weeks, that will.'

'How much?' asked Prydain.

'That depends what you are paying with,' said Calder.

'Coin,' said Prydain.

'Copper or silver?'

'Gold,' said Prydain.

Calder stared at Prydain and his eyes narrowed suspiciously.

'You've got gold coin?' he asked.

'I have,' said Prydain. 'Don't ask how because I won't tell you.'

'No business of mine,' said Calder. 'Be you brigand or merchant, business is business and for a golden coin I will throw some extras in.'

'Like what?' asked Prydain.

'Couple of hearts,' said Calder, 'some kidneys and you can have that sheep's head if you want. Killed fresh this morning.'

'Throw in that goose outside and we have a deal,' said Prydain, 'but you can keep the sheep's head.'

'Agreed,' said Calder and wiped his hand on his apron before holding it out for the promised coin.

'Meat first,' said Prydain.

Calder hesitated.

'Let me see,' he said.

Prydain pulled a leather pouch from beneath his cloak and extracted a gold coin.

'I'll go and get the goose,' said Calder. 'Do you want it killed?'

Prydain nodded. A few minutes later Calder returned with the limp body of the goose over his shoulders. Once it was in a fresh sack, he turned to Prydain once more.

'The coin?' he said.

Prydain flicked it over and watched as Calder used his knife to check it was indeed gold.

'Can't be too careful,' he said once he was satisfied.

'Where can I get bread and biscuit?' asked Prydain.

'There are many bakers on the far side of the village,' said Calder, 'but surely there is no bread worth a gold coin?'

'You can't eat gold, Calder,' said Prydain as he hoisted the sack over his shoulder.

'If you have gold, who needs to eat?' said Calder.

'I think we are done,' said Prydain and ducked out of the doorway to find Heulwen.

Calder watched him go before pulling out the gold coin again. Only Romans or brigands had such riches these days and that man was no Roman. Without another thought he followed him out of the hut and down the lane before disappearing down a side alley.

–

Prydain made his way back toward the centre of the village, looking all the while for Heulwen. Though he couldn't find her, he wasn't unduly worried and after dropping the meat sacks off at the stables, made his way to find the street of bakers. During his time at the slaughter-house, the village had become busier and children were playing in the central clearing while their families laid out their wares on sack cloth around the edges or offered their skills to whoever passed them by. Tailors stood behind hand barrows, hoping that a brand-new tunic would be preferable to the second-hand rags offered by many of the desperate people around the square. Farmers brought turnips and field greens from their farms as well as live sheep and baskets of eggs, while brewers lifted buckets of stale smelling ale onto trestles confident their particular commodity would sell quite well.

Covered carts parked against walls, each offering the more private services that could be found in busy markets such as these. Soothsayers, Shamen and magicians offered the older people hope, while the younger men hung around the whores' wagons, summoning the courage to venture into the welcoming silks of their perfumed boudoirs.

Children taunted the many loose dogs around the square, their joint cacophony being exaggerated by the scolding of the adults and Prydain knew this scene could be anywhere in the Khymru if it hadn't been for one differentiating fact, the presence of a dozen or so Roman Auxiliaries wandering in pairs through the crowd.

Prydain walked amongst the busier part of the crowd, hoping to blend in unnoticed as he crossed the square. Within moments he was in the relative safety of a side street as he made his way toward the welcoming smell of warm bread. This time there was more urgency in his manner and he wasted no time in buying a sack of biscuits from the nearest dealer before making his way back toward the stable. A disturbance had broken out in the square and a crowd gathered around two men arguing over an unpaid debt, obviously hoping it would break into a fight. Prydain took the opportunity to make his way toward the stable, keeping to the side of the square as much as possible but had gone no more than twenty paces when a voice called out, stopping him dead in his tracks.

'You there,' said the voice. 'Hold still.'

Prydain looked around and his heart sank as he saw a large man with a scarred face standing next to the slaughter man he had done business with less than an hour earlier.

'That's him,' said Calder to the armed man. 'He has more gold on him than you or I will ever see. I tell you, there's something strange going on there.'

Prydain looked around quickly, hoping for a quick escape but the thug stepped toward him.

'Don't even think about it, stranger,' he said. 'Just back up against the wall and show me the purse.'

'My purse is my own,' said Prydain, 'and no business of anyone but me.'

'Wrong,' said the thug. 'Tales of brigands abound in these parts and I do not know your face. Perhaps the contents of your purse are not of honest origin.'

'Just stick him,' said Calder, 'and we will share the contents. I will vouch he reached for a blade.'

'Wait,' said Prydain. 'It is true I have coin and you can have it.' He reached beneath his coat and pulled out the purse. 'Let me leave freely and this is yours.' He tossed the purse over to fall at the man's feet.

'Check it,' said the thug and Calder leapt forward to pick up the leather pouch. Within seconds he had undone the leather lace and poured some of the contents into his hand, the gold coins glistening in the sun.

'Told you,' he said, stifling a laugh, 'we are rich. Let's get out of here.'

'Give it to me,' snarled the man.

Calder handed over the purse.

'Equal shares,' hissed Calder. 'We had a deal.'

'Where there's one purse, who's to say there aren't more?' asked the man.

'There are no more,' said Prydain. 'You have what you want, now let me go.'

'Not going to happen, stranger,' said the thug, drawing a large cleaver from beneath his cloak. 'This isn't your lucky day.'

As the huge man strode forward Prydain dropped the sack of biscuits and drew his own sword, much to the surprise of both attackers.

'Back off,' snarled Prydain, 'or it is you who will die this day.'

The man paused but did not withdraw.

'We will see,' he said and lunged forward to the assault, swinging his heavy blade at Prydain's head.

Prydain deflected the blade but the strength of the blow forced him back, causing him to lose his balance and drop his own weapon to the floor. The thug instantly followed up his advantage, forcing Prydain up against the wall. It took all of Prydain's strength to hold the blade from his throat but he knew the bigger man's strength would soon tell.

'Stick him,' hissed Calder. 'Do it quick before someone notices.'

The man's hand crept closer and though Prydain strained to hold the blade away, within seconds he could feel the edge against his throat.

'Goodbye, stranger,' hissed the thug through rotten teeth and despite his imminent death, Prydain gagged at the stench of his fetid breath.

Suddenly a shout rang out.

'Prydain!'

The thug turned his head quickly to assess the new threat but didn't release the pressure.

'Don't worry,' shouted Calder, 'it's just his woman. Do it!'

Out of the corner of his eye, Prydain saw a flash of movement from Heulwen and a second later, a blade span through the air to sink deep into his attacker's throat with a sickening thud. The would-be assassin's eyes widened in shock and he staggered backward, clawing at the weapon in panic. Prydain reached down to retrieve his own sword from the dirt and without pause, plunged it through the man's chest. He turned to face Calder but the old man was already shuffling toward the crowd.

'Come on,' said Heulwen, 'we have to get out of here.'

Prydain picked up the purse and retrieved Heulwen's knife.

'I think this is yours,' he said and tossed it over to the girl. Together they walked quickly through the square toward the stable.

'The horses are ready,' whispered Heulwen, 'at least the boy has honour, unlike his kin.'

'It is a disease spread by the presence of the Romans,' said Prydain. 'In their eyes, everything in this world is measured against monetary value and as such can be bought, even loyalty.'

Within moments they reached the stables where the horses were waiting for them, looking fresh after their attention from the stable boy.

'Sir, I did what you requested,' he said as they approached. 'Fed and watered as you asked. You said I could have an extra coin?'

'And you shall,' said Prydain mounting his horse. 'Is there another way out of this village?'

'Down there,' said the boy pointing down a side alley. 'It takes you to a ford in the river.'

'Good,' said Prydain. 'One last task, boy. If anyone asks, tell them we rode toward the main gate. Can you do that?'

'I can,' said the boy, 'but…' His sentence went unfinished as a gold coin fell at his feet.

'But that's…'

'It's the price of loyalty,' said Prydain. 'Will you do it?'

The boy nodded and picked up the coin.

'Thank you, Sir.'

'Spend it well, boy,' said Prydain and without looking back, led Heulwen and the pack horse down the narrow alley away from the village.

'That was close,' said Heulwen when they had crossed the river.

'Too close,' said Prydain. 'From now on I think we will rely on our hunting bows. Civilisation is too dangerous.'

Chapter Sixteen

The Lands of the Iceni

Rianna struck her sword over and over again against the trunk of a tree. Her wounds were tightly bound and she felt confident the freshly healed skin would hold when it came to conflict. They had been encamped in the forest for over a week and each day brought another level of strength to her sword arm. She knew that the day was rapidly approaching when her life may depend on her skill with blade.

Her training session was mid flow when a disturbance back amongst the queen's tents made her spin around in concern. People were running everywhere and raised voices added to the confusion. Rianna wiped the sweat from her brow and started to run toward the camp, afraid that they were under attack. As she approached, she heard the voice of Boudicca raised above the rest, issuing commands to all those around her, but though Rianna had heard her queen like this many times before, this time there was something different about her voice. There was fear.

Rianna ran amongst the tents, trying to work out what was happening and within moments came across Boudicca talking to one of the clan's scouts. As she approached, the scout wheeled his horse and rode away, closely followed by his ten men.

'Boudicca,' called Rianna as she approached. 'What's happening? Are we under attack?'

Boudicca turned and stared at Rianna for a moment before answering.

'Attack? No, nothing like that,' she said 'It's Lannosea.'

'What about her?'

'She's gone,' said Boudicca. 'Nobody has seen her since last night.'

-

Lannosea stumbled through the depths of the forest. Her legs were lacerated from the thorn bushes and her hair fell in a tangle of untended knots about her face. Despite her exhaustion, she knew she had to find water and if possible, something to eat. She had been walking for two days without any food or water, except that which she sucked from the occasional muddy puddle she found amongst the forest debris. At night she sought shelter from the beasts amongst the higher branches of the trees.

It wasn't supposed to have been like this. Her sister seemed to be handling the memory of the abuse well but Lannosea couldn't get it out of her mind. Every minute of every day since the assault, she had thought of nothing else. The pain, the shame and the overwhelming stink of the soldier's breath on her face as they tore into her body was relived in her mind over and over again. By night her nightmares were replays of the assault while by day she searched her memory to see if she could have done something different to avoid it happening. Her head felt as if there was a beast within trying to escape and despite the care of the Shamen and indeed her mother, Lannosea finally could take no more and had run from the camp to seek solace.

She hadn't meant to go far, just to find a secluded spot amongst the trees, away from the constant battle preparations happening all around her but she had kept on walking and by the time she realised she had gone too far, it was too late. She was lost. That had been two days ago and she had tried in vain to find her way back to the camp with no success. Her feet dragged through the leaves and her face was smeared with blood where she had fallen countless times, once smashing her head against a rock.

'No more,' she mumbled to herself as she went. 'By the gods, no more!'

She stumbled again and lay amongst the rotting under-growth, too weak to even cry. After a few moments, a sound reached her ears and she tilted her head slightly, hoping fervently that it was voices. For a few seconds she wondered what it was but then realised though it wasn't the people she craved, it was something just as important – the sweet sound of running water.

Lannosea pulled herself to her feet and pushed onward, each painful step taking her closer to the welcome sound and she finally emerged onto the banks of a wide stream flowing sweet and clear amongst the trees. Sobbing to herself she stumbled down the bank and dropped to her knees, leaning forward to suck up the freezing, life-giving liquid. The water was painful on her throat at first but she drank deeply. Finally she lifted her head and stared at the reflection below, unable to recognise the face that stared back up at her. Her hand reached forward slowly and touched the surface, sending ripples across the pool and hiding the image from her gaze. For a few seconds she let her fingers play in the gentle current, and her mind wandered to what might have been but within moments reality came flooding back and she smashed her hand into the pool over and over again, screaming as loud as her voice would allow.

'No, no, no...'

Lannosea jumped to her feet and ran downstream. Again and again she stumbled on the stones beneath the surface and finally fell headlong onto the rocky stream bed, screaming in pain as her forearm snapped beneath her. Only the freezing water stopped her from passing out and once again she dragged herself to her feet, following the water downstream, in the hope of finding a village or at least a hut.

Just as she thought she could go no further, the trees started to thin out and within moments the stream fell away and the whole world opened up before her.

She realised she was at the top of an escarpment and stared out over a vista of unbroken tree canopy as far as the eye could see. At first the beauty astounded her but the more she stared, she realised there were no signs of life. No trails cut through the trees and there were no tell-tale wisps of smoke, showing any civilisation where she could find help.

For an age she stared, realizing that the beauty was also her death sentence. Despite this her heart seemed strangely calm and she stepped closer to the edge of the waterfall, looking down toward the misty pool far below. Amongst the rocks the watery mist had formed a rainbow and despite her terrible state, Lannosea smiled at the beauty. She knew she could not go on much further and night was approaching fast. With her broken arm there was no way she could climb a tree and without the safety the boughs would offer, she would likely be killed by a bear or a wolf pack before the dawn broke. If that happened, her spirit would never rest.

Exhausted and weak from hunger her mind was settling. For the first time she found herself thinking of other things away from the assault. The colours around her seemed brighter, the smells crisper and the birdsong louder. The beauty of the scene flooded her brain and the rainbow beckoned her as if it was a gateway.

Lannosea knew what she had to do. It was better to stride through the gateway to the afterlife with head held high, than to become a spirit of the night, forever wandering the forests of the beasts. The way was clear and she felt for the necklace her mother had given her as a child. For a second her smile faded as she realised she had lost it during one of her falls but despite this her mind was set. Her time was done and the after world waited for her.

She pictured her family in her mind and after taking a deep breath, held her arms out wide before stepping out over the cliff edge.

–

Miles away, Rianna rode into the camp, exhausted from the twenty-four hours she had spent in the saddle. She slid from her horse and after allowing a slave to lead the spent animal away, made her way over to Boudicca's tent. As she approached, Heanua emerged and looked at Rianna with hope in her eyes. Rianna just shook her head silently and the young girl's face fell along with her hope.

'Is your mother here?' asked Rianna.

'She is inside,' said Heanua and stepped to one side.

Rianna ducked into the tent expecting to see Boudicca briefing fresh search parties. It had been a week since Lannosea's disappearance and thousands of warriors had been deployed in all directions to search for her but with no success. For the first few days Boudicca had been frantic and had ridden amongst the search parties, desperately seeking her daughter, as indeed had Rianna, but over the past day word had been sent to all the searchers to return to camp. Rianna looked at Boudicca expecting to see a drained woman, beset with grief but what she saw was completely different.

Boudicca stood at the far edge of a crude table with a deerskin map spread before her. Around the table edge stood several warriors, most of whom Rianna recognised by sight as chieftains of the larger tribes in the area. Boudicca herself was wearing a leather tunic over a chainmail undercoat and her flowing red hair was tied back out of her way as she pored over the map.

'My Queen...' started Rianna and Boudicca looked across the table at her friend.

'Rianna, you have returned,' said Boudicca. 'Good. You are just in time to hear the news.'

'About Lannosea?' asked Rianna.

'No,' said Boudicca after a pause. 'Lannosea is dead. It is time to move on.'

Rianna stifled a sob and her hand flew to cover her mouth. For a few seconds she struggled to keep her emotions in check in front of the warlords but gradually she trusted herself to speak again.

'Where is her body?' she asked.

'There is no body,' said Boudicca, 'live or otherwise. I have called off the search.'

Rianna's brow lowered in confusion.

'But if there is no body, how can you be sure she is dead?' she asked. 'She could be wandering around out there as we speak, weak and frightened.'

'It has been almost eight days,' said Boudicca, 'and there has been not one sign of her. Either she has been captured by the Romans or taken by the beasts. Either way, she is beyond our help.'

'But...' started Rianna.

'Don't you think I hurt, Rianna?' shouted Boudicca. 'Don't you think I hate myself for my actions? There is a pain in my heart greater than any blade could inflict but I have to face the truth. The gods are punishing me, Rianna and have seen fit to take her from me. If I do not make my peace with them, Heanua could be next.'

'Punishing you? Why would the gods punish you? I do not understand.'

'The Shamen have cast the bones, Rianna, and they show anger at my indecision in the face of the enemy. Too often I have doubted my role in this and as we speak, I have allowed myself to waste more time while the enemy lick their wounds and gather their strength. This uprising is bigger than me, Rianna, and bigger than Lannosea. She is gone but our destiny remains and with it, a resolve reborn. It is time to seek the trail forward and continue that we started.'

'But...'

'Enough, Rianna. See to your needs and pass the word for the army to prepare. I have news that the Roman Governor Suetonius approaches Londinium with the Gemina legion and if we move quickly, we can trap him there. It is done, Rianna, we ride with the dawn's light.'

Boudicca returned her attention to the map alongside her warlords and after a few second's pause, Rianna left the tent to seek some much-needed food. Her head was throbbing with the implications and her heart was heavy. But despite it all, she knew that Boudicca was right. Their task was greater than any one individual and if Boudicca was willing to put the future of Britannia before her own daughter, then who was Rianna to argue. What was done was done. Lannosea was dead, but the revolt was very much alive.

Fifty miles away Cassus looked back down the lines of his cohort. They were strewn along either side of the pathetic track the Britons had the audacity to call a road. Cassus knew that had it been a Roman road they would have been at their destination two days earlier but the pull of the mud had slowed them as efficiently as any heavy pack. Almost a quarter of his men had fallen by the wayside, each a victim of the terrible pace he had set them and though they would be picked up by those coming behind, their sword arms were lost to him in the event of a fight. The pace had been hard with only minimal rest breaks to eat or drink. Blistered feet had been treated with the ointments of the Medicus and bandaged tightly but many of those still with him were now limping.

A party of riders galloped back down the path toward him and Cassus stood up as he recognised the lead officer. It was Attellus, the Tribune who doubted him back at the Cerrig of the Deceangli. Cassus could see the urgency on the man's face and realised he was the bearer of bad news.

'Hail, Attellus,' said Cassus as the Tribune reined in his horse. 'Do you have word of the Ninth?'

'I do,' said Attellus. 'Do you have water? We have ridden hard.'

Cassus beckoned a slave with a goatskin of water and gave it to the now dismounted officer. Attellus drank deeply before passing the skin to the next man in line.

'Cassus,' said Attellus, staring at the soldier. 'I have news of the worst kind.'

'Then spit it out, Attellus,' said Cassus.

'It's the Ninth,' said Attellus, 'they have suffered a great defeat.'

'At whose hands?' asked Cassus, already guessing the answer.

'Boudicca,' spat Attellus. 'It would seem her army is as great as the ants beneath our feet.'

'How many casualties?' asked Cassus.

'They were wiped out, Cassus, almost to a man.'

'You are sure of this?'

'Our scouts have picked up some survivors,' said Attellus. 'Their tale is one of devastation.'

'And the Eagle?'

'Nobody knows,' said Attellus. 'The standards are missing as is Legate Petillius. We can only hope he escaped though I fear his head adorns a heathen saddle as we speak.'

'Then our march has been in vain,' said Cassus, looking back along the column of men.

'You have pushed them hard,' said Attellus.

'They are Romans,' said Cassus. 'It is what we do.'

'Exhausted men are weak in the fight,' said Attellus.

'Not these men,' said Cassus, 'they are the best Rome can offer. I would trust my life in any of their hands, no matter how weary.'

'It may come to that,' said Attellus.

'How?' asked Cassus. 'Surely Suetonius doesn't expect us to face this woman alone. The fate of the Ninth would suggest there is only defeat on that path. We should seek the strength of the other legions before drawing swords.'

'Are you afraid, Cassus?'

'Of death, no, of defeat, yes,' came the reply. 'This woman presents a threat long dormant but always there, the unification of Britannia. Unchecked she will unite the tribes but strike too soon and their horizons will know no bounds. What does Suetonius say?'

'He orders we change our route and head for Londinium,' said Attellus. 'He makes his way there as we speak and looks to find a position of strength from which we can defend against the horde. You are to make haste to support him while I rally the rest of the legion to his side.'

'How far is Londinium?' asked Cassus.

'A day and a half march,' said Attellus. 'You should start as soon as possible.'

'And are the enemy there?'

'Not yet, though our spies say they are no more than a few days away.'

'Then I will allow my men a few hours' sleep,' said Cassus.

'Suetonius is waiting for you,' said Attellus.

'From what you say, a few hours won't make much difference,' said Cassus.

Attellus remounted his horse.

'You are right,' he said. 'It seems the gods have set us on a great road where every sword will be needed before this thing is done. Look to your men, Cassus, and let them know that from this day, we are the ones who are the oppressed.'

'We will never be oppressed,' said Cassus, 'we are Romans.'

'We are but three legions, Cassus. Boudicca has mobilised a nation.' Without another word he pulled on the reins and wheeled his horse to gallop further down the line. Cassus watched him go before calling over his Optio.

'Gather the Centurions,' he said. 'The stakes have changed.'

Taliesin woke beneath the red cloak of the Roman he had killed days earlier. They had stripped the corpse of everything useful and both he and Finian were adorned in various items of the dead man's clothing. The dead soldier had half a bag of biscuits and dried meat in his leather pouch and the two men had used it sparingly to keep them going as they continued their quest to find Boudicca. Though they knew they were headed in the right direction, there was still no sign of the Celtic army and the going was slow due to the continued presence of the odd Roman survivor still wandering the forest. Finally they had crawled beneath a thorn bush and wrapped themselves in the cloak for warmth as they faced yet another night in the forest.

Checking there was no danger, Taliesin left the thorn bush and after urinating against a tree, made his way over to the nearby stream to drink. A flash of silver caught his eye and he realised the stream was teeming with fish. He allowed himself a smile, for one of the things he had enjoyed as a boy was fishing in the streams of his people and he had garnered a bit of a reputation at his continued success. At last there was a chance of some meaningful food and he followed the flow downstream until he found a suitable spot where the bank overhung the water. Laying on his stomach he slowly lowered his hand into the water and moved it beneath the overhang. The gods were with him and almost immediately he felt the cold scaly skin of a resting fish and he had to calm himself in case he scared it off.

'Steady, Taliesin,' he murmured to himself, 'take it easy.'

Gently he used the tips of his fingers to tickle the fish body, knowing full well that as long as he didn't make any sudden movements, the fish would happily stay there and enjoy the sensation. Bit by bit he moved his fingers along the body toward the head until he could feel the openings of the gills. Taliesin took a deep breath. This was the important part; get this wrong and the fish would be gone in a flash. Finally he made his move and with a dramatic lunge, he grabbed the body of the fish while digging his fingers into the gills to get better purchase.

His target thrashed violently but it was too late. Taliesin swung his arm over his head and threw his catch onto the bank behind him. He jumped to his feet and turned to see a fish as long as his forearm thrashing amongst the bracken.

Using the hilt of the knife he had taken from the dead Roman, Taliesin killed the fish before starting to gut it. He knew the catch would go a long way to replacing some of their strength, at least for a day or so and where there was one fish, there had to be others. Finally he had it cleaned and was about to return to Finian when he heard a noise in the woods coming toward him. Quickly he lay down amongst the bracken with the knife in his hand. Though he was weak, he would fight to the death if need be. There was no way he would become a slave once more. Quietly he waited as the threat approached, and he tightened the grip on his knife in anticipation.

The intruder burst into sight and ran past his hiding place. Though it made Taliesin's heart jump, he quickly realised this was no threat. He paused, not sure what to do but within seconds was on his feet again, following the imagined aggressor downstream, realising that far from being a would-be assassin, the intruder could in fact prove to be their salvation.

For several minutes he followed the runner downstream, catching occasional glimpses of the retreating figure. He considered calling out but a combination of caution and fear made him hold his voice; he still wasn't sure what was happening here. Finally he ducked under a thicket and stopped dead in his tracks. The runner was just a few yards ahead and had also stopped.

Taliesin ducked back amongst the thicket and watches as events unfolded. The runner was facing away from him and obviously breathing deeply from the exertion while they contemplated the next step.

At first Taliesin was confused but as it became clearer what was about to happen, he stepped out quietly and approached the person from behind, careful not to startle them. He quickened his pace, unsure if he would be in time, but finally he reached his target and just as the person was about to step forward, he put his hand on their shoulder and spoke a single word that would change his life.

'Don't!'

Petillius stalked the ramparts of his thinly manned fort. The trickle of survivors had dried up and he believed that all those who were able to reach the fort had done so. The wounded had been tended and the men were rested but their predicament was dire. He had no more than a hundred men left alive, from a strength of over five thousand and most of those carried wounds of some description. There was food enough in the camp for a few days but it did not change the fact they were dangerously understrength in the middle of hostile territory. The size of the perimeter meant they would be unable to defend the whole camp should an attack come and they did not have enough able men to construct a smaller palisade. The one good thing was that they had over fifty fit horses due to the amount of cavalry who had managed to escape and there had been no sustained attack as of yet.

Despite this, Petillius knew it was only a matter of time before the assault came. Already, small groups of barbarians were testing the perimeter with feints, seeking the weaker points of the palisade and drawing the attention of the defenders.

The few bows that were left in the fort were handed out amongst the troops but as stocks of arrows were small, each man was instructed to keep their firepower for when the attack came.

Dellus approached him carrying a wooden platter.

'My lord, I have some hot food,' he said.

Petillius looked at the thick slab of meat and his mouth watered at the aroma.

'Have the men eaten?' he asked.

'We killed a lame horse, my lord. The beast has made a hearty broth but I saved this cut for you.'

'An unnecessary luxury, yet welcome all the same,' said Petillius drawing his knife. 'Thank you.' He took the platter from the young Tribune and cut slices off the horse steak.

'Share this with me,' said Petillius, offering the plate.

Dellus speared a slice with his own knife and both men fell silent, chewing thoughtfully as they stared at the tree line a hundred paces away. Finally Dellus spoke again.

'My lord, can I ask you a question?'

'Of course.'

'What are the chances of us getting out of this alive? I'm not afraid of dying, but I was thinking about writing a letter to my parents in case I fall. Perhaps those who follow behind may find my body and send the letter back home.'

'First of all,' said Petillius, 'I would write the letter for nothing is guaranteed. Also I would make peace with your gods, Dellus. There may not be time later. However, saying that, this fight is not yet done and the outcome is uncertain. If Boudicca turns her attention on this fort, it will fall within the hour and our fate is sealed. However, I hope that she sees us as a distraction only and has eyes on a bigger prize. Yes she may send a smaller unit to deal with us but man for man we are far better than the Celts in any battle.'

'Do you think we have a chance?'

'It is not their swords that worry me, Dellus, but our lack of resources. We have enough for a few days maximum and cannot get out of here to seek fresh supplies. Even now I see shadows amongst the trees but have no idea how many are out there. There may be a hundred, there may be a thousand. Time will tell but it is the one resource we lack most of all. Unless something happens in the next two days, my arm will be forced.'

'You have a plan?'

'I do, but it is dangerous and possibly suicide.'

'I assume it is the best one you have?'

'It is the only one I have,' said Petillius and handed back the platter. The conversation was over.

Chapter Seventeen

Londinium

Suetonius rode through the narrow streets of the vast trading town, ignoring the beggars that pestered him from either side. Ordinarily his personal guard would clear the way but with most of his legion spread out over the previous twenty miles, most of the men with him had other things on their mind.

As he passed the dirtier outskirts, the standards of the area changed and the influence of Rome was easily seen. Women in bright colours walked arm in arm enjoying the all too rare Britannic sunshine, while retired Evocati strode in groups of similarly minded men, reliving past battles during their service in the armies of Rome.

All around traders bartered their wares from carts or open doorways and Suetonius recognised many items catering for those with Roman tastes. Bowls of green and black olives joined amphorae of wine, making tables groan under their weight and coloured linens competed with rich silks for space on wooden racks. Exotic fruits added a rainbow of colours and the smell of spices wafted through the air reminding him of the markets of home. Overall it was a sign of a thriving market town and the people went about their business without a care in the world.

Suetonius made his way to the site of an old fortress on the banks of the Tamesas. The riverside fortress had long been dismantled and replaced with a villa that would not have been out of place back on the outskirts of Rome and was the residence of the Procurator, Catus Decianus.

Suetonius and his party pulled up outside the gates of the villa and looked up at the guards in the gate towers.

'Open the gates,' he called.

'On whose orders?' asked the civilian in charge.

'Do you not recognise the banner of the governor?' roared a Centurion at Suetonius' side. 'Open the gates immediately or suffer the consequences.'

The man's face fell and he disappeared from view. A few minutes later the giant gates creaked open and the impatient riders galloped into a courtyard. Servants were running everywhere in panic at the unannounced arrival of the governor of Britannia. Suetonius dismounted and grabbed the nearest servant.

'Where is Catus Decianus?' he growled.

'There,' stuttered the man, pointing toward an outside terrace surrounded with carefully cultivated fruit trees.

The Legate threw the servant to the floor before striding toward the terrace. Behind him he could hear the cries of the gate guard as the Centurion beat him mercilessly with his Vitis. On the terrace, various minor officials stood in groups making small talk as they sipped from ornate wine glasses and several beautiful women sat upon silk covered dais' each draped in the finery only the wealthy could afford. Catus Decianus was standing next to an elaborate pool with his own goblet of wine in his hand, obviously being briefed by a stressed servant about the unexpected arrival.

The Procurator looked up at the sound of the governor's hobnailed boots on the flagstones and his look of concern instantly changed to one of contrived delight.

'Governor,' he said warmly. 'How wonderful to see you. If you had let me know of your impending arrival, I would have laid on a suitable celebration.'

The false smile fell slightly as Suetonius continued his purposeful stride and before he could react, the governor smashed the Procurator across the face with the back of his fist, sending the fat man sprawling on the floor.

Screams echoed around the walls as the women jumped to their feet and the officials shouted their disapproval.

'Silence,' roared Suetonius. 'I am Gaius Suetonius Paullinus, Governor of Britannia. Get out of my sight or suffer the same disgrace, woman or man.'

The news took a few seconds to sink in but as one they all picked up their belongings and left the terrace as quickly as they could. When they had gone, Suetonius turned his attention back to the Procurator sprawled at his feet.

'Get up,' he snarled.

'I will have you hauled before the senate for this,' growled Decianus.

'I look forward to it,' said Suetonius and reached down to grab the collar of the Procurator's toga.

'Unhand me,' shouted Decianus as he was hauled upward.

Suetonius threw him onto a nearby chair before reaching for the small amphorae of wine on the table. Without taking his eyes off the Procurator, he filled his mouth with wine, before spitting it out across the terrace.

'Road dust,' he said before lifting the amphorae again, though this time drinking deeply.

'What do you want, Suetonius?' asked the Procurator quietly.

'I will tell you what I want in good time,' said Suetonius. 'First of all, tell me about Camulodunum.'

Decianus shrugged.

'What of it?'

Suetonius stared in disbelief.

'You don't know do you?'

'Know of what? If you are referring to an uprising from some petty tribal queen, then of course I know and I am awaiting word from Petillius about his retribution. I would imagine the body of that crucified queen surveys her slaughtered army even as we speak.'

'Oh, there are certainly dead bodies, Decianus, thousands of them. Though you would struggle to find a barbarian amongst them, for most are of Roman descent. I would send a unit to count them for you but as this petty queen, as you call her, has razed the city to the ground it would be difficult to find them all, don't you think? Besides, the legions are short of manpower at the moment, as the bodies of five thousand legionaries rot in some cursed field. Five thousand of our countrymen who will never see the seven hills of Rome again.'

'But I don't understand,' stuttered Decianus. 'I know nothing of this.'

'How can you not know, Decianus? I was in the Khymru fighting the Druids, yet I knew.'

'To be fair, you have a network of messengers throughout Britannia,' said Decianus.

'As should you,' shouted Suetonius. 'You are the Procurator, Decianus. It is your duty to know of such things before they happen and to act accordingly. Our Evocati, our citizens, hell, even our client tribes look to you for protection yet while they are slaughtered like cattle you surround yourself with wine and food like a pig at a trough.'

'I never knew,' repeated Decianus, struggling to take in the implications. 'I thought they were nothing but an irritation to be scratched.'

'They are more than an irritation,' said Suetonius, 'they are a gaping wound and while my men die to protect you, you and your kind frolic with whores.'

'What do you want me to do?' asked Decianus.

'Tell me of your defences here,' said Suetonius. 'Brief me about your strengths and weaknesses. What defensive walls do you have? The armouries, the units, any artillery you have in store. Anything you think may be of value. I need to know if we are to protect this town.'

'I'm not sure,' started Decianus, 'I think there are some private units along the Tamesas and of course there are the Evocati but...'

Suetonius shook his head in amazement.

'You don't know,' he said.

'Suetonius, you have to understand this is a trading town and we have little need of such things.'

'You have every need of such things,' shouted Suetonius. 'We are invaders in a lawless country and you live in an insignificant trading post surrounded by barbarians who would behead you as soon as look at you. How can you not be prepared? Even as we speak there is an army tens of thousands strong on your doorstep. They have already slaughtered a legion and will be here within days.'

'I am sorry,' grovelled Decianus, 'I never dreamed...'

'You are unbelievable,' interrupted Suetonius before pacing around the courtyard, his face creased with concern. Finally he returned and faced the Procurator once more.

'You and I have unfinished business, Decianus,' he said 'and there will be a day of reckoning. Until then, I need you alive to limit the amount of blood that is yet to be spilt. This is what I want you to do.'

For the next ten minutes Suetonius instructed the Procurator on what to do. As he did, the fat man's face fell as the implications sank in. Finally Suetonius sat back down and stared at Decianus.

'Is there no other way?' asked Decianus.

'Not that I can see,' said Suetonius. 'My men are the best legion in Rome's army but they are tired from a demanding march across country and would be no match for Boudicca at the moment.'

'The people won't like it,' said Decianus.

'They can do as I say or take their chances. Either way, the choice is theirs. I do not have time to play at politics anymore, there is a war to be won.'

Decianus nodded.

'I will make the arrangements,' he said. 'The heralds will travel the town first thing in the morning.'

'See that they do,' said Suetonius and stood up. 'Do this well, Decianus, and you may still keep your position in the equestrian order. Make a mess of it and I will personally see you stripped of your titles.'

Decianus watched Suetonius leave before calling a slave to bring a bowl of warm, scented water. He needed to summon the heralds but before he did, the cut mouth he had received as a result of the Legate's back hander needed bathing.

'I don't know who he thinks he is,' said Decianus to the few friends who had returned. 'My father is high in the senate and will know of this outrage within days. Nobody strikes me and gets away with it.'

—

The following day Suetonius rode back down to the edge of Londinium and waited for one of the heralds to arrive. He was accompanied by two of his bodyguard but this time he was draped in a cloak of nondescript brown covering his uniform. He wanted to be as invisible as possible amongst the crowd. Within an hour of the dawn the gathered crowd made way for a herald who walked up to the platform and withdrew a parchment. He waited for the noise to die down before making the announcement.

'Citizens of Londinium,' he started. 'This is a proclamation from Gaius Suetonius Paullinus, Legate of the Fourteenth Gemina Martia Victrix and Rome's governor of these islands of Britannia. Let it be known that Camulodunum has fallen to the swords of a heathen hoard to the north. Despite a heroic action by the Legio Nona Hispana, the defeat was total and there are no survivors.'

The crowd talked amongst themselves, unsure how to take the news.

'Furthermore,' continued the herald, 'it is known that these murderers are headed for Londinium and will be here within days.'

This time the disturbance was greater as the crowd realised their safety was at risk.

'Let it also be known,' shouted the herald above the din, 'the legions of Rome are otherwise engaged and are unable to defend Londinium. Rome advises that all who are able should leave the town immediately and seek shelter amongst the forests and hills.'

This time the unease turned to shouting and people started calling out.

'Where is Suetonius?' called one. 'He is the governor. Where are the troops our taxes pay for?'

'Where are we to go?' called another. 'The forests are full of brigands. We will be surely killed.'

'I have no more information save this,' said the herald. 'Rome's legions will not defend you here. Leave this place now or risk the consequences at the hands of Boudicca.' Despite the continued questions, the herald was finished and descended from the platform. Across the square the hooded general turned to the similarly disguised Centurion by his side.

'It is done,' he said. 'Decianus has done his job. Similar announcements are being made as we speak across Londinium.'

'Do you think they will leave?' asked the Centurion.

'Some will,' said Suetonius, 'others will think they are safe and the worst will never happen.'

'Perhaps they are right,' said the Centurion. 'Most of those who dwell within the town are of Britannic descent.'

'They are,' said Suetonius, 'but when an army as big as this is mobilised it is very difficult to reign them in. Especially as they have tasted blood. We cannot face this Boudicca yet and need time to form a strategy. Londinium is just a jumble of huts and can be rebuilt.'

'And the people?' asked the Centurion.

'They have been warned,' said Suetonius, 'and their fate is in their own hands. Come, we have a legion to tend and a battle plan to make.'

The two men returned to the forest edge where riders were holding their horses and without further ado, galloped back to join their legion.

Chapter Eighteen

Fifty miles North West of Londinium

Cassus approached the tent of the governor. The legion had reformed in an open valley and they had established a secure fort on a nearby hilltop. The steep slopes and clear fields of view meant there was no chance of any surprise attack but even so, the auxiliary cavalry had been deployed to form a circular perimeter over a mile away and roving scouts roamed further afield, keeping abreast of any developments in the local villages. The men within the fort walls took full advantage of the enforced break and tended to the injuries received from the battle on Mona and during the enforced march. Suetonius had summoned his officers to his command tent to discuss the military situation.

'Gentlemen,' he said when everyone was present. 'As you know, Boudicca is on the outskirts of Londinium with an army the size of which this island has never seen before. Many residents have left Londinium but many more have decided to stay in the mistaken belief they would be safe.'

'How do we know they are not?' asked an officer.

'We have Exploratores amongst Boudicca's ranks,' answered Suetonius, 'and their intelligence tells us the mood is one of retribution, but even if we had the numbers, it does not make sense to risk Roman lives on what is a mere trading town. This Boudicca is a wounded animal and there is no greater risk in my eyes.'

'So what do we do?' asked another officer.

'First of all we wait,' said Suetonius, 'and watch how this woman operates. Our scouts will learn her tactics and along with the intelligence from the Exploratores, we will build a picture of her methods. Hopefully the fire in their bellies will burn itself out with the destruction of Londinium and her army will disperse back to whence they came, however, whether she leaves or not, our knowledge will grow by the day.'

'And if she attacks here?'

'If she attacks this fort, she will find nothing but a burning palisade and horse shit,' said Suetonius.

A gasp rippled around the room as they realised what he was proposing.

'You mean we will run,' said the officer in amazement.

'If that's the way you want to see it, then yes, we will run.'

'Since when has any legion done so before a sword is drawn?' shouted a Tribune. 'It is a shame no legionary will bear.'

'It is but a tactic toward a greater goal,' said Suetonius, 'victory.'

'You can dress it as you will,' said the Tribune, 'but they will still see our backs running before them. My father served in the Gemina as did his father before him and never have they turned their backs on an undefeated enemy. I see no reason why such an illustrious legion should do so now.'

'The Gemina will do as I say,' shouted the general, and the room fell silent at the unexpected outburst. 'This woman is a greater threat than we have realised. Already she has laid waste to a city and slaughtered an entire legion. The Ninth Hispana have battle honours as great as the Gemina and Petillius is a war-hardened Legate, yet she swatted them aside as if they were horse flies. What makes you think the Gemina will fare any better?'

Another gasp rippled around the command tent. It was unheard of for a Commander to publicly doubt the abilities of his legion.

'So what do you propose we do?' asked the Tribune.

'First of all we will go firm here,' said the Legate. 'We will lick our wounds and rebuild our strength. At the same time we will send our spies amongst them and learn how her mind works. When I think we have enough information, then and only then will we formulate our plans. I have no intention of letting this woman drive us from Britannia but at the moment we are in her lands fighting on her terms and that has to change. We will send immediate messages to the Augusta and Victrix legions requesting support and by the time we are ready to face her, we will have almost twenty thousand men at arms.'

'What about Londinium?' asked a voice.

'Londinium is already lost to us,' said Suetonius, 'but it is no more than a trading town. Camulodunum was a far greater loss.'

'What are our orders?' asked a Tribune.

'Keep the perimeter guard refreshed at a distance of one day's march,' said Suetonius. 'Make sure they have fresh horses and if Boudicca's army turn this way, I want to know about it within hours. Allow the wounded men to heal but instigate battle training immediately for those who are fit. I want every able man ready for the battle to come, whether that be next month or three months from now.'

For the next half hour Suetonius outlined his defensive requirements until finally the tent emptied and the Legate was left alone with Cassus.

'You disapprove?' said Suetonius, pouring a goblet of wine.

'On the contrary, I support your strategy,' replied Cassus.

'Really? You surprise me. I thought an out and out soldier like you would want to plough in with Gladius drawn.'

'The time will come for such action but now is not that time.'

'Wine?' asked Suetonius, offering an empty goblet.

'Thank you. No. I remained behind as I have a proposition.'

'A proposition? I am intrigued.'

'My lord, the location you have chosen here is excellent and affords adequate measures for defence. The extra training you have requested is well within the abilities of the other Centurions and as you have mentioned on more than one occasion, I am no parade ground soldier.'

'That you certainly are not,' said Suetonius. 'So what are you proposing, Cassus?'

'My lord, as you know I spent six years in the Exploratores. I propose you allow me to ride out and infiltrate the ranks of Boudicca. I speak their language as well as a native and with a good disguise, I reckon I can breach her outer ranks.'

'To what end,' asked Suetonius, 'assassination?'

'I fear there is no time to gain the trust to get that near,' said Cassus, 'besides, I think assassination will only rally her troops. We need to inflict a crushing victory on her army if we are to put down this rebellion effectively.'

'I agree,' said Suetonius, 'but I fail to see what you hope to gain. There are already Exploratores within her ranks and I am briefed regularly.'

'I realise that, my lord,' said Cassus, 'but they see with detached eyes and have no knowledge of our needs. I have lived with these people and understand how they think. I also know the strengths and weaknesses of our own men. If I can see this army's tactics for myself, then it gives us an advantage in any future conflict.'

'But if you are found out, I lose a Primus Pilus.'

'I will not be found out,' said Cassus.

Suetonius paused and drank from the goblet while he considered his response.

'How long do you need?' he asked.

'One month,' answered Cassus.

Again Suetonius considered carefully before answering.

'You can have ten days, no more.'

'But…'

'I need you here, Cassus. The men look up to you. Within ten days, most will be fighting fit again and I want you to lead their training by example. Ten days or nothing.'

'Ten days it is,' said Cassus and turned to leave the tent.

'Don't you go and do something stupid like getting yourself killed,' said the Legate. 'It has been five years since you were an Exploratore.'

'It's the last thing on my mind,' said Cassus, 'and besides, Exploratore training stays with you forever.'

–

Forty miles away, Petillius was sleeping under a cover of furs when a commotion dragged him from his slumber.

Quickly he jumped up and grabbing his Gladius, ducked out of his tent. Ten riders had been let through the gates and the soldier in charge was talking to Tribune Dellus. Petillius recognised the insignia on the saddle blanket.

'Let him through,' he said, 'he is from the Gemina.'

The men moved aside and the cavalry man rode forward, dismounting before the Legate.

'Hail, Petillius,' said the rider, 'I am Decurion Conatus of the Gemina scouts. Suetonius will be relieved to learn you still live.'

'The governor knows of our plight?' asked Petillius.

'Only the outcome of the battle,' said the rider, 'not of your survival. The Gemina marched as fast as we could from the lands of the Deceangli but were too late to offer help.'

'Come inside,' said Petillius and led the way into the tent. 'What news of the campaign against the Druids?'

'The campaign went well,' said Conatus, 'and the island has been laid waste. The battle was an overwhelming victory.'

'An outcome not shared here,' said Petillius.

'I hear the enemy were tenfold your number,' said the scout.

'Even so,' said the Legate, 'the taste is sour in my mouth. Tell me, how you are here? Is Gemina camped close by?'

'No my lord. The legion has gone to ground in the west. The situation with Boudicca changes by the day and Suetonius garners his strength before facing the hoard.'

'So why are you here?'

'My unit was sent to find any survivors,' said Conatus, 'and we saw your camp smoke from the hills. We thought the fort may be overrun but decided to check anyway.'

'Thanks to the gods that you did,' said Petillius, 'but how did you get through the enemy lines?'

'There are no enemy lines in the forest,' said Conatus. 'Yes there are pockets of barbarians dotted throughout the area but the main army is camped on the outside of Londinium.'

'That explains it,' said Petillius.

'Explains what, my lord?'

'Why we haven't been overrun,' said the Legate. 'This devil queen eyes the greater prize and sees us as a minor distraction. Tell me, how strong are the enemy in the woods?'

'Hard to say, my lord. A few thousand I suppose, but they are well spread out.'

'Good,' said Petillius, his eyes wide with excitement. 'This is exactly the opportunity we were hoping for. Get your command fed and rested, Decurion. Before the sun rises, they will need every ounce of strength they have.'

–

Deep in the forest, Lannosea spun around in fright and stared at the boy who had pulled her back from the edge.

'Who are you?' she asked.

'I am Taliesin of the Deceangli,' he answered. 'Who are you?'

Lannosea looked around nervously.

'I am Lannosea of the Iceni,' she said. 'Daughter of Boudicca.'

Taliesin's eyes widened in shock. For a moment he didn't answer but looked at the bedraggled girl for a few moments before smiling.

'If you say so,' he said. 'Now why not step away from that cliff before you fall.'

'What do you mean, if I say so?' asked Lannosea with a frown. 'I am who I say I am and will have you whipped for not believing me.'

'Well, you don't look like the daughter of a warrior queen,' said Taliesin.

Lannosea looked down at herself. Her dress was torn and covered in mud and she knew her hair was a tangled mess.

'I am Lannosea,' she repeated quietly, 'and I am the daughter of Boudicca.'

Before Taliesin could answer, the girl collapsed and fell headlong into the current. Taliesin realised the danger and jumped in to grab her before the water carried her over the edge. With one hand holding a tree root, he pulled the girl to the water's edge but was unable to drag her up the bank.

'Wake up,' he shouted, trying to rouse the girl from her stupor. 'Lannosea, I can't do this by myself, you have to help me.'

Lannosea slowly responded and placed her feet against the stream bed, pushing hard as Taliesin pulled her out. Finally they both lay on the bank, the girl crying in pain as Taliesin gasped for breath. After a few moments he sat up and looked at the girl.

'Seriously,' he said, 'who are you?'

'I spoke the truth,' said Lannosea, 'Boudicca is my mother.'

'If that is the truth,' said Taliesin, 'why were you about to throw yourself from the falls?'

Lannosea looked up at him and shook her head.

'I can't tell you,' she murmured, 'it hurts too much.'

'Does the Queen know you are here?'

Lannosea shook her head.

'I have wandered this forest for days,' she said, 'and have no idea how to get back.'

'You are lost?'

Lannosea nodded.

'When was the last time you ate?' asked Taliesin.

The girl shrugged her shoulders.

'I don't remember.'

Taliesin stood and wandered down the bank until he found the fish he had caught earlier. He returned to Lannosea and sat beside her before using the knife to cut slices from the fish.

'Here,' he said, passing her some of the pink flesh. 'I know it's not cooked but it is food.'

'I can't,' said Lannosea.

'You must,' said Taliesin. 'Take small chunks and swallow them whole.'

Lannosea did as she was told and though she gagged, she managed to keep it down. Taliesin took a slice for himself and chewed on the fibrous flesh as he watched the girl.

'Are you truly the daughter of Boudicca?' he asked.

Lannosea nodded.

'I am,' she said.

'She must be worried if you have been lost all this time.'

'Perhaps,' said Lannosea, 'but she has other things on her mind.'

'Like what?'

'The attack on Londinium,' said Lannosea.

Taliesin swallowed the piece of fish in his mouth before staring at her again.

'Boudicca is going to attack Londinium?'

'Yes, why?'

'Because we have been looking for her but had no idea where she was, but if she is going toward Londinium, we should be able to find her.'

'How?'

'A while ago we were being held in a Roman fort…'

'We?'

'A friend of mine,' explained Taliesin. 'Anyway, we were prisoners there and I overheard a rider saying he had ridden half a day from Londinium in the east. That means if we walk south east, we could be there in less than two days.'

'But why would you do that?' asked Lannosea.

'I left the Khymru to seek Boudicca,' said Taliesin. 'If what you say is true, then she is no more than a few days away. Find her and I can help rid this country of the Roman filth.'

'Are you sure?'

'Absolutely, but first we have to get you dry and look after that arm. Come on, Finian will know what to do.'

Chapter Nineteen

The Outskirts of Londinium

Boudicca left her tent and looked around the gathered warlords waiting for her. Together they stood in silence until two warriors led a white bull into the clearing, holding it still while the Shamen anointed its head with oils and flowers. Boudicca stepped forward and stood in front of the bull. More men helped hold the animal still while yet another pulled the harness, forcing it to extend its neck. Boudicca lifted her head to face the heavens.

'Andraste,' she called, 'I offer this bull in sacrifice to your name. Drink deeply of its pure liquid for surely this day, the rivers will be soiled with Roman blood.'

Another warrior with an enormous sword stepped forward and lifted the weapon high above his head.

'Andraste, lead us to victory in your name,' shouted Boudicca and the warrior swung the sword downward cutting cleanly through the neck of the young bull.

The strike was true and the animal's head rolled away in the dust but the body remained upright, held in place by the warriors on either side. Fountains of blood from the severed arteries sprayed over Boudicca, and she opened her arms in supplication, welcoming the sign from her God.

The surrounding warlords shouted their appreciation at the clean kill and when the warriors finally let the animal fall, the Shamen fell upon the still twitching corpse, desperate to examine the entrails for divination. Above the cheering Boudicca heard the sound of horses and watched Rianna ride the war chariot into the clearing.

'Ready, my Queen,' she said, when the chariot came to a stop.

Boudicca looked around at her warlords, every one of them cheering their leader. Finally her gaze fell on Heanua watching from the edge of the clearing. For a second Boudicca thought she saw a hint of disapproval in the girl's eyes but finally, Heanua drew her sword and lifted it to her mouth before raising it high.

'In Andraste's name,' shouted the girl and Boudicca's heart leapt. She had failed one daughter but this one was behind her. She climbed aboard the chariot and turned to face Rianna.

'It is time, friend,' she said, 'let them go.'

Rianna cracked a whip and the spirited horses leapt forward. Within moments they were clear of the treeline and galloping out onto the plains. A deafening roar rose from the massed ranks of the Britannic warriors and though she knew her army was large, seeing its sheer size for the first time astonished her. Rianna pulled hard on the reins and sent the chariot flying along the front of the cheering army and as she passed the massed ranks of warriors, Boudicca held up a spear in recognition of their strength. Surely no army on earth, Roman or otherwise could withstand such a force.

Behind her rode a hundred warlords, each carrying the banners of their tribes and the cheers increased as factions of the army recognised their own colours. Finally Boudicca's chariot topped a small rise and Rianna reined in the four lathered horses. Though Boudicca knew her words wouldn't reach the majority of the army, she knew the warlords would pass them on. She climbed up onto the edge of the chariot, using one of the spears for balance as she addressed the cavalry and chariots before her.

'People of Britannia,' she called. 'For almost twenty years we have been downtrodden by the invaders from across the seas. They have raped our women and enslaved our men. They have killed our priests and burned our temples. They have grown fat while our children have starved but today we say, no more. We have already laid waste to their false city and slaughtered the legion sent to destroy us. Those men witnessed at first hand the strength of our resolve but that was just a lover's caress compared to the wrath we are about to unleash. Even as I speak, Nero's best hides from us, trembling in fear at the sound of our marching feet. They cower like scared dogs behind palisades of puny timber in fear of our ire. Make no mistake, in the days to come there will be a reckoning but until then, we will send them a message they will never forget. Look to your front for before us is a symbol of everything they stand for. Do not hold back this day for the only thing Britannic about Londinium is the soil upon which it sits. Harden your hearts and send it the way of Camulodunum. Spare nobody for everyone within that forsaken town is tainted by Roman hands.'

She lifted her spear high and aimed it toward the sprawling town before her. Her hair blew in the wind and bulls blood dripped from her chin.

'For Andraste and Britannia,' she screamed.

'For Andraste and Britannia,' answered those in earshot and the roar spread down the ranks of chariots like a wave.

Rianna cracked the whip again and the horses bolted forward, closely followed by hundreds of war chariots, each bearing scythe-like blades on the hubs of their wheels. Behind them the roar was taken up by the foot soldiers and fifty thousand warriors raced down the hill toward the Roman trading town. The assault on Londinium had begun.

—

A mile away, hundreds of people stood before the tented village that made up the outer edges of Londinium. Families with children huddled together to stare at the black masses in the distance, not sure what to do. They had heard Boudicca was coming but hadn't quite believed it; besides, they were also Britons and Boudicca wouldn't kill her own people… would she?

At first, they wandered toward the hoard as it started moving, keen to greet their fellow Britons but as the impetus became clear, realisation dawned and they started to retreat back toward the town. Within moments the intention of the approaching army became clear as the chariots thundered toward them. All doubt of Boudicca's intentions disappeared and the people turned in panic, seeking the safety of the wooden houses and narrow streets of the town.

Those who were too old or stubborn to run held their arms out in recognition, pleading for mercy but any hopes they held were shattered by crushing hooves and spinning blades as the chariots smashed into them. The air was torn asunder by the screams of women and children alike but the riders took no notice and vented their pent-up rage on anyone within range. Within minutes the chariots split up and wheeled in two directions, following the ill-defined perimeter to the south and north respectively. Those who had escaped their ferocity, either by luck or subterfuge picked themselves up from the dust and stared after them in shock. For a fleeting moment they thought they had been saved by the gods but soon realised that all hope was lost as they returned their gaze to the oncoming foot soldiers.

The army ripped through the remains of the tented village, slaughtering any who had survived the chariots. The impetus went unabated and within minutes they were at the edge of the town, venting their fury on anyone and anything that moved. Hundreds upon hundreds of warriors followed each other between the wooden buildings as they headed into the town, cutting down everything in their path. Those behind kicked down doors and rampaged through the buildings, murdering man and woman alike in their blood lust. Children suffered a similar fate and babies were thrown from upper windows to be crushed beneath the rampaging army's feet.

Boudicca's chariot had pulled up before the main gates and she watched as the main army poured past her. The scythes on her chariot were scarlet from human blood and her spear arm was tired from use.

'You,' she shouted toward a passing warrior wearing the colours of the Iceni, 'attend me.'

The warrior ran over, his sword still un-blooded.

'My Queen,' he gasped, out of breath from the run.

'Can you drive a team?'

'I can.'

'Then climb aboard, I have a task for you.'

Rianna looked at Boudicca in confusion.

'Boudicca, what are you doing?'

'Surely you don't think our part in this day is done,' said Boudicca, selecting a short-handled spear from a scabbard, 'those who have fallen beneath our wheels are only a symptom of the disease that wracks our country. The infection lies within the streets before us and I, for one, intend cutting it out. You can join me or chase down those that flee.'

Rianna handed over the reins to the young warrior and drew her sword.

'I am at your side, my Queen,' she said with a grin.

Boudicca turned to the warrior.

'Take my chariot back to the camp. I will see that you are well rewarded for being denied the battle.'

Both women jumped from the chariot and watched it disappear back toward the camp.

'Ready?' asked Boudicca.

'Always,' said Rianna and both women joined the seemingly never-ending ranks of soldiers racing toward the town.

—

The Celtic army descended on the town like a tidal wave, killing everything in its path. The forward ranks of armed men were followed by those bearing make-shift weapons, constructed from whatever they could find. Wooden cudgels or simple skinning knives were borne by younger boys and women alike, each just as desperate to seek not only retribution but the promise of plunder from the stored wealth of the traders. Older men and those who suffered from infirmity also limped along in their wake and the massed ranks of warriors were soon replaced by thousands of ordinary tribal members, spread across the plains as far as the eye could see.

It was this disorganised throng that helped one man merge amongst them without fear of his true identity being found out. Centurion Cassus Maecilius had donned the garb of the Catuvellauni and stayed within the dark shadows at the edge of the enemy camps, listening to campfire talk of the soldiers. Much of the talk was typical soldier bravado but occasionally he picked up a snippet he could possibly use against them but overall, it was more or less what he had expected. Cassus had fought the Britons on many occasions and though this was the first time he had encountered the northern tribes, they seemed very similar to those he had fought for almost twenty years across the south of Britannia.

Cassus had been away from the legion for five days and was considering returning with what little information he had but something happened that changed his mind. The mood in the camps had changed and the rumour was that Boudicca had arrived and the attack was imminent. The word spread like wildfire and the change in everyone's mood was tangible. Confirmation soon came in the form of runners from the queen's tents, bearing messages from the warlords.

'Make peace with your gods, for tomorrow we assault Londinium.'

Warriors set to sharpening their swords with renewed vigour and carefully stored rations were used up in feasting to the gods, showing trust that the day would be won. Men made love to their wives with renewed vigour while those still single drank ale and sang battle songs with exaggerated bravado. Throughout the forests, animals were slaughtered in homage to the gods and the mood of the army heightened with anticipation for the coming battle. Few men slept that night and as the ale flowed, Cassus moved freely amongst them, joining in their revelries as if a fellow Celt. By the morning the army was high on alcohol and almost rabid in their eagerness to engage the enemy. Cassus knew this was an opportunity too good to miss for the prospect of being amongst the enemy forces as they assaulted a fixed position was a perfect chance to see them in action and understand their tactics at close hand. The sheer numbers meant that apart from their own clan comrades, most men didn't know the countless new faces around them and as Cassus spoke the Britannic tongue as well as any native, his presence was never questioned. So it was, that when the second wave of screaming Barbarians reached the outskirts of the Roman trading town, Cassus was deep amongst them, to all intents and purposes, one of Boudicca's warriors.

–

Deep in the heart of Londinium the news spread like wildfire and the population took to the streets. Crowds jammed the narrow walkways and many were trampled underfoot as they desperately sought escape from the onslaught. The numbers swelled as they flowed back and fore throughout the town, desperately seeking an exit only to find their way blocked by others fleeing the carnage in every direction. Smoke filled the air as Boudicca's men torched the outskirts of the town and the spring winds helped spread the flames from building to building almost quicker than the hoard could do it themselves.

On the southern edge of the town, the River Tamesas thronged with vessels of every size, each taking advantage of the high tide to carry the rich away from the slaughter. Boats had been ferrying people away from the town for days, most just going to the far side but the larger ones taking the nobles and the rich downstream to the relative safety of the estuary. Vessels of all sizes from rowing boats to trading barges did what they could, each vying for position amongst the horror and the smoke but amongst them all, one ship sat serenely alongside the dock as if immune from the panic.

The ship was a Bireme, a warship of the Roman navy manned by a Contubernium of well-trained marines and another of legionaries. In addition, a hundred and twenty professional oarsmen sat at their stations within the giant hull, waiting for the command to leave. Their brute strength and practised skills meant that when the command came, they would be midstream within minutes and driving the ship toward the safety of the sea, complete with their important cargo, but each also trained in the use of various weaponry and if there was need of conflict, every man would bear arms in defence of the vessel.

–

Trierachus Verres, the ship's captain walked nervously back and fore along the deck. He had been in the Navy for twenty-five years and in that time, the gods had been kind to him. He had only seen serious action once and even then, a minor flesh wound from an enemy arrow had meant he spent most of the time below deck with the Medicus, missing the ferocious fighting that had ensued on the shore. Since then, a mixture of guile and fortunate postings had meant his service had been relatively safe and he was only one year from retirement and the journey back home.

He never had a wife but his substantial wealth, accumulated by fair means and foul, meant he was rarely without a bedfellow, either woman or boy and he knew that his father's inheritance along with his pension would combine to ensure he enjoyed a comfortable retirement back in Rome. All he had to do was survive this godforsaken posting for one more year.

Verres approached the rail and peered down to the dock side, his face alive with worry.

'Where is he?' he asked for what seemed the hundredth time. 'He should be here by now.'

'He will come,' said a voice beside him and Verres looked over at the ship's Centurion, Galeo.

'He should have been here at dawn, Galeo,' said Verres. 'Something could have happened to him.'

'We will wait as long as possible,' said Galeo. 'Our orders are clear, to evacuate the Procurator and his entourage from the city.'

'I still can't believe the Nauarchus gave this man the time of day,' said Verres. 'Decianus could have left days ago but instead he has dragged his feet and put one of Rome's best ships at risk.'

'The Nauarchus is the fleet commander and his orders are final,' said Galeo. 'Besides, I would wager that there's a nice little reward for providing this ship for the Procurator. Decianus is a very rich and powerful man. It is said he has the ear of the Emperor himself.'

The two men fell silent and watched the crowds milling around the dock. Galeo's legionaries and twenty of the Milites from the rowing decks formed a guard around the gangplank, ensuring no desperate refugees tried to access the ship. Smoke billowed across the roof tops and screaming could be heard in the distance.

'This is ridiculous,' said Verres. 'If he isn't here in the next few minutes, I will give the order to sail.'

'You will do no such thing,' said Galeo.

'I am the captain of this ship,' snarled Verres, 'and I will do what it takes to keep her safe.'

'You forget your place, Verres,' answered the Centurion. 'As you well know, during conflict, command of this ship transfers to me and it becomes a warship.'

'We are not in a battle,' said Verres. 'Your role remains subordinate.'

'We are under orders to rescue Roman citizens from a marauding army,' said Galeo, 'and this vessel is indeed in danger. If that isn't a qualifying conflict, I don't know what is. Now stand aside. I am assuming command.'

Verres stifled his angry response for he knew Galeo was right. In times of conflict, each ship's Centurion assumed command.

'Optio,' shouted the Centurion.

Down on the dock, his second in command looked up at him.

'Yes, my lord.'

'Take ten men and follow that street north and look for the Procurator's group. Go no further than a thousand paces and if there is no sign, return here immediately. This ship will not leave without you.'

'Yes, my lord,' shouted the Optio and within moments, his unit was marching into the city.

Galeo turned to Verres.

'I have done what I can,' he said, 'but this ship stays until I say otherwise. I suggest you ensure the men below are ready to move at a moment's notice.'

Verres didn't answer but walked away in silence. There was nothing he could do.

–

Deeper in the town, Decianus was getting frantic. He and his wife were in a litter being carried by twelve slaves and though they had left it quite late before leaving, they had been confident of reaching the ship in time. What they hadn't allowed for was the sheer number of people in the streets. Decianus lifted the side curtain.

'What is the hold up?' he shouted. 'Get a move on.'

'The crowds are heavy, my lord,' answered Beacan, the head of the household servants leading the way. 'It is difficult to get through.'

'Use your cane,' shouted Decianus, 'beat them until they move.'

Suddenly the litter lurched as one of the slaves fell and within moments his fellow bearers all ended up on the floor as they tripped over each other.

Decianus and his wife, Sura, lay tangled within the litter, until Beacan reached inside to help them out.

'Get them up,' screamed Decianus as soon as he was out, pointing at the injured slaves. 'Get on your feet, you miserable filth.'

As the men struggled to their feet, one stayed down, his ankle obviously broken.

Decianus pulled a riding crop from beneath his robe and started whipping him about the head.

'Get up,' he screamed, 'I will have you crucified for this.'

The cowering man screamed in pain as the crop cut deep into his flesh and the other slaves backed away in fear.

'Beacan, get them back,' shouted Decianus. 'Get this litter upright immediately.' His tirade was cut short as he felt a hand on his arm and the soft voice of Sura addressing him.

'Decianus,' she said, 'look.'

Decianus looked around and saw the crowd had fallen silent. Hundreds of faces stared at him in anger and a clearing had opened up, with him and his entourage at the centre.

'What are you looking at?' shouted Decianus. 'Back off or you will suffer the same fate as this man.'

'Really?' shouted a man from the crowd. 'How many whips do you have, Procurator?'

A well-built man stepped forward and pulled a knife, closely followed by several others.

'It is his fault we are in this mess,' shouted another, 'and if we are to die today, then it is only fair he should share our fate.'

'Get back,' shouted Decianus. 'I am the Procurator and can have you all crucified for this.'

'Go ahead,' shouted a voice from the crowd and though there was a nervous laugh, the faces on the crowd were deadly serious.

Sura gripped his arm tighter.

'Beacan, do something,' shouted Decianus.

Despite being a Celt, Beacan had spent his entire life in servitude to the Romans and knew no other way of life. His entire existence had revolved around looking after people such as these and at last, this was an opportunity to discard the yoke of slavery. Behind him he could hear the soft sobs of Sura as she realised there was no way out.

Sura had always been kind to him and if it hadn't been for her, he would have gladly stepped aside but the amount of beatings she had saved him from over the years meant he owed her his protection, even if only for a few futile moments. He pulled the small knife his position of privilege allowed him and stepped forward to stand between the Procurator and the threatening mob, knowing full well he was about to die.

'You heard the man,' he said, 'get back.'

For a second the mob paused and then started to laugh.

'So what do you intend to do with that pig sticker?' shouted a man. 'Kill us all? Get out of the way, man. Let this Roman and his whore get what they deserve.'

For a few moments nothing happened, but finally one of the men started forward, blade in hand, but before he reached Beacan, a commotion to one side made them all turn in panic. At first, they thought Boudicca's army had reached them but were proved wrong when a unit of heavily armed legionaries broke through the crowd and into the clearing.

'Soldiers,' shouted Decianus, 'thank the gods.'

'What's happening here?' shouted the Optio as his men formed a loose perimeter facing the crowd.

'They threatened us,' said Decianus, 'kill them.'

'With respect, my lord,' answered the Optio, 'we are but a Contubernium, not a legion. We are outnumbered and the ship is about to sail. We have to get out of here.'

Despite the shock of the arrival of the soldiers, the crowd soon realised they were only ten strong and the mood darkened once more.

'They are but a handful,' shouted the main protagonist, 'and there are a thousand of us. We will probably die today anyway; let's take some Romans with us.'

The Romans drew their swords, forcing the crowd back once more.

'My lord, do you have anything of value on you?' asked the Optio.

'What do you mean?' asked Decianus.

'Coins, jewellery, anything of value.'

'No,' said the Procurator.

'Yes we do,' said Sura, contradicting her husband. 'You have the monthly tribute from the traders.'

'Sura, shut up,' said Decianus. 'I will not give a fortune to barbarians.'

'It is that or die,' said the Optio. 'Choose quickly for I will not let my men die needlessly for a rich dead man.'

Decianus still paused but Sura reached around her neck and removed a beautiful gold necklace encrusted with precious stones.

'Here,' she said, 'take this, the rings too. It is all I have but Decianus has a purse of golden coins beneath his robe.'

The Optio stared at the Procurator.

'Rich and dead, or poor and alive. Your choice.'

'I will have you whipped for this,' growled Decianus and reached beneath his robe to retrieve two large leather pouches. He handed them over and the Optio cut away the leather ties before addressing his men.

'On my mark, we head back to the ship,' he said and turned to Decianus. 'In a moment, my men will cut a hole through the crowd behind us. We will form a square with you at its centre. Stay with us and do not falter. I am about to buy us some time but they will be behind us within seconds. Are you ready?'

Decianus and Sura nodded silently.

'Right, get ready.' He turned to the soldiers.

'Prepare to move,' he shouted. 'Hollow square formation, double time.'

Opening the purse necks wide, he poured the gold coins into his hands and scattered them into the crowd.

For a moment nothing happened, but within seconds there was pandemonium as people fell over each other in their panic to get rich.

The Optio threw the last of the coins into the crowd before turning to his men once more.

'Let's get out of here,' he shouted, 'move.'

The unit quickly formed a square and with swords drawn, ran toward the few people blocking their way back to the ship. Many jumped out of the way but those too slow were smashed by the shields of the Romans, the metal bosses in their centres breaking jaws as if they were eggs. Any foolish enough to try and stop them were bloodily despatched by Gladius and within a minute, the group had broken free into a relatively quiet side street.

'Keep running,' shouted the Optio, 'they're right behind us.'

Chapter Twenty

The Forests to the North of Londinium

Finian finished binding Lannosea's arm to a stick, knowing that the bone would set fairly straight.

'I am no Shaman, girl,' he said. 'It's the best I can do.'

Lannosea just nodded, her face streaming with tears of pain from the well-meant but rough treatment.

'Are you alright?' asked Taliesin.

Lannosea nodded again and wiped the tears from her eyes.

'Why did you do it?' she asked eventually.

'Do what?'

'Stop me jumping off the cliff.'

'Oh that,' said Taliesin. 'Just a natural reaction I suppose. Anyone would have done the same. Anyway, you are far too pretty to die yet.'

A hint of a smile played about her face.

'Now you flatter me,' she said. 'I have seen my reflection and I look like an old witch.'

Taliesin shuffled over and sat before her.

'It is true, a bathe and a comb would enhance your appearance,' he laughed, 'but no amount of mud can hide your grace.' He held out a large leaf containing a slice of the raw fish. 'Not exactly the golden platter the daughter of a queen would expect, but all I can provide at the moment.'

'Our platters are wooden like yours,' said Lannosea, 'and anyway, a more welcome meal was never more gratefully received.' For a few moments they both made small talk and even laughed a little at their predicament. Finally, Finian strolled over and interrupted their conversation.

'Right,' he said, 'when you two have stopped your nonsense, we have to get moving. By my reckoning we are just over a day away from Londinium and if this wench is who she says she is, I think we may be in for some sort of reward for bringing her home safe.'

'I am who I say,' said Lannosea, 'and I will make sure you are suitably rewarded.'

'I seek no reward,' said Taliesin, 'just the chance to serve and help drive the Romans from our soil.'

'If we find my people,' answered Lannosea, 'I will ensure the queen places a thousand men under your command.'

Finian snorted in derision.

'A thousand men?' he laughed. 'This one needs to learn how to look after himself first.'

Taliesin smiled.

'He is right,' he said, 'I have a lot to learn.'

'Then you will learn at my mother's side,' said Lannosea.

'Enough talk,' said Finian. 'Time to get moving.'

Taliesin and Lannosea stood up and followed Finian southward through the forest. For the first time in weeks, Taliesin realised he was getting very close to Boudicca.

Prydain and his party of travellers were camped deep in a wood north of the city of Verulamium. As another town dominated by a Roman presence, many retired soldiers chose to make their homes there at the end of their military service, especially those who had married local girls. The effect on the city over the years was one of improvement and a better lifestyle. Roads were wider and laid in stone and temples to the many Roman gods were peppered throughout the city. The proximity to Londinium in the south meant it enjoyed its fair share of luxuries from the continent and the lifestyle was comfortable. Again though, the natural lean toward slavery meant that already there was a distinct ruling class within its population and those of Roman descent had carved out positions of power over the original inhabitants.

Knowing this, Prydain's intention had been to give the city a wide berth but they had become lost in a particularly dense forest and when they had finally come across a woodsman, who could give them directions, they found they were miles out of their way.

Three of the travellers sat around the campfire deep in a ravine cutting through the forest. A small deer brought down by one of Heulwen's arrows earlier in the day hung above the flames, and their mouths watered from the aromas.

The sound of approaching horsemen made each check his weapon, but as expected it was Taran and Cullen returning from their scouting mission.

'Hwyl, Prydain,' called Cullen from the ravine edge above.

'Down here,' answered Prydain. 'There is a track a hundred paces to your front. Follow it down to the river then come back upstream.'

Ten minutes later the two men rode into the camp and tethered their horses alongside the others before joining their comrades at the fire.

'We were beginning to wonder if you had been killed,' said Prydain holding out his arm in greeting.

Taran gripped the forearm of Prydain in return.

'We almost were,' he said. 'The forest around here is alive with refugees. The word is Boudicca intends to sack Londinium and many people fled the town to take refuge in Verulamium only to be turned away by the city's militia.'

'Boudicca intends to attack Londinium?' gasped Prydain. 'Surely she eyes that which is too great to achieve.'

'You would think so,' said Taran, 'but this trek has kept us from momentous news. Not only has she laid waste to Camulodunum but she has also defeated one of the legions in an open battle.'

'Impossible,' said Prydain.

'Yet true,' said Taran. 'While we were out, we took up with a column of traders for a day and the news was rife. She has slaughtered a legion, sacked a city and now intends to attack Londinium. If she is successful, she cuts one of the main supply routes from Rome and the remaining three legions will be isolated.'

'They have Rutupiae on the coast,' said Prydain.

'A three-day journey for the supply columns,' said Taran, 'and one that invites attack from Boudicca's allies or even brigands. In Londinium the ships sailed straight into the heart of the town and the stores were distributed quickly. Make no mistake, if Londinium falls it will be a massive blow to Rome's presence here.'

'And you believe she will do it?'

'There is word that even as we speak, the skies above Londinium burn red.'

'She has fired the town?' gasped Heulwen.

'It would seem so.'

'So what does this mean for us?' asked Gildas. 'Obviously it is good news that the Romans are tasting Britannic steel but how does it affect our mission?'

'I'm not sure,' said Prydain. 'We have much to talk about but first we will eat. Your return is timely for the deer is almost done. See to your horses and we will talk with full bellies.'

Half an hour later, each man handed over their wooden bowl and Heulwen filled them with strips of the roasted deer. Everyone ate in silence, savouring the still bloody freshness of the red venison.

'Good meat,' mumbled Gildas, through his full mouth.

'A welcome change from the pig,' agreed Taran.

Each leaned forward as their bowls emptied and cut off fresh slices, agreeing they would finish off the deer tonight rather than save it for the morrow. They still had enough dried pork and biscuit for a few days travel and the deer was a welcome treat. Gildas cut off an entire leg and ate direct from the bone, mumbling in satisfaction as the grease ran down his chin.

'He looks happy,' laughed Heulwen quietly to Prydain.

'Easy man to please,' said Prydain. 'Fill his belly and he will travel to the ends of the earth for you. Accompany it with ale and you have a friend for life.'

'A deer I can manage,' said Heulwen tapping the bow at her side. 'Ale is harder to source.'

'On the contrary,' said Prydain, 'we have the finest ale in the world right at hand.' He nodded toward the shallow river. 'When a man is thirsty, he needs nothing else.'

They fell quiet and watched as the other men finished their meal.

'Do you think we can actually do this?' asked Heulwen eventually.

'This was your quest, Heulwen,' said Prydain. 'Surely you are not doubting the outcome?'

'When I sought your aid, it was simply a quest to rescue a boy from his own stupidity,' she said. 'Now we are in the midst of unfamiliar territory, not knowing our final destination and walking into a battle of no concern to us.'

'Are you suggesting we stop?'

'I am suggesting that you stop,' she said. 'I intend to carry on but you and your comrades are not indebted to me in any way.'

'That would be stupid,' said Prydain.

'Costing the lives of four good men on a fool's errand is no less stupid,' answered Heulwen.

'These men are the best there are,' said Prydain. 'So far you have seen the quiet side of them only, a trait born of necessity. Should the time come to defend themselves they will not fall short of what is expected. The Silures are like no other Britons, Heulwen. Their strategy is avoidance, subterfuge and ambush. As long as our people or lands are not directly affected, they will watch from the shadows but if threatened, then their wrath is incalculable.'

'You say "they"! Why is that?'

'What do you mean?'

'Do you not count yourself Silures?'

'I do but these men have learned the ways since leaving their mother's breast. I have returned to my heritage only in the second half of my life and stand in awe of men such as these. If I die with half the mettle of my comrades, then I will rest an honoured man.'

'So you don't think we should at least offer them the opportunity to return home.'

'No, but if it makes you feel better, I will ask the question.'

'It will,' said Heulwen.

Prydain half turned to the men and called out.

'Taran, Gildas, Cullen. Heulwen fears for our safety and recommends you return to your families. What say you?'

'Hell no,' said Gildas, still concentrating on the deer's leg.

'With my sword still clear of Roman blood?' asked Taran. 'I think not.'

'What of you, Cullen?' asked Heulwen.

'These men are my family so I am already home,' came the answer.

'But you could die out here,' said Heulwen.

'We all die, lady. Today, tomorrow or as old men, it matters not. The outcome remains the same.'

'Well, that was straightforward,' said Heulwen with a laugh as she turned back to Prydain.

'Now that is settled,' said Prydain, 'we should agree our strategy.' He called the men over and they sat in a loose circle, finishing their meals. Prydain turned to Taran.

'Taran, share what you have seen these last few days.'

'First of all, the woodsman was right,' said the young man. 'We are nowhere near where we thought we were. One day's ride in that direction lies Verulamium, a city heavily influenced by the Romans who have made it their home. Londinium lies on the far side so we have to either go straight through the city or around it if we are to find Boudicca.'

'We can't risk going through it,' said Prydain, 'any strangers will stand out from the crowd.'

'True,' said Taran, 'but veering off track also has risks.'

'How so?'

'The refugees from Londinium I told you about, many have been refused entry to the city and wander throughout the forests seeking shelter and food. Some are desperate and have turned to murder to meet their needs.'

'There have always been such people,' said Gildas, 'brigands hold no fear for me.'

'Nor I,' said Taran, 'but their numbers are unknown. Our clothing and accent make us stand out from the locals and we would be targeted immediately.'

'How far do they extend?' asked Prydain.

'Mainly from here to the eastern edge of Londinium,' said Taran.

'Then we go west,' said Gildas.

'That way lies a greater danger,' said Cullen. 'Somewhere to the west of us, the Gemina legion lays up preparing for battle. Their scouts will be watching like hawks and probably many locals willing to give us up for a rusty coin.'

'So, we can't go forward, east or west,' said Prydain.

'That only leaves back the way we came,' said Gildas.

'We do not go back,' said Prydain, 'until we get what we came for.'

'So what do you propose?' asked Taran.

Prydain thought for a while before answering.

'Tell me,' he said. 'Why does this legion lie up while Boudicca lays waste to Londinium?'

'The word is that it gathers its strength to confront her.'

'And yet she carries on regardless.'

'Boudicca has no fear of the Gemina,' said Taran. 'She has already defeated the Hispana with half the amount of men she has now. I think she is taunting him and wants him out in the open.'

'I agree,' said Prydain, 'and it raises an important question. Where will this battle take place?'

'Nobody knows,' said Gildas.

'Not yet,' said Prydain, 'and there are only two people who can influence that decision, Boudicca and Suetonius.'

'So?'

'So by the time we get to Londinium, she could be miles away and we could spend months chasing her around Britannia,' said Prydain. 'However, if we stay close to Suetonius, they will eventually face each other across the battlefield and wherever she is, Taliesin will be close by.'

'So we wait?' suggested Taran.

'Exactly,' answered Prydain. 'We will find somewhere secure close by, yet watch the movements of Suetonius closely. When a legion moves, it leaves a trail like a storm across the land and can be easily followed. Stay close to it, and eventually we will find Boudicca.'

The group looked at each other in turn until finally Gildas spoke up.

'Well it is a plan,' he said.

'It is,' said Prydain, 'and plays on our strengths. All we have to do is be patient.'

'Then it is agreed,' said Taran. 'Tomorrow we will go to ground and await the will of the gods.'

–

Petillius left his tent and walked toward his waiting men. It was still dark and the only light came from a burning cart in the centre of the camp. Only two soldiers remained on the ramparts of the marching camp as lookouts and would leave it until the last possible moment before joining the remains of the legion. Petillius climbed up onto another upturned cart and addressed the gathered men.

'Fellow legionaries of the Ninth,' he started. 'In the last few days we have had the misfortune of witnessing the demise of our beloved legion, but this is just a setback. In the years ahead, our banners will writhe in the winds of battle and our Aquila will witness glorious victories once more. Our dead will live strong in our memories but it is time we move on. It is time we lift our heads and show these barbarians that though our numbers are few, our resolve is great and we will return to suffer our vengeance upon the heathen in our comrades' names. To do this we must leave this place as soon as possible and at last, opportunity has arisen. The risk is great but the rewards are greater still.'

He paused and looked around the few men left from his command.

'Stay here,' he continued, 'and we will surely be overrun but leave and we run the risk of ambush. I for one would prefer to meet my gods while taking the assault to the enemy.'

A murmur of approval arose from the men, happy at last to be taking action.

'There is, however, a problem,' continued the Legate. 'We number a hundred and ten men in total and only fifty-two horses between us so not all can ride. There are an unknown number of barbarians within the forest around us but we have no way of knowing how many, so this is what we will do. Each horse will have one rider on his back, armed with a Pugio. Another man will run at the side of the horse, with his hand tied to the saddle. Where necessary this will be repeated on the opposite side so each horse conveys up to three men. The aim is to break out of the fort as fast as possible and plough straight through them without pause or thought. Hopefully by the time they realise what is happening we will be deep into the forest. Are there any questions?'

'My lord,' said a Decurion. 'Surely the horses will tire quickly with such a load.'

'They will,' said the Legate, 'so every man will discard their armour to make the load as light as possible. The only armament needed by the runners will be a Gladius.'

'No armour?' said another. 'We will surely be easy meat for barbarian blades.'

'Our aim is to escape, not fight,' said Petillius. 'If we are forced to stop by sheer numbers, no amount of chain mail will be enough.'

'If we are to be tied,' said the Decurion, 'and someone does fall to a blade or arrow, won't they hold the horses back?'

'They will,' said Petillius, 'and that is why the rider has a blade, to cut away the ties holding the injured man.'

'We leave them behind?' asked the soldier.

'We have no other choice,' said Petillius. 'The needs of the many outweigh the needs of the few in this instance but hopefully it won't come to that. The trick to this is speed and balance. As soon as the gate is open, use the horse's momentum to carry you forward and do not falter. The scouts from the Gemina who joined us yesterday will afford some protection on the flanks and lead the way out of the forest. With the gods' will, we will join Suetonius before nightfall. Any more questions?'

The men remained silent.

'Good,' said Petillius. 'Aquilifer, recover the Eagle and make it shine like it has never shone before. Whatever fate lies before us, it will be met under the emblem of the Gemina. The rest of you, make your peace with your gods and get ready to move; we ride at first light.'

Back in Londinium, Galeo heard the returning patrol before he saw them. The sound of the Optio's voice rang out over the general sound of panic, demanding the crowd clear the way or suffer the consequences.

Verres waddled to the Centurion's side and stared over the crowd.

'At last,' he said, 'now we can get out of here.'

'Prepare to raise the plank,' shouted Galeo, 'release the ropes. Verres, pass the word below, ready the oars.'

The ship burst into frantic activity and men ran everywhere preparing the ship to sail.

'The wind is favourable,' shouted Verres, 'stand by the sail.'

The crowd on the dock parted before the oncoming squad of Romans. In their midst, Galeo could see the Procurator, his wife and one of his household. There was no sign of the others. He watched as they climbed up the gangplank and onto the deck, closely followed by all the remaining guards from the dock.

'Raise the plank,' shouted Galeo. 'Verres, get us out of here.' He walked over to the group, all catching their breath from the sustained run.

'Procurator Catus Decianus,' he said, 'I am Centurion Galeo and have been tasked with your transport to a place of safety. Welcome on board the Minerva.'

'Good to be here, soldier,' said Decianus.

'My lord, I thought there would be more in your group.'

'My fellows left a few days ago,' said Decianus. 'I had to stay to call in some debts before leaving.'

'Really?' said Galeo. 'They must have been important to risk your life so.'

'They were,' said Decianus, 'not that it's any of your business.'

'And your staff?' asked Galeo.

'Mere Britons,' said Decianus. 'I left them behind. Plenty more slaves in Rome.'

'They will probably be killed,' said Galeo.

Decianus stopped and stared at him.

'Listen, Centurion,' he said, 'I appreciate you sending your men for us but my business is exactly that, my business. I answer to the Senate only not some jumped up street rat who kills for money. The slaves were mine to do with as I please and today, I chose to let them die. Now get out of my way.'

The Procurator barged past the soldier and headed toward the captain's tent at the far end of the deck. Galeo felt the ship lurch as the first pull of the oarsmen powered the Bireme toward the centre of the river but before they had gone more than a few lengths, a voice cried out from the dock.

'Procurator Decianus, please take me with you.'

Galeo turned and saw a woman running along the bank.

'Who is she?' asked Galeo.

The Optio shrugged his shoulders.

'One of his whores I expect.'

'It's Cara,' said a voice, 'Sura's handmaiden. She must have followed us through Londinium.'

Galeo turned and saw Beacan, the Procurator's head of household standing behind them.

'We have to help her,' continued Beacan. 'Can we take the ship in?'

'We will do no such thing,' shouted Decianus, overhearing the conversation. 'Captain, keep to your course.'

'But my lord,' answered Beacan, 'she has been a loyal servant to you and your house for years. Surely you owe her something.'

The Procurators' eyes blazed with anger at the slave's impudence and he walked forward until he stood toe to toe with Beacan.

'I owe her nothing,' he said. 'I own her as I own you. How dare you raise your voice to me.'

'But my lord...'

'Shut your filthy slave mouth,' growled Decianus, 'I am speaking. Now turn around.'

Beacan turned and stared out over the rail toward the shore and the still-running girl.

'That slave is nothing to me,' said Decianus, 'I throw away rotten food that is worth more to me than her. Do you understand?'

Beacan remained silent.

'She is worthless to me and is easily replaced, as indeed are you. Long service does not earn you loyalty, Beacan, it is simply a measure of my kindness that I allowed you to stay. However, I am not an unreasonable man and in this case I will make an exception. You are no longer of use to me, Beacan. You can go.'

'My lord, I do not understand,' said Beacan.

'It's not difficult,' said Decianus, 'I am setting you free. Go and join her.'

Beacan was sweating in fright at the implications.

'My lord, I can't swim,' he said.

'Not my problem,' said Decianus before turning to the two nearest soldiers.

'Seize him,' he said.

The men grabbed Beacan and held him fast.

'It's very simple,' said Decianus, approaching him, 'reach the bank and you and that whore can set up a nice little slum somewhere and rut to your heart's content.'

'But my lord,' shouted Beacan, his voice shaking with fear.

'Throw him overboard,' shouted Decianus.

The two soldiers dragged the struggling man to the rail but just before they pushed him over, Decianus called out again.

'Wait.'

Everyone stopped and the Procurator walked up close to the servant.

'I forgot to give you something for your journey,' he said.

'Please let me go, my lord,' pleaded the slave, 'I will not survive the river.'

'Too late, Beacan,' said Decianus, 'but before you go, I have a gift for you.'

'A gift?'

'Yes, this,' he said and plunged a knife into the man's stomach.

Beacan gasped in pain and his eyes widened.

'Do it,' said Decianus and watched as the two soldiers threw the mortally wounded man over the side.

Decianus looked over the rail and started laughing as Beacan struggled in the current.

'Look,' he said, pointing excitedly, 'he's actually trying to swim.' He clapped his hands in glee as the ship left the man far behind. 'Good luck, Beacan,' he shouted, 'I hope you enjoy your freedom.'

When the slave finally disappeared from view he turned around and saw everybody on the upper deck looking at him in disgust.

'What are you staring at?' he shouted, 'I am the Procurator of Londinium and my word is law. Get back to your duties.'

For a few moments nobody moved, but finally Centurion Galeo's voice rang out across the deck.

'You heard the Procurator,' he said, 'there is work to be done. Get to it. Trierachus Verres, take us to Rutupiae.'

'Wait,' said Decianus, 'our destination has changed.'

Both Galeo and Verres turned to stare at the Procurator.

'My lord, we were told to take you to Rutupiae,' said Galeo. 'Though Governor Suetonius is in the field, he has ordered a temporary headquarters set up at the port. He will surely want to meet you there when the conflict is over.'

'I have no intention of meeting Suetonius,' said Decianus, 'and my passage has been approved by men of high station within the senate. My orders are clear, Centurion, take me to Gaul.'

Chapter Twenty-One

The Trading Town of Londinium

The evening sky glowed red, reflecting the raging fires below. Screams of pain echoed through the night and warriors rampaged the streets, killing at will. Cassus watched from the shadows as the city fell around him. The carnage was total and drunken warriors used the bodies of the dead as temporary resting places. Everywhere Cassus looked, the population was being rounded up and tortured or killed in every way imaginable. Women were passed from man to man for their sexual gratification, while orphaned children ran crying through the streets, often silenced by a blade before they had gone too far. But rape and murder were the lesser evils for the residents of Londinium, for those who were proved to have Roman blood suffered far worse. Roman men were nailed to doors and had their knees smashed, while others were genitally mutilated and left to die a slow and lingering death. The women were gang raped by the warriors before being killed but that was nothing compared to the fate suffered by those left to the barbarian women. At first the Roman women were just killed with knives or strangulation but as the night continued, the degradation increased and many had their breasts hacked off and made to run naked through the streets. Some even had parts of their breasts stuffed into their mouths and their lips sewn together, watched by hysterical, drunken crowds. The longer the night progressed, the more varied the torture became and both women and men were impaled on wooden stakes driven between their legs, before being hoisted high above the crowds as macabre trophies. Others were covered with animal fats and used as living torches to light the squares where the atrocities took place.

Through all this, Cassus maintained his detachment. He had seen such things before and there was nothing one man could do to stop the horror. It was as if he had stepped into Hades itself. Finally he had seen enough and made his way back toward the edge of the city but as he walked down a darkened alley, a man lurched out of the smoke and fell against him. Both men fell to the floor and though Cassus immediately rolled away and drew his Pugio, it soon became evident he was in no danger.

'Please, help me,' gasped the man.

Cassus paused, waiting for his heartbeat to steady once more.

The man scrambled to his knees.

'Please,' he said, holding out both arms, 'whoever you are, please help me.'

Cassus squinted in the fire lit gloom, seeing dark shadows on the man's face.

'What's the matter with you?' he asked.

'My eyes,' said the man, 'they have taken my eyes.'

Cassus realised the shadows were the blood stains and remains of soft tissue hanging down the man's face.

'They tore them out,' sobbed the man, 'with their bare hands, then let me go. I can't see, please help me.'

'Why you?' asked Cassus. 'What link do you have with the Romans?'

'Nothing,' cried the man, 'I was enslaved to those filth. You don't understand, I had no choice but to serve. Please you have to help me.'

'You call them filth?' said Cassus, walking around the man.

'Yes,' gasped the man, his head turning as he tried to locate where Cassus's voice was coming from. 'I recognise your accent, friend. I too am of the Catuvellauni. We are brothers, you and me. We above all know the weight of Roman oppression and you must believe me, though I was a slave, I did everything I could to make their lives hell.'

'Like what?' asked Cassus.

'Small things,' said the man, 'I stole their food and pissed in the wine. Sometimes I even poisoned the horses. Over the years it must have cost them a small fortune. See, I am a true Briton and I need your help. Please take me from here and let me speak to your queen. She will understand.'

'I have no queen,' said Cassus quietly. 'I have an emperor.'

The man's head turned in confusion.

'I don't understand,' he said, 'I thought...'

'You thought wrong,' said Cassus. 'I am not a Briton but a Roman, perhaps even one of those who drank your piss-laced wine.'

'I didn't mean it,' gasped the man, 'I was lying, I thought you were one of the attackers.'

'Enough,' shouted Cassus. 'I have heard enough of your lies.'

'What are you going to do?' sobbed the man.

'You are in luck,' said Cassus, 'I have seen enough cruelty for one night. I have no intention of leaving you here to wander in permanent darkness.'

'What do you intend to do?' asked the man with renewed hope.

'I will help you see again,' said Cassus.

'But... that's impossible,' said the man.

'It is in this life,' said Cassus, 'but I have no doubt your gods will allow you your sight in the next.'

'I don't understand,' said the man but before he could say anything else, Cassus grabbed his hair from behind and pulled back his head, exposing his throat.

'Accept my mercy, barbarian,' said Cassus, 'your suffering is over.' His knife sliced deep through the blind man's throat and Cassus pushed him forward into the mud.

The man's hands clawed at the wound as his blood spurted between his fingers but within moments his struggles ended and Cassus wiped his blade on the dead man's tunic before disappearing into the darkness.

—

Three days later Boudicca stood at the edge of the forest, looking back at Londinium. The town was still smouldering and crows argued over the scarred remnants of the population. The smell of the fires reached her on the breeze and countless spires of smoke climbed up into the morning air.

The fields before her were littered with thousands of smaller fires but not from destruction; these were the fires of her army, built in the open for the first time since the call to arms. Their numbers were growing daily and for the first time there was a feeling of invincibility about them. They had defeated a legion and destroyed two of the most important Roman population centres in Britannia.

Rianna rode up on a horse and dismounted before her.

'Boudicca, it is a momentous morning.'

'It has merit,' agreed Boudicca.

'Merit worth shouting to the gods,' said Rianna, 'another blow dealt to the invader. Suetonius must be quaking in his boots as we speak, as must any of Roman descent throughout this country.'

'This campaign has just begun,' said Boudicca. 'We should not get carried away celebrating victories in battles not yet fought.'

'A fair point,' said Rianna, 'but we should still enjoy those that have been won.'

'How are the men?' asked Boudicca.

'Nursing their hangovers and counting the spoils. The storerooms of the traders were generous.'

'I thought as much,' said Boudicca. 'What about casualties?'

'No more than a hundred, and half of them were from fights within our own ranks.'

'A curse of the victorious,' said Boudicca.

'I don't understand.'

'If we are not careful those who have gained the most will return back to their lands while those with the least will covet their spoils and seek to gain them for themselves. Gold can be as destructive as a blade.'

'It is our way,' said Rianna. 'There isn't much you can do about it.'

'Yes there is,' said Boudicca, 'we can keep up the momentum. Summon the warlords.'

Rianna mounted her horse and galloped away while Boudicca continued to stare down at the devastated city.

An hour later, Boudicca stood in a clearing along with almost fifty tribal chiefs, some of whom she hadn't met before.

'Fellow Britons,' she said. 'I call you here first to pay homage to you. Your blades have again proved the better of our enemy and the Tamesas runs red with Roman blood. The gods sing of our victories and more people flock to our cause every day.'

'A bloody few days,' answered one.

'Yet profitable,' said another and the whole group burst out laughing.

'Both descriptions are true,' said Boudicca, 'and our people deserve to enjoy the celebrations, but we must call them to an end and press forward.'

'What's the rush?' asked a voice.

'The rush is to ensure the enemy have no time to consolidate and build their defences,' said Boudicca. 'We have them on the run and it is important that situation remains. I have been informed that many fled to Verulamium and sought refuge there. Verulamium is yet another city that has been infested by their touch and many ex legionaries who have completed their service now call that place home.'

'Surely it can wait,' shouted a voice.

'No it can't,' said Boudicca. 'We no longer have surprise on our side. As we speak, they will be building their defences and the better their defences, the more of our people will die in the assault. Verulamium is an important target and we can't afford to leave it behind us or it will become a focal point for reorganisation. So I ask you, tell your men to replace the stoppers in their wine jugs, sharpen their blades and march on Verulamium without delay.'

'Don't forget,' added Rianna, 'Verulamium is heavily populated by retired legionaries and as such, is rich in gold and spices. Londinium's wealth was but pennies in comparison.'

The possibility of a richer plunder made many of the men listen harder and Boudicca glanced at Rianna with gratitude.

'Rianna is right,' said Boudicca. 'Already clan argues with clan over the sharing of the spoils but they need not do so. Take Verulamium and there will be enough for all, irrespective of allegiance.'

'What about the legions?' asked one of the men.

'They hide like frightened children,' said Boudicca, 'and after we have taken Verulamium, we will turn our attentions on them. Tribes flock to our banner by the day and even if the Romans combine all their legions to face us in battle, they will be swatted like flies. So what say you?' shouted Boudicca. 'Do we sit and drink at the destruction of a mere trading town, or do we face the walls of Verulamium as a liberating army and send a statement to Rome they will never forget?'

The gathered men shouted their allegiance once more and for the next few hours, Boudicca outlined her plans. By midday, they had left to join their own clans, all agreed that the following morning, they would march on Verulamium.

Chapter Twenty-Two

The Gemina Fort

Suetonius stood on the palisade of the fort and watched the lone rider approach. The very fact that the rider had got within a mile meant he was Roman and the outer patrols had let him through.

'It's Cassus,' he said quietly to the Tribune at his side. 'Have a hot meal prepared, I am guessing he will be hungry.' The Legate clambered down to the fort floor.

'Open the gates,' he ordered, 'the Primus Pilus returns.'

The gates opened and a few minutes later, Cassus entered the safety of the fort.

'Cassus, as usual you take your own path,' said Suetonius.

Cassus dismounted and saluted his commander.

'Hail, Suetonius,' he said. 'Your words confuse me.'

'I said ten days yet the thirteenth has dawned,' said Suetonius. 'This could be seen as insubordination.'

'It could,' said Cassus, 'and I offer no apology except that circumstances demanded I linger.'

'Hopefully these circumstances were fruitful,' said Suetonius.

'They were,' said Cassus.

'Then come to my tent,' said Suetonius, 'and share the knowledge. I have organised some food to be prepared.'

The two men walked through the camp, talking the talk of soldiers. Finally they passed the two guards at the entrance to the large command tent. Inside, they removed their capes and handed them to the ever-present slaves.

'Sit,' said Suetonius and signalled the attending servant to pour two goblets of wine. Cassus sat in a wooden chair lined with sheepskin.

'So,' said Suetonius, taking his own seat. 'Fill me in on the relevance of this journey, Cassus, for truth be told, I struggle to make a strategy with regards to this woman. Do I ride out and face her while she drinks the wine of Londinium or wait until her army is formed up on the plains and make use of our cavalry?'

'I fear neither strategy will work here,' said Cassus. 'Her army is too big.'

'You surprise me, Centurion,' said Suetonius, 'since when has my Primus Pilus proclaimed anything but victory?'

'Since he saw a foe he knows cannot be beaten,' said Cassus, 'at least with normal tactics.'

'Our histories are fat with defeats of greater armies,' said Suetonius, 'what makes you think these barbarians offer a greater threat than those whose bones litter the ancient battlefields?'

'This army is greater than any I have ever seen,' said Cassus, 'and has no knowledge of structure or tactics.'

'Surely that is a good thing,' said the Legate.

'You would think so,' said Cassus, 'but in open warfare their assault would be unpredictable and their lines could easily surround the entire Germina a hundred deep. If they followed expected formations then there would be a chance but their numbers preclude a battle of tactics.'

'I struggle with this,' said Suetonius. 'I have a full-strength legion under command and we fear no one. Superior numbers are a consideration but nothing else. One of our men is worth ten of theirs in battle.'

'I agree,' said Cassus, 'and I think there are ways to defeat Boudicca but there are other factors to be taken into consideration.'

'Which are?'

'First of all, our own numbers. Do we have the support of the Augusta or Valera Victrix?'

'I have sent messengers to both,' said Suetonius, 'and have received word that the Victrix already march to our aid.'

'And the Augusta?'

'Prefect Postumus hasn't replied yet and I admit to having concern. He is known to have ambition above his station and may see this as an opportunity to see me fall.'

'Surely refusal to aid the governor is treason?' said Cassus.

'Perhaps,' said Suetonius, 'but that is a matter for another day. We know we can count on ourselves and the Victrix as well as some vexillations from around the colonies. In all, we have over ten thousand swords under my command.'

'Still a number less than a tenth of the enemy,' said Cassus, 'but hope is not lost.'

'Explain,' said Suetonius.

'Their strength is their numbers,' said Cassus, 'and at first glance it is impenetrable, yet I think I have seen a chink in their armour.'

'Which is?' asked Suetonius.

'Their numbers,' said Cassus.

Suetonius frowned.

'You jest with me, Centurion. You just said their numbers were their strength.'

'And they are,' said Cassus, 'except in one circumstance, one where they become an unbearable burden.'

Suetonius signalled for the servant to pour more wine.

'At last your tone lifts my spirits, Cassus,' said the Legatus, 'and you find a willing listener. Share what you have for one way or another, this situation will be brought to a conclusion.'

For the next few hours Cassus shared what he had learned as well as his thoughts on a strategy for defeating Boudicca's army and by the time dawn approached, Suetonius's mind was set. At last they had a plan and though it was risky, if the gods were willing, they would have a chance of victory and for Suetonius, that was the best he could hope for.

—

While Suetonius and Cassus shared wine in their stronghold, another Legate was preparing to run the gauntlet of an unknown enemy with little more than a century of men. Petillius looked around at the column of horses and the runners alongside them. The sun was still just below the horizon but the clouds above were reflecting just enough light for them to see where they were going.

'Aquilifer,' he said, 'raise the Eagle.'

The standard bearer complied and every head turned to stare at their emblem.

'Look well, men,' said Petillius, 'for though today we are few, a hundred thousand spirits ride beside us. Every man who has ever looked up at this Aquila rides alongside you today and though their sword arms are denied us, their spirits strengthen our resolve. Today, the Eagle of the Ninth will stand alongside that of the Gemina or we will die in the attempt. Legio Nona Hispana, despite our numbers we are still a legion and I expect every man to do his duty. Today I ask that you forget your own mortality and take this legion's name into the annals of history.' He turned to the two men still left at the gate. 'It is time,' he said. 'Open the gates.' The two wooden gates creaked open, and Petillius peered into the gloom outside the fort.

'We will take it easy at first,' he said, 'and perhaps we will get past their lookouts without discovery. Decurion, lead the way.'

The scout commander flicked his heels and his horse walked forward, through the gates, closely followed by the others. For over a mile the column walked through the forest without opposition and Petillius allowed himself a faint hope that they would be successful without blood being spilt. Finally they broke free of the trees and followed a small valley toward the distant hills.

Out in the open, the lack of trees meant it was considerably lighter and as the sun broke over the horizon, the scout leading the way reined in his horse.

'What's the matter?' asked Petillius.

'An enemy camp before us,' said the scout. 'It wasn't there a few days ago.'

'Which way lies our path?' asked the Legate.

'There is only one way,' said the scout, and pointed toward the barbarian camp. 'Straight through.'

Petillius took a deep breath and paused before answering. Finally he drew his Gladius.

'Then so be it,' he said. 'The camp still stirs from sleep and we have surprise on our side.' He turned to the rider behind him. 'Pass the word back,' he said. 'Draw Gladii and stiffen sinew, there is blood to be spilt.'

The sounds of swords being drawn whispered down the line and battle-hardened men said silent prayers to their gods.

'No time to waste,' said the Legate. 'Take us through them, Decurion, before their drunken eyes see the gleam of our Eagle.' The scout drew his own sword and urged his horse forward, followed by the rest of the column. Those without mounts clung on tightly, their feet hardly touching the floor as they were carried along and as they reached the edge of the enemy lines, the first calls of alarm echoed around the camp.

The tents stretched as far as Petillius could see but the columns pace meant they were deep amongst them before any serious threat emerged. By now, the shouts echoed around the camp and people were emerging from their tents, unsure what was happening.

'Romans,' screamed a woman in her own language, 'we are under attack!'

'Ignore her,' shouted Petillius, 'keep going.'

To their front men scrabbled for weapons and ran to intercept the column, but most were simply barged aside before they presented any real threat. Those men running beside the horses gasped for breath as they swung their swords toward any barbarian managing to get close and by the time the enemy realised what was happening, the column were more than halfway through. A scream rang out and Petillius swung his horse to one side and peered back down the galloping column. A horse lay in the dust with a spear sticking out of his side. The rider lay motionless beside the animal, his neck obviously broken from the fall, and another man struggled to his feet, his face covered in blood. For a second Petillius considered riding back to get him but as he watched, a spinning axe embedded itself into the man's back and he fell to his knees.

Other riders pulled up with the intention of helping their comrade but Petillius's voice rang through the morning air.

'Leave them,' he screamed, 'there is nothing we can do. Keep going.' The riders realised the Legate was right and kicked their horses once more to continue the headlong advance, leaving their comrade behind to be enveloped in a crowd of screaming warriors. More men fell to spears as they ran but still the desperate column galloped on.

Though the camp was awakening, the early hour and the total surprise meant that the column was virtually unchallenged and though they lost another ten men in the charge, they finally burst clear of the tents and onto the plains beyond.

'Keep going,' shouted Petillius, 'we need to make as much ground as we can before they follow.' Exhausted men clung desperately to the saddles and the horses frothed at the mouth as they galloped as fast as they dared across the plain. For an hour they pushed both animals and humans to the limit until finally the Legate gave the order to halt at a stream. Everyone fell to their knees in relief and drank deeply as Tribune Dellus approached the Legate.

'Dellus, you made it through,' said Petillius.

'I did, my lord, but how, I will never know.'

'What of our men?'

'Eleven lost and three wounded my lord. An outcome we could only dream of.'

'The gods were smiling on us,' said Petillius, 'but we are not clear yet. Those barbarians won't be far behind us.'

'We can't go on much further, my lord, the horses are about to drop through exhaustion, as are the men.'

'We have to,' said Petillius, 'if that horde catches us there will only be one outcome.'

'We will do our best, my lord,' said Dellus.

'Riders approach,' shouted a voice, making every man jump to their feet in fear.

'Shit,' cursed Petillius, 'surely they can't have caught us up already?' He reached for his Gladius and ran up to the man who had sounded the alarm.

'To our front, my lord,' said the soldier.

Petillius heart sank. In the distance he could see a dust cloud, raised by the hooves of many horses.

'We are surrounded,' he said quietly. 'It looks like our journey ends here.' The remainder of the legion walked up beside him, a hundred exhausted, bloody men, bedraggled and pathetic remnants of a once great legion.

'Look to your gods, men,' said Petillius, 'for today we dine with our ancestors.'

'I think not my lord,' said the Scout Decurion, the only man still astride his horse, 'for if I am not mistaken, they carry the Boar standard before them, the emblem of the Valeria Victrix.'

'I don't understand,' said Petillius, 'it can't be a Victrix patrol, they are in the south.'

'Suetonius sent word for support,' shouted the scout in excitement. 'It looks like the request was heeded, my lord. It's not a Victrix patrol, it's the entire fucking legion.'

For a second the news didn't sink in, but as the vanguard of the oncoming legion became more discernible, the remaining men of Petillius's unit started to laugh and cheer, waving their swords in the air at the oncoming relief.

'Silence,' shouted Petillius. 'Sheath swords and form up, double ranks. Aquilifer, stand forward and present the Eagle. We may be few but we are still the Ninth Hispana and we will welcome the Victrix as such. I thought this day was done but I was wrong – it has only just begun.'

Chapter Twenty-Three

Verulamium

Once more, terrifying screams echoed through smoke-filled streets and mutilated bodies lay in rivers of blood as Boudicca's army slaughtered men, women and children in the name of freedom. This time, the slaughter wasn't taking place in the town of Londinium but the city of Verulamium and due to its high population of ex-Roman legionaries, the initial defence had been strong and bloody. However, the final outcome was never in doubt and eventually the never-ending ranks of Britannic warriors swarmed through the streets in a frenzy of violence, hacking every living thing in their path. In amongst them was Boudicca, flanked by Rianna and Heanua, and all three women were just as committed to the slaughter as the rest of the Britannic army. No quarter was shown to the enemy and bodies lay everywhere, dead and dying from the brutal onslaught of the barbarian hoard and by the time the night was over, thirty thousand corpses lay in the streets.

Once again, the rampaging warriors took out their frustrations on those unlucky few spared the massacre, and the screams of tortured souls filled the night air as they suffered unspeakable atrocities at the hands of the barbarians.

Boudicca stood at the back of a crowd, watching silently as they strung up their prisoners on wooden frames, before torturing them with burning brands on their naked flesh. Heanua ran up beside her, breathless from the exhilaration of the battle.

'Mother,' she cried, 'look what we found in that burning villa.'

Boudicca glanced down at the golden necklaces hanging around her daughter's neck.

'Very pretty,' she said and looked back toward the tortured men. Heanua followed her gaze and fell quiet as she witnessed the horrifying acts being inflicted on the screaming prisoners.

'What are they doing?' she asked.

'You can see what they are doing, Heanua,' said Boudicca quietly, 'and you should look well for this is the true face of warfare. The victors wear the baubles while the losers die screaming.'

'A fate well deserved,' snarled Heanua.

'Really?' asked Boudicca. 'What did they do to deserve such a fate?'

'I don't understand,' said Heanua. 'Today we fought alongside each other and I lost count of the men slain at your hands. Why do you now doubt our cause?'

'There is no doubt, Heanua, our cause is true.'

'Then why worry about those who die at our people's hands?'

'To kill or indeed die in the heat of battle is an honour,' said Boudicca, 'but no man deserves to be tortured so.'

'The Romans crucify our people,' said Heanua, 'is that not as vile a death?'

'It is,' said Boudicca, 'but since when do we measure ourselves by them? Our people have always settled argument by trial of arms but any death is swift and with honour. A death such as that before us is an abomination before the gods.'

'They are still the enemy,' said Heanua, 'and deserve to die.'

'Those who bleed before us are just symptoms of the disease,' said Boudicca, 'the infection is yet untouched.'

'Boudicca,' called a voice and the queen turned to see Rianna running toward her, accompanied by a younger man.

'Rianna,' said Boudicca, 'I trust your sword arm is weary?'

'It is,' said Rianna, 'but there is no time for celebration – this man has news.'

'Speak,' said Boudicca.

'My Queen,' said the man, 'I have ridden with a message from Maccus. The legion of Suetonius has left its fort and is marching across country as we speak.'

'To here?' asked Boudicca.

'No, they march north,' said the young warrior.

'Why would they march north?' asked Boudicca. 'They have no strongholds in that direction.'

'We know not,' said the man, 'only that their fort burns behind them.'

Rianna turned to stare at Boudicca.

'If they have burned their fort, it means they have no stronghold to bolt to. Perhaps they return from whence they came and seek refuge in the hills of the Khymru.'

'Possibly,' said Boudicca, 'but to reach them they have to pass through the lands of the Trinovantes, lands that are ideal for open battle. This is the opportunity we have waited for, Rianna. Suetonius has made a grave error. If we move quickly, we can catch him before he reaches the

Khymru and send his cursed legion the way of the Ninth. Send word to the warlords. Withdraw their men back to the river. We march with the dawn.'

–

Suetonius rode at the head of his legion. They had left the temporary fort the previous day and had marched just ten miles in over twenty-four hours. The pace was frustratingly slow but if his plan was to succeed, it was essential that Boudicca took the bait and pursued him north. The Primus Pilus rode alongside him and together they talked over the details of the plan.

'Are the men ready, Cassus?' asked Suetonius.

'As ready as they will ever be,' said Cassus, 'though I fear their strength will be of little use in open battle.'

'Let's hope that isn't necessary,' said Suetonius. Before he could continue, Cassus indicated a group of riders galloping toward them in a cloud of dust.

'A patrol approaches,' he said, 'and it looks in a hurry.'

Suetonius gave the order for the column to halt and ten of their own cavalry rode out to meet the oncoming party. A few minutes later both groups rode in toward the legion and one rider detached to approach the general.

'Hail, Suetonius,' he said. 'I bring message from the Valeria Victrix. Our legion marches parallel to yours a day's ride away.'

'Excellent news,' said Suetonius. 'Are you at full strength?'

'No, we are three thousand strong though we are joined by the survivors of the Ninth Hispana. A unit not exceeding a hundred men.'

'Does Petillius live?'

'He does, my lord, and has taken temporary command of the Vexillation. He is hungry for retribution and awaits your orders.'

'Tell Petillius to continue north west until he reaches a wide river,' said Suetonius. 'Go firm there and we will join him as soon as possible.'

'I also have news of a graver nature,' said the man. 'It is said that Verulamium burns and everyone within has been slaughtered.'

Suetonius glanced at Cassus before shaking his head.

'There is nothing we can do,' he said. 'We continue with the plan.'

'Shouldn't we send a patrol to see if there is anything we could do?' asked the rider.

'No, we will need every man if this madness is to be brought to an end. Verulamium is lost to us. Tell Petillius we will join forces before the sun sets tomorrow and make a stand against this woman.'

'Yes, my lord,' said the man and turned his horse to return to his unit. Within moments they were galloping away across the plains.

'Events are closing in fast,' said Cassus.

'They are,' said Suetonius, 'and truth be told, it is a situation I welcome. It is time we steeled our hearts and showed this woman the real strength of Rome.'

–

Prydain and Heulwen lay hidden in the bracken, cold and tired from their long day's hunting. So far, they had managed to get nothing more than a wood pigeon but finally they had struck lucky as less than fifty paces away was a deer grazing at the edge of the forest. Slowly they crawled forward, each desperate to fell the creature that would feed their party for several days. Finally they slipped into a ditch, out of sight of the animal.

'Stay here,' whispered Heulwen, removing the wrapped bow from her back. 'I will get closer on my own.'

'I am no stranger to hunting, Heulwen,' said Prydain.

'We can't afford to get this wrong and with two of us there is twice as much chance of being noticed.'

'You flatter yourself,' said Prydain but sat back as Heulwen strung her bow. She peered over the lip of the ditch.

'Still there,' she said. 'I will go up as far as that bush. It is downwind and from there I should get a clear shot.'

Prydain watched her crawl over the edge and adjusted his position to watch events unfold. It was essential the hunt was successful as the group was out of meat and the heavy Roman presence in the area meant they couldn't risk entering a village to buy supplies. Despite his jibe, he was well aware of Heulwen's prowess as a hunter and her skills with both bow and knife were unrivalled. Truth be told, he had no doubt her aim would be true and they would dine again on venison that night.

Heulwen crept forward, keeping as low as possible. Inch by inch she covered the ground, pausing only when the deer looked up nervously.

'Steady,' whispered Prydain to himself as she took aim but he knew there was no way she would miss from that range. Suddenly the deer's head flew up startled at some unseen danger.

'Shoot,' gasped Prydain again, even though he knew Heulwen was too far away to hear but despite the imminent flight of the deer, Heulwen lowered her bow and stood up. Immediately the deer bolted and Prydain cursed out loud before running over to join Heulwen.

'What's the matter with you?' he shouted. 'You could have taken that deer easily.'

'Forget the deer,' said Heulwen without facing him, 'look there.'

Prydain followed her gaze and at first thought there was a grass fire out on the plains, but after a few moments he could make out that what he thought was smoke was actually dust. Dust from the feet of tens of thousands of marching people.

'Who do you think it is?' asked Heulwen.

'There is only one army as big as that in Britannia,' said Prydain, 'it has to be Boudicca and it looks as if they are travelling with purpose. Come on, we have to go.'

'Where?' asked Heulwen.

'To get the others,' said Prydain. 'If Taliesin is anywhere, he is amongst that throng. I think it is about time we joined the cause.'

The two ran back through the woods to get the rest of the men while back on the plains, a team of four black horses pulled a chariot holding a Britannic Queen at the head of an army over a hundred thousand strong.

Taliesin and Finian walked through the depths of the forest leading a horse carrying the exhausted Lannosea. They had found the horse earlier that morning standing by its dead rider, a Roman cavalry man with three arrows in his back and since then their pace had quickened. The further they went, the more people they saw in the woods, each making their way as fast as possible in the opposite direction but every attempt to make conversation was ignored as the refugees concentrated on their plight. Finally a woman and child passed close enough for Finian to run her down.

'Please don't hurt us,' screamed the woman, covering her young child with her body.

'Why would I hurt you?' asked Finian.

The woman looked up in confusion.

'You are not Roman?'

'Me, of course not,' said Finian, and then looked down at the red cloak draped around his shoulders.

'Shit, I forgot about this,' he said. 'Don't worry, I took it from a dead man. I am Khymric and hate the invaders as much as you. I mean you no harm.'

The woman stood but kept her child held tightly against her side, still unsure about the stranger.

'Tell me,' said Finian, 'who are all these people and why are they running?'

'You don't know?' asked the woman.

'Know what?'

'Boudicca has sacked Londinium and Verulamium. Both cities lie in ashes and they say the bodies stack higher than a hill.'

'She has sacked Verulamium as well?' gasped Finian. 'Her army must be impressive.'

'She has an entire nation on the march,' said the woman, 'and that is why we run. That many people need feeding and her warriors take everything in their path, food, horses, even women.'

'Why would they rape their own?' asked Finian.

'It is said the army has become so great that Boudicca's warlords struggle to keep discipline. It takes a rider half a

280

day to ride from one flank to another. She has become as much a threat as those she wishes to depose.'

'Where is this army?' asked Finian.

'An hour's ride west,' said the woman. 'I have heard others say the Romans lie that way also, and there will be a reckoning within days. Can I go now?'

'Of course,' said Finian. 'Thank you.' He returned to Taliesin and Lannosea who were sharing the last of the water.

'Well?' said Taliesin.

'There is good news,' said Finian, 'Boudicca lies less than a day west of here. The only thing is it seems she intends to face Suetonius, so we must be careful not to fall victim to either side.'

'Why would my mother's people be a risk to us?' asked Lannosea.

'Those who are loyal will probably be true,' said Finian, 'but the army has outgrown her influence and many see this fight as a means to riches and glory. They forget the true cause preached by your mother.'

'Nevertheless, our fate is likely to be safer amongst the Britons,' said Taliesin, 'and I think it is a risk we should take.'

Finian nodded.

'Then we should move as quickly as possible,' he said, 'and return the girl before battle is joined.'

'Why?' asked Taliesin.

'Think about the omens,' said Finian. 'The return of the queen's daughter on the eve of battle will send raptures through her lines and add strength to their sword arms. They may be a rabble but they are a Britannic rabble and we will need every advantage possible to defeat the

281

Romans. Now, if you are both agreeable, we need to get going.'

The Gemina legion formed a defensive position while Suetonius rode forward flanked by a cohort of cavalry to meet with Petillius at the river edge. The two legions had camped a mile apart along the river and the governor wanted to see for himself the strength of the Victrix and even more importantly, the state of Legate Petillius' mind. The man had just lost one legion and Suetonius wanted to make sure he was in a fit state to command.

The general rode toward the camp, passing squad after squad of mounted guards placed at strategic points along the route. He noticed with satisfaction that they seemed alert and focussed, obviously fully aware of the perilous situation their legion was in. Finally he rode through the outer limits of the marching camp, leaving his escort waiting on the outside. Minutes later he was shown into the command tent of Petillius.

The Legate immediately stood and saluted the general.

'Hail, Suetonius,' he said. 'Your arrival is timely and welcome.'

'Sit,' said Suetonius abruptly, 'our time is limited for such formalities. I need to know what happened to the Ninth and what strengths the Victrix offer.'

For the next half hour Petillius briefed the general about the demise of his legion. Suetonius listened carefully, often interrupting the Legate with pointed questions regarding tactics. Finally he sat back and stared at Petillius.

'I hear only a hundred men survived,' he said eventually.

'A few more have been subsequently found by our patrols,' said Petillius, 'but we fear there are no more.'

'And when you were found, you immediately took command of the Victrix,' said Suetonius. 'On whose authority?'

'Nobody's,' said Petillius. 'They marched without their Legate who is laid low with illness. He sent what strength he could spare under the command of his Tribunus Laticlavius. A keen young man but with no battle experience. I felt that in the circumstances, I was better able to ensure the legion's effectiveness. Of course, if you wish me to stand down...'

'That won't be necessary,' said Suetonius. 'We do not have time for petty politics; your reputation speaks for itself. No doubt there will come a time when you will have to answer to a greater authority regarding the fate of the Ninth, but in the meantime, I need your experience alongside me. What forces are under your command?'

Petillius breathed a silent sigh of relief. He wanted a chance to redeem himself and had taken a chance assuming command of the Victrix, but it was a gamble that had paid off.

'Two cohorts of heavy infantry,' he said. 'Another two of auxiliary light infantry and five hundred cavalry.'

'Any archers?'

'Two centuries only,' said Petillius.

'Artillery?'

'Ballistae and Onagers, twenty of each.'

'Scorpios?'

'Just under a hundred,' said Petillius.

'A depleted force but it will have to do,' said Suetonius.

'General,' said Petillius, 'I have to reiterate the dangers of facing this woman in open battle. I have never seen such numbers and I fear even our combined strength may not be enough to claim victory.'

'And that is why I have no intention of meeting this woman in open battle,' said Suetonius. 'In fact, my plan is quite the opposite. Listen well, Legatus, for our fate lies not in brute strength or overwhelming numbers but in the most basic of legionary skills. Discipline.'

For the next hour Suetonius outlined his plans and by the time he had finished, the temporary commander of the Victrix Vexillation knew exactly what was expected of him.

'Send out patrols immediately,' said Suetonius, 'and instruct them to report back no later than nightfall tomorrow. My own patrols are scouring the area as we speak and it is essential we find a suitable location as soon as possible. I am informed that Boudicca is on the move and trails us no more than two days behind. This is it, Petillius, this is the time of reckoning. We will face this woman with Britannia itself the spoils. Before we are finished the fate of this country will be decided.'

-

Suetonius returned to his horse and made his way back to the Gemina lines. Everything relied on the success of the patrols sent to choose a suitable killing ground. Successful selection meant they had a chance, but if they got it wrong, he knew both legions would be slaughtered and Rome's influence in Britannia would come to a crashing end. The consequences were unthinkable. He could not afford to fail.

Chapter Twenty-Four

The Plains of the Trinovantes

Boudicca paused atop a small hill and gazed over the darkened plains in front of her. These were the lands of her childhood and she recognised the low rolling hills with longing in her heart. Those childhood days when she and Rianna rode these vales for hours on end without a care in the world seemed several lifetimes away. Thoughts back then were of freedom and fun, with occasional glances at the attractive boys of the village. Oh, how they had teased them and played them along, knowing full well that as the daughter of a king, there was no way she would ever choose one of them but nevertheless, the baiting had been fun.

These days her thoughts were of mayhem and slaughter. Her nights were wracked with nightmares and her days were taken up discussing the best way to kill thousands of fellow human beings. Her soul was split in two for despite her regret as to the necessity of killing, her heart knew it was the only way. She had no doubt that many more thousands had to die on both sides if Britannia was ever to be free. A terrible price but one worth paying.

'Does your mind race back?' asked Rianna at her side.

'It does,' said Boudicca, 'and plays in the streams where we swam as children.'

'A happy time,' said Rianna.

'It was,' said Boudicca, 'and it saddens me to know that somewhere out there, the plains where we made daisy chains and raced the clouds' shadows are now soiled by the feet of the invaders. Where there was grass is now mud and birdsong has been replaced with the sound of marching feet.'

'Then it is our duty to remove them,' said Rianna, 'and return these plains to our children.'

'It is,' said Boudicca, 'and I accept this burden placed upon me. They are out there somewhere and I intend to find them.' She looked back at the army amassed under her banner. Though the night was dark, the myriads of campfires paid testament to the numbers willing to die in the name of freedom. 'Look at them, Rianna,' said Boudicca, 'every fire represents a yearning to be free. Men, women, the old and the young all desperate to laugh again. Those who are long dead or have died in the course of this campaign are owed our victory. They earned it while those not yet born deserve it. We cannot afford to fail, Rianna, Andraste herself demands a victory.'

'Surely no army in the world can withstand an army so great,' said Rianna, gazing over the countless fires. 'Our numbers alone will see them crushed like ants beneath our feet. This is your time, Boudicca, this is where you release Britannia from her yoke of slavery.'

'We have to catch them first,' said Boudicca. 'If they reach the Khymru, we will never get them out and our warriors will ultimately disperse to their homes. This is our only chance.'

Rianna glanced around and saw a group of men carrying burning torches making their way up the hill.

'We may be in luck,' she said. 'Perhaps our scouts have news.'

The group reached them and Boudicca recognised the face of Maccus in the light of his burning torch.

'My Queen,' he said, 'we have momentous news. Today we watched as Suetonius left the river and led his legion north. They were joined by a lesser force but nothing to cause us alarm, we have twenty times their number.'

'So what other news brings you up here breathless from the ride?' asked Boudicca.

'My Queen, they have passed the Crag of Eagles and into Wolf's Pass.'

Boudicca paused as the information sunk in.

'I don't understand,' she said, 'that way lies nothing but impenetrable forest. The vale closes in and if they continue, they will be forced to retrace their steps or be trapped.'

'They obviously do not know this country like we do,' said Rianna, 'and have made an error of judgement. This is our chance, Boudicca; if we can move quickly, we can close the neck of the valley and the Romans will be trapped. They will have nowhere to go.'

Boudicca turned to Rianna.

'You are right,' she said, 'the gods have sent us a gift. Pass word to the warlords. Extinguish all fires and get the army moving.'

'Through the night?' asked Maccus.

'Yes,' said Boudicca, 'and make sure they carry no fire torches. I want to be at Wolf's Pass by dawn without any Roman scouts sending word to Suetonius. Tell them to wrap their weapons to dull any sound of steel on steel. Only the warriors are to march tonight, the carts and the rest of the people will follow at sunrise. This so-called governor has made a grave mistake and he will pay the price.'

–

Prydain and his fellow travellers headed toward the outskirts of Boudicca's camp. Though they had long ago joined the throng, the camp followers were spread out over many miles and it had taken far longer than they had thought it would to reach the main warrior core.

'Hold, stranger,' said a voice in the darkness. 'State your business.'

Prydain looked at the levelled spear aimed directly at his chest.

'I am a friend,' he said, 'and would seek permission to pass.'

'Beyond here are the campfires of the warriors,' said the man. 'Your voice is strange to me, what clan are you from?'

'The Silures,' said Prydain.

'There are no Silures here,' said the warrior, 'they hide in their forests like frightened children while real warriors fight for liberty.'

Gildas took a step forward but a hand from Taran held him back.

'Hold,' whispered Taran, 'they are nothing but cheap jibes. We cannot afford meaningless conflict now; we are too close.'

'He insults our people,' snarled Gildas, 'and should pay the price.'

'In another life, friend,' said Taran. 'Besides, he would not provide much contest and is not worth drawing your blade.'

'Our clan opposes the Augustan legion in the Khymru,' said Prydain to the guard. 'Be comforted that many Romans lose sleep in fear that they feel Silurian steel in the night.'

'Meaningless words,' spat the Guard. 'State your business.'

'I seek audience with Boudicca,' said Prydain.

The man laughed out loud.

'You and ten thousand others,' he said. 'Be gone and stop wasting my time.'

'My business is of great importance,' said Prydain.

'Then share it,' said the guard, 'and I will see it reaches her.'

'It is for her ears only,' said Prydain.

The man lifted his spear to rest against Prydain's throat and once more Taran had to restrain Gildas from leaping forward.

'Listen, friend,' said the guard. 'You come in darkness and speak in an accent strange to me demanding audience with the queen. As far as I know you could be an assassin sent from Nero himself. Now, I am very tempted to kill you and your comrades right here for wasting my time but I have fed well and am in a good mood. So what I suggest is this – either you tell me your message or you return from whence you came. Choose quickly or I'll stick you like a pig right now.'

For a few moments there was a standoff until finally Prydain spoke again.

'You are right,' he said, 'the circumstances are indeed suspicious. We will withdraw and make suitable representation in the light. I apologise for wasting your time.'

The man grunted and lowered his spear.

'Go,' he said, 'before I change my mind and don't think of using a different route. I will pass the word and if you are seen again this night, there will be no questions asked. You will die on the spot.'

'Thank you,' said Prydain and took a step backward before walking away, closely followed by his comrades.

'You should have let me kill him,' said Gildas.

'To what end?' asked Prydain as he walked. 'There are another fifty thousand in that camp and even you would struggle with those numbers, Gildas. Besides, we have no quarrel with Boudicca.'

'So what do we do now?' asked Heulwen.

'We find a place to sleep,' said Prydain, 'and try again in the morning.'

—

Suetonius stood at the entrance to the long valley. On either side were steep slopes heavily wooded and tangled with undergrowth, while underfoot the ground was treacherous and broken. To his front the valley continued for about a mile, sloping gently downhill before flattening out between the flanking hills. To the far end the ground started to rise again before meeting another steeply wooded slope, again impenetrable to any large bodies of men. It was a dead end and the only way out or into the valley was back the way they came.

'My lord, there is no way forward,' said Tribune Attellus. 'Do you want me to turn the legions around?'

'On the contrary, Attellus,' said Suetonius, 'here lies the only way forward. Advance the legions to the far end of the valley and go firm there. This is where we make our stand, Attellus, there is where history will be made.'

The Cornicines gave the signal to advance and Legate Petillius joined Governor Suetonius to one side as the two legions marched past.

'Petillius,' said Suetonius, 'I want you to set up the Onagers on the edge of the far wood line. Use the archers on either flank but set them back amongst the trees. The rest of the men will form up in line abreast. The Gemina will form the front lines while the Victrix will provide the reserve. Get the men as far up the slope as they can while maintaining a sure foothold; I want any attackers to be out of breath when they reach our lines.'

'Yes, my lord,' said Petillius and rode off.

As he rode away, Cassus approached and reined in his horse alongside the governor.

'So, Cassus,' said Suetonius. 'Does this suit?'

Cassus looked around the valley.

'It does,' he said. 'The scouts have done well.'

'I am informed that Boudicca has taken the bait,' said Suetonius, 'and will be here by the dawn.'

'Then we must make haste,' said Cassus, 'and prepare the men. They have time to eat and sharpen their swords. Boudicca will not attack in the dark but I want every man alert and in position before the sun rises.'

'And what of you, Cassus? How do you see your role in this?'

'My lord?'

'I would prefer you by my side, Cassus, but know you still smart from the attack on Mona.'

'There is only one place that I need be and that is amongst my men in the front line,' said Cassus.

'I thought you would say that,' sighed Suetonius. 'So be it, Cassus. The first cohort will provide the centre of the line. This is a task no other has taken before you and I need you to show those behind the meaning of discipline. The outcome of today will lie on the shoulders of your men. Do they have the strength to carry such a weight?'

'They do, my lord,' said Cassus, 'as do I.'

—

All through the night Boudicca's army marched across the open vale toward Wolf's Pass, until finally the queen stood on her chariot at the entrance to the valley, watching the sun's rays creep slowly across the ground.

'Where are they?' asked Rianna.

'They are there,' said Boudicca. 'Andraste will reveal them soon enough.'

Suddenly a glint in the distance caught their eye and slowly the sun's reflections on the Roman armour revealed the enemy position.

'The scouts were right,' said Boudicca, 'and Suetonius is trapped. He has nowhere to go.'

'They have formed defensive lines,' said Rianna.

'Of course they have,' said Boudicca. 'What else could he do? He knows he is trapped and has no option but to defend himself. But it will be in vain, Rianna; we outnumber him twenty-fold and he has nowhere to run.' She looked back the way they had come to witness the rest of her army stretched out far to the rear. Beyond them lay the countless wagons bearing their families and the supplies for the frontline warriors.

'It seems as if the whole of Britannia wants to witness this day,' said Boudicca, 'our people cover the plains like corn.'

'It is a momentous day,' said Rianna, 'for when these two legions fall, there will only be the Augusta left and they will waste no time leaving our shores or suffer the same fate.'

'Boudicca,' shouted Maccus, 'my men are impatient to bloody their swords. How long do we wait?'

'Advance them into the valley, Maccus,' said Boudicca, 'but stay out of range of their catapults. It will be a while before all our people arrive and I want them here to witness our victory.'

'And if the Romans attack?'

'They won't attack,' said Boudicca. 'Suetonius is no fool and his only hope is in defence. Tell the men to be patient and I promise before the sun is at its highest, they will blood their blades.'

Maccus gave the order and the front lines of the Barbarian army descended into the valley, making their way toward the silent Roman lines.

'Prydain, wake up,' shouted Heulwen, 'it seems like the whole world is on the move.'

Prydain discarded the blanket and jumped to his feet.

'What's happening?' he asked.

'Boudicca advanced in the night and faces Suetonius across a battlefield,' said Heulwen. 'Her people move at haste to witness the battle. Come on, there is little time to lose.'

The five comrades saddled their horses before riding out and joining the seemingly endless migration of people across the grassy plains. The going was good at first but as they caught up with the main body of people and carts, their pace slowed to a walk.

'It's no good,' said Prydain, 'we have to leave the horses. It will be quicker on foot.' He looked around the masses of people before spying a family whose cart had lost a wheel. 'Over there,' he said, 'follow me.' They rode up to the cart and dismounted. A woman stood alongside three young children; their faces dejected at their predicament.

'I see you are having difficulty,' said Prydain.

'The wheel has snapped,' said the woman in frustration, 'and my man fights alongside Boudicca. The cart contains all we own and I cannot leave it unattended. I fear we will not be there to share his glory.'

'There is another glory to be earned,' said Prydain, 'should you wish to offer aid.'

'What aid do you seek?' asked the woman.

'We have to get to the battlefield,' said Prydain, 'yet cannot risk our horses. If you look after them for us until we return, I will ensure you have enough wealth for ten such carts.'

'How?' said the woman. 'The only plunder from the enemy this day will be their heads and armour.'

'We have no intention of fighting,' said Prydain, 'and we have our own gold.' He pulled out the purse and poured the contents into his hand.

'There are ten coins here,' he said. 'One is yours now as a sign of my trust. The rest are yours upon our return.'

The woman's eyes widened in shock and she took the offered coin carefully before looking up at Prydain.

'You race toward the battle yet proclaim against fighting,' she said. 'What foolishness is this?'

'We look to return a runaway boy to his people,' said Heulwen. 'Nothing more.'

'Your offer is indeed generous,' said the woman, 'but what if you do not return?'

'Then you will have five fine horses to sell,' said Heulwen. 'All we ask is you wait until dark and if we are

294

not back by then, you are free to leave with the coin and the horses. Will you do this?'

The woman stared for a while before nodding.

'I will wait until dark,' she said, 'but no longer. The night is a dangerous time, especially when men are dying all around.'

'I understand,' said Prydain. He tied the reins of his horse to the immobilised cart before calling his comrades. 'Leave the horses here,' he said. 'We will pick them up later.'

'What is your name?' he asked the woman.

'Lora,' said the woman, 'and I hope you are successful in your quest.'

'So do I, Lora,' said Prydain, 'so do I.'

The woman sent her children into the safety of the cart before watching Prydain and his comrades run into the surging crowd heading toward the battle.

–

Taliesin, Finian and Lannosea crested the lip of the valley and stared at the sight before them. At the far end they could see the scarlet lines of the Roman ranks squashed between two steep hills, their armour glittering in the morning sun.

In the centre of the valley, thousands of Britannic warriors faced them across the open slopes, screaming their insults and banging their weapons against their shields. Lone warriors took the opportunity to run from the stationary ranks to taunt the Romans before returning to their comrades and continuing the tirade. Behind the front ranks of warriors thousands more people added their voices to the challenge, while on the slopes leading into the valley, countless carts vied for the best positions to witness the slaughter.

'Never have I seen such an army,' said Finian in awe, 'their numbers are like sand upon a shore and the Romans are but a red stain before them.'

'The Roman's fate is surely sealed,' said Taliesin. 'Not even a horse fly could escape this valley. The day is already ours.'

'Their leader must be stupid,' laughed Finian. 'In the open they had a chance to escape but, in this place, they are as wine within a jug.'

'And these people are the stopper,' laughed Taliesin, shouting above the din of the hoard around them.

'Look,' shouted Lannosea, 'there's my mother.'

All eyes stared forward and they could see the black chariot being ridden wildly across the front lines of warriors, closely followed by riders bearing the banners of the clans preparing to do battle.

'Come on,' said Lannosea, 'let's go.'

'Wait,' said Taliesin. 'Where are you going?'

'To join her of course,' said Lannosea. 'I have wronged her and she needs to know I admit my mistake. My burden was not inflicted by her but by those about to die by her hand. My place is with my mother.'

'But you are injured,' said Taliesin. 'What aid can you offer?'

'My support, my heart and my love,' said Lannosea. 'They alone will be worth a thousand arrows to my mother.'

Before Taliesin could argue further, Lannosea ran down the slope, intent on joining the battle.

'Well, what are you waiting for?' asked Finian. 'Isn't this why you came?'

Taliesin grinned and drew the Gladius they had taken from the dead Roman days earlier.

'It is,' he said, 'and whether I live or die this day, let it be said that Taliesin was present on the day Boudicca freed Britannia from Roman tyranny.'

Both men stepped forward and followed the girl down the slopes, their heads full of victory and hearts full of valour, each a tiny part of an army greater than any ever before seen in Britannia.

Chapter Twenty-Five

The Valley of the Wolf

'Report,' ordered Suetonius.

'My lord, the artillery are well dug into the rear,' answered a Tribune. 'We have several hundred rocks and double that number of fire pots.'

'What about the flanks?'

'Two cohorts of auxiliary infantry deployed across the slopes and amongst the trees. If they try to outflank us our men have been ordered to hold the ground at all costs. They will gain no advantage that way.'

'And the rear?'

'Covered by our reserve,' said the Tribune. 'Petillius commands the high slopes, and beyond, the forests are too dense for any surprise attack. No, the only way they pose any threat is head on.'

Suetonius stared across the valley. The enemy seemed to be rolling down the opposite slopes like a thick black liquid, expanding to fill every piece of open ground. Already they had reached over halfway and still they came. The front lines had halted less than a thousand paces before the silent Roman formations screaming their insults across the broken ground that would soon echo with cries of a different sort.

'Primus Pilus, what is the mettle of our men?' asked Suetonius.

'Quiet,' said Centurion Cassus. 'Their eyes are filled with superior numbers and they are in danger of putting quantity above quality.'

'I agree,' said Suetonius. 'This is where we earn our rations, Centurion. Mount your horse for it is time to join our men.' He turned to Tribune Attellus.

'Attellus, should I fall, you will assume command.'

'My lord, surely you are not going down there. Your place is here to oversee and command as necessary. One sword arm won't affect the outcome.'

'Normally you would be right,' said Suetonius, 'but not this day. Today the men are outnumbered twenty to one by a barbarian army such has never been seen. Today they need their commanding officer amongst them. I am the direct representative of Nero on these islands and our continued dominance revolves around this one battle. I have been awarded the title 'Governor' of these islands and today, Attellus, I will earn that honour.'

Attellus silently saluted his general.

The governor turned to the rest of the officers gathered around him.

'You have all been briefed,' he said, 'and know what to do. You are the best Rome has to offer and should we all die this day, then I expect the last man standing to be holding our Eagle as he meets his gods. This is it, gentlemen, the greatest battle you are ever likely to face. In the name of your gods, your emperor and your legion, I General Gaius Suetonius Paullinus, Legatus of the Fourteenth Gemina Martia Victrix, and governor of Rome's Britannic islands salute you.' He paused as he looked around the gathered officers, each a man he would entrust with his very life. Finally he spoke again, 'Gentlemen,' he said, 'it has been an honour.' He extended his arm in the legionary salute and in return every man in earshot returned the tribute, shouting out his name in respect.

'Cassus,' said Suetonius over the noise, 'lead the way. Our men await.'

The two men rode between the massed ranks and down to their forward lines. As they did, they were followed by the shouts of cheering men as the army realised their general was going to lead from the front.

-

Across the valley, Boudicca watched as the unmistakeable figure of the Roman general rode across the front of his pathetic army. The Romans were formed up in straight ranks across the valley floor from slope to slope but were no more than twenty deep. Behind them she could see squares of reserves on the higher slopes and beyond them rows of Ballistae and the tell-tale plumes of smoke that meant they had the liquid fire which would be used against her own warriors. It was a fearsome weapon but she knew it could only be used at distance and though many of her warriors may fall to its fiery embrace, the numbers would be slight compared to her overall strength.

Boudicca stood on her chariot, one of many spread out across the valley before the main body of men.

'This is it, Rianna,' said Boudicca. 'The day we pay back Rome for every life taken, every Briton enslaved and every temple burned.'

'My heart races like Andraste's hare,' said Rianna, 'and my arm aches to wield steel.'

'Before this day is out, the gods will be sated with enough blood for a thousand lifetimes,' said Boudicca, 'and I will gain revenge for my people and my daughters.' She looked across at the next chariot. Heanua glanced back, feeling her mother's eyes upon her. Heanua's face was rigid with determination and her leather armour was proudly emblazoned with the emblem of the Iceni. Boudicca nodded gently, offering encouragement.

'This day will be sung about by the bards forever more,' said Rianna, her hair blowing in the breeze, 'and your name will be immortalised alongside Andraste.'

'I do not seek immortality, Rianna, only freedom for my country and release from my torment.'

'What torment is this?' asked Rianna with confusion in her eyes.

'The torment of a mother who failed her daughters,' said Boudicca, and without another word rode her chariot forward before turning to face her people. A seemingly never-ending sea of faces lay before her, men and women alike each desperate to spill the blood of the invaders. Sunlight reflected from thousands of weapons and behind them in the distance, the slopes were alive with the families and carts of the camp followers, each jostling for position to see the slaughter of the Romans. It seemed to Boudicca that every citizen of Britannia was present on those slopes and she knew that the gods had favoured her with an unbeatable advantage.

The cheering was deafening and finally she held up her hands for silence. For an age nothing happened but finally the noise died and the army strained to hear her words.

'People of Britannia,' she shouted. 'Today, we are not Iceni or Trinovantes. We are not Brigantes, Dobunii or Catuvellauni. We are one people, fighting for one country. Durotriges fight alongside the Belgae and Coritani call the Deceangli brother. Today our traditional enemies are friends and scores are put aside to face the one true enemy we all share, the Romans.'

A cheer ripped the air apart before she continued.

'For too long they have raped our women and killed our men and our children have been taken to far off shores, a never-ending life of slavery before them. Our gods have been ridiculed and our temples burned. We have all heard tell of the fate befallen Mona where our holy people perished at the hands of the invaders. Our healers and holy men, the seers, the poets and the bards, all were slaughtered by the blood thirsty actions of Rome and the man responsible stands before you.' She pointed toward the Roman lines. 'There lies the one called Suetonius, the one who calls himself 'Governor'. Before this day is over, I will bathe in his blood and these lands will return to our ancestors. Today we rid our lands of this pestilence and never again will we allow them or any other to step foot on our shores. From today onward we are no longer an island of tribes but one people, fighting as one, the Britons.'

Once more the crowd cheered and Boudicca knew the time was almost upon them when she would unleash her overwhelming ferocity upon the Romans.

–

A few hundred yards away, Lannosea was forcing herself between the massed ranks of the warriors, desperate to get to her mother's side before the battle started, knowing full well that her presence would add strength to Boudicca's resolve.

'Let me through,' she shouted over and over but to no avail, the deafening cheering and almost rabid desperation for battle to be joined meant that most ignored her, each eager to enter the fray. Behind her, Taliesin and Finian also fought their way through the throng, trying as hard as they could to stay near the girl but within moments her frail figure was lost amongst the crowd.

'Where is she?' shouted Taliesin, 'I can't see her.'

'Nor can I,' replied Finian. 'Just keep going forward and look for Boudicca's chariot. She will try to reach her mother.'

With renewed energy Taliesin forged forward between the screaming crowd but gradually the noise lessened once more as Boudicca called for silence. Taliesin stretched upward and could just see the queen's red hair above the sea of heads. In one hand she held aloft a sword while in the other was a round shield.

'What's happening?' asked a voice.

'Boudicca has just released a hare from beneath her cape,' shouted another, 'and it ran toward the enemy. It is a sign from Andraste herself – the way has been shown.'

–

Across the valley Suetonius was also addressing his men, though he did so from horse-back.

'Men of Rome,' he called. 'Before us stands a barbarian army the like of which has never been seen before, but do not let this weaken our spirit. They have numbers only and that is not enough. They do not have the training we have, nor do they have the discipline instilled into each and every one of us since the day we took the Sacramentum. Each one of us is worth ten of them and it is this that will win us this day, discipline and controlled aggression. Every moment of our military lives have led toward this battle, for here we prove to these islands once and for all that resistance is not an option. Today we will send a message to every corner of these lands that Rome is all powerful and they resist at their peril.

'Our plans are clear,' he continued, 'and if you follow the commands of your leaders, this barbarian hoard will spear themselves on our waiting swords. Our culture is with us, our ancestors are with us and our gods are with us. Do not fight for yourself this day, fight for the man alongside you and his family for they are what we stand for, a brotherhood of strength and glory.' He drew his Gladius and stood up in his stirrups.

'Men of Rome,' he shouted, 'Legionaries of the four-teenth Gemina Martia Victrix, fellow soldiers. Stiffen resolve and do your duty for today, we create history.'

Even Boudicca's horses knew that something was about to happen and they strained against their reins, desperate to gallop across the plain before them. The barbarian army was already inching forward and Boudicca knew it was time to unleash them.

'Warriors of Britannia,' she shouted, 'behold the last of the invaders. Spill their blood and we can once again be free. Our fight is just and Andraste herself champions our cause.' She held up her spear so the whole army could see it above their heads.

'For Andraste,' she screamed, 'for Britannia and for freedom.'

'For freedom,' roared the army and as one, a line of war chariots raced forward, leading over a hundred thousand warriors surging toward the Roman lines.

'Here they come,' shouted Cassus. 'General, step into the line.'

Suetonius dismounted and gave the reins to another cavalry man to take it back up to safety. The front rank shuffled sideways to allow the general to stand amongst them.

'My lord, you should go to the rear,' said a Decurion.

'You are wrong, soldier,' said the general as someone gave him a Scutum, 'today my place is amongst my men. The rest is in the hands of the gods.'

Chapter Twenty-Six

The Battle of Watling Street

Boudicca raced her chariots headlong toward the Roman lines, determined to use their weight to smash holes in the Roman defences. Painted warriors, both male and female screamed from the platforms, brandishing spears they would release as soon as they were in range. The massed ranks of the Britannic tribes raced in their wake, wielding their own weapons of death. Behind them Prydain and his comrades crested the hill and looked down into the valley in astonishment.

'What's happening?' gasped Gildas, catching up with the fitter men.

'The battle is about to start,' shouted Cullen. 'Boudicca's chariots race free from her army.'

'The Roman force is tiny in comparison,' said Heulwen, 'Boudicca's warriors will smash them with ease.'

Prydain took in the scene in an instant, remembering the constant training he had undertaken in his days with the legions.

'No,' he shouted in alarm, 'what is she doing? Chariots are pointless in these circumstances.'

'How so?' asked Cullen.

'The Romans are in a defensive formation,' said Prydain. 'They expect this attack and will have taken steps to guard the approach from any sort of cavalry.'

'How?' asked Cullen. 'They have had no time to build defensive palisades.'

'They have endless means,' said Prydain, 'at the very least the approach will be covered by archers.'

'Well, we will soon see,' said Gildas. 'The first blows are about to be dealt.'

—

The chariots hurtled toward the Romans, and for a few seconds it seemed they would crash into the enemy lines with devastating effect but suddenly, and without warning, the horses started to crash to the floor, screaming in agony and causing the chariots to smash into smithereens, killing or injuring the riders within.

Boudicca watched in horror as her chariots disintegrated around her but before she could realise what was happening, one of her own horses screamed in pain and crashed to the floor, dragging the other three down behind it. Boudicca and Rianna were flung from the chariot and landed face first in the dust of the valley.

—

Back up on the hill, Prydain witnessed the destruction of Boudicca's chariots.

'What's happening?' shouted Heulwen. 'They are falling like autumn leaves.'

Prydain scanned the field furiously. He could see no defences of timber spikes or ditches and there were certainly no lines of spear throwers in range.

'The archers hold their cords,' said Prydain. 'They are confident the attack will fail. That means there must be a hidden threat, one that will bring down any horse-borne warrior.'

'What sort of threat?' asked Heulwen.

'Unless I am mistaken,' said Prydain, 'I suspect they use the Tribulus.'

'What's a Tribulus?' asked Heulwen.

'A set of four spikes arranged in such a way that when they are strewn across the ground, one spike always faces upward while the other three provide a solid base. It is no more than the size of a fist and difficult to see amongst the grass so when a galloping horse steps on one, it pierces its hoof and brings the beast crashing down. They are lethal against cavalry and chariots alike.'

'But surely Boudicca would have expected such a weapon?'

'Don't forget, Heulwen,' said Prydain, 'this is a peoples uprising and perhaps she has not yet encountered such things.'

'The army slows,' shouted Gildas. 'They have seen the threat and pick their way amongst the dead.'

'And that is exactly what Suetonius wants,' said Prydain, and looked over to the treeline on the flanking slopes. Almost as if summoned, lines of archers appeared from the trees and aimed their arrows high into the sky.

'By the gods,' shouted Cullen, 'they will be picked off like fish in a pool.'

The skies above Boudicca's army darkened with the flights of Roman arrows and within seconds, hundreds of men dropped to the floor, their bodies pierced with lethal barbed arrows.

Volley after volley followed and the killing zone filled with the dead and dying. Behind them the main army faltered, but within moments thousands of fresh warriors pushed through the throng to take the place of those already fallen. These men were heavily bearded and carried longer shields similar to those used by the Romans. Their leaders screamed their commands and the fresh warriors broke into a run, clambering over their fallen comrades and negotiating their way between the thousands of lethal spikes strewn across the valley floor. Again the skies darkened but this time they were expected and every time a volley was fired, the Celtic warriors dropped to their knees to take shelter behind their shields and although some arrows got through, only a few men fell as a result of the onslaught.

'Boudicca, are you alright?' shouted Rianna. 'Boudicca, wake up.'

Boudicca's eyes opened slowly, unsure of where she was. The taste of blood and dust in her mouth soon brought reality flooding back and she gasped in pain as all feeling returned.

'Rianna,' she gasped. 'We live still.'

'We do,' said Rianna, 'and are sheltered from the Roman archers by the bodies of the horses.'

Boudicca could feel the rapidly cooling corpse of one of the magnificent beasts behind her, its body now riddled with arrow shafts.

'Loyal unto death,' muttered Boudicca and tried to sit up.

'Stay down,' ordered Rianna. 'We are within range of their archers and that red hair of yours would present too rich a target.'

'We can't stay here,' argued Boudicca.

'Our people will be here any second,' said Rianna. 'The first wave fell around us but the Trinovantes send their shield bearers.'

As she spoke, the first of the men passed their position and made their way slowly toward the Roman lines. One of the men threw the women a spare shield from a fallen comrade before carrying on behind his comrades. Rianna picked up the shield and helped Boudicca to her feet.

'Come,' she said, 'we need to get you back.'

'I am not going back,' said Boudicca, 'my place is with these people.'

'I know,' said Rianna, 'but you won't go far like this.'

Boudicca looked down and saw an arrow sticking out of her side. She grimaced at the sight, realising that though it probably wasn't fatal, it had to be removed and to do that safely, she needed a Shaman.

'Alright,' she said, 'but only to sort this out, then we will return.'

Rianna nodded and helped the queen back toward the main army. Behind them, the Roman archers had exhausted their supply of arrows and were running back toward the defensive lines. In the meantime, hundreds of women and children from the Celtic army spread across the valley, picking up the metal spikes that had caused so much carnage and stacking them into easily visible piles. Before long the way was clear and the main body of the army advanced once more.

-

'Open the lines,' shouted Cassus, and the ranks parted for the running archers to slip through and take up positions in the rear with swords and small shields. They would now make up the remainder of the rear guard as the battle evolved, unless required as a reaction force to guard the flanks.

'The advance has slowed,' said Suetonius.

'A momentary respite, I fear,' said Cassus.

'I agree,' said Suetonius before turning his head to shout over his shoulder.

'Ready the fire,' he shouted and a flag bearer waved the signal to those on the slopes behind the legion. The Tribune in charge of the artillery saw the signal and passed the message down the lines.

'Ready Onagers,' he roared, and every trigger man held a little tighter on the rope that when pulled, would release a ball of fire high into the morning sky.

--

The enemy were now only a hundred strides away and had formed up into lines that spread from slope to slope across the valley. A large warrior stepped forward and raising an axe high, gave the command to charge. Right across the valley, thousands of screaming warriors started running toward the Roman lines, knowing that at last, the battle would be joined.

--

'The false fight ends, Cassus,' shouted Suetonius. 'Make peace with your gods for the enemy are upon us.' He raised his Gladius high into the air.

'Onagers,' he shouted, 'time to show these heathen the real meaning of war. Release fireballs.'

His sword arm dropped sharply and seconds later the thud of dozens of wooden catapults echoed across the valley, closely followed by the whoosh of air as fireballs left trails of black smoke in their wake, before falling amongst the massed ranks of the enemy.

'Fireballs,' shouted one of the warriors seeing the approaching threat. 'Take cover.'

Almost as one the attackers took cover behind their shields, not realising they would offer scant protection from the fiery death. Clay pots of burning oil smashed amongst them and those not hit directly were splashed with the sticky substance, screaming in pain as they struggled frantically to extinguish the flames on their skin and clothes.

Each fireball caused dozens of deaths and many more were severely burned as the blazing oil stripped skin from flesh. Hair and beards burst into flame and eyeballs burst from the searing heat, causing the bravest of warriors to scream in agony as they clutched at their faces in terror. Yet despite the numbers of dead and wounded, the attack continued unabated and the gap between the armies closed rapidly.

–

'Front rank, prepare Pilae,' roared Cassus, and the first line of soldiers hoisted their spears to shoulder height.

'On my command. Ten paces and release. Advance!'

The men ran forward and launched the spears high into the sky, sending the lethal weapons amongst the front lines of the rapidly approaching barbarians. Almost every spear found a target and the impetus of the attack slowed.

'Re-join,' screamed Cassus and the legionaries raced back to the lines.

The barbarians dropped to their knees, revealing massed ranks of archers a hundred paces to the rear.

Within seconds, the skies darkened again as they seized the opportunity to aim their own arrows at the Romans.

'Testudo,' roared Suetonius and legionary shields lifted to provide a cover impenetrable to enemy arrows. Beneath the shields, Romans sweated in fear as arrows thudded into their wooden shields like a hailstorm. Many arrow heads smashed through the wooden shields and some reached the neck or faces of the men beneath.

'Lift them higher,' screamed another centurion and the shields were hoisted to arm's length.

For several minutes the deadly rain continued but as it eased, the noise was replaced with something far more deadly; the deafening roar of ten thousand men as they raced to combat.

'Lower shields,' shouted Cassus. 'Third and rear ranks only, launch Pilae.'

Thousands of spears flew above his head, striking deep into the front lines of the warriors and though thousands more warriors fell, this time their impetus hardly faltered.

'Front rank present Scutum,' shouted Cassus, 'second rank present Pilae. Brace for impact.'

Each legionary in the front line lapped his shield over the one to his right and braced his shoulder into the concave face of his shield. The second rank placed their remaining spears over the shoulders of the front rank and leaned against the men before them. Each man knew the first impact was crucial and it was essential not to give ground; the whole battle could depend on it.

'*Ready*,' screamed Cassus from behind his own shield, '*brace!*'

'There is no way we will find Taliesin amongst that lot,' said Gildas, 'the valley is crowded.'

'We have to try,' said Heulwen. 'We need to go down there.'

'No,' snapped Prydain. 'The sheer numbers are a threat in themselves. They allow no room for manoeuvre.' He looked around the valley edge. 'Come,' he said, 'we will follow the ridgeline around and get closer to the battle. At least we will have a better view.'

'Won't those forests be guarded?' asked Cullen.

'They will,' said Prydain, 'but we have little choice. If we don't do something quickly our journey will be wasted.' Prydain turned and ran along the ridgeline, closely followed by his comrades. As they neared the treeline, they could see many warriors were already engaged with the auxiliaries amongst the trees.

'Don't stop,' shouted Prydain, 'head for the lower slopes.' Within seconds they were amongst a running battle. There was no room for tactics or formations; up here man fought against man in a deadly duel with only one possible outcome, the death of one combatant.

Prydain drew his sword and leapt over the dead bodies in his path, and though men of both sides fought desperately all around him, he knew this was nothing compared to the main battle unfolding in the valley below.

–

'*Hold*,' screamed Cassus, straining against the enormous force being exerted against the Roman lines. '*Not a step backward.*'

Each man in the Roman lines strained every sinew, but despite being close to the enemy, not many casualties were caused in those first few moments of contact. Closed shields meant few blades could reach them and the massive numbers meant the front lines of warriors were crushed against their shields. For several minutes both sides drove their weight against the enemy, the barbarians desperate to cause a breach and the Romans equally desperate to hold them out. Finally the pressure eased and the sounds of horns ripped through the air – Celtic signals to withdraw.

Slowly the warriors retreated but no more than fifty paces. The Romans gasped with relief, each man exhausted from the strain.

'We did it,' said a soldier. 'They have pulled back.'

'A momentary respite,' snarled Cassus, before stepping out of the line and turning to face his cohort.

'Do not relax your guard,' he ordered, 'prepare for another assault. Again they will be met with a wall of shields.'

'Look out,' screamed a soldier, and Cassus spun around just in time to avoid a spear hurled at his back. He pulled it from the ground and facing the Celtic army, snapped it across his knee.

'Come on barbarian filth. The day has just started and we haven't even broken sweat.'

His challenge was met with a roar and again the massed ranks raced forward to engage the Romans. Cassus regained his place in the line.

'Same again. Close ranks, present Scuta!'

The barbarians crashed into the Romans once more, though this time with even more ferocity. The Roman lines staggered backward but held firm until once again the barbarians withdrew to a safe distance. Over and over again the attacks came and each time the assaults were repelled. During the clashes, axes smashed through shields and attackers were despatched by the defenders. During another withdrawal, Suetonius came over and offering Cassus his flask, took the Centurion to one side.

'Cassus, the men are exhausted. We can't go on like this. The lines may be holding but with each attack we lose more men and though their losses are greater, they can well afford them, we cannot.'

'I agree,' said Cassus, staring at the enemy ranks. They too were tired and were being affected by the midday sun. 'The beast's ferocity has been tamed and it is time to show them our own resolve. Now we take the battle to them.'

'Then give the signal, Centurion,' said Suetonius, 'I tire of these games and would rather fall with Gladius drawn.'

Cassus saluted and marched to the front of his command.

'Legionaries of the first cohort,' he shouted. 'These past hours you have seen the mettle of the enemy. They are nothing but unwashed barbarians with little knowledge of battle. We, however, do have such knowledge and it is time we taught them how a battle should be fought.' He drew his Gladius and turned to face the enemy. '*First cohort,*' he screamed, '*Cuneus formation. Prepare to advance.*'

Behind him the centre of the lines marched forward to join the Centurion, and the flanks followed, a few paces behind.

All along the lines the order was repeated and men marched into well-drilled formations. Within moments, the recent flat line of the legion defences had transformed into the arrowhead shapes favoured for Roman attacks.

–

Up on the hill the artillery commander saw the tactics change and turned to his command.

'Onagers, use all remaining ammunition available to you. Ballistae and Scorpios, target their front lines. On my command, fire at will and reload faster than you ever have before. Any man found slacking will fall to my sword. Those below are relying on us. Prepare to fire.'

The Roman infantry below fell silent and faced the enemy across the corpse littered battlefield. The front lines of Boudicca's army were tired and though their numbers filled the valley, the confusion meant few fresh warriors could make their way forward. The Romans, on the other hand, had refreshed their ranks after every assault.

'My lord, the first cohort are ready,' shouted Cassus.

'Then do what you were born to do, Centurion,' shouted Suetonius, 'and lead us to victory.'

Behind them the artillery opened up with their devastating bombardment and the air was torn apart by volley after volley of giant arrows from the Ballistae and the smaller crossbow bolts from the Scorpios. Fireballs and giant boulders from the Onagers smashed amongst the barbarian ranks causing devastating casualties, but despite this, the tribe leaders rallied their own lines in defiance and sounded the charge toward the Roman advance.

Cassus raised his Gladius high above his head.

'*First cohort*, no prisoners, no retreat, no quarter. *Advance!*'

As one, over six hundred heavily armoured legionaries stepped forward and marched toward the oncoming enemy. The manoeuvre was repeated across the entire valley and two proud nations crashed into each other in a bloody battle that would determine the future of Britannia.

-

Lannosea was caught amongst the throng in the middle of the valley. Despite the crush she continued to push forward, determined to reach her mother's side. Far to her front she could see the trails of black smoke as the dreaded fireballs fell amongst those clans leading the assault and she knew that many would die. As she pressed forward, a ripple of angst seemed to flow through the crowd and a wail of fear rose from the throats of many women.

'What's the matter?' shouted Lannosea. 'What's happening?'

'Boudicca has fallen,' shouted a woman, 'hit by an enemy arrow.'

'No,' gasped Lannosea, stopping in her tracks. 'It can't be true.'

The shouts increased as the rumour spread.

'Boudicca has fallen,' came the call. 'The queen is down.'

Lannosea shook herself from her momentary stupor.

'Is she dead?' she called. 'Does anyone know her fate?'

A warrior with severe burns limped past her, heading toward the carts to the rear.

'The queen is alive,' he said. 'At least she was when last I saw her.'

'Where is she?' gasped Lannosea.

'They have taken her to the Shamen,' said the warrior. 'They need to remove the arrow.'

Lannosea looked around the slopes of the valley, searching for the carts she knew would be there. At last she spotted the covered cart with the strange designs typical of all Shamen and knew her mother would be taken there. She changed direction and forced herself into the crowd again.

'Out of my way,' she screamed above the din. 'I have to get through.'

–

Both armies crashed into each other with mutual hatred and though the Celtic army was immense, the wedge-shaped formations of the Romans cut into their ranks like spear heads. The frustrations of many weeks added strength to the Roman sword arms and they hacked their way through the enemy ranks with impunity. The disciplined army kept its shape and each man protected the one to his left as they slowly split the barbarian army apart.

Cassus took the lead at the head of his elite first cohort and his mind was lost amongst the battle lust. Over and over again his blade met barbarian flesh and his shield smashed into the faces of those stupid enough to confront him. Lakes of blood turned the battlefield into red mud and any wounded man unlucky enough to fall at the Romans' feet had their faces caved in by hobnailed Caligae, their brains joining the cloying mess of the valley floor.

The artillery had raised their aim and now fired the remaining missiles deep into the main body of the barbarian masses, causing mayhem and panic amongst the families of the warriors. Women and children fell in flames as the fireballs landed and the giant boulders from the Onagers smashed through flesh and bone, irrespective of age or sex.

The disciplined assault and controlled aggression caught the clans by surprise and though many took the battle to the Romans, they were soon cut down by the relentless advance. Faced with their own certain death some of the younger Britons turned and ran from the Romans, causing even more confusion amongst their ranks.

'*Hold your lines*,' screamed Maccus. 'The day is not lost.' He grabbed at those running past him and threw them back toward the relentless Roman advance. 'Do not shame your people,' he cried, 'face the enemy and die like men.'

The older men resumed their attack with renewed ferocity and though they counted for many enemy lives, far more Barbarians fell than Roman. Finally Maccus found himself isolated from any of his comrades and knew his time had come.

'*Come on!*' he screamed, and waved his enormous axe around his head. 'My gods await me with open arms, Romans. Who amongst you will join me?'

The nearest legionaries faltered, knowing that the first to approach would undoubtedly fall to the giant blade before he could be overcome. Suetonius stepped forward, knowing he had to do something quickly.

'Pila,' he ordered and a legionary handed him a spear.

'Get out of my way, heathen,' shouted Suetonius, 'and meet your gods alone.' He launched the Pila and watched with satisfaction as the steel shaft smashed into the man's chest.

Maccus dropped his axe and staggered backward. He looked up and saw several Romans running toward him with swords drawn and, knowing his fate was sealed, opened his arms wide to stare at the sky above.

'Andraste,' he roared, 'I attend thee in...'

Before he could finish, a sword plunged into his stomach and he fell to his knees. The sole of a Caligae smashed into his face and as he fell backward, the face of Suetonius appeared above him.

'Pathetic,' said the general and plunged his Gladius through the face of Maccus. 'Continue the advance,' shouted Suetonius withdrawing his sword, 'the enemy are turning. Press home the advantage.' He stepped over the corpse and forged forward, leaving the body of Boudicca's lieutenant behind him.

–

All across the battlefield the Romans unleashed their fury and though the enemy were immensely superior in numbers, the narrowness of the valley meant they could only ever deploy the same amount of men as the Romans at any one time. Slowly the barbarians were forced back, leaving hundreds of their dead behind them and gaps started to appear in their lines as many turned to escape the slaughter.

Within moments the malaise spread like a fire and warriors across the valley turned to flee. Many Romans continued but were astonished to hear the sound of the Cornicines sounding the halt. Men stopped in their tracks, gasping for breath, blood dripping from their swords.

Suetonius stormed up to the Cornicen, the young officer who had given the signal.

'What do you think you are doing?' he shouted. 'The enemy is in retreat.'

'I was ordered to sound the halt,' said the Cornicen.

'On whose command?'

'On mine,' said a voice and Suetonius turned to see Cassus removing his helmet.

'The enemy has turned, Centurion,' growled the general. 'Since when do we allow a foe to escape?'

'With respect, my lord,' said Cassus, 'the enemy are going nowhere.' He nodded toward the far end of the valley and slowly Suetonius saw the mayhem unfolding before him. The retreating army had run into those massed behind them and confusion reigned as tens of thousands of people struggled to escape. To add to the chaos, the many carts on the far slopes stopped any clear passage and the continuing arrival of those who had missed the battle meant pandemonium reigned.

'The men need a few minutes to reorganise, my lord,' continued Cassus. 'Then we can send the enemy to hell.'

Suetonius nodded silently and sheathed his sword. Cassus turned to face the ragged front lines of the legion, thousands of men looking at him in expectation, their hearts still racing from the conflict.

'Close your lines,' shouted Cassus as he strode along before them with Gladius drawn, 'and remember your training. You are legionaries not barbarians. Those with wounds fall back and seek the Medicus. Second and third ranks to the fore, I want fresh blades for what is about to unfold. Every man will drink deeply of their water bottles. Drain them and cast them away for there will be no time to drink in the hours ahead.' He turned to look at the panic ensuing at the far end of the valley. 'The next time we rest will be at the top of that ridge.'

The lines of Romans reorganised and straightened their formations. Within minutes silence fell, and Cassus returned to the front of the first cohort. The men were ready for the final battle and this time, there would be no stopping.

'My lord, we are ready,' he said.

Suetonius drew his bloody Gladius and held it up. This time there was no morale boosting speech – the men knew exactly what was expected of them.

'Soldiers of Rome,' shouted Suetonius, '*advance!*'

The legion stepped forward as one and within minutes, the massacre of Boudicca's army began.

–

'Leave me alone,' screamed Boudicca, 'I have to get back down there.'

'There is nothing you can do,' said Rianna, 'the tribes have turned and fight amongst themselves to escape the valley.'

'This can't be,' said Boudicca. 'The signs from Andraste were clear. This day should be ours. Our army still outnumbers theirs tenfold. We have to turn them around.' She tried to get to her feet but gasped in pain at the arrow still through her side.

'Boudicca, the day is done,' said Rianna. 'We have to get out of here.'

'*No*,' screamed Boudicca, 'the signs were right. Bring me the Shaman.'

Within moments the old woman was dragged in by her hair and cast at Boudicca's feet.

'Tell me old crone,' gasped Boudicca, 'why has Andraste turned her back?'

'Andraste stays true, my Queen,' said the woman, her head facing the soil.

'No,' snarled Boudicca, 'you took the dream root and she showed you a vision. Are you saying the vision was false?'

'The vision has come to pass as promised,' said the Shaman. 'The gods do not lie, but it is for us to interpret the visions as we see fit.'

'The vision was clear, hag,' said Boudicca, 'the minnow turned and consumed the pike. How could this have been interpreted in any other way?'

'Boudicca,' said Rianna quietly. 'I fear we looked too far into the future. The vision was about this battle only and indeed reflects the reality.'

'How can you say this?' shouted Boudicca. 'The Romans are the pike and we are the minnows.'

'Not today,' said Rianna and turned to stare into the valley. Boudicca followed her gaze and realisation dawned. The sheer size of her army compared to the Romans meant that her own people had become the predator and the Romans the prey. The vision had been true and now the Britons would pay with their lives.

'By the gods,' whispered Boudicca, 'how can I have got it so wrong?'

'You weren't to know,' said Rianna. 'All we can do now is salvage as much as we can and regroup for another day.'

They both looked up as a commotion broke out the other side of the ring of guards around the queen.

'Boudicca,' shouted a voice, 'I need to see you. I have important news.'

'Let him through,' shouted Rianna.

A warrior fell at Boudicca's feet and gasped for breath.

'My Queen,' he said. 'I have seen your daughter. Lannosea lives.'

'What?' gasped Boudicca. 'Are you sure?'

'Yes, my Queen. I have seen her with my own eyes.'

'Where?'

'In the valley,' said the man. 'She was caught up in the crowd but it was her, I swear.'

'Take me to her,' shouted Boudicca.

'No,' shouted Rianna. 'You need to escape this place. I will get your daughter.'

'As will I,' said a voice and both women looked over to see Heanua; her leather armour was covered with blood and her sword hung loose in her hand.

'Heanua,' said Boudicca, 'you made it. Come to me.'

'No,' said Heanua. 'Rianna is right. You are the queen and Britannia needs you alive. If you succumb then there is no hope. Rianna and I will take the best men and find my sister. This I swear.'

Boudicca tried again to rise but collapsed once more.

'We have to remove the arrow,' said the Shaman, 'or it will be too late.'

Boudicca nodded and turned to her daughter.

'You are no longer my little girl, Heanua,' she said, 'for you have grown into a fearsome woman. Go then and do what I know you can. Bring your sister home to me.'

Heanua nodded and spoke to the messenger.

'Show me where she was seen,' she said, 'and make no mistakes. Your life depends on it.' The man nodded and led her down the hill.

'You men come with me,' shouted Rianna and followed Heanua back into the fray, along with a hundred of Boudicca's best warriors.

_

'There she is,' shouted Taliesin and pushed his way through the masses to reach Lannosea.

'Taliesin,' she shouted, recognising the boy. 'What's happening? The army is in retreat.'

'I fear the day is lost,' shouted Taliesin, 'we need to get out of here.'

'But my mother is wounded,' cried Lannosea. 'We have to reach her.'

325

'She will be fine,' said Taliesin. 'We will find her another day. The warriors fall like scythed hay and there is no hope. We have to escape this valley.' Lannosea allowed herself to be led toward the flanking hill, as Finian and Taliesin fought their way through. At first, they made good headway but within minutes their way was blocked by a fight between a hundred or so warriors taking on an auxiliary Roman unit.

'This way,' shouted Finian and they ran up through the undergrowth, frantic to find a way out.

—

'I see him,' shouted Heulwen. 'By the gods, fortune smiles on us.'

'Where?' replied Prydain.

'At the base of that oak,' shouted Heulwen. 'He is with a girl and another man. It seems they are surrounded.'

Down below, many auxiliaries were laying waste to the remaining warriors and it would be a matter of moments before they reached Taliesin.

'Quickly,' shouted Prydain, 'there is no time to lose.' All five comrades raced down the hill and fell upon the rear of the light infantry with unbridled aggression. Many fell before they realised what was happening and Prydain fought his way through toward Taliesin.

Cullen fought like a madman and soldiers fell in their dozens all around him but finally his sword dropped to the floor and he looked down at the spear point sticking out of his chest.

'I am done,' he said and fell to the floor, his heart cut in two by Syrian steel.

'Nooo!' shouted Gildas, and stormed into the enemy like an enraged bull, casting them aside as if they were children. Taran joined him and together they slaughtered the rest of the patrol as Prydain at last reached the boy.

'Taliesin,' he shouted as he broke through. 'Come with me.'

'Who are you?' shouted Taliesin above the noise of the approaching slaughter. 'How do you know my name?'

'I was a friend of your father,' said Prydain, 'but there is no time to explain, we have to go.'

Heulwen joined them and ran up to Taliesin.

'You are bleeding,' she said, 'are you wounded?'

'Heulwen,' gasped Taliesin, recognising the woman who had brought him up. 'What are you doing here? What is going on?'

'No time to explain,' said Heulwen. 'The Romans will be upon us in seconds.'

Taliesin grabbed Lannosea's good arm and followed Prydain back up the hill. Taran and Gildas stayed out to either side, fighting off any Romans that came near.

'We have to find Boudicca,' shouted Lannosea as they ran.

'We have no time,' answered Prydain, 'we need to get as far from here as possible. We may yet be too late and I take no orders from a girl.'

'But it is important,' cried Lannosea.

'Our lives are important,' said Prydain. 'Now keep quiet or I will throw you back down the hill.'

'You will do no such thing,' said Taliesin and stopped dead in his tracks.

'Taliesin,' said Prydain, 'you do not know what is at stake here and it is too complicated to explain. If the girl wants to stay then let her. You are coming with us.'

'I will not leave her,' shouted Taliesin, 'and neither will you.'

'I will do as I want, boy,' shouted Prydain. 'I have already lost one friend in your name and will lose no more.'

'She is the daughter of Boudicca,' shouted Taliesin.

Prydain stared at Taliesin and the girl in turn, his mind racing. The revelation threw him momentarily off guard and he was at a loss what to do. His focus was Taliesin but the fact that he was now responsible for the daughter of the Queen of Britannia complicated the issue. He thought frantically, trying to make sense of the situation. Should they flee as planned or try to find Boudicca? Before he could make a decision, Taran returned from the slopes above.

'There is no escape that way,' he shouted, 'the upper slopes swarm with cavalry.'

The massacre in the valley below continued and the Romans killed at will. Warriors died in their thousands and when their lines thinned, Roman blades fell on anything that moved. Women and children did not escape the slaughter nor did the old or even the animals. Blood flowed down the slopes in rivers and bodies covered the valley from ridge to ridge. The air was filled with screaming as flesh was hewn from bone and mothers fought with bare hands to protect their terrified children, only to see them cleaved apart by Roman steel. The feet of so many people turned the slopes to mud and thousands more struggled to escape its cloying embrace, knowing that death was only minutes behind. The slaughter was unrelenting and for many, there was simply no escape.

'We can't go back down there,' said Gildas, 'the battle-field belongs to the Romans.'

'We have no choice,' said Prydain, 'we have no chance against cavalry. At least some of Boudicca's army still gives fight. If we can reach them, we may have a chance.' He turned to the girl. 'Listen,' he said. 'I don't know if you are who you claim to be but it matters not either way. From here on in we move like lightning and you either keep up or you don't. Our only hope is surprise so we have one chance at this.' He turned to face the others. 'We will go straight through the fight at the base of this hill. Do not falter. If any of us fall, then the others carry on regardless. Our sole aim is to get Taliesin away from here and we have come too far to fail now. If the gods are with us then our task will not have been in vain.'

'Wait,' said Taliesin. 'You have come here just for me? I do not understand.'

Prydain glanced at Heulwen and she nodded in return.

'Taliesin,' he said, 'the gods act in strange ways and it turns out you are the last true blood Deceangli prince. The Khymru is in turmoil and needs a king's lead. You are that man and we have to get you back.'

'But that's wrong,' stuttered Taliesin. 'I am no prince; my father was Gwydion of the Blaidd who died at Caer Caradog and I was raised by Asbri.'

'It is true, Taliesin,' said Heulwen. 'Your mother was Gwenno, daughter of Erwyn and as such you have true lineage to kingship.'

'I know of Erwyn, he was a tribal leader only,' said Taliesin.

'He was,' said Heulwen, 'but all other bloodlines have either been killed in the war against the Romans or in petty fights between clans. The gods have decided to spare only you so like it or not, the burden rests on your shoulders.'

'But...'

'Enough,' shouted Gildas. 'You can have your little chat later, we have to get out of here. Now either you do as Prydain says or I swear I will kill you myself and spare the Romans a job.'

Taliesin paused and guessed that the huge warrior might actually carry out his threat.

'We are ready,' he said finally.

'Good,' said Prydain and pointed across the battlefield. 'Boudicca's army seem to be holding out there. Between us there are many Romans but in no formation. They seem to be the wounded or the relieved. Make no mistake, any of them will still give us a fair fight. We run as fast as we can, avoiding all conflict. Do not stop, do not falter. Our aim is to seek the support of Boudicca's men. If this girl is who she says she is, we may just get it. Are we ready?'

Everyone nodded.

'Right,' said Prydain. 'Let's get this done. Gildas, you know what to do.'

Gildas turned and started to run down the slopes, closely followed by the rest. Within moments they reached the valley floor and they increased speed, covering the ground quickly. Where possible they used the dead ground out of the enemy's sight but were soon forced out into the open and it wasn't long before they were seen.

'Here they come,' shouted Prydain, 'keep going.'

A group of ten men ran toward them with swords drawn and Gildas altered the angle of his run to avoid them. One was closer than the others and it was obvious he would intercept them but before he could reach the running group, the man fell headlong into the dirt with Heulwen's knife lodged deep in his throat.

330

'Spears,' shouted Taran and the group glanced over their shoulders to see their pursuers pause to launch their Pilae. The metal headed spears landed amongst them but luckily, none found a target.

'Keep going,' shouted Prydain. 'They are heavily armoured and we can outrun them.'

The gap widened between the two groups and it seemed the Celts would escape but their flight had now been seen by many and several groups tried to cut them off.

'Shit,' gasped Gildas coming to a sudden halt.

'What's the matter?' gasped Prydain.

'It's no use,' said Gildas. 'The way is blocked.' Prydain followed his gaze and saw a unit of ten cavalry galloping across the valley floor to block their escape. Prydain looked back the way they had come and saw dozens of auxiliary infantry closing in fast.

'Keep going,' he shouted.

'We can't take on cavalry,' answered Gildas.

'I agree but we can't stop here. Those are Syrians behind us and they will take no prisoners. If the cavalry are Roman, I may be able to beg mercy. Our task may have come to an end, Gildas, but they may spare the women. We press on.' They started running again but Prydain's heart sunk as he recognised the garb of eastern horsemen. The cavalry blocked their path and the group came to a halt.

'It's no use,' said Heulwen, 'we will never get past them. The day is done.'

'No it isn't,' said Lannosea, 'look.'

Prydain followed her gaze and saw a heavily armed group of warriors racing toward the rear of the horsemen.

'Who are they?' he asked.

'It's my mother's personal bodyguard,' gasped Lannosea, 'and they are led by Heanua, my sister.'

A hundred yards away, the warriors fell on the rear of the unsuspecting cavalry with unbridled savagery, slashing their swords against the horses' legs to bring them crashing down before falling on the riders with their blades. Within moments the riders were slaughtered and though others had seen the attack and raced to join the fight, the safety of the treeline was now in reach.

'Heanua,' shouted Lannosea and ran to embrace her sister.

Heanua returned the embrace almost crushing the air out of her sister's body.

A panting Rianna stood to one side but although she smiled at the girl, her attention was elsewhere, seeking a way from the battlefield.

'I thought you were dead,' said Heanua to Lannosea.

'I almost was,' said Lannosea, 'but Taliesin found me in time.'

'Who's Taliesin?'

'Time for that later,' shouted Rianna. 'We are still not safe. Make for the treeline, our people still hold the slope but not for long.' They continued the flight but could see there was another group of soldiers closing in fast to intercept them.

'Legionaries,' gasped Prydain, 'and it looks like a full Century.'

Rianna stopped and stared at the new threat before turning to face the group.

'We will never make it,' she said, 'unless we slow them down. You men, follow me, the rest of you make for the woods on the slope and get the girls away from here.'

'What do you think you are doing?' asked Heanua.

'We will confront them,' said Rianna, 'and gain you some time.'

'No,' said Heanua, 'we stay together.'

'Not this time,' said Rianna. 'There is no way we can get through, at least this way you will survive.'

'What do you mean?' asked Heanua. 'My place is with you.'

'No,' said Rianna, 'these people need you to show the way.'

'I will not leave you,' shouted Heanua.

'You will do as I say,' shouted Rianna, but then caught her breath and spoke in a calmer voice. 'Heanua, your mother is wounded and your sister carries an injury. If neither survives this day, Britannia will need someone to lead them and that may well be you. This day is lost but if there are to be others you have to survive. Do you understand?'

'But...'

'Heanua, I have no time to argue. You are no longer a child but a Britannic warrior. Show me now the mettle needed for such a title and make the decision we know must be made.'

Heanua wiped a tear from her eye and nodded.

'I understand,' she said. 'We will never forget you, Rianna, is there anything we can do?'

Rianna hugged the girl tightly.

'Just live your lives the best you can,' she said, 'and one day, if you are blessed with daughters, perhaps you can name one after me?'

'I will, Rianna,' cried Heanua, 'I swear.'

Rianna turned to Lannosea but hesitated before the girl's gaze. Lannosea didn't say anything but just walked forward to embrace her. Rianna squeezed as hard as she dared and her own tears came flooding down her face.

'Am I forgiven?' whispered Rianna.

'There was never anything to forgive,' sobbed Lannosea.

'Rianna, we have to go,' shouted a warrior, 'the Romans are almost upon us.'

Rianna released Lannosea and gave the two girls one last smile.

'Lead these people to safety,' she said, 'and tell your mother I will await her in the fields of the sun.' Without another word she turned to the men under her command.

'In the name of Andraste,' she shouted, 'let's show these invaders the weight of Boudicca's wrath.'

The unit screamed their support and followed Rianna as she ran to confront the Romans racing toward them.

'What's she doing?' asked Heulwen.

'Buying us some time,' said Prydain. 'Come, we have to move.'

'Not me,' said Gildas.

Prydain turned to see the man staring after the warriors.

'Gildas, this is not our fight,' said Prydain.

'Perhaps not,' said Gildas, 'but my blade will gain you even more time. Take the boy quickly, Prydain. If the gods are kind, I will join you back in the Khymru but if I fall, then at least it will be with Roman blood on my blade and I will travel to my ancestors' campfires with honour.'

'And I will join him,' said Finian. 'My body is too weak to keep going and if I spill one drop of Roman blood, I will die a rich man. Look after her, Taliesin,' he said nodding toward Lannosea, 'and don't be in such a rush to die. You need to live a little first.'

'Travel well, Prydain,' said Gildas and before Prydain could answer, the two men raced after Rianna and the rest of the warriors.

'Come,' said Heanua, 'it is a painful task but we have to go.'

The group continued to run toward the hill, leaping the dead bodies in their way and ducking the random arrows falling around them. Within minutes they reached the treeline and as Heanua led them up into the relative safety, Prydain paused to look back across the battlefield. Most of the warriors had already fallen to arrows and Pila and the fight was already over. The century of heavily armed legionaries surrounded the few remaining warriors and in the centre Prydain could see the giant frame of Gildas still swinging his axe. For a second, Gildas looked toward the hill and Prydain raised his sword in salute.

Gildas raised his axe in response and his voice echoed across the battlefield.

'Live long, Prydain,' he shouted but before he could say any more, a Pila thudded into his chest and he fell to his knees. The Romans closed in for the kill but a command ripped through the air, stopping them dead.

'Hold your weapons,' ordered the Primus Pilus and the men held back as the officer pushed through to the front rank.

'Report,' shouted Cassus.

'My lord,' said the Centurion in charge, 'we were attacked by a unit of barbarians but have put them to the sword. Their leader lies wounded over there.' He pointed to Rianna lying face down in the mud.

'Who is this man?' asked Cassus pointing at Gildas.

'Just another barbarian,' said a soldier.

'What was the name he just called?'

The Centurion shook his head.

'I don't understand the language,' he said.

'I do, my lord,' said a soldier. 'He said "live long Prydain."'

'I thought so,' said Cassus. He stared at the warrior on the hill, his memory racing as he recalled the man he used to call friend. Surely fate hadn't brought them together once more? There was one way to find out. He dropped to his knees beside Gildas.

'You have fought well, barbarian,' he said, 'but the time to die is upon you.'

'I welcome death, Roman,' said Gildas between gritted teeth. 'Do your worst.'

'Oh, I will, barbarian,' said Cassus, 'and when I am done, I will pursue your friend and feed his heart to the ravens.'

'It will take more of a man than you to better Prydain,' said Gildas.

'Really? Then tell me, why is this man so special to you?'

'I will tell you nothing,' said Gildas, coughing up blood from his pierced lung.

Cassus knew the man was dying but it was imperative he found out if his suspicions were correct. He took a gamble.

'You don't have to tell me anything, barbarian. I already know. He is a filthy traitor who deserted from the Roman army many years ago to fight alongside the Silures in the Khymru.'

'He did not desert,' gasped Gildas in pain. 'He took his true place amongst his father's people.'

Cassus nodded as his suspicions were confirmed.

'I thought as much,' he said. It was the man he had sworn to kill seventeen years earlier, and at last the gods had delivered him into his hands. He stood up and stared up at the hill. 'Get me a horse,' he said quietly.

'Yes, my lord,' said the Centurion.

Moments later Cassus was astride a fresh horse and joined by ten other riders.

'What about the prisoners?' asked the Centurion as Cassus turned to ride away.

'You know the orders,' said Cassus over his shoulder, 'no prisoners, kill them all.'

He kicked in his heels and galloped across the field heading toward the last place he had seen Prydain. It had been a long seventeen years but at last, it was payback time.

Chapter Twenty-Seven

The Fate of Britannia

Taran and Heanua led the way, closely followed by the rest. Prydain brought up the rear and they panted heavily as they made their way up the steep slope. All around them, individual battles still took place but they fought their way through to reach the plain on the other side. As they broke free of the forests the true scale of the defeat became apparent as tens of thousands of Celts raced away from the slaughter.

'By the Gods,' said Heanua, 'Andraste has truly turned her back on her people this day.'

They joined the crowd and pushed their way through as fast as they could. Women sobbed as they helped their wounded men, and orphaned children wandered aimlessly amongst the throng, seeking the parents who would never come.

Throughout the exodus, Roman cavalry rode at will and people ran screaming before them or fell to sword or lance, but soon even the bloodthirsty cavalrymen tired of killing and settled for rounding up the survivors for slaves.

Heanua led the group down into a stream bed and away from the fields and though the going was slower, they were out of sight of any pursuers and were still undetected as night fell. Through the hours of darkness they pressed on until finally they reached another forest, though this time, vast and welcoming. The group collapsed at the base of a giant oak and fell into an exhausted sleep.

–

The sun was high when Prydain woke and for a while he sat against the tree reliving the events of the last few days. His comrades were still fast asleep and as they were miles away from the battle, he decided to let them rest. They would need every ounce of strength if they were to survive the next few days.

He knew they would need food and took the opportunity to scout the way forward. Hopefully they would find a village which could give them food enough for travel but if not, they would have to rely on what they could steal.

He nudged Taran gently.

'Taran, I will be back by noon. Guard them well.'

Taran nodded.

'Be careful,' he said.

Prydain walked along the stream bed and away from the temporary camp. They had found the boy but he had lost two of his best friends in the process. He hoped the boy was worth it.

For an hour he walked through the wood but dropped to the floor when he heard someone coming toward him. He pulled his knife slowly from its sheath, fully expecting a Roman to emerge from the undergrowth, but the man who appeared was no more than a local hunter and across his shoulders he carried the carcass of a young deer.

Prydain stood up and stepped out to face the man.

'Hail, friend,' he said.

The man stopped and stared at Prydain with suspicion.

'Friend, you say,' said the man, 'yet you brandish a knife like a brigand.'

Prydain glanced down and, realising he still held the knife, placed it back in the sheath.

'I am sorry,' he said, 'but I thought it was you who may be a brigand or worse still, a Roman.'

The man still did not move.

'I have need of your aid,' said Prydain. 'I have friends back in the wood who are weak from hunger. I see you have made a fine kill and would beg a share of the meat for a fellow Briton.'

'Why should I share my kill?' asked the man. 'Hunger is the bedfellow of many and this deer will feed my family for many days.'

'You have a family?' asked Prydain.

'A woman and a child of four years,' said the man. 'We live in the woods and trouble no one.'

'Then you too are in danger,' said Prydain. 'You must get them and leave this place immediately.'

'Why would I do that?'

'You don't know?'

'Know what?'

'About the battle back amongst the hills.'

'I know of no such battle.'

'Boudicca has suffered a terrible defeat at the hands of the Romans,' said Prydain, 'and they scour these lands for slaves as we speak. You and your family are at risk and at the very least would be enslaved if not killed. Join with us and we will take you to the Khymru.'

'How do I know this is not a ruse to free me of my kill?' asked the man.

Prydain sighed and realised he was wasting time.

'Look,' he said. 'I tell the truth. I have an injured girl and six hungry mouths to feed. As a fellow Briton I am asking for your aid. In return I can offer only good advice. That is all I have.'

The man stared at Prydain for a while before throwing the deer to the ground.

'Like I said,' said the man. 'I know of no such battle but hunger is a pain I know only too well. We will not join you, however, I will not see you go hungry.' He nodded toward the deer. 'Use your knife, stranger. A haunch will last you three days if you eat sparingly.'

Prydain sighed in relief.

'Thank you,' he said and walked over to the dead animal to carve away one of the legs. When he had finished, he turned to the man again.

'Are you sure you won't join us?' he asked.

'I am sure,' said the man, 'our home is here and rest assured it is well hidden.'

'Then at least take care,' said Prydain, 'for the world just became a far more dangerous place.'

'It has always been such,' said the man. 'Journey safely, stranger.' He picked up the deer, and disappeared into the forest once more, leaving Prydain staring after him.

—

Prydain knew he was nearing the place where he left the group and was about to call out when a noise stopped him in his tracks. Slowly he crouched down amongst the bracken and listened again. There it was, the sound of a horse snorting after a hard ride. He put the venison aside and crawled forward to see the source, knowing full well there were no horses within his group. Within moments he saw a Syrian cavalryman astride a horse, obviously keeping watch over the path leading through the wood. Prydain knew that could mean only one thing; his comrades had been compromised. He retreated back into the undergrowth, his mind racing as to what he could do. Eventually he realised he had to have better information and made his way through the denser parts of the forest, giving the guard a wide berth, and made his way back to where he last saw his comrades. Finally he crawled forward and peered down into the clearing.

What he saw made his heart sink. Taliesin was tied against a tree, his hair matted with blood and one eye closed from the beating he had obviously received. Heanua, Lannosea and Heulwen were sitting next to each other, their hands and feet bound and their mouths stuffed with gags. There was no sign of Taran.

Prydain took in the scene quickly. Four men stood guard around the clearing astride their horses and he knew at least one more was guarding the path. He knew there would probably be more but it wasn't the number of riders that caught him cold, but the man sat nonchalantly on a fallen tree to one side. It was Cassus Maecilius, his boyhood friend. They had spent their childhood growing up amongst the vine covered slopes of Picenum and had set out together as young men to seek glory in the legions until fate had intervened and sent them on separate paths. Since that day, Cassus had sworn to kill him.

-

Prydain stayed hidden for as long as he could, forming plans over and over in his mind, each discarded as the futility became clear. There was no way he could better ten men and even if he could, he knew Cassus was a formidable fighter and was more than a match for him. If he wanted to survive, he knew he had to run, to get as far away as possible while he had the chance but below him, he had a situation no man could walk away from. There were two daughters of Boudicca, a boy destined to be king of the Deceangli if not the Khymru and a woman he had grown to love over the past few weeks.

The thought shocked him. Until now he had simply enjoyed Heulwen's company, but suddenly the thought of losing her hurt more than any of the battle wounds he had ever suffered. He savoured the unbidden thought for a few moments before realising that he could no more run away than fly like a bird. No, he had to do something and had to do it quickly. He crawled back through the bracken knowing what he had to do. It was risky, but it was the only plan he had.

Cassus stared at the women before looking up at the sun. It was already well on its way to midday and he knew Prydain should be back by now. He swallowed the last of his Buccellatum and washed the dry biscuit down with some water from his bottle. He looked at the women again and caught the youngest staring at his food pouch.

'Hungry?' he asked.

Lannosea looked away quickly.

Cassus reached in the bag and retrieved some dried meat. He walked over and crouched before the women, carving thin slivers of the meat and dangling it in front of their faces.

'Plenty of food to be had,' he said. 'In fact, tell me what I want and I will get one of my men to make a broth. How does that sound?'

Lannosea looked away and Cassus laughed as he saw the hatred on her face.

'What I don't understand,' said Cassus, 'is why Prydain is so far away from his so-called people and risked his life to lead you right across a battlefield. What is so special about you, eh?' He placed the point of his knife under Heulwen's chin and forced her head up. 'Your face is familiar to me,' he said. 'We have met before.'

Heulwen stared back, meeting the Roman's gaze.

'I am Heulwen of the Asbri, true natives of these lands. We were here before you came and will be here after you are gone.'

'The Asbri?' said Cassus. 'I remember you. You are the woman who nursed my wounds in the household of Madoc. You were also the one who robbed me of my revenge the last time Prydain crossed my path.'

'You knew the arrangement, Cassus,' said Heulwen, 'a life for a life.'

'And the debt was paid,' said Cassus. 'This time there will be no such burden to stay my sword. So tell me, Witch, why are you here and where is Prydain?'

'I have nothing more to say to you,' said Heulwen.

'Not yet perhaps,' said Cassus, 'but you will.' He stood up and walked over to the tethered Taliesin. The boy's head hung limply on his chest and Cassus grabbed his hair to lift it up. Taliesin's face was a mess and he mumbled through swollen lips.

'Shame about his pretty face,' said Cassus. 'The boy has spirit but little skill.' He looked over at Heulwen and saw the fear on her face.

344

'I see this boy means something to you,' he said. 'Let's see if we can loosen your tongue. Now, where is Prydain?'

'I don't know,' said Heulwen.

'Wrong answer,' said Cassus and smashed Taliesin across the face with the back of his hand. The boy's head flung sideways and fresh blood poured from his mouth.

'Stop,' shouted Heulwen, 'I tell the truth. He left before we awoke. He could be miles away by now.'

'I don't believe you,' said Cassus and smashed the boy again.

'Stop it,' screamed Lannosea, 'she tells the truth. Hurting him more will not make the truth change. Can't you see he has had enough?'

'Perhaps,' said Cassus, 'but I have only just started.' He drew his Pugio, spinning the knife in his hand while staring at the women. 'Ever seen a man with his tongue cut out?'

'No, don't,' begged Lannosea. 'Please, there is no point. Killing him or us cannot make the unknown, known. Spare his life and I will sacrifice mine in his place.'

'A girl's life has no worth to me,' said Cassus.

'I'm not an ordinary girl,' sobbed Lannosea.

'Lannosea, be quiet,' shouted Heanua.

'What do you mean?' asked Cassus. 'Speak quickly or he dies.'

'I will give you a gift worth a fortune,' said Lannosea, ignoring the shouts of the other two women. 'My true identity.'

Cassus stared.

'Speak,' he said, 'or he dies right now.'

'I am Lannosea, daughter of Boudicca,' she said quietly.

Cassus stared in silence, taking in the astonishing fact. Her capture would be worth a fortune.

'So that's it,' he said at last, 'the reason he tried so hard to save you.' Before he could say any more, a shout made him turn in alarm.

'My lord, a rider approaches.'

Cassus ran across the clearing and watched as a horse walked slowly into the clearing, a body draped across its saddle.

'It's Ashur,' shouted one of the guards.

Cassus recognised one of the riders he had posted as an outer sentry and he ordered the tethered man cut from the horse's back. The man was wounded but conscious.

'What happened?' asked Cassus.

'I was struck from behind,' said Ashur, 'and fell to the attacker's sword.'

'Where is the wound?'

Ashur indicated his shoulder, a place unlikely to be fatal.

'Why did he spare you?'

'He gave me a message,' said Ashur. 'He said he is the one you want and he is willing to give himself up in return for the freedom of your captives.'

'He said that?' said Cassus quietly. 'And why should we trust him?'

'He said he gives his word and swears on the memory of Karim.'

Cassus fell quiet. Karim was the man who had saved Prydain as a baby and had brought him up as his own son. He knew that whatever he was, Prydain would never sully his father's memory with a false promise.

'What else did he say?' he asked.

'He said to send your men away and release the prisoners. When he sees both parties on opposite horizons, he will meet you one on one.'

Cassus stared at the man, his mind racing with the implications. At last his quarry of seventeen years was within his grasp.

'Do it,' he said.

'My lord,' said one of the riders, 'the girl is Boudicca's daughter. She alone is worth a fortune in gold. Surely this man can wait?'

'I have waited long enough,' said Cassus, 'and it is time to bring it to an end. Release the prisoners and give them a horse for the boy.'

'But my lord.'

Cassus turned around and punched the Syrian, sending him sprawling in the dirt.

'I am the Primus Pilus,' he shouted, 'and you will do as I command. Release the prisoners and take your unit back to the legion or suffer the consequences.'

The man stood up and saluted the officer.

'Yes my lord,' he said and turned to carry out his orders. Ten minutes later both parties were heading in opposite directions leaving the Centurion on his own. Cassus watched them go before sitting back on the fallen tree. He drew his Gladius and retrieved a small whetstone from a pouch. Slowly he drew the stone along the blade's length anticipating that soon, it would be needed to end a burden he had lived with for too long.

—

Prydain stared down into the clearing. Cassus sat waiting for him but Prydain had to be sure there was no trickery. Finally he saw the riders appear on a far hill and he knew Cassus had kept his side of the bargain. He climbed down from the tree and after saying a prayer to his ancestors, walked down the slope and into the clearing.

Chapter Twenty-Eight

Resolution

Cassus stood up and watched Prydain approach. For an age, both men stared at each other in silence before Cassus finally spoke.

'So, you were stupid enough to come after all,' he said.

'I am a man of my word, Cassus,' said Prydain, 'we made a bargain.'

'A one-sided bargain,' said Cassus.

'How so?'

'I will ride away from here today while your corpse will be left to rot alongside your friend there.' Cassus pointed to a corpse half hidden in the undergrowth. Prydain recognised the body of Taran and his heart sank.

'He put up a good fight but was no match for my blade,' said Cassus.

'You killed him?'

'I did. Is that a problem?'

'He was a good man,' said Prydain, 'and deserved better.'

'He died with honour,' said Cassus. 'A trait I admire in any man.'

'So what is this about, Cassus?' said Prydain. 'What burns you so much that you still require I die, after all this time?'

'You know why, Prydain,' said Cassus, circling around the clearing. 'You have brought disgrace on my family's name by deserting and joining the enemy all those years ago.'

'You know that is not true,' said Prydain. 'I simply joined my father's people.'

'You were a legionary,' shouted Cassus, 'and took the Sacramentum.'

'An oath based on the unknown,' answered Prydain. 'I believed I was as Roman as you and fought alongside you as brother. But when I found out I was killing my own people, how else could I react? You surely would have done the same.'

'Never,' growled Cassus. 'I have too much honour to betray my comrades, no matter what the reason.'

'Really, Cassus?'

'Do not mock me, Prydain,' said Cassus, 'and enough talking. Draw your sword for this ends now.'

Prydain slowly drew his sword and stood opposite the Centurion.

'Have your sport, Cassus, for I know I am no match for you. Even on those sun-baked slopes of Picenum as a boy you were always the victor and I expect no different outcome.'

'You already talk defeat,' spat Cassus. 'What trickery is this?'

'No trickery,' said Prydain, 'just realism. I fully expect to die this day though will use everything in my power to delay that moment.' He paused. 'We were close once, Cassus. Boyhood friends growing strong together in the hills, above the Adriatic. Where are those allegiances, Cassus? Are they not stronger than any false oath?'

'The Sacramentum is an oath of honour,' shouted Cassus.

'It was once,' said Prydain, 'now it is no more than a promise to slaughter thousands of innocents so one man can amass more wealth than he could spend in a thousand lifetimes. What honour is there in that?'

'You play with words, Prydain,' said Cassus, 'but only delay the inevitable.'

'Then let's do this,' said Prydain, 'for I tire of you justifying that which cannot be defended.'

—

Both men circled each other slowly with swords drawn, Cassus in his full Lorica Segmentata armour and Prydain in his leather tunic. Ordinarily Cassus would be confident of the outcome and he knew his skills far outweighed those of Prydain. His time in the Exploratores had seen to that and he could probably better Prydain with his bare hands. But something was wrong. Prydain's words had struck a chord and he found his mind racing as he relived them over and over again in his mind. Yes, the emperor was getting richer but that was how it was. Soldiers fought, enemies died and emperors got rich. It was how it had always been since the days of the republic.

Cassus himself had killed more men than he could remember and knew he could despatch Prydain with ease, yet when the anticipated lunge came, he simply deflected it and stepped to one side.

Prydain spun around and resumed the assault, relying on speed and strength to break through the Centurion's defence but every blow was deflected easily, without as much as a single counter. Over and over again Prydain returned to the attack and the forest rang with the clash of metal on metal, as both men matched each other in skill and strength. Finally Cassus took the initiative and stepped forward into the attack. The speed of his sword was astonishing and Prydain realised Cassus had been toying with him. Cassus forced Prydain backward and despite Prydain's desperate defence, Cassus knocked the sword from his hand with ease. Prydain backed up against a tree and Cassus leapt forward to place the point of his sword against Prydain's throat.

Prydain gasped for breath and stared into his executioner's eyes, realising there was nothing he could do. He was about to die.

Cassus breathed heavily as he watched a tiny trickle of blood run down Prydain's neck from the point of the Gladius. For half a minute nobody moved and both men stared deep into each other's eyes.

'Do it,' said Prydain.

'I take no orders from a traitor,' growled Cassus.

'You owe me nothing,' said Prydain. 'The fight was fair. End this madness once and for all.'

After a few more moments, Cassus stepped back and lowered his sword.

'I have what I want, Prydain,' he said.

Prydain swallowed hard.

'I don't understand,' he said.

'I could have killed you any time, Prydain, but held back the final blow. Whether you believe me or not, I am a man of honour and your earlier words have merit. Despite our differences there was a time when I called you brother. Those times may be long in the past but a man's worth is only the sum of his days. Killing you would be no more than killing the memories we once shared and proves nothing. Giving you your life proves my humanity. I am a Roman legionary and as such have become a sword of Rome, but let it not be said that Rome owns my very soul. I am the master of my own destiny, Prydain, and today I chose compassion.'

Before Prydain could speak, a scream echoed around the clearing and Cassus's whole body arched backward in pain as he fell to his knees with a sword sticking out of his side. Behind him, the battered face of Taliesin grimaced with rage as he withdrew the Gladius from Cassus's back.

'Taliesin, no,' screamed Prydain and lunged forward to stop him striking a second blow.

'What are you doing?' shouted Taliesin. 'He was going to kill you.'

'No,' said Prydain. 'The fight was done. It is over.'

'I came back, Prydain,' said Taliesin. 'The women hide in the forests and I used the horse to return.'

'And I am grateful,' said Prydain, 'but now is not the time.' He reached down and cradled his old friend in his arms.

'Not the outcome I expected, Prydain,' gasped Cassus. 'You have prevailed.'

'You don't escape that easily,' said Prydain. 'The wound has missed your heart. There is yet a chance you will live.'

'I seek no chances, Prydain. You were right. I tire of all the killing and am desperate for the peace that death brings. Leave me here to meet my gods.'

'No,' said Prydain, 'once more there is a debt between us and we always pay our way.'

'Your life is my gift,' said Cassus, 'there is no debt to pay.'

'I talk of the greater debt between us,' said Prydain. 'The debt we have denied each other for too long. Twenty years of friendship should not fall foul to the stupidity of war. I will not see you die, Cassus, not like this. There are people back in the Khymru who can heal this wound.'

'The Khymru?' said Cassus with a weak smile. 'I was at my happiest when I shared the household of Madoc for those few months before the battle of Caer Caradog. There was a girl...'

'Sioned,' said Prydain.

'You know her?'

'I have met her once,' said Prydain. 'She lives there still.'

'I loved her, Prydain,' said Cassus, 'the only woman I have ever loved. She thought I died a hero at Caer Caradog and though I watched her from the trees for many nights after the battle, I knew I had to leave. My true identity meant I could never be with her.'

He gasped as Prydain stuffed strips of fabric against his wounds.

'It's not too late, Cassus,' said Prydain. 'You can go back and make your peace. Leave this bloodshed behind and seek happiness.'

'And how do you think the arrival of a Centurion will be welcomed in the Khymru?' laughed Cassus weakly. 'I think the welcome will be somewhat cold, don't you?'

'I think you could be surprised,' said Prydain. 'Ordinary people are often detached from the politics of warfare and compassion is difficult to keep down.'

'A pretty dream, Prydain,' said Cassus, 'but there have been too many bad things done by these hands. I fear I am beyond redemption.'

'Let the gods be the judge of that,' said Prydain as he secured the bandages. He turned to Taliesin.

'Bring the horse,' he said. 'We need to move quickly.'

Cassus' eyes closed and he slumped into Prydain's arms.

'Is he dead?' asked Taliesin.

'I don't think so,' said Prydain. 'Help me move him. We have to get him to a Shaman.'

'Why should we help him?' asked Taliesin. 'He is our enemy.'

'He was,' said Prydain, 'but he was also once a friend.' He turned back to the unconscious man.

'You may be right or you may be wrong, Cassus, but one thing is certain. I am not leaving you here to die.'

Taliesin helped Prydain put the wounded legionary on the horse.

'Come,' said Prydain, 'we will take him to the Asbri.'

'Not me, Prydain,' said Taliesin, 'at least, not yet.'

'Why not?' asked Prydain.

'I need to be with Lannosea,' he said. 'I know the Khymru needs me and men have fallen in my name, but my heart needs Lannosea and without her, I will be nothing. I am sorry.'

Prydain stared at the boy for an age but eventually nodded in acceptance.

'I understand,' he said. 'Be safe Taliesin and hopefully our paths will cross again one day.'

'I am sure they will,' said Taliesin. 'Goodbye, Prydain and thank you.'

Prydain nodded and without another word, led the horse from the clearing to head toward the Khymru.

Chapter Twenty-Nine

Legacy

Boudicca lay on a pile of furs at the back of a leaking hut. She and her entourage had escaped the wrath of the Romans and had managed to seek refuge with a local tribe, and though the battle had ended over a month earlier, her wound had become infected and the Shamen had struggled to find a cure. Her strength and demeanour had improved briefly when Heanua and Lannosea returned but it soon became apparent that she was deteriorating fast. Finally the Shamen admitted they had no more magic and told the queen to prepare for the afterlife.

'Bring me my daughters,' she said weakly.

Several minutes later both girls entered and sat alongside the queen's death bed. With them were Taliesin and Heulwen, both now fully recovered from their ordeals.

'My girls,' said Boudicca. 'My time here is over but I need you to promise me something.'

'Anything,' said Heanua through her tears.

'Heanua,' said Boudicca. 'You have the heart of a wolf and are a true warrior. Yet you have to bury these traits and become a leader to our people. The Iceni need a queen, not to fight the Romans but to make sure no more bleed in my name. We had our chance, Heanua but the gods have a different path for us. Take this strength and ensure our people survive. It will be a greater feat than any battle and I do not know if it can be done but if anyone can do it, you can. Will you do this for me?'

Heanua nodded and wiped the tears from her eyes.

'Lannosea?' said Boudicca.

'I am here, Mother.'

'Lannosea, I fear I was not there for you. For that I am truly sorry. I gave up on you when you needed me most. I thought you were dead, when you wandered alone and hungry.'

'It's alright, Mother,' sobbed Lannosea. 'You weren't to know.'

'I should never have given up, child, but my eyes were blinded by glory and that is unforgiveable.' She looked toward Taliesin. 'This boy was there for you when I was absent. I have seen the way you look at each other and know what is right. Taliesin, take my daughter back to your lands and become the man she deserves. Treat her well and remember she is the daughter of a queen. Take the fight back to the Romans in the lands of the Khymru and one day, when your sons wield Britannic steel above a defeated legion, let them know it is Boudicca's blood that holds the blade. This will be my legacy.'

'We will, Boudicca,' said Taliesin, 'in the name of Andraste I promise your legacy will live on.'

Boudicca coughed, her face screwed up in agony as the infection coursed through her veins and before the night was over, her body was carried out to lay on the funeral pyre prepared in readiness. As the dawn rose, three riders crested a hill and looked back down to the village they had just left. The pyre was still burning and Lannosea saw the solitary girl standing to one side, knowing she would probably never see her sister again.

'Come,' said Heulwen, 'we have a long road ahead of us,' and she urged her horse forward, closely followed by Lannosea and Taliesin.

Hundreds of miles away two men rode toward a small farmstead deep in the heart of the Khymru. The journey had been long but at last they had reached their destination. One rider was strong but the other nursed a wound to his back and was weak through blood loss.

'Wait,' said Cassus and reined in his horse.

'Does your wound give trouble?' asked Prydain.

'No more than usual,' said Cassus, 'but this is a situation I have never foreseen and I need a moment of reflection.'

'We have discussed this,' said Prydain. 'Despite the circumstances it is something that needs to be done.'

'And you are sure she will be here?' said Cassus.

'As sure as I can be,' said Prydain.

'I loved her once,' said Cassus, 'but too much has happened to rebuild the past. How can I ever ask her to understand?'

'Start by being honest, Cassus,' said Prydain. 'At the very least, she deserves that. Besides, there is something I haven't shared with you, something that will change your life forever.'

'Which is?'

'It is not for me to say, Cassus,' said Prydain. 'For I may be wrong, but if my suspicions are correct, the truth will unfold.'

They started riding again and stopped at the outskirts of the farm. Prydain helped Cassus dismount and they walked between the buildings. An old man ducked out of a hut and walked toward them.

'Hwyl, strangers,' he said. 'Welcome to our home in peace.'

'It is peace we seek, Madoc,' said Prydain.

'I recognise your voice,' said Madoc. 'You travelled with Heulwen many months ago.'

'I did,' said Prydain.

'Is she with you?' asked Madoc.

'No,' said Prydain, 'and I have no news of her fate.'

'A sad day,' said Madoc. 'And who is this?'

Cassus removed his hood.

'You know me too, Madoc,' he said. 'I shared your hospitality ten years ago.'

Madoc's eyes narrowed as he struggled to recognise the man.

'My memory is not as good as it once was,' he said, 'and I struggle to remember your name.'

'I remember,' said a voice.

The men turned to see Sioned standing to one side.

'Sioned,' said Cassus. 'You remember me.'

'I remember,' said Sioned. 'You are the man I once loved. The man who left to fight at Caer Caradog and was reported dead. For ten years I have honoured your memory, yet now you return as if it was yesterday. What cruelty is this?'

'I intend no cruelty, Sioned,' said Cassus. 'There were things I did not tell you and it was better you never had to face the truth.'

'What truth could mirror the pain of your reported death?' snapped Sioned.

'I am not the person you think I am,' said Cassus.

358

'Who is it, Mother?' asked a voice, and a young boy appeared from behind a wall. 'Do you know him?'

Cassus stared at the boy before looking back at Sioned with confusion in his eyes.

'Just a traveller, Allyn,' said Sioned. 'He is just passing through.'

'Is that what you want?' asked Cassus.

'All I want is security for my son,' said Sioned. 'Your lies have given me ten years pain – what is to stop you leaving again?'

'You are right,' said Cassus. 'There has been too much pain on all sides and the time for healing is here. If you give me a chance, I can be the man I once was. The man you once had feelings for.'

'I don't know, Cassus,' she said. 'If there is to be any chance at all, there has to be honesty between us. Are you able to do that?'

'I am,' said Cassus, 'though to do so there will be more pain before there is comfort.'

'Then that is the price to be paid,' said Sioned. She turned to her son. 'Allyn, come here.'

The boy walked over and stood in front of his mother, facing the stranger.

Prydain stared at the boy's prominent features and knew his assumption had been correct. He had seen that face before, not just on the fleeting visit a few months earlier, but many, many times in the vineyards of his youth.

'Allyn,' said Sioned, 'there is something you should know. I have always told you that your father fell at Caer Caradog, but it seems I was wrong. This man before you is your father.'

The gathering fell silent as the news sunk in. Finally, Allyn walked forward to stand before Cassus.

'Is it true?' he asked. 'Are you my father?'

'No more lies, Cassus,' said Sioned quietly.

Cassus glanced toward Prydain and received a slight nod of encouragement. Cassus returned his attention to the boy and dropped to his knees.

'It is true, Allyn,' he said, 'I am your father, but there is something you should know.'

He paused and took a deep breath.

'My name,' he said, 'is Cassus Maecilius... and I am Roman.'

Author's Notes

Though many versions of Boudicca's campaign abound there are very little references from the time. The Roman historians, Tacitus and Dio both refer to her reign briefly though exact details are not available. Some things are however generally agreed by many historians and the notes below reflect the history, as far as current research can ascertain.

The Treatment of Boudicca and her daughters

After the death of Prasatagus, Seneca the Younger called in the debts of the Iceni and despite the wishes of the dead king, a deal for power sharing was rejected. Boudicca and her two daughters were beaten and raped. This seems to have been the catalyst for the uprising.

The Island of Mona

Mona (Anglesey in modern day Wales) was the headquarters of the powerful Druids and was under siege from the Gemina legion when the uprising started. Governor Gaius Suetonius Paullinus was in command of the IV Germina legion at the time and led them across country to Londinium as soon as he could. Once there he decided that defence was impossible and left Londinium to face Boudicca's army alone.

Boudicca's Victories.

Boudicca seems to have laid waste to three major population centres at that time, Camulodunum, (Colchester) Londinium, (London) and Verulamium (St Albans) During the campaign she also defeated the Ninth Hispana legion, probably her greatest victory.

The Brutality of Boudicca

There are some notes recording the brutality of Boudicca's army and records show that many of those depicted in this book actually happened at the time. In reality, as in many historical battles, the reality was probably much worse.

Catus Decianus

Catus Decianus was the Procurator at the time and it seems he failed to see the seriousness of the revolt, sending only a force of two hundred men to relieve Camulodunum. He later escaped to Gaul, thus avoiding the rout of Londinium.

Quintus Petillius Cerialis.

Petillius was in command of the Ninth Hispana, though when the legion was defeated, he escaped the slaughter and in later years, went on to become a Governor of Britannia.

Poenius Postumus

Poenius Postumus was the Praefectus Castrorum of the Second Augusta legion at the time and though his aid was requested by Suetonius, it seems the request was ignored. Subsequently, at the end of the campaign he committed suicide by falling on his sword, presumably in shame.

The Final Battle

The exact location of the final battle is unknown though many believe it is somewhere along the Roman Road known today as Watling Street.

Military numbers vary for the battle but it is generally agreed that Suetonius had approximately ten thousand men under his command, made up from the Gemina, the remains of the Hispana, part of the Valeria Victrix and several vexillations (smaller units) from around the country.

Numbers for Boudicca's army range from a hundred thousand to two hundred thousand and though we will never know the exact figure, it is agreed the Britannic army vastly outnumbered the Romans.

Despite this superiority, the narrowness of the carefully selected valley meant Boudicca could only deploy the same amount of men as the Romans at any one time and her numerical superiority was thus nullified. The Roman tactics and discipline won the day and when they turned the native army, Boudicca's warriors were caught amongst their watching families and the carts they had brought to witness the anticipated victory. Tacitus reports that over eighty thousand Britons died that day compared to only four hundred Romans.

Nero was the Emperor at the time and he seriously contemplated abandoning Britannia. If Boudicca had prevailed in the final battle, it is likely Roman occupation would have ended and our history would have been vastly different.